A Promise to Die For

AN EVANGELINE RAINES MYSTERY

A Promise to Die For

Jacqueline Pelham

FIVE STAR

A part of Gale, Cengage Learning

GALE
CENGAGE Learning

Farmington Hills, Mich • San Francisco • New York • Waterville, Maine
Meriden, Conn • Mason, Ohio • Chicago

Five Star™ Publishing, a part of Cengage Learning, Inc.

LIBRARY OF CONGRESS CATALOGING-IN-PUBLICATION DATA

Pelham, Jackie.
A promise to die for : an Evangeline Raines mystery / Jacqueline Pelham. — First Edition.
pages ; cm
ISBN 978-1-4328-3055-7 (hardcover) — ISBN 1-4328-3055-4 (hardcover) — ISBN 978-1-4328-3052-6 (ebook) — ISBN 1-4328-3052-x (ebook)
I. Title.
PS3566.E383P76 2015
813'.54—dc23 2014047843

First Edition. First Printing: May 2015
Find us on Facebook– https://www.facebook.com/FiveStarCengage
Visit our website– http://www.gale.cengage.com/fivestar/
Contact Five Star™ Publishing at FiveStar@cengage.com

Printed in the United States of America
12 3 4 5 6 7 19 18 17 16 15

To my family for their continued loving support.
They are the lifelines to my heart.

ACKNOWLEDGMENTS

I have been blessed in my writing journey with a unique blend of friends and authors who have offered support, expertise and encouragement in numerous ways. Thank you, Guida Jackson, author and dear friend, without whom I would never have completed my first novel; Ida Luttrell, author and dear friend, whose smile makes it all better; my sweet buddy Patsy Ward Burk, now deceased; Julia Mercedes Castilla, who perseveres; Louise Gaylord, multi-published author; Vanessa Leggett, who can do it all: write, perform, and parent; Irene Bond, who recently published her first novel; Karen Stuyck, multi-published; and Lynn Gonzales, our resident poet.

A huge thanks to my Thursday critique buddies, for without their patient line editing and plotting input, I would be lost. Each one contributes an expertise that is invaluable to the writing process: Jeana Kendrick, Joy Ziegler and Beverly Herkommer. Our bond is strong, our lunches fabulous.

A special thanks to my daughter Linda Jones for the book photo and for the fun we had.

Thanks to the Five Star Mysteries group who helped bring Evangeline to life, especially Denise Dietz, Tiffany Schofield, and Tracey Matthews.

My family is what I live for. It is the root, the lifeline, the beginning, and the end all.

Chapter 1

Evangeline Raines double-timed her steps along the steep San Francisco street, wishing she had taken a taxi from the hotel. But wanting to enjoy the local color, she had ridden a streetcar and was now late for the appointment that could change her life.

The afternoon shower had dwindled to a fine mist, but the pavement was slippery and the sky a hard, cold slate. At the corner, she checked the map clutched in her hand, turned left, bent into a blustery wind, and entered the gloom of a narrow, canyon-like row of buildings with cracked panes and peeling paint. A black cat crouched in a shadowed doorway, its eyes like melted spheres of gold daring her to pass.

"Oh, brother, right out of a gothic novel." But like her mother always said, when encountering an immovable object, go around it, so she circumvented into the street. She wasn't overly superstitious, but one could never be too careful.

In the middle of the deserted block, a prickle crept up her spine and her eyelid twitched, a definite sign of trouble. She glanced over her shoulder and pulled up her collar—a sound or movement, footsteps that stopped as she turned, her own thumping heart, or an overactive imagination?

She probably shouldn't have come alone, but several hours of daylight remained, and she was going to a public place. She looked up to the leaden sky. *Grandmother, the promise I made to you might be more than I bargained for, especially if the telephone call this morning is any indication.*

Although the voice had sounded digitally altered, squeaky high, and impossible to tell if male or female, she could quote it verbatim. "Miz Raines, some things are better left buried. If you continue your search, be prepared for the consequences."

So cliché, she thought at the time, and told the prank caller to stick it where the sun didn't shine. Realistically, prank calls usually occurred late at night, not at five o'clock in the morning. And who could have known she had an appointment in San Francisco to view a painting that might be one stolen from her family during World War II? But it wasn't so much what the caller had said, as the emphasis on reaping the consequences.

She breathed heavily, swallowed hard, and searched storefront addresses. She found the faded numbers and stopped at the dingy security-barred door of a small art gallery. Its hand-painted sign, dangling by uneven rusty chains, creaked in the strong breeze blowing in from the bay.

Now she had arrived, what would she say to the proprietor? "Gee, Mr. Rossini, are you trading in stolen art?"

After a whiff of salty air, she said, "Here we go!" She reached through the bars, took hold of the doorknob and twisted. It did not give.

"No! Come on. You have to be kidding me. It can't be locked." She knocked; no answer. She knocked again, rapped on the little square door pane, which rattled at her touch, wiped at the grimy glass and peered inside. A woman leaned against the doorjamb to a poorly lit back room. Her drab clothing and fleshy skin seemed out of place among the colorful framed landscapes and portraits of richly gowned women, hanging from the walls.

In thick Italian, the woman said through an intercom, "What do you want?"

"I'm Evangeline Raines from Houston. I spoke with Mr.

Rossini yesterday and made an appointment for today."

The woman buried her face in her hands and muttered, "He's dead. A car accident this morning."

Evangeline's stomach lurched. "Oh, my word. How terrible."

"Please leave! I can't talk right now." She backed into the room and disappeared from view.

The air whooshed out of Evangeline. She had been so certain this trip would actually lead somewhere. But why should today be any different? Her life had poetically been in the toilet since Nicky left.

She stood at the door, shoulders hunched, hands hanging by her sides, not knowing what to do, because this was another episode of déjà vu. Whenever she thought she might be getting closer, the door slammed and she had to begin again. And she wanted to believe Mr. Rossini's death was a horrible accident and happened coincidentally on the day of their meeting, but a niggle at the back of her mind worried that someone wanted to sabotage her search, didn't want her to succeed. If so, how far would that person go to stop her? Was the call a real warning? Maybe she had been watching too many movies, reading too many mysteries and letting her imagination run amok. And was the phone call even a reference to her search for her grandmother Delacroix-Ravel's artwork?

In today's market, the family heirlooms would be worth a small fortune—no, a monstrous fortune. Heat roiled up inside and into her face. Before her grandmother had died, Evangeline had promised to continue the search for those treasures, and if they were anywhere on this earth, she vowed to discover their whereabouts no matter the consequences.

Chapter 2

In Houston the next morning, Evangeline shuffled around like a little old lady with arthritic joints. She nursed jet lag and was also late for work. Although not required to punch a time clock, she tried to be diligent at whatever task was set before her.

Her mind still couldn't grasp yesterday's events, whether the telephone call or Mr. Rossini's death were connected to her search for the paintings, but one thing was certain, she would be watching for other incidents to prove it one way or another.

She rinsed the coffee dregs from her mug—a souvenir from a restaurant she and Nicky had visited—and placed it in the dish drainer, her fingers lingering on its warm surface. She scrunched her mouth, deciding it was time to put the past behind her. She would begin with a new mug, one with a funny saying, maybe one with her astrological sign.

She grabbed her leather-fringed shoulder purse from the kitchen island, stumbled out the back door to the detached two-car garage and climbed into Atlas; no sissy name for her black Ford Bronco. She pulled the visor mirror down, checked the eyeliner around her amber-colored eyes and smacked the lipstick she had forgotten to blot. Other than a moisturizer under a foundation and a little hairspray to help control the frizz in her curly auburn hair, she went au naturel. Mamma always said less was better, which Evangeline had found to be good advice, but she did love her Bohemian clothes. Today she wore a black heavy-crocheted ankle-length skirt, aqua-colored tunic and black lace-up granny boots. The outfits seemed to change her outlook, provided her with insouciance, like playing a character from one of her black-and-white movies.

Thank goodness the summer heat was practically over. Another sweltering Houston day and she would fly back to San Francisco for respite. She lowered the window to enjoy the cool, humidity-free October crispness, tucked into place the wayward curly strand of hair tickling her forehead, clicked the remote iron-gate opener and backed into the street. Atlas's right rear tire plunged into a pothole and the car hit bottom.

Her stomach flip-flopped. "Crud! Bet I broke my tailpipe." She had called the county, but since she was becoming more resourceful, she would buy a package of cement mix and fill it in later.

"Well, this is a rotten way to start the day. Come on, Atlas, prove me wrong." She gunned the engine and the Bronco bounced out of the hole and purred right along. She patted the dashboard and said, "Way to go, big boy."

Nicky had been dubious when she bought the vehicle already sporting a hundred-thousand-mile odometer reading. It fit her perfectly, and from the day she drove it off the lot, Atlas had never missed a beat.

Thankfully the automobile was okay, because she couldn't do without transportation and certainly couldn't afford to rent a car. At the corner, she saw the girl lounging on the curb, ankles crossed and legs extending out over the gutter. Evangeline had noticed her several days before and decided she must be from the homeless shelter nearby.

The waif stared intently at her and then smiled. Evangeline quickly turned her head. It was hard enough to keep oneself in check. The last thing she needed was to get involved with a hormonally charged teenager. They took too much out of you, especially a runaway like that one appeared to be. And, too,

Evangeline had a soft spot for these kids, because one never knew the circumstances behind their plight. Lord knew, she'd been in difficult situations because of the way she was raised. She didn't consider herself an enabler, but liked to think of herself as being compassionate. Now wasn't the time to complicate her life with such matters.

She turned west where the bumper-to-bumper traffic headed toward the Loop 610. She planned to go around to Rembrandt's rear parking lot, so she wheeled onto a side street and slammed on her brakes at the loud clatter of trashcans tumbling, a dog barking and a man's voice shouting, "Stop or I'll shoot!"

"What in the world?" She scanned the area but saw nothing unusual. Seconds later a man darted from the hedges, banged into her front fender, glanced off, dashed up the street and disappeared around the corner.

Instinct told her there was more to come, and she waited for the pursuer to show. A big black poodle came next, barely missing her Bronco, and in what resembled a playful romp, bounded off in the direction of the first man. A uniformed policeman burst from the hedge and banged into the passenger-side door. He appeared dazed, then recovered and sprinted after the dog. The whole episode was comical, but it seemed to be serious business. She clamped her mouth shut to suppress a giggle, but then erupted into laughter.

Should she stick her nose where it didn't belong or let the situation alone? "What the heck." She was trying to be more spontaneous, the way she was before.

She stepped on the gas and pulled up to the street corner. The policeman in sergeant stripes was bent over, breathing hard, and the dog was sniffing at oleanders growing through a sagging wire fence. Since the plant was poisonous if ingested, she started to yell, but the animal quickly lost interest and urinated on a small patch of grass nearby.

The officer snapped his fingers and bellowed, "Get over here, right now." The dog's ears perked up and it bounced over and sat on its haunches before him, wagging its nub without a care in the world. "Zelda, this is not playtime. You have screwed up royally."

Evangeline called, "Sergeant, need any help?"

He glanced up in surprise and waved her off. She waited in the car until he caught his breath and spoke into his shoulder phone. She opened her door, hopped down and approached.

Perspiration soaked his blue shirt around the armpits, and sweat rivered a deep crease in his brow and plastered his curly blond hair to his head like glue. Cheeks resembling ripe peaches told her that, although he looked fit and had not a sign of a policeman's roll, he could not keep up with a dog.

She extended her hand. "I'm Evangeline Raines with Rembrandt Art Investigations."

A glimmer of recognition crossed his face at the mention of Rembrandt, and they shook hands. "I'm Sergeant Arlo Strecker," he said, and nodding toward the dog, added, "this is Zelda, and she's flat no good for police work. I've done everything I know of, and she still messes up."

"Uh, may I ask what happened here?"

"Why not? Can't hurt. I had two drug suspects cornered and gave Zelda the command to find the stuff. She downed in front of one, so I searched him and didn't find a thing. I started to pat down the other perp, but he took off, Zelda lost the scent, and I lost both the suspects."

The panting and chuffing dog watched Evangeline with interest. She said, "She's beautiful, though."

"Yeah, beautiful won't cut it in police work. We never use poodles. But the trainer felt good about her, so the chief went along. My gut told me it wouldn't work, and this proves it."

He removed a handkerchief from his pocket, wiped his brow

and blew his nose. "Besides, she needs lots of grooming, and the chief doesn't cotton to spending budget money on frou-frou."

"I can understand his reluctance, and I'll bet it takes a chunk of one's time."

"I drop her off at the groomers. No big deal. She's a sweetie, and smart. Or maybe I should say so instinctual it's spooky. Basically, I do believe she thinks it's a game. This is probably her swan song, though." He shook his head, and his arctic-blue eyes gazed adoringly at Zelda. "I'd keep her but I'm dog poor already and I'll have to board her replacement. Don't know what will become of her. She's too young to be put out to pasture, and I can't let her go to just anyone."

Zelda was still on sit command. Evangeline gazed into her intelligent black eyes that seemed to beg for another chance. When the poodle dropped to her stomach and inched toward her, she squatted, adjusting her skirt to drape over her knees. Gently, she clasped the dog's head in her hands. Stars shone back.

"See," he said. "She's on sit-stay command, but pretty much does as she pleases. The kicker is she's usually right."

Think about it, Evangeline. Don't do anything foolish. But her own reflection waved to her in those dark liquid eyes, and if she had a choice before, it had completely washed away.

She looked up at the sergeant and quickly said, "I'll take her." *And you too, cutie.*

The sergeant's eyes widened. "You're kidding, just like that?"

An image of Aunt Olinda popped into her mind, and she said, "Spooky is right up my alley."

CHAPTER 3

At Rembrandt Art Investigations, Evangeline said good morning to the receptionist. Babs was so tiny, the U-shaped desk practically enveloped her like one of those bouncy infant seats. The writing on her pale pink T-shirt read "Don't Blame Me. I Was Born Awesome."

"Nice tee," Evangeline said.

Babs wasn't the sharpest knife in the drawer, possessed a vivid imagination, and jabbered constantly about her night-before escapades, but she was dependable, arrived on time every day, and Evangeline liked the little toot. Barbie was her real name, but nobody in the offices called her that. Their boss, Julian, didn't seem to mind the way she dressed.

At her desk, Evangeline absently thumbed through the stack of fluorescent-orange phone messages Babs had handed to her. As soon as Julian came in, she would tell him about the mysterious phone call yesterday morning and Mr. Rossini's death.

And what about the dog? What was she thinking? It would take time to care for one, and the thought of leaving it home alone was distasteful. She would fret about its welfare, and there would be food and vet bills and grooming fees, and money was tight. Maybe the captain wouldn't agree to her adopting Zelda. Maybe Sergeant Strecker wouldn't call, but if he did simply to say hello, that would be fine. Maybe she worried for no reason, although worrying was her mission in life. She'd been accused of being a borderline pessimist, but that was only after she learned the truth about her father.

In trying to be more spontaneous, maybe she had gone over the edge with the dog issue. If she were truly pessimistic, wouldn't quitting a prime job teaching art history and joining an investigation firm that specialized in art theft, which was owned by one of the wealthiest men in Houston, be the last thing she would do? Mamma wouldn't have believed it, but Grandmother would have. She shook away the dull ache. Maybe Zelda was what she needed: a distraction at the end of the day.

She reached over, slid out the bottom file that called to her from the in-box, and submerged herself in mundane work. The antique clock in the outer office was chiming eleven when Babs buzzed Evangeline's line. The entire morning she'd dreaded answering the phone because it might be the police captain about the poodle. Her fears were answered.

After a lengthy conversation, with him interrogating her as though *she* were a criminal, she agreed to go by the station later to get the dog. *God, what have I done?*

She checked with Marion in the art gallery across the hall to see if Julian had shown, but evidently he was out entertaining a client. She told Babs she was leaving for the day, and in the parking lot behind the building, she felt a crunch under her shoe, looked down and gaped at shards from her Bronco's side-view mirror scattered on the concrete.

"Well, phooey, what's going on here?" She walked to the back of the car to inspect it for other damage and saw the red taillight shattered on the pavement, as if someone had possessed such rage he or she wanted to pound it to dust. A vandal getting rid of frustration by destroying her personal property really ticked her off. In fact, it made her so mad, she spat between her front teeth. Why couldn't things always go the way they were supposed to?

Now she would be late to the police station, but the taillight must be repaired. A ticket would cost money she couldn't afford. Luckily, when she arrived at the auto parts store, a serviceman installed a new light fixture; the side mirror had to be ordered.

She entered the police precinct a few minutes later than scheduled. Zelda, who lay on a flowered doggie pallet near the door, rose to her haunches and watched Evangeline as if aware of the adoption. *She can't be that smart, can she?*

Because of the once-overs and catcalls from several of the policemen lounging or sitting at their respective desks, she glanced down to the buttons on her blouse. She wasn't offended because she got initiated into such teasing when taking her investigative courses, innocent ways to fill a boring day or to deal with an especially stressful one.

One of the policemen yelled through the intercom, "Hey Streck, your chick is here about Zelda."

Evangeline tried to suppress a smile. *Your chick.* Cute.

Another uniform with a face too babyish for its owner to be packing a gun or wearing a badge, lounged back in his desk chair, patted his chest and said, "Be still my beating heart. An angel walked in the door."

Evangeline winked and threw him a kiss. The whole room burst into laughter and guffaws, and the young policeman turned crimson.

Sergeant Strecker entered the room carrying a basket containing dog paraphernalia. Evangeline noticed he was handsomer when he wasn't flushed and gasping for breath.

He set the basket on a desk and shook her hand. "The captain had an emergency. Authorized me to handle the adoption, so after you sign some papers, I'll help take this stuff to your car."

"Thank you. But I could actually use advice on commands and such."

He glanced at the wall clock. "This afternoon is out, but give me your address, and I'll come by tonight and run through a few moves to get you by."

A policeman within hearing distance said, "Oh, yeah, you'll show her some moves, all right."

Strecker growled, "Can it, you guys. Show some respect," then he returned speaking to Evangeline. "Not much to know. As I said before, she pretty much does as she pleases. Real smart little gal. In fact"—he indicated the room—"smarter'n some people I've come across. She'll do you good. Understands body language and such." He looked at Zelda with a loving, somber expression. "Never kept her in a cage like I was supposed to." He pointed to the one against the wall. "It's for show."

Evangeline sighed. "Great. All I need is a talking dog that does as it pleases."

Zelda still occupied the pallet and watched them. The sergeant made a hand movement, and the animal rose from its haunches and padded over, nub wagging. She sat in front of Evangeline, cocked her head, and Evangeline swore she grinned. The dog raised her paw, Evangeline melted and shook the offered appendage.

"Darnedest dog I ever saw," Strecker said. "Beats me how she's aware of what's going on. It's a shame she's too much of a lightweight for police work. I'm kinda jealous of the way she's taken a shine to you."

"You may visit any time. And if you need a serious Zelda fix, be my guest at dog-sitting."

"I'll take you up on that. It relieves my mind she'll have a good home, someone to love her. We all need love." He raised an eyebrow and his arctic-blue eyes twinkled.

Is he flirting with me? No, he's being sensitive. Evangeline knelt and scratched Zelda's neck, cradled the animal's head in her hands and looked into her bright, expectant eyes. Strange she had not noticed exactly how beautiful and perfect the animal was.

As if she'd had a fresh grooming, her dense, curly black coat was lustrous, clipped short and smelled of coconut. If not for the sparkle in her dark oval eyes, and her good-natured attitude, one might assume her aloof and haughty. Evangeline prayed she kept her playful side and adapted to her new surroundings. And since the dog was trained for action, she hoped isolation, which she knew too much about, didn't send the animal into depression.

"Well, girl, I'll try if you will. Let's go home and see what kind of damage we can do."

Zelda woofed.

Chapter 4

The Montrose area Evangeline called home nestled inside the Loop 610 near downtown. Platted over one hundred years ago, it had become one of the most diversely populated areas in Houston. She enjoyed walking its wide boulevards and marveled at the lush foliage. If she let her imagination go, she could almost hear the streetcars that used to traverse the district.

Evangeline's corner house was in an ideal location and in one of the better neighborhoods. She and Nicky had bought the old 1920s two-story stucco on the oak-lined boulevard with intentions of refurbishing it the way many new homeowners in the near-downtown area had done. Nicky's leaving threw a monkey wrench into those plans. For security, they had managed to install a wrought-iron fence with a driveway and entrance gate in front and a wooden one around the rest of the property. With a new central-air-and-heat system, re-plastered walls and refinished oak floors, the sparsely furnished house sat waiting until she decided what to do with the rest of her thirty-year-old life.

To arrive home before dark for a change was a relief. At night, loneliness lay like a blanket over the house. The absence of sound was the worst: no faucet running, no toilet being flushed, no loud television or the forlorn wail of Nicky's saxophone. It was as though the house was paying homage to a death by the occasional creak of a wooden beam as the structure cooled and settled.

Then other houses came to mind, so many she couldn't count them, and days and nights so bleak and silent when her mother was gone on a date. Evangeline would pace the floor and talk to herself for comfort.

Realistically, she could do little about it. After the divorce from Evangeline's stepfather, and probably even before, Mamma's philosophy was that by burning bridges she would find again the sweet scent of love. Each new vista opening before her brought her nearer to a wonderland beaconing its promise beyond the horizon. In other words, "a good life might be waiting around the corner."

Evangeline kept a suitcase packed with her few prized possessions, touchstones of the past she would not leave behind. Felicia eventually made her discard them all, so by the time Evangeline went to live with Grandpop, she possessed one duffel bag with two changes of clothes, a toothbrush and a pair of rain boots. Felicia would say that wherever they landed they would be provided with what they needed.

Youth was not conducive to understanding such grownup viewpoints, or for discerning why they traveled a ribboned highway to another fairyland town that would "surely appreciate us" and "where our lives will be so much better."

Their lives never were.

For years Evangeline thought *New Kid* was part of her name. Unless someone experienced living like that, it was impossible to imagine how the emptiness dug inside you, sucked at you and never let go, like a leech draining your life's blood.

Her one burning desire was to fit in and acquire a best friend. But the new kid must prove herself, and parents watched and fretted about where these new people came from, who their family was, and what values they held. Would these vagabonds lead their babies astray?

Evangeline's mother never knew how she felt. Not then, nor

the day she died. The unspoken rule was simple—what was past was past. But some things were better left unsaid, and deep inside, Evangeline realized talking to her mother would not have changed the situation. Their one confrontation, the one that mattered, the one where the secret was revealed, came much later.

"Shake it off, Evangeline. It'll barrel back when you least expect it." Maybe her new companion would help alleviate the focus on herself and, according to the therapist she went to for a few months after Nicky left, her fear of rejection. At a hundred dollars a pop, the therapy helped her forgive, but deep-seated feelings were hard to change.

Buckled up in the back seat, Zelda woofed as the gate swung open.

"Yes, this is home."

Evangeline waited until the gate closed automatically to exit the Bronco, a precaution Nicky had insisted upon in case someone followed her in and tried to accost her. She opened the rear door and released Zelda's safety belt. The dog sailed out and bounded around the yard with the sprightliness of a puppy, disappeared, and reappeared from around the other side, panting.

Evangeline scratched the dog's head between her ears. "Hope you took care of business."

Zelda woofed, wagged her nub, and looked at her proudly.

"Yeah, right. You really understood what I said, didn't you?"

The poodle wagged its nub again.

After she unlocked the glass storm door and the wooden door leading into the kitchen, and turned off the alarm, Evangeline stowed the dog supplies in the pantry and puzzled over where to put the bed. She should have realized it wouldn't be a problem as Zelda settled under the desk that sat next to the back door. Evangeline knew the canine species possessed a primordial instinct to snuggle in dark warm places, so she snapped her fingers, motioned for her to come out, and placed the bed there. The extra-wide kneehole allowed for a nice fit. She patted it; Zelda obligingly ducked and climbed in, settled down again, and through contented, sleepy eyes watched Evangeline move about the kitchen.

This might work after all, she thought. Zelda could alert her to a prowler or a fire or be here when she arrived home. And, although logically she knew it was impossible, she could swear the dog was familiar with the house. Maybe canines had a sixth sense. Sort of the way she did, the way Aunt Olinda did.

She clicked on the wide-screen television to watch the six o'clock news, a habit she'd cultivated to diffuse the quiet. When Nicky had moved out, she kept the house, its mortgage, the new television (also mortgaged), her free-and-clear old Bronco, a few pieces of her grandmother's antique furniture, personal items, and their library of old black-and-white movies she and Nicky had loved watching. She would have fought him all the way out the door for those. He probably knew he would be too busy to watch them with his new job at Fallana B's.

She opened the bag of dry dog food, and at the clink in the stainless-steel bowl, Zelda came out of her cave and sat, waiting expectantly. When the animal finished daintily crunching the food, Evangeline realized she, too, was hungry.

She scrounged in the pantry and found a can of chicken-vegetable soup. She zapped it in the microwave, and placed the hot bowl and some saltines on a plate.

"Not much of a meal," she said and glanced at Zelda.

Zelda woofed.

She rolled her eyes at the dog. "Okay, okay, you're a smarty."

With her legs propped on a bar stool, Evangeline sat at the oversized butcher-block island separating the kitchen and family room, and sipped the soup. The news was the same: murder, mayhem, and border patrol problems. She picked up the remote to click over to another channel, but her house phone chimed and she jumped, sloshing soup onto her blouse. "Stupid schmuck."

When she saw *Unknown Caller,* she hesitated. Ridiculous; she had to get over her fear, couldn't continue to worry about one prank call.

"Hello," she said cautiously. Silence. "Okay, who is this and what do you want?" Heavy breathing. "Don't call here anymore." She punched disconnect so hard she dropped the phone.

The phone chimed again and this time she was ready. She picked it up and said, "Okay, creep, let's talk about this."

Chapter 5

Sergeant Strecker said, "Okay, what do you want to talk about?"

Evangeline sputtered, "Oh, Sergeant, I'm sorry, thought you might be—never mind." She did not want to mention the phone call to the police, because they would laugh her out of the precinct if all she had to go on were two measly prank calls.

"If you're having problems, I'll be glad to listen."

"No, just kids prank calling. Nothing important."

He said he would be by shortly, and she tried to shake off her concern, but instinctively she knew she did have a problem, that the calls were not simply pranks. Someone was seriously trying to frighten her, and they were succeeding.

Strecker arrived about fifteen minutes later, and after he and Zelda greeted each other, Evangeline offered him a beer. He declined because of a later commitment.

Secretly, she felt disappointment. "I appreciate your taking the time to help me. It's above and beyond—"

"Not a problem. I enjoy the whole process, a dog lover to the max."

They decided to go into the backyard and get right to the training. The outside vapor light Nicky had installed on a pine tree illuminated most of the yard, giving them a clear view to work in.

Strecker said, "A dog responds to your tone of voice. It usually tells the animal what's expected, whether you're being firm, displeased, playful, commanding obedience, wanting affection, or whatever. It's especially important to stay calm, because dogs respond to your energy level. An anxious pack leader lends to an anxious canine."

"I might have trouble with that, since my emotions tend to rule my head. All Grandpop's hound did was sleep and eat." Thoughtfully, she said, "Never considered myself a pack leader. I like it."

Strecker grinned. "And Zelda will help you. She's very accommodating."

Zelda woofed.

Evangeline whispered, "Do you think she understands what we're saying?"

He placed his hand over his mouth and whispered, "I wouldn't bet a ten-penny nail she doesn't."

"I like the way you think, and maybe I'm not completely imagining things."

"What things?"

"Really, it's nothing."

A feeling of being watched rolled over Evangeline. She glanced up at the Bernowitzes' window and waved as the curtain fell back into place.

Strecker followed her gaze. "Nosy neighbors?"

"Mr. and Mrs. Bernowitz are a mixed blessing. At least I'm never completely alone."

"But you have no real privacy."

"Exactly."

"Think of it as a good thing with you living alone. Can't be too careful, and Zelda is an A-one watchdog. Anyway, anything special you'd like to know about her or dogs in general?"

"I've heard animals need to keep up with training or they lose initiative."

"You always have me for backup."

"Uh-huh." *Thank you, God.*

"Okay, let's try another approach."

Zelda sat waiting for a command. Strecker said, "Zelda, watch me." He pointed to his eyes with two fingers, and the dog focused on his face. "You won't have to point, she understands the words. I'm showing how we trained her."

"Now I'll give her a non-verbal command to come." He waved her forward with his hand. She came and sat before him. "Good girl," he said and massaged her ears. "See, I praise her when she does what I ask. Dogs love praise. They live to please the pack leader." He chuckled. "Although most do it for treats, our Zelda does it for affection. Treats are a bonus." Then he said casually, "But I don't have to tell you about affection."

Our Zelda? Heat rose to Evangeline's face. "I see you're passionate and good at what you do."

The compliment flustered him as if only he were allowed to dole them out. He said, "I'll show you a few more non-verbals in case you're in a situation where silence is needed. Being a PI."

Surely his words weren't meant as a put-down, for that would go against his nature.

After Evangeline performed the hand movements and commands for come, sit, stay and a few others, Strecker said, "Each of our dogs is trained to attack to its own individual word. Zelda's is," he whispered in her ear, "crush. She'll sense danger and will usually respond, but don't use the word carelessly."

"Gotcha. So much to remember."

"Try visualizing a crushed orange."

Zelda looked at him as though disgusted with the whispering. "She knows what you're saying, doesn't she?"

"Yeah, that's the problem. I can't put anything over on her. But you're a quick study, already learned the basics. When you're comfortable with those, I'll show you some neat tricks Zelda's learned. She's a very special dog. Full of surprises." He paused and stared at Evangeline with his arctic-blue eyes.

Evangeline felt weak-kneed.

"You realize I wouldn't let her go to just anyone. I knew immediately I could trust you. Zelda did too."

She felt a blush, but couldn't control it. "Thank you, kind sir, and Zelda," she said, and performed a slight curtsey. "Living up to your expectations won't be easy, or remembering your instructions, because right now, my brain is fried."

"Like I said, Zelda will help you." He glanced at his watch. "Now, though, my other job is calling. Twice a week I'm a security guard at a hormonal teen club. If I was ever that rowdy, my parents should've institutionalized me."

They laughed, and Evangeline said, "You grew up fine, and if truth be known, teens haven't changed so much. It's the opportunities available to them that have multiplied."

She thanked the sergeant for his help, they shook hands, and his touch warmed her. She and Zelda followed him to the front gate, and the animal watched forlornly as he left. His car disappeared around the corner and the air swooshed out of Evangeline. She was physically and mentally exhausted, and it felt like a vise was squeezing her head.

But she was buoyed up by the satisfaction of becoming familiar with the basic dog commands, and when walking Zelda on a leash, to keep her to her left side in an imaginary box.

Hopefully she would never be in a situation to issue attack orders, because Zelda acted so mild-mannered it might not be in her nature to show aggression.

To become skillful, Evangeline needed to learn much more, and they both would benefit if she took a course in obedience training. Zelda knew it all, but she wasn't a mind reader. When Evangeline bungled a directive, the dog would look smug and disgusted, which could mortify one's ego.

Actually, she needed to share this new development with

someone. Aunt Olinda stayed up late, and desiring to keep her privy to changes in her life, Evangeline dialed her number at their small East Texas home.

Olinda said, "Hey, child. What be happening?"

"I got a dog. She is so beautiful. You'll love her—she's smart, and her name's Zelda."

"I knew someone new be coming into your life. Didn't reckon on a dog."

Evangeline ignored the insinuation. "Are you okay? Having any more trouble with your stomach?"

"I be fine, girl. Don't you worry 'bout Aunt Olinda. Take care of you and find dose treasures you been searching for. We need to get rich."

Evangeline laughed and said teasingly, "What's this *we* stuff? You think what's mine is yours?"

"Watch it, or I'll put a heebie-jeebie on you."

"Right back atcha."

Before they disconnected, Aunt Olinda said, "I decided. Be looking for a sign and don't fight it. Hear me?"

Evangeline humored her, not believing in Aunt Olinda's hocus-pocus. Still, she didn't discount the woman's beliefs, but kept an open mind for the sake of harmony.

"Make it good."

Evangeline stretched, tapped her thigh and said to Zelda, "Okay, girl, time for bed. I've a busy day at work tomorrow. Taking advantage isn't in my genes, and I've done enough of that to Julian. First, let's go outside for your constitutional."

Zelda's ears pricked up and she padded over to the desk and pointed to the red retractable leash.

"Nope, we won't need the leash. A few turns around the yard should do it. We've both had enough activity for one day."

They went out to the patio and she glanced up at the window

in the house behind hers. On many occasions she'd noticed Mr. or Mrs. Bernowitz watching her from there. If they hadn't always done it, she would think they were watching for her to bring home a lover. At the rate she was going, they'd have a long wait with not one prospect in her future.

Tonight the lookout window appeared empty. Maybe they got bored with the dog training session. In the distance, a flash lightened the dark sky. Good, rain would be there soon. She loved the patter of it at night.

Evangeline noticed Zelda sniffing the impatiens, the one kind of flower she could grow. "Don't you dare," she commanded.

The dog turned, gave her a snooty glance, padded away from the flowers and over to the walking stones Nicky had lain. She trotted around the corner of the house and disappeared. Evangeline sat in the fold-up chair by the back door, and as the breeze stroked her cheeks, she enjoyed the tinkle and music of the many wind chimes she had hung under the eaves and in the trees. With the slightest wafting, they danced and harmonized. The cacophony was simply the lovely soothing sound of home.

At a blast of thunder, she flinched, crossed her arms in front and hugged herself. That one hit too close for comfort, so she stood and surveyed the yard for Zelda. The dog's black coat blended so well with the dark, Evangeline almost missed seeing her squatting behind the fig tree. At night that tree reminded her of a huge hulking monster with a thousand arms practically gutting the south side corner of the yard. When ripe, the figs tasted delicious, so she left the tree alone. Not long ago, lightning hit the tall skinny pine closest to the house, but she hadn't had the time or the inclination to have it removed.

"Come on, girl," she called. "We need to go inside."

Suddenly, Zelda streaked along the wooden fence, growling and barking ferociously. Evangeline's blood turned to ice and she stumbled back, plopping into the lawn chair and almost tipping it over. She pitched forward, reeled to her feet and yelled, "Zelda, what is it?"

The dog, now on its hind legs, was scratching at the boards and growling. Evangeline reached for the door handle to escape inside, her heart pounding in her chest, but as suddenly as Zelda's antics had begun, she sat on her haunches and stared at the fence.

"My gosh, you scared me to death," she said, and placed her hand over her thumping heart. "It must have been one of the homeless people walking by."

A shrill crack vibrated the air, rattled the windows and played havoc with the wind chimes. In unison, a blinding bolt hit the pine and sizzled up its base. The pressure threw Evangeline back against the door. Zelda froze in place, her legs stiff, smoke seeming to waft from her body.

"Oh, no! You're hit."

She rushed to the dog, almost afraid to touch her, and then, relieved, saw that the smoke wafted from the pine tree, along with a strong acrid odor. Zelda shuddered, shook herself, sneezed, and skinned her lips back from her teeth in what resembled a foolish grin.

Shaken, Evangeline crumpled in front of the dog and patted the ground. "Oh, Zelda, you could've been killed. Come here, girl." The dog dropped to its stomach, scooted closer to her and whined softly as if agreeing. Afraid to move the limp animal immediately, Evangeline hugged her, ruffled and stroked her coat, testing for any noticeable wounds.

And then the strangest thing happened. The action of holding the dog against her evoked an odd, almost spiritual, indescribable feeling, as if the two were enveloped in religious communion, drawing strength from the other. *Aunt Olinda? A heebie-jeebie sign? Nah, it can't be.*

The moment passed and she whispered, "We'll see the vet

tomorrow. I'll call about the tree, but you come first, sweetheart. You come first."

Zelda whined pitifully.

Evangeline patted her head. "Let's go inside and I'll check every inch of you. And to think I believed the old saying 'Lightning never strikes the same place twice.' "

From habit, she glanced up at the Bernowitzes' window and saw the curtains move. She guessed the old couple had nothing better to do than spy on her. One of these days she would shock them and dance naked in the backyard. She'd heard celibacy had its advantages, but for the life of her she couldn't think what they might be.

Without warning, the bottom fell out of the sky. Sheets of rain pummeled down, so they dashed for the house. Evangeline had never been so close to witnessing a death and wondered if it was an omen. The episode at the fence pushed to the back of her mind, she decided it was time to visit Aunt Olinda at the old homestead.

Chapter 6

The next day, Evangeline made an appointment with the veterinarian Arlo Strecker had recommended. On the way to work, the craziest urge to return home struck her. She'd had the dog one day, but they had made a connection she could not explain. It was as though the animal were human, as though she knew Evangeline's thoughts in advance.

She had studied anthropomorphism, whereby people became so attached to their pets they gave them human emotions or characteristics. And she'd read animals had no soul. Wouldn't it be amazing if Zelda were imbued with one-of-a-kind intelligence?

She braked for a red light and thought, *Can't put my finger on it, but since the storm, Zelda's different.* When Evangeline awoke that morning, the dog lay snoozing inside her bedroom door, blocking the entrance. Maybe her trainer or Arlo taught her to guard her master. While Evangeline dressed, Zelda stood at the window on her hind legs with forepaws on the sill and occasionally sniffed the air. When Evangeline asked what was wrong, Zelda whined low as if she wasn't quite certain. Or maybe her actions were caused by the trauma of the lightning strike. Maybe it had singed her brain or traumatized her in some way.

But when Evangeline moved the curtain to the side and peeked out, a car was turning the corner and Zelda growled deeply. Chills zipped up Evangeline's back and she quickly let go of the curtain. "What was it, girl?" But Zelda had already left the window and waited at the bedroom door. Evangeline said, "Get real. Why am I so spooked?"

At the red light, she realized her knuckles had turned white from gripping the steering wheel. "Ridiculous. Get hold of yourself," and shaking her head, she controlled the urge to turn the car around.

The light changed and a horn blared behind her. She muttered, "Hold your britches." Then she pressed the gas pedal hard and almost burned rubber.

When she arrived discombobulated at the office, Babs was popping gum and said Julian wanted to see her immediately. She winked. "Unless he took an early lunch."

Evangeline refused to contribute to office gossip and ignored the insinuation. Julian's philosophy was that money begets money, so an affluent appearance was mandatory. In Rembrandt Art Investigations' outer office sat two plush brown velvet loveseats and two barrel chairs covered in deep-burnished-red tapestry. A seventeenth-century clock in its original Chinese black lacquer base stood near the door. A Poussin landscape hung behind Babs' desk, red-hued Persian rugs lay in the offices, and an important sculpture occupied each desk or sideboard. The décor in the investigative office could not compare to the gallery across the hall.

With the many important art pieces in Julian's building, the security system was one of the best—as good as or better than any bank. An armed security guard patrolled the premises night and day, and only Julian knew the combination to the walk-in vault. Once, Evangeline had glimpsed inside and noted wall-to-wall paintings and objets d'art.

She waved to Kreshon, the daytime security guard sitting at his post at the front of the long, wide hall, the floor of which was paved with white marble imported from a villa in Italy. The hall divided the two businesses and provided client entry to the building. Beveled-glass double doors opened to the gallery with two ancient ceramic foo dogs flanking each side as if guarding the temple.

The less obtrusive investigation-firm door had "Rembrandt Art Investigations" printed on the etched glass. The back entrance from the parking lot admitted employees and deliveries, with inside doors directly across from each other leading from the hall into the rear of each business. These doors remained locked, with only Julian and his employees having keys.

She entered the art gallery by the main door and automatically reached to her right and rubbed the stone Buddha's huge belly. *Need all the luck I can get.*

Julian was with a client, so she stopped and spoke to Marion, the receptionist/sales person. Then she poked her head into Lydia's office. Lydia was Julian's private secretary and accountant, and keeper of the keys to the kingdom. Evangeline tolerated her standoffish, generally flustered and frustrated attitude, but it wasn't easy. Lydia needed to delegate some responsibilities, but from some skewed sense of superiority, she acted as if her job were too secret or important to share.

At almost fifty, the woman should have learned nobody was indispensible and, according to a permanently pinched brow, if she continued on her present course, a popped blood vessel would be her reward. Evangeline hadn't heard her speak of a lover, so maybe she needed a little spooning, as Grandpop used to say.

After one-sided amenities with Lydia, Evangeline milled around until Julian's client left, and then she approached.

"Do you need me?"

He beckoned, "Let's go into my office. I've an assignment you'll like."

He shut the door and motioned her to one of the matching

antique hand-carved leather Tuscan chairs in front of the desk. He settled in the buttery-soft brown leather behind it and took a manila folder from a bottom drawer.

Julian, who was in his mid-fifties, stood an inch or so shorter than Evangeline's five feet nine, but his physical stature wasn't significant. Impeccably dressed, when he came into a room, one felt the electricity crackle, as if an important figure had entered. She was sure he hadn't had hair implants and admired the thick wavy gray framing his tanned but surprisingly unlined face.

Cobalt eyes pierced her as though he was privy to her hidden thoughts, and it wouldn't surprise her if he were. He might have had liposuction around his middle, but with more money than the United States Mint, he could afford anything he wanted and usually got what he desired. Long lunches were fodder for the gossip mill, but for every intent and purpose, he was a single man. His wife of thirty years, fed up with his work ethic and philandering, finally told him to move out. Julian parked his town car and bought the champagne-colored sports car. Divorce didn't seem to be in their future, probably because he would have to split his fortune and she would have to give up the prestige. The arrangement worked for them, so it was nobody's business.

Julian leaned back in the chair and clasped his hands behind his head. "How does a trip to Manhattan sound?"

She sat forward expectantly. "Fantastic."

"I thought you'd like that. Blendell's will auction off a Vermeer day after tomorrow, and I want a representative there. I can't—prefer not to—go, and Lance is leaving for Mexico City tonight. This is the second painting by Vermeer to surface in the last eighty years."

"Could it be Grandmother's?"

"Sorry. I've seen photos. No resemblance."

She clenched her hands in her lap. "I studied Vermeer some,

but need a refresher."

For all his friendliness, Julian enjoyed flaunting his expertise, and proceeded with an elementary history of the artist. "Johannes Vermeer was a Dutch artist who lived in the seventeenth century. He died young and wasn't a prolific painter—thirty-five in all. His last painting, which, by the way, was in dispute for decades, sold for millions."

She plopped back in the chair. "Art *is* big money."

Julian grinned. "A nice sum for a little eight- or ten-inch painting. And although this new one has been technically analyzed, and pigments and the warp and weft of the canvas match those Vermeer used, I'm still skeptical."

"I don't blame you. But Julian, what will I be looking for?"

Julian sat up straight and scooted the chair to his desk. "Any inconsistencies. Try viewing it the day before, and personally, I don't care if we get this one or not. My gut tells me there's a conspiracy going on." He looked into space. "My appraiser, who is a connoisseur on Vermeer, swears this one is an original. We'll see."

Since it would be her first real task without Lance, she felt queasy. She'd attended auctions, but had never been a bidder. "Should I bid?"

"I want you there for appearances. We have to keep abreast. To answer your question, ten million tops. Peanuts for a painting that could go as high as fifty, sixty million or more."

"You trust me with this?"

"Of course."

"But why not one of the more prominent auction houses? I've never heard of this one."

"Probably will support more bidders, or they've leased a larger space for the occasion. Not sure why. Anyway, your plane leaves tomorrow about noon. Lydia has your round-trip ticket and hotel reservations." He glanced at his gold calendar and moon-phase wristwatch, and with his middle and index fingers slid the folder across his desk to her.

"Photos and short bios of collectors who will probably be there. Study them because I'll ask you who bid what. And Evangeline"—he paused, and a smile tilted the corners of his mouth—"after the auction, feel free to pursue your other interest."

Heat rose to her face. "Thank you, Julian. You are too good to me, giving me so much time off with no questions asked. How can I ever repay you?"

"Consider it an investment, and if you find even one painting, you'll be a wealthy woman." The meeting ended, he pushed his chair back, stood and walked her to the door.

Somehow the phone call and Mr. Rossini's death didn't seem important at the moment.

Chapter 7

Since Evangeline would be gone for several days and needed to see her friend Dahlia, who had returned from Europe, she called and made a date for lunch at their favorite restaurant. Upon her arrival, Dahlia was already there, waving to her from an aisle table.

They hugged and Evangeline, wrapped in the warm embrace of a friend she trusted with her life, felt a soothing wave of calm. After amenities, she asked Dahlia about her recent trip. Her friend recounted her escapade with an Italian count, and left nothing to the imagination.

Her friend's bravado and cynicism were pretenses to hide the pain and grief she endured after losing Carlo. They met in Madrid one summer while Dahlia toured with a study group. Carlo became her one focus, and she never returned to the university. When he and their two children were killed in an automobile accident, it was as though Dahlia's own heart had been torn from her. At least with Carlo's estate, she had become independently wealthy.

Evangeline and Dahlia had known each other since high school. Dahlia and Aunt Olinda were her confidants when Evangeline learned the true circumstances of her birth. Later, both Evangeline and Dahlia married for love, and ironically they were back where they started, except Dahlia's loss was tragic, final.

The waiter came and, without perusing the menu, Dahlia

ordered grilled salmon and a vodka martini with three olives. Evangeline ordered the daily special salad and a Chardonnay spritzer.

Dahlia said, "What's been happening here? Is Nicky still finding himself?"

"Definitely. It gets easier for me as time goes by." The statement was only half true. She scrutinized Dahlia, whose countenance appeared relaxed and whose heavily defined green-and-gold flecked eyes were bright and clear. The vacation had agreed with her.

"Dahlia's home now. You will be fine." She patted Evangeline's hand as if being there was enough. She flipped her brick-red neck-length bob, took a compact from her designer purse, patted powder on her nose and whined, "Even in October this god-awful humidity is terrible. Dahlia takes a bath, fixes her hair, and in fifteen minutes feels like a wilted banana peel. You're lucky. Wash and wear."

Evangeline laughed heartily, because even wash-and-wear hair needed care. "You are totally nuts. And you are totally glowing. What's your secret?"

"Sex, my dear. You should try it."

Evangeline raised an eyebrow. "I have tried it, just not lately."

"Have any prospects?"

"Not really. Been too busy."

"Well, Dahlia has a prospect in mind for you, but we need to take a vacation first."

Probably because her friend wanted to be the person she was before her husband's death, she often referred to herself in the third person, and spent the long, hot Houston summers touring Europe. In the fall she returned to her roots, and this year, for a change, with no plastic surgery—well, maybe an eyelift, but Evangeline didn't ask. And although Dahlia traveled in affluent social circles, she was a born and bred East Texas woman, and played up its twang and dialect to the max, possibly a ploy to set her apart from the establishment. Those East Texas idioms sneaked into Evangeline's vocabulary occasionally, but since she moved to the area as a teenager, they were not as dominant.

Dahlia stared silently into space, and Evangeline wondered where she had gone.

She waved her hand in front of Dahlia's face. "Hello, where are you? I got a dog. Am I pathetic, or what?"

Dahlia raised one eyebrow. "What kind of dog? Lord almighty, not one of those yappy little froufrous."

"It's a pedigreed standard poodle, papers and all. Doesn't shed. Smart as the dickens. Almost human." She didn't mention Zelda having been a police dog.

"Now don't go imagining again. You get downright paranoid."

Indignant and embarrassed, Evangeline pulled up and said, "I mentioned ghosts once, and you and Nicky will never let me live it down."

The ghost thing had begun when they moved into her present home. She felt an immediate connection with the house at first sight. And if it held a ghost or two, they were at least friendly. Upon several occasions, she swore she had seen a movement, or a shadow on the stairs. And she had encountered cold places and swooshes of air. The experiences hadn't been frightening, but more like welcomings.

Nicky said she had a vivid imagination, had been around Aunt Olinda too long. She didn't really believe in ghosts, but her thought processes were open to offbeat ideas, including the supernatural. It didn't matter how realistic she intended to be; Aunt Olinda's ways and a couple of classes she took in college had given her fodder to chew upon.

In the one real conversation with her neighbor Mrs. Bernowitz, the woman mentioned that a neighbor had told her a previous owner had died in the upstairs front bedroom. In the past, dying at home was often preferable to going to a hospital, so Evangeline didn't view it as unusual. In fact, it was proving to be psychologically more appealing to spend one's last days at home rather than in a hospice room.

Dahlia drawled, "Your aunt Olinda has certainly done a number on you." She swished her hand in the air. "Ghosts be gone! Dahlia's in the mood for a party."

The waiter brought their cocktails and Evangeline sipped the spritzer. She was not in the mood for one of Dahlia's parties; each one proved to be the same: guests drank too much, names dropped off tongues, and transparent gaiety tended to make personal agendas more noticeable. As different as a mountain is from a cave, how she and Dahlia had remained friends was beyond reasoning.

"Can't do it," Evangeline said. "Blendell's in Manhattan is having an important auction and I have research to do. Another Vermeer surfaced and is going on the auction block. This is the second undocumented painting to surface. Julian wants me to check it out."

Visibly disappointed, Dahlia said, "A forgery?"

Evangeline shrugged. "For some reason, Julian respects my opinion." She grinned sheepishly. "To tell the truth, I'm the only one available. The Vermeer will go for millions and I'm flat not qualified to handle such an assignment. Thank God we're bidding low. Probably get knocked out on the first round." She ran her fingers through her hair. "Don't know if I can take the pressure."

"Yes you can. Dahlia believes in you." She rimmed the glass with her finger. "How *is* Julian, anyway? Has he hooked up with anyone?"

"Don't even go there," Evangeline said, and gave Dahlia a disapproving glare. For her friend to become involved with her boss would be the bitter end. Keeping her professional life separate from her personal life was important to her.

"Oh, pooh, just asking."

Unaccountably Evangeline's neck hair bristled. She quickly scanned the room, but nothing seemed out of the ordinary. Filled with the crème de la crème of Houston high society passing the usual backyard gossip, the restaurant was first-class.

Dahlia glanced around. "What is it, hon? See someone you know?"

"No, an odd twinge is all." But the eerie sensation of evil afoot, as Aunt Olinda would say, pervaded her senses.

Satisfied, Dahlia asked, "How long will you be gone?"

"Two nights. I'm taking an extra day to check out some leads. The one in San Francisco didn't pan out." She made a mental note to call Mrs. Rossini.

Dahlia leaned back and studied her. "You need to give up on that, Evie. You spend so much energy obsessing over stolen art, you can't see how lucky you are. Maybe you need to step back and take a long look at what's important, what you're doing to yourself. Dahlia would in your circumstances."

To Evangeline, it sounded like an attack, so she didn't mention the unsettling phone calls or Mr. Rossini. She wiped at the sweat on the spritzer glass and chose her words carefully. "Grandmother Delacroix-Ravel never gave up, and because I made a promise, neither will I." She paused. "It still doesn't make sense, the way she died. It was a miracle I spoke to her the same day—to say good-bye—make the promise." Her throat caught and tears brimmed.

Dahlia patted her hand. "It hurts, sweetheart, and you can't help how you feel. It took me forever before I could carry on a conversation without tearing up. But your grandmother was getting old. Her heart wasn't pumping right, and for your own sake, you need to let go. A whole new world is out there waiting to be explored. Uh, along with a boatload of men." The serious talk ended, she grinned, wiggled her martini glass at the waiter, and then gazed deep into Evangeline's eyes. "Let's say you find all the art, what then?"

"Maybe I'll feel worthy."

CHAPTER 8

Abner Jacobson had lived quietly since retiring from a private museum near Washington, D.C. He had maintained a low profile so as not to draw attention to himself, and felt proud of his discretion and control of occasional impulses for extravagance. Other than a few fishing trips, his one reckless spending spree took him on a recent European vacation. But traveling wasn't what it used to be with all the airline restrictions and rules, especially at his age, and he was glad to be home on US soil. His small condo had never looked so good, and it would take a bulldozer to get him abroad again. The trip was necessary in order to make it right.

He rested a few days and then needed to shop for essentials. He also yearned for friendly conversation, so he drove into town, and after completing his errands, stopped at Rudy's.

There, he ordered a draft beer in a frosty mug from Joe the bartender, took a sip and welcomed the warm glow. "Hey Joe, is Rudy here?"

"Nah, Abner, he left on a family matter. Should be back soon, though."

Disappointed at first because he wanted to share his exploits, Abner knew there would be another chance.

He ambled through the maze of tables to his usual at the rear, nodding to several regulars as he went. He leaned back in the chair, and surveyed the familiar interior with its scarred tabletops partially covered with white plastic, and the comfortably padded straight-back chairs with rollers that glided smoothly on the aged tile floor. Not the most glamorous place, but homey and relaxed, no pretense of being other than what it was.

He had spent hours at this same table listening to gossip and watching the small overhead television set, now a recently purchased, large flat-screen, and Rudy and Joe knew him by name. They weren't close friends, for Abner could not afford to confide in or get too close to anyone. Occasionally they discussed ball games, election results, the weather. Abner felt part of a family at Rudy's. When his family was alive, home was the center of his existence. Now, he substituted as best he could.

He remembered his retirement as if it were yesterday. If upper management thought the pitiful plaque given him at the luncheon was compensation for his years of loyalty, they were utterly mistaken. It had read: "To Abner Jacobson for a Lifetime of Faithful Service." He had disdainfully left the plaque in his locker, but like a lost dog, it had shown up in the mail a few days later without a note of hello, how are you, or go to hell. He dropped it in the trash with the rest of the garbage. To their credit, they did allow him to remain years beyond retirement age because he was *good old dependable Abner,* and as the director said with emphasis on the word, *almost* indispensable.

He smiled. *If they only knew.* Except for Abner's one indiscretion, which he was convinced was his entitlement because of the many years he had given to the museum, he had led an exemplary life, been an asset to the community.

Strange how fate decided his destiny long before he realized where it would lead. Someday he would think about what might have been if he'd taken another path, if, after his discharge from the army in the forties, he had not offhandedly applied for the driver and mechanic job for the museum. At the memory, he became almost as giddy as when he touched a Renoir for the first time those sixty or more years ago—he wasn't sure which, since time seemed irrelevant now. And sometimes, in the solitude of his room, the desire to share his story overcame him so strongly that he felt like a helium balloon filled to the max and ready to explode. He wanted to shout to the world that he wasn't some pitiful, lonely old man taking up space, waiting to die, but one who took opportunity by the horns and, in his estimation, succeeded in pulling off one of the biggest charades of this or any other century.

Abner listened to the banal chatter around him, and wondered what it would be like to join in on the camaraderie, but knew it would never—could never—happen. Except, maybe one day soon, when the time was right, he would contact her, make her privy to what he had done, and they would sit down like two old friends and have one helluva discussion about stolen art and World War II.

Chapter 9

Evangeline's itinerary was to land at the Newark airport and take a taxi to Blendell's before going to the hotel. Except for a slight delay taking off at Bush Intercontinental, the flight had been uneventful, smooth, and the seat next to her unoccupied, allowing for a relaxing trip. Julian spared no expense for his employees, so flying first class could spoil one.

The male attendant plastered on a smile as he cleared the coffee cup from the tray table and offered her more. She shook her head. When he ambled on down the aisle, Evangeline leaned her head back, tested her seat belt, closed her eyes and let the past wash over her like an incoming wave.

It had been a stomach-churning, hot flash of a roller coaster ride to learn her life was a lie. Actually, she felt relieved to finally lift the veil of silence fluttering around her but of which she couldn't catch hold. When she entered a room where her mother, Felicia, Grandpop or Olinda were talking, the conversation died and immediately started up again in a flustered, caught-with-a-hand-in-the-cookie-jar kind of way. Or when she asked a question about her father, Felicia and Grandpop would look aside and begin talking about the weather or an impersonal subject. At the time, she figured they were discussing grownup stuff.

The truth was, at seventeen, her mother met a young man at Mardi Gras, had a two-day affair and became pregnant. Grandpop sent her away—to school, for those who asked—and she gave birth to Evangeline. Not able to abide giving her up for adoption as Grandpop wanted, Felicia married a traveling salesman and returned home for an occasional family function.

When growing up, Evangeline had no reason to doubt her biological father was a war hero killed a few months before her birth. Even after Felicia remarried, she displayed, like a shrine, a photo of her with a soldier purported to be Evangeline's father. Heat rose to her face when she remembered how she had often held the framed photo close, even planted sweet kisses on its glass shield, trying to conjure up feelings for the handsome soldier.

Grandmother Delacroix-Ravel's arrival on the scene forced Felicia to confess she had asked a stranger to join her in the picture. Evangeline figured her mother told the lie so often, it became true in her mind, or at least she wanted it to be so.

A chill went up Evangeline's back as if somebody had walked across her grave, as Grandpop used to say. She craned her neck, noting that other passengers seemed occupied with their seatmates. She pressed her back against the cushion, attempting to disappear into it, crossed her arms tightly against her stomach and swallowed hard.

God, being the new kid was traumatic; trying to remember names and faces over and over again, having no history with her peers, always the outsider fighting to get in—one way to get a quick education in rejection. Felicia divorced after six on-the-road years, but nothing changed—traveling ran in her blood. Until the day she died, she never stopped running, burning bridges, never looking back, as though fleeing from an unknown enemy. Old acquaintances were seldom mentioned again, as if talking about them tainted the now.

Evangeline frowned, tried to bring into focus a face from those years, but not one friend, enemy, or teacher came to the forefront. She'd never stayed in one place long enough for names to become embedded in her psyche. Towns and special events were enigmas.

A month after her fourteenth birthday, Felicia dropped her off to live with Grandpop and Aunt Olinda while she worked—or, as Evangeline suspected, so she could be free.

Grandmother Delacroix-Ravel found her there and her world changed forever. Evangeline vividly remembered the doorbell ringing and hurrying to answer it, believing Dahlia had come to wish her a happy seventeenth birthday. Instead, a tall, straight elderly woman stood there smiling, her honey-brown eyes glittering with brimming tears that spilled over and ran down her cheeks.

She said, in what Evangeline recognized as a French accent, "You are even more beautiful than your photographs, and you have our eyes."

Evangeline felt the burn on her cheeks and courteously mumbled thank you. With too-full lips, frizzy auburn hair, and a slim boyish figure, she thought of herself as anything but beautiful.

The visitor extended her arms as though expecting Evangeline to fall into them. Evangeline scrutinized the woman's face and said stiffly, "Are you a friend of my mother's? Do I know you?"

"*Ma chère,* I will come right out with it. I am your father's mother. You are my granddaughter."

Evangeline took hold of the doorjamb. "No way." Then she gazed deeply into the woman's serious amber eyes, and saw her own. Hours later, she was convinced, but in shock. Through the years, she believed her father's relatives were dead. Even now, that day seemed like a fairytale with a godmother bestowing gifts and hopes for the future.

Grandmother's name was Danielle-Patrice Ancelina de Delacroix-Ravel. Her son, Aubert, was Evangeline's biological father. After a fatal automobile accident while driving home to

Connecticut from Mardi Gras, he regained consciousness once before he died. He told his mother about meeting the loveliest girl named Felicia, and his sorrow at losing her among the crowd of revelers. Grandmother Ravel promised she would find the girl, and spent years searching for the last person who had formed a connection with her son.

With only a first name to go by, her detectives pursued many dead ends, but when Felicia returned to East Texas to live, somehow they found Evangeline. With DNA coming into its own, a paper cup she had thrown in the trash proved she possessed a genetic link to the Delacroix-Ravel bloodline.

Evangeline's eyes flashed open, and she glanced at the still-empty seat beside her. Even so, she could not shake that odd feeling of someone watching her, the same weird sensation she had experienced prior to meeting her Grandmother Ravel. And since that encounter flipped her world upside down, it unsettled her that another life-changing revelation might be waiting.

Chapter 10

Julian suggested Evangeline examine the painting at Blendell's the night before the auction. The plane's delay in landing prevented her from making the last viewing, although her taxi driver had broken many traffic laws in getting them there. The location was a warehouse in a seedy part of the city, but the facade had been newly finished, so space was probably the contributing factor for Blendell's to conduct the auction.

She tipped the taxi driver generously at the entrance to the Waldorf Astoria, its flags ruffling in the slight breeze. Julian's thoughtfulness never ceased to surprise her. He must have remembered she would like to stay there because of its history.

After she checked in, a smallish bellhop escorted her through the plush, quiet lobby to the bank of elevators and then to a room on the fifth floor. He hung the black garment bag on the closet rack and set her tote on a chair. She deposited what she thought to be a generous tip onto his outstretched palm, but his frown indicated otherwise. Tough, she thought and raised an eyebrow. She worked for a living, too.

When he left, she surveyed the spacious business-class room with a Park Avenue view. What did she ever do to deserve this? Unzipping the garment bag, she removed her black flats lying at the bottom and changed shoes.

With a busy schedule ahead of her tomorrow, she should retire early, but her stomach growled, and she had promised Lydia to see the Broadway show in which an old friend was appearing. Not wanting to be obliged to a certain date, she did not call ahead for reservations, but decided to take a chance at the ticket booth or in the lobby immediately before curtain time. Often, there were last-minute cancellations, and tickets were sometimes available.

She plopped on the edge of the queen-size bed and accessed Julian's number on her cell phone. "I'm sorry, Julian, because of traffic, I didn't make it to the viewing. Hope it isn't a problem?"

"No, there's probably nothing to report I don't already know."

"Lydia asked me to go to the Broadway play she talked about. I'll have a quick dinner and then try to get a ticket at the booth. Uh, my phone will be off for a few hours."

"Enjoy yourself," he said. "I'll talk to you tomorrow."

She dialed Arlo Strecker, who had agreed to keep Zelda.

He said, "Zelda is fine and having a blast playing with my other dogs."

"I feel guilty about leaving her so soon. I promise not to make it a habit."

"We made an agreement I'd dog-sit whenever you needed."

"I should be home tomorrow night, if that's okay."

"We'll see you when you get back."

Satisfied the animal was happy, she went downstairs, and after a quick dinner at one of the hotel's restaurants, hailed a taxi to 45th and Broadway. In her rush to the ticket booth, she collided with what felt like a semitruck. It took a second for her and the man to recover, and simultaneously shove their credit cards under the glass at the booth. The girl behind the glass smiled toothily and said they were in luck. She had two seats available together.

Each took a ticket and rushed across the faded flowered carpet and through the doors, where an old, wrinkled usherette showed them to their seats two rows from the back. The man graciously gave Evangeline the aisle seat, while he squeezed into the one beside her; his legs were bent in front of him like a marionette. The lights dimmed and the red velvet curtain rose.

Aware of the man's predicament, at intermission Evangeline offered to trade places.

"Thanks," he said. "Don't think I could handle this through another act."

Evangeline smelled mint and peered into penetrating coal-black eyes. His dark good looks, cheekbones and strong jawline reminded her of a film star. "Are you . . . ?"

"Sorry, no, I'm not an actor."

She felt her cheeks flush, excused herself and quickly went into the lobby, where she called Lydia to report that her actor friend was fantastic. When the loudspeaker announced the second act, her aisle companion already occupied her vacated seat. He stood and she slipped into the one beside him. Although engrossed in the play, she sensed his presence and, at times, suspected he was more interested in watching her than the performance.

As the curtain lowered, he gallantly blocked the aisle, allowing her to exit first, and it might be imagination, but she thought he followed her to the street where a row of taxis waited for the after-hours theater crowd. He attempted conversation, but Evangeline entered the nearest cab and pulled the door closed, shutting off communication to the outside. She wasn't desperate or stupid enough to pick up a total stranger in Manhattan or anywhere else. A woman would have to be a complete idiot to do that.

Through the safety of the window glass, she smiled at her seat companion standing at the curb appearing somewhat confused and disappointed. *Sorry, fella. You are downright adorable.*

★ ★ ★ ★ ★

Fate had a way of getting what it wanted. The next afternoon, in the large Blendell room on the warehouse's second floor, Evangeline sat several rows from the back with Fay, an acquaintance from a Houston art gallery. They were deep in conversation about the Vermeer, when that familiar sense of her space being invaded crept over her. She glanced up.

The stranger from last night said, "Well, hello there. My luck is holding. Looks like we travel in the same circles."

She blinked, flustered and surprised. Fay pressed Evangeline's thigh with her knee and rolled her eyes, her face displaying a where-did-you-meet-that-hunk expression.

"I'm sorry," Evangeline said, "but I don't know your name."

He laughed and extended his hand. "Maximilian Forbes."

After introductions and an explanation to Fay about their encounter the night before, she learned he owned a small gallery in Dallas, flew his own plane and had registered at a nearby hotel until the next day. She opened her mouth to ask him to join them, but he waved at someone behind her and said he must speak with a client. Hesitantly, he said, "Would you ladies honor me with cocktails and dinner after the auction?"

Intrigued, Evangeline threw caution to the wind. "I'd be delighted."

Fay said, "It'll have to be you two. I've another commitment."

Selfishly, Evangeline was pleased.

While she and Fay talked, Evangeline scoped out the filled to capacity auction room, noting the famous, the infamous, and the not so famous. In Julian's folder were photos and short biographies of serious collectors whom he knew would attend and those he presumed would. It was quite an impressive list.

In suit, tie and horn-rimmed glasses, and now taking a seat

on the third row, was the software whiz who would soon outmaneuver the richest men in the United States. About midway down sat the son of an Arabian oil magnate flaunting his lineage in flowing robes and headgear. On the back row, and included in Julian's list, sat a reputed New York crime boss literally surrounded by a crew of tough-looking bodyguards. *It takes all kinds.*

Across the aisle to the right lounged a famous European, and behind him, the son of one of the wealthiest families in Switzerland. Also represented were museums, gallery owners, socialites—the world's crème de la crème. Those wishing to remain anonymous had positioned agents, such as her, among the crowd, and others would bid by phone.

Such excitement for a fourteen-by-sixteen oil painting by an artist who might or might not have painted it three hundred years ago. If Evangeline ever doubted art was big business, this event should prove it. Out of her league, she felt like a country bumpkin. And Julian, simply by his absence and by sending a novice in his place, made a brazen statement of doubt about the Vermeer's authenticity. The art world would be buzzing about it for months.

Shake it off, Evangeline and enjoy the moment. She thumbed through the catalog Blendell's had prepared especially for the occasion, a classic midnight-blue suede cover with gold engraving. Only registered bidders were privileged to hold one. In bold lettering, a provenance of each painting was printed on the page adjacent to a colored photograph.

"I see the best is kept for last," Evangeline whispered to Fay, pointing to the photograph of the Vermeer. "Eleven lots will go up before this does, and I'm already as nervous as a wiggle worm in a bowl of gelatin. When my turn comes, I'll be sick to my stomach."

Fay patted her arm. "You'll do fine if you remember to picture the spectators naked. It works every time."

Evangeline laughed lightly. "So I've heard. There must be two hundred people in here. To picture all of them naked will produce sexual overload."

She pinpointed a couple of spotters. "How in the world can spotters keep up with all the bids? Seems impossible in an auction this important."

"Practice, practice, practice," Fay said. "Pretty sure they're drilled to the max and trained to recognize every serious bidder's nuance. I don't know for sure, but I think each spotter is assigned a section."

"So these paddles are for show?" Evangeline said, indicating the one in her lap bearing the number 221.

"New bidders use them because they haven't perfected a recognizable bid movement."

"I'll have to remember that." Not that she could afford to participate on her own in anything of such magnitude.

Evangeline glanced toward the double doors leading into a hall crammed with onlookers. Maximilian stood there engaged in an intimate conversation with an older woman, blond pageboy coiffed, jeweled, with a mink stole draped casually over one shoulder. A twinge of jealousy flitted through Evangeline. Ridiculous. She'd only met the man and shouldn't be feeling anything. "Let's get this show on the road. I'm getting claustrophobic."

Fay nudged Evangeline. "Looks like they're ready to begin. The easel is in place and the spotlight came on over the dais."

"Since you've been here before, do you know the main auctioneer?"

"Benoit. The best for this one."

"If I embarrass Julian, I'll die."

The auctioneer, tall and regal in a velvet dinner jacket, primly traversed the three steps up and took his place behind the dark lacquered podium. He tapped the microphone and waited for silence.

After clearing his throat, he greeted the room. "We will begin with Lot Number One, a Diego Velázquez with a reserve bid of . . ."

Evangeline realized she should pay attention to the bidding, should watch as it was raised in increments by the subtle nod of a head, movement of a finger, touch of an ear, lip, chin, or the slight wave of a hand. But her concentration waned and she was aware of only portions of the proceedings while imagining flub-ups she could make during her meager bid for the Vermeer.

Eleven lots and an interminable intermission later, Benoit finally called for Lot Number Twelve. A hush fell over the room as two white-gloved men carried in the painting and gingerly positioned it onto the easel. Evangeline took a deep breath and steeled herself. She would be knocked out of the bidding early, which was fine with her.

Benoit did his spiel and set the reserve at ten million with a minimum bid of five. It would go for much more and the room crackled with anticipation. At the last minute her phone vibrated. It was Julian raising his final offer to twenty-five million. She left the phone line open so he could hear the proceedings, and whispered each bidders name and their bid.

She had kept an eye on Maximilian seated four rows ahead of her and to the right. She figured out he made an offer by tapping his chin with his index finger. She would have to use the paddle, the perfect reveal of a virgin attendee.

Benoit said, "Do I have fifteen million?"

To get the feel of it, Evangeline raised her paddle, and the spotter indicated to Benoit she had an offer of fifteen million.

"Do I hear twenty?"

Several people took the bid but Maximilian was the first, so he was up for twenty.

"Do I hear twenty-five?"

Adrenaline pumping, Evangeline raised her paddle first, but her twenty-five was upped quickly, with a bid of thirty-five. The spotter eyed her, she shook her head, and breathed an audible sigh of relief that her part was over, although she was finally getting into it, easy when it wasn't her money.

When the final gavel fell and Benoit said, "Sold for sixty million dollars," the silence was palpable as necks craned to see who won the prize. The Arab rose, turned, grinned at the spectators, gave the peace sign and headed for the door, his entourage following like cattle.

"God," Evangeline muttered to Fay. "That was the most nerve-racking but exciting thing I've ever been part of." Now it was over, she wished it could have lasted longer.

In the event Julian didn't hear, she whispered, "The Arab, sixty mil."

He said, "I heard. Hope he enjoys it. A huge amount for a speculative Vermeer."

Chapter 11

Evangeline and Maximilian were seated at a table in a little Italian restaurant near the Waldorf. Even as she spoke, she wondered why baring her soul to a man she hardly knew felt so right. Could she be so hungry for companionship she threw herself at the first male who appeared attracted to her and her work? Or did she and Maximilian simply hold common interests? What possible difference could it make? Long-distance relationships seldom worked. *Relax, Evangeline, and enjoy the moment.*

Maximilian said, "You couldn't work for a better organization. Julian Krystos is highly respected."

"Tell me. I count my blessings every day."

"I visited the gallery a few months ago, but didn't see you there."

"The detective agency is across the hall. Probably just missed each other."

"Probably, because I would have remembered you."

Evangeline pretended to blush. "Thank you, kind sir."

"I've heard of the Delacroixs," Maximilian said, sipping his Cabernet Sauvignon. She watched how he savored it on his palate. "In fact, if memory serves me correctly, Claudine bought a painting from me last summer."

Evangeline's cousin Claudine was the great-granddaughter of Jacques-Avenall Delacroix. Due to a misunderstanding, she had become Evangeline's supreme adversary. "Claudine has exceptional taste."

After a moment of silence, Maximilian said, "I enjoy your company. May I call you sometime?"

"I'd like that."

"And please, I'm Max to my friends."

Evangeline smiled and said, "Max."

"This will sound like a line, and I'm sure you hear it often, but you have the honest-to-goodness most unusual eyes. What's the color? They're honey-hued one minute, then a hint of green."

Heat rose to her face. She *had* heard it before but never in such an expressive way. "They change according to what I wear," she said, indicating the forest-green knit under her jacket.

"Not mine, they're bland. Black doesn't change into anything."

Turning the conversation around, she said, "Actually, your eyes are what I first noticed about you."

Now seeming embarrassed, he changed the subject. "Evangeline is a beautiful name. It fits you. Is there a story behind it?"

With so many compliments, she felt her cheeks turning a deeper shade of red. "I grew up believing Mamma simply liked the name. Years later I found out she named me after the poem *Evangeline.* Do you know it?"

"Every kid in the world had to read it. Evangeline and her lover were separated when the Acadians were expelled from Nova Scotia and sent to southern Louisiana. In other words, the Cajuns. Evangeline searched for and finally found her lover and soon afterward they both died."

"Mamma told me when she became pregnant at Mardi Gras, and Grandpop shipped her off to a home for unwed mothers, her high school class had been reading the poem. She felt such kinship with Evangeline, she decided that would be her baby girl's name."

"Kind of a sweet gesture, if you think about it."

She shrugged. "I hated the name after I found that out. What can you do? I certainly wasn't going to change it." Pensive, Evangeline stared at her plate. Looking up, she said, "You know what? Maybe in Mamma's travels she was searching for my father. If so, her actions make more sense. Uh, you do realize I came into the Delacroix family late. I'm actually a bastard."

He belly-laughed. "You don't look like one."

She grinned, and then her gaze flitted toward the door. There it was again. What was going on? Why was she so on edge? Whatever had her spooked better make its presence known soon, or she would go bonkers.

Max followed her gaze and raised an eyebrow. "What is it?"

"For weeks now, I've had the strangest feeling someone is watching me. Can't explain it. A chill I get or a shadowy movement, and then it's gone. And I did receive several threatening phone calls." *He's going to think I'm a dingbat if I'm not careful.* Abruptly she said, "My Aunt Olinda has premonitions." She did not say what they really were.

"Intuition often proves true. Trust it," he said, sipping the wine.

"Lord, I hope it's good, whatever it is."

"What about the phone calls?"

"I'm embarrassed to even mention it, but the morning I was to leave for an out-of-town business trip, an anonymous caller said if I didn't stop looking for my grandmother's treasures I would be very sorry. And more calls came later on."

He frowned. "Strange, but it could be a prank—bored kids. I did a few hang-ups in my foolish youth."

She tipped her glass. "We all probably did. And you're probably right, except how would a kid know of my search for lost paintings? It's been a while, so I'm hoping someone wanted to play an unfunny joke."

"Evangeline, I don't want to pry, but what lost paintings are you talking about?"

Flustered, she said, "I'm sorry. It's such common knowledge I forget not everyone knows. Are you sure you want to hear about it tonight?"

"I want to know everything about you."

Pleased at his interest, she said, "Well, you asked for it." She took a sip of water and cleared her throat. "It's an intriguing story, not only because it's family history, but it was a perilous time period, especially for such a naïve young woman."

"Now you've really piqued my interest."

"While in Paris during World War Two, the Nazis forced my paternal grandmother Delacroix-Ravel to work for them documenting looted artifacts. My grandfather recruited her into the French underground as a spy."

Max leaned closer on his elbows. "How fascinating. I've never known anyone who knew a real spy."

"A German officer became infatuated with her and learned where they had hidden the family's art. He sequestered Grandmother, stole the art and planned to kill her and Grandfather, but she turned the tables on him."

Max's eyes glinted. "She must have had great courage."

"Yes, I agree. Grandmother searched for years, but never found the treasures. Before she died, I promised to keep looking." She waved her hand in the air. "So far, I don't have a clue."

"A real-life crime drama, to say the least. Do you have the provenances, photos, descriptions, anything as proof?"

"Some grainy photographs and the provenances. I've had a few leads, but nothing panned out."

"This sounds challenging, and I love a challenge. How about we work together? Two heads are better than one, as the saying goes."

Evangeline shook her head. "Oh, Max, I appreciate the offer.

Really I do, but we just met and I don't want you involved."

"I'm already involved," he said, reaching over and fingering back the unruly curl trailing down her forehead. "More than you realize."

For the second time, heat rose to Evangeline's cheeks, and she lowered her head toward her plate like a bashful schoolgirl. *Maximilian, you don't know what you're getting into.*

With Max's promise to call her the next morning, they strolled to the Waldorf Astoria, where a message to immediately contact Julian waited. "Duty calls," she said, and Maximilian said he would ring her tomorrow.

Her cell phone indicated a low battery, probably why Julian couldn't reach her. In her hotel room, she plugged the charger into an outlet and accessed his contact number. Since she had spoken to her boss earlier about the auction, she wondered what was up.

He answered on the first ring. "Evangeline, this may be another dead end, but one of my spies called and saw a painting in a gallery in upstate New York that might be one of yours."

She plopped onto the bed. "Oh, my God! Where?"

"The Muñoz Gallery. You should check it out ASAP."

"Which painting? Did he say?"

"The El Greco."

"I'm on it right now." She disconnected and then punched in the airline to change her reservations, but couldn't get a flight until morning. She wouldn't sleep a wink, so decided to prepare for a quick departure. She packed nonessentials and laid out her makeup bag, black corduroy jeans, a heavy wool pink sweater, black suede cowboy boots and her new long black cashmere coat.

After a hot bath and quick relaxing meditation, she removed from her purse the folded partial list of treasures her grandmother had made, and scanned it briefly.

Crystal dog collection consisting of 36 (1- to 5-inch high dogs), sentimental value.

Gold tiara encrusted w/diamonds, rubies and pearls.

Various coins, jewelry, medals, small collectibles.

8 old masters paintings and a triptych consisting of 3 panels.

A partial list, Evangeline wondered if she would eventually find even one. She compared it to looking for a special feather in a down mattress, a daunting task. Could she, should she, spend her life searching for items she might never find? Were Dahlia and Nicky right? Should she forget the whole thing and live her life as if her inheritance didn't exist or matter? Maybe so, but she was not ready to give up, not just yet.

She returned the list to her purse, and thumbed through an art magazine purchased at a kiosk near the hotel, but her mind wandered. Max had said he would call in the morning, except she would check out early and had forgotten to get his cell phone number. He could certainly find her if he wanted to, and she sincerely hoped he would. He was the first real interest she'd had since Nicky left. It would be nice to have a dinner or movie partner, and it would be a plus if Max enjoyed black-and-white films. She made a mental note to mention it if he called.

She dismissed the man from her mind, scrunched down into the covers and tried to sleep. Thoughts of treasures, legacies, and the promise to her grandmother to continue the search invaded the night. Maybe this lead would be a good one, although with the many disappointments, she tried to hold anticipation in reserve. Julian sounded more excited than she, his voice almost euphoric.

Chapter 12

Evangeline took a taxi from the airport directly to the Muñoz Gallery, where she asked the driver to wait. To think she might finally find one of her grandmother's paintings was so overwhelming she had difficulty breathing and took several deep breaths for composure. If the owner became suspicious, the painting might go underground and be lost forever.

The area was living up to its reputation. Snow wasn't falling, but the freezing wind bit right through her cashmere coat. One of Dahlia's minks or sables would come in handy, except Evangeline would buckle under the pressure if accosted by an animal rights advocate.

A handsome young man wearing a black thick-ribbed turtleneck sweater over stonewashed jeans, who, she imagined, watched and prayed for a customer, opened the door and quickly shut it behind her.

"The cold," he said, offering a handshake and a smile that revealed the whitest teeth she'd ever seen.

"I'm Raphael Muñoz. My father is away on business, but I'll be glad to help you."

In her best southern belle accent, she said, "A friend told me about your lil' ol' gallery and I promised to visit if I came this way."

He seemed pleased but did not ask about her friend, although she had an explanation ready.

"Lordy," she said. "It's the end of October and cold as the dickens."

Evidently amused at her strong accent, he suppressed a smile that tried to break the corners of his mouth. "We did have an early cold snap. Supposed to warm up tomorrow." He turned the small talk back to a possible sale. "Are you looking for a particular artist?"

She laughed. "My daddy says my tastes are much too expensive and one day our oil wells will dry up and then what'll I do? But the sweet dear can't say no to me. If you don't mind, I'll browse. See if anything catches my fancy. It'd be a shame to go home empty-handed."

His interest piqued, he offered her a glass of red wine and indicated a cheese tray with party crackers laid out on a small side table draped with white linen. She passed on the cheese, but accepted the room-temperature wine, and hoped she wasn't overdoing the southern belle bit.

A PhD in art history with a Flemish art emphasis enabled her to recognize various artistic techniques and styles, but her grandmother's El Greco had been handed down for generations. Other than an old provenance, the only proof she had to send out to sources after the war was a grainy photograph. All Evangeline had to rely upon were her instincts and an enlargement of the photo she had examined a thousand times.

Occasionally tipping the glass to her lips, pretending to sip, and trying to appear interested in several paintings, she nonchalantly perused the forest-green art-laden walls and partitions—nice backdrops for the artwork. When she reached the rear of the gallery, the painting had not appeared, and she decided she'd reached another dead end.

Then, displayed alone in a small nook, there it was—and her spirits crumbled. Although of the same scene, this painting supposedly by El Greco was a mediocre imitation. Even a layman could tell. The figures of Christ carrying the cross and Mary Magdalene on her knees reaching up adoringly to touch his robe weren't elongated and flowing enough, and the pale brilliance wasn't there in the yellows, blues and pinks. El Greco would have been appalled. Still, a niggle started at the back of her mind.

She motioned to Raphael and, playing inexperienced, said, "Is this an El Greco?"

"I wish. Then I could retire and travel for the rest of my life."

"Where did it come from?"

"One of our colleagues has a friend who imitates the old masters, and we purchased from him simply to give our clients options."

Not wanting him to think her totally naïve, she said, "Isn't that illegal?"

He sputtered, "We would never provenance it as an original. Our gallery is above reproach. Look," he said, pointing to a signature in the lower right corner. "Abner Jacobson signed and dated it. The gallery tag plainly states 'Not an Original El Greco. Painted by Abner Jacobson.' "

And then the niggle presented itself. To copy an original was nothing new. The question was how would Abner Jacobson know to paint this particular scene? And if such were the case, how could he do it with such detail if all he had to go by was Grandmother's black-and-white somewhat fuzzy photograph posted on stolen art registries? Could he have access to the original?

"I like it," she said. "If displayed on a high wall or behind glass, nobody could tell it's a copy, could they?"

"I suppose not." He frowned. "Please don't mislead people to believe the Muñoz Gallery sells fakes as originals."

"*¿Cuánto cuesta?* How much?"

Startled, he sputtered, but quickly recovered. "Although a

copy, it is good, don't you agree?"

Smooth, she thought, and screwing up her face, looked at him questioningly to let him know she knew he was full of baloney.

He winked. "Five thousand. A fair price for an El Greco."

"Raphael, you and I both know this painting isn't worth fifty dollars. I'll give you five hundred."

"Sold," he said.

"I'll call Daddy and get back to you in a few hours."

She left the gallery and asked the waiting taxi driver to take her to the motel where Lydia had made reservations. In the first-floor room, she settled in and called Julian.

As before, he seemed more disappointed than she. "I've never heard of this Abner Jacobson. What else can you tell me?"

"Not much, except the scene is the same as my grandmother's photograph, and even though it's second-rate, it's still too detailed to have been painted from a black-and-white photo."

"I'll take a look. Find out where to send the money, and I'll wire it to their bank today."

"Thank you, Julian. If I hadn't maxed out my credit card, I wouldn't ask. I owe you big-time."

Sometimes she wondered if Julian had an ulterior motive in wanting her to find the lost paintings or if he was simply being a good friend and father figure. He certainly gave her free rein to pursue any lead, and often footed the bill. She would pay back the money. Five hundred dollars was nothing to him, but after everything else he'd done for her, it was not an obligation she wanted to be under.

Almost forgetting to use her accent, she called Raphael, wrote down the necessary bank information for the deposit, and said she'd be there before closing. Then she called Julian back with the wire transfer information.

With negotiations finished, she was exhausted but excited

that she might finally be onto a real lead. With a few hours to kill, she wiggled out of her suede boots, plopped onto the bed and slid into a warm, weightless episode of Nicky asking if he could come home.

Nicky's voice slipped away to the sounds of sirens, a horn blaring to vacate the rooms, and the smell of smoke. *Fire?* Heart pounding, she sat straight up and shook the cobwebs from her brain. Barefoot and groggy, she wobbled from the bed, groped for her purse, and gathered her boots and coat in a bundle. The rest could burn. She reeled to the door, grabbed for the knob and jerked her hand away. The knob was scorching, and heat from outside threw her back. *My God! What will I do? How will I get out? Can they get to me? Do they know I'm in here?*

"Help!" she screamed.

A light exploded through her brain and a shot of adrenaline gushed through her veins like liquid mercury—the fight-or-flight syndrome on high. She rushed into the bathroom, dropped her belongings and fumbled with the latch on the window over the toilet. "Damn, it's stuck." Frantic, she stumbled back into the bedroom, jerked a lamp cord from its wall socket, took aim and hurled the lamp through the bathroom window. The glass shattered but shards clung to the frame like stalactites and stalagmites, blocking her exit. Not wanting to cut or maim her right hand, she wrapped a fluffy white towel around her left hand and arm and broke out the rest of the windowpane.

She pitched out her boots, coat, and purse, shinnied through, and dropped into the strong arms of a fireman.

"Ma'am, are you okay?"

She collapsed against him and tears brimmed. "Thought for sure I was a goner."

The fire was quickly extinguished and with minor arm scratches, Evangeline was allowed to return to retrieve her belongings. Either her nostrils had become accustomed to the smoke or her clothes had escaped damage. The establishment furnished her keys to a room at the opposite end of the motel, and later at the police station, she was shocked when told the fire appeared to be arson and had originated at her door.

At the base of the "V," or what they called the cone, they found a pile of ashes and the outline or pour pattern of an accelerant, probably some kind of petroleum. A no-nonsense officer asked many questions she had no answers for, especially the insinuation someone might want to cause her harm.

She said, "Not logical. I arrived in town today, and nobody knows me here. Why would they want to hurt me?" And there it was. The dread that evil was afoot was real. And she knew, as surely as the area was in the throes of a cold snap, her world had tilted and would never be the same.

Chapter 13

Evangeline and Julian sat in his office, and she said, "I was so sure Abner Jacobson did a paint-over on an original El Greco."

"I thought so too, but my experts used infrared reflectography to see beneath the visible layers and determined nothing appeared unusual about the canvas except that an untalented artist painted it."

I could've told them that.

"My source said a black chalk sketch was all that was under the paint."

"Well, it's back to the drawing board. No pun intended."

"Evangeline, I promise you, if another one surfaces, we'll definitely investigate Abner Jacobson, whoever and wherever he is."

Evangeline's finer qualities did not include patience, and the more she thought about it, the more she wondered about Mr. Rossini's accident. Especially since he was killed on the exact day she went to view the Seurat.

Back at her desk, she dialed the Rossini Gallery. A youngish voice answered on the first ring. Evangeline introduced herself and asked to speak to Mrs. Rossini.

A muffled conversation ensued and a woman said hello.

"Mrs. Rossini?"

"Yes." A pause. "Do I know you?"

Evangeline chose her words carefully. "I'm the one who came

for an appointment the day of Mr. Rossini's accident, and although I'd never met him, please accept my condolences."

The woman thanked her, and Evangeline said, "If you're able to talk about it, I'd so much like to know how it happened."

"What business did you have with my husband?"

"I'd heard your gallery has, or at least had, a copy of a Seurat, and I wanted to view it for possible purchase. Is it still available?"

"My daughter sold the painting the day after my husband died. The police are still investigating the death, but my family believes it was deliberate—a homicide. Why would anyone want to harm my husband? We've done nothing wrong. No enemies who would want us dead. I don't know what to think." Her voice broke. "I'm sorry, I can't talk anymore."

The line disconnected, and Evangeline immediately strode across the hall to the gallery and to Julian's office.

He appeared as confused as she. "They say it might be murder. I'll see what my friend in the San Francisco PD knows."

At the end of the workday they still had not heard anything, and Julian promised to call her if he did. She was entering the back door of her house when her cell phone chimed.

Julian said, "Evangeline, my source said Rossini was a hit and run. Witnesses said he was parked in front of another art gallery loading a painting into the backseat on the street side when a black SUV sped up, swerved and ran him over. One witness said it seemed intentional. They couldn't get a license number because mud caked the plates, and darkly tinted windows prevented a visual of the driver."

He paused, and she tried to absorb the implications.

Gently, he said, "I don't want to worry you, but they haven't ruled out homicide. I'm sure it had nothing to do with your visit, but you need to be careful."

Evangeline's knees buckled and she grabbed for the back of a bar stool. Then it was true. She *was* in danger.

She needed to talk to someone, and Dahlia entered her mind. She dialed her friend's high-rise and spoke to the answering machine. She then dialed Dahlia's cell and listened to a ridiculous message about taking a cruise on a private yacht in the Caribbean, and cha-chaing with the deck hands.

She slammed down the phone. "Where are you when I need you?"

Nicky was the next one who came to mind. She grabbed her purse, rushed to her car, and headed for Fallana B's, a nearby cocktail lounge.

The drive calmed her somewhat, but when she thought about seeing Nicky, her stomach did flip-flops. In the beginning, she had thought she would never recover from the divorce, but the Lord worked in mysterious ways. She had started night school for her private detective license and plunged headlong into her new job. Although her heart would always lie with Nick and teaching, and the new job could be stressful because of the learning curve, it served a purpose. She had commission opportunity and, with Julian's generosity, enough freedom to pursue her quest.

At Fallana's she sat at a table in a secluded corner as the band members assembled on the small stage. Nicky took the microphone and said a few words of introduction. Even now, her heart palpitated at the sound of his voice, and she remembered their first meeting.

After midterm exams, she and several girlfriends had gone to a local bar and were causing a small scene with their silliness. Nobody paid attention to the combo until the bluesy strains of a saxophone began playing a tune Evangeline's mother always hummed. Perhaps the smoke, the music and the drink influenced her, but when she glanced up and saw him standing before the microphone wailing that lovely melody, she was smitten, and the man was so beautiful, she practically drooled.

He had a nice physique—not too muscled—and a boyish grin. But what really attracted her was his attire: he wore suspenders versus a belt, a white starched shirt with French cuffs and two top buttons open, and black horn-rimmed glasses. To her friends, it was a nerdy appearance; to her, a complete turn-on, and could he ever make love. Her heart broke from missing him, and the image of him with someone else made her ill. Who was Evangeline without Nick? They belonged together, and all the therapy in the world wouldn't change that.

Why did she still turn to him when a problem arose? After the pain he had caused, why didn't the days and nights of utter misery matter? Maybe it was habit, enduring college together: late-night cramming, junk food, pooling their money and trying to decide what to do with the rest of their lives. Much had transpired in the last fourteen months, and she couldn't recapture what they had, but he had been part of her world for almost ten years and, although he had thrown away their love like so much garbage, she still trusted him with her life and could not seem to let go.

"God, get over it." Instant decision: *this is a mistake and I have to make a break for it.* She scooted the chair back from the table and headed for the door. At the sound of her name over the loudspeaker, she bolted for the exit.

His hand on her arm was restraining.

"Wait," he said. "I'm glad you're here."

Knees like jelly, she said, "It was dumb."

"You are anything but dumb."

His insight into what she wanted to hear was remarkable.

His face serious, he said, "I've been going to call."

"But you didn't."

"You know how it is."

"Yes," she said. "I do."

"Want to talk?"

"Maybe."

"I'm here for you."

What a crock; but she didn't reprimand. "Shouldn't you be on stage to finish the set?"

"Fallana and the customers will understand."

I'll bet.

"You smell so good," he said, evidently referring to the fragrance bottled by a perfumer they had found in New Orleans—the scent was an aphrodisiac he couldn't get enough of. The bottle was empty now, so the atomizer was useless, but by poking her little finger around inside, she still got enough out to dab onto her wrists. *Mental note: check to see if the perfumer is still in business.*

Nicky's hand was warm as she surrendered and he led her back to the table. He ordered club soda. She, requiring a stiffer brew than a spritzer, but not one to dull her senses, ordered coffee with a liqueur. What a contradiction, a stimulant and a depressant.

To break the ice, he said stiffly, "Seen any good black-and-whites lately?"

They were once on the same wavelength, with a love of jazz and blues music, and old movies, especially those made in the forties. Nicky accused her of being naïve, but he could be worse. Basically an utter romantic, he valued anything vintage, and to her, ten years spoke of vintage. That was why his leaving had brought her to her knees.

"I miss our playacting," he said, nursing the club soda.

She and Nicky would pretend to be characters in a movie. Nothing kinky, simply an enjoyable evening of make-believe. She wrapped her fingers around the mug, and ignoring his attempt at sentimentality, blurted out, "I almost died yesterday."

He grabbed her arm and she winced as hot liquid sloshed onto her fingers. She fumbled for a bar napkin and quickly wiped her hand. And realizing it sounded worse than the reality, she started to backtrack, but quick on the uptake, he swiped his hands down his cheeks. "God, Evie! How? A car accident?"

"It happened in upstate New York."

His eyes lowered and his face clouded over. He had never condoned her second career, said it was dangerous and partly blamed her fixation on the search for the Delacroix paintings for them not reconciling. Not true, of course, because until he left, all she had done was research the Internet and interview a few people. It was his way of easing his conscience.

"Do you want to hear, or not?"

He nodded.

She related the details of the fire and what the police insinuated, omitting the part about meeting Max.

"I knew it. Someone's trying to stop you."

"There's more."

He shook his head in disbelief, and she told him about the auto accident and Rossini's death. "Julian is convinced I'm in real danger."

"Sounds like this person, these people, mean business and will stop at nothing."

"If true, I must be getting close." She paused and raised her right eyebrow. "Wouldn't you think? Besides, maybe whoever it is wants to scare me. If they intended to hurt me they could have already. I'm an open book."

"I give up. I gave up, couldn't watch you go through the disappointments and depression. Couldn't watch your obsession consume you."

"Was I so bad? I don't see it."

Silence ensued and she took a cue the discussion would be

the same, two hard heads with different opinions. Try as she might, she couldn't resist. "I see you've abandoned *your* obsession."

"What obsession?"

"Your dream of following the music scene to New York or California or Nashville. Anywhere except Houston, Texas."

He ignored her rebuff and a smile played at the corner of his mouth—all she could think of was his beautiful, kissable lips. *Get a grip, Evangeline. Remember he dumped you.*

"An opportunity came up I couldn't refuse." He looked down and rimmed his glass. "Fallana's asked me to become her business partner and I said yes."

Well, that's that. The conniving witch got what she wanted. He would never admit it, but she was convinced he was seeing Fallana before they separated. The transition was too easy. She figured when a man moved out as effortlessly as Nicky had, he usually had somewhere else to go or someone else to sleep with.

"I see. So you're shelving your desire for a successful music career to become a lounge lizard. It seems like a step down to me."

"You've never understood. Eight-to-five was suffocating, slowly but surely killing me. This way I'll own my own business and play the music I love."

"Love? You drop the word like a hot potato."

She needed to get out of there before spouting off any more choice words she would regret, so she pushed back from the table and rose. "This was a big mistake, but it won't happen again."

As she turned to leave him sitting there with a ridiculous look on his face, she tossed over her shoulder, "By the way, I adopted a police dog named Zelda from a very handsome policeman." *So there, who needs you?*

CHAPTER 14

Abner missed seeing Rudy the last time he visited the café, and was glad he was there today. He waved. Rudy waved back.

Abner settled at his favorite table in the back corner and waited, hoping Rudy would join him. He didn't want to appear needy and pretended to scan the menu but sensed the man heading his way.

"Hey, Abner, how the heck are you?" Rudy squeezed Abner's shoulder and said, "It's good to see you back safely. How was the vacation?"

Abner grinned. "Can't beat it, but I missed the camaraderie here, and, of course, the great chow."

"May I?" Rudy asked. Not waiting for an answer, he turned the chair around and straddled it. "I've got a few minutes and want to hear all about it. I'll bet you have some stories to tell."

Abner smiled. "I did visit a few interesting places."

"You were gone long enough. What, two months?"

Abner laughed. "About six weeks."

"I'll bet you went to every museum you could find."

"Practically, and the birthplaces of several of the old masters."

"Figures. Where were your favorites?"

Abner took a deep breath. "I made home base at a château, and took side trips. Besides Paris, I loved Florence. The sculptures, frescoes, and architecture were all I imagined."

"I had a chance to go to Florence once, but decided on the Riviera. My mind was on women and a good time."

"Nothing wrong with that. At my age, the cultural aspect intrigued me. Didn't have time to see all I wanted, but I visited every museum in my path."

Abner's heart began to beat faster, and he felt a little twinge. *Oh, God, not now.*

Rudy's face took on a concerned look. He reached over and placed his hand on Abner's arm. "Are you all right?"

Abner breathed shallowly and counted to twenty before releasing a deep breath. Thankfully, the pain dissipated. "I'm fine, just a little indigestion."

"Wouldn't want you to get sick."

Abner dismissed the comment with a wave of his hand. "Are you familiar with Rembrandt?"

"Well, I've seen pictures of his art, but don't know much about him."

"No artist captures the light like Rembrandt. He had an, umm,"—he grasped for the right words—"intrinsic sensitivity. Maybe that's what makes a painting a masterpiece, intrinsic sensitivity."

Abner surprised himself sometimes by how knowledgeable he proved to be. "A few of the great painters had it. Da Vinci, for one. Everybody's heard of the *Mona Lisa.* Hard to believe he painted it in the fifteen hundreds." He lingered over the name. "To say it boggles my mind."

Abner noticed Rudy's interest fading, and decided to change the subject. But what would they talk about? Art was all he knew, and he needed conversation.

He quickly said, "Were you ever in the war?"

"I missed out on all of them. Either too young or too old, or didn't get my number called. Nah," Rudy said, "I wasn't dumb enough to volunteer."

"I enlisted in the big one," Abner said, noticing for the first time Rudy's slightly cocked right eye and chinless face, reminding him of a squashed pumpkin.

"World War Two," Rudy said matter-of-factly, his overly full lips slightly pursed.

"Yes, sir." Abner neglected to mention he arrived in Germany at war's end and saw no real action. "After the conflict, there wasn't much to do except clean up and hold. I had turned sixteen, but lied and said I was eighteen on enlistment papers. Lots of guys fudged on their age, and to tell the truth, I don't think the military really cared. I did have a knack for automobile mechanics, so by the time I received my discharge, I could repair any vehicle and could drive the hell out of a small, big, or in-between one."

"But how did you get into the art field? Automobile repair seems a far cry from that."

"Strictly by accident. I answered an advertisement for an experienced driver for our local museum. That led to part-time warehouse work, then advancement into framing, and after a couple years of proving myself, I became the warehouse custodian, overseeing all aspects of maintenance, repair, etcetera. It was no secret that I had no formal education or training in the arts. Never even finished high school, but by watching from the sidelines, I sucked up knowledge like a sponge—how to identify an artist's style and technique, the differences between an original and a fake, paint usage, and so forth, and it all led up to my lifetime job at the museum doing something I loved."

Pull back, Abner, be careful what you reveal.

His heart thumped loudly and he paused, breathed deeply and counted to twenty again, an exercise he learned from one of his neighbors. Rudy raised an eyebrow, waiting for him to continue. When his heart slowed, Abner said, "It was as though the paintings were mine, that I had brushed on the color, or knew the subjects and places." He mused. "Time stands still in a painting. Know what I mean?"

"Sort of, but never really thought about it till now."

Abner leaned back. "If I have one piece of advice for the younger generation, it's to be receptive to new experiences. If you've never been exposed to a situation, how do you know you won't enjoy or like it? When an opportunity presents itself, take it, because it could lead to an amazing career. And although I'm retired, I won't be far from art, and you can count on it."

Chapter 15

Saturday morning Evangeline decided to visit Aunt Olinda at the old homestead in East Texas. It was a three- or four-hour drive according to how heavily her foot pressed the accelerator, and how many trucks traveled the highway. Since she did not plan to spend the night, she left Zelda at home with Strecker's promise to check on her. For such emergencies she had hidden a house key in the mouth of a stone frog sitting in a flowerbed by the back patio. Although a ridiculous thought, she didn't want to chance Aunt Olinda putting a heebie-jeebie on Zelda.

An occasional glance in the rearview mirror assured her nobody followed. *This is stupid. I'm not in danger.* But she could not shake the uneasy feeling plaguing her. The feeling she was being watched and not knowing where to look.

She rounded the last curve on the blacktop, and saw Olinda waving from the front porch of the cedar-shake house. Olinda wasn't blood kin, being from Haiti with a black mother and white father. Grandpop saved her from a burning death somewhere in the swamps when she was about eighteen. Photography was one of Grandpop's many hobbies, and he had hired a guide to escort him into the wetlands to photograph wildlife for a magazine spread. Upon hearing screams, they found Olinda tied to a tree surrounded by a blazing fire. He and the guide managed to cut her loose before anyone returned. Olinda told him human traffickers kidnapped her, and brought her to America where she escaped into the marsh. As an outsider, she defended herself against a swamp clan, but they accused her of a crime and sentenced her to death by burning.

Oleander was her real name, but Grandpop shortened it, and the truth gradually unfolded. Her mother was a mambo, a voodoo witch doctor, and Olinda had learned some rituals from her. Since the traffickers took her from Haiti as a teenager, she never had the opportunity to become a full-fledged mambo, but instead practiced root magic. In other words, she was a hoodoo woman, also known as a conjurer or root worker. Supposedly, a hoodoo is limited to making charms, potions, casting spells, conjuring up stuff and doing general protection magic. Olinda played the role to the max.

While Grandpop lived, their clashes sometimes caused problems, because he was a dyed-in-the-wool Southern Baptist. He made her promise never to implement any of her "witchcraft" under his roof. The situation worked well for everyone, and Olinda became like one of the family, nursing Grandmother Beene, who had developed breast cancer. Evangeline wished she had known the woman, because their community respected her immensely. She had already passed and Grandpop was in his early sixties when Evangeline went to live there.

Seeing Olinda on the front porch reminded her of the first time she became aware of conjuring and other rituals. One evening while searching for blackberries in the deep woods behind the house, she found partially hidden candles in the hollow of a tree, and on the ground squiggly snake prints traced out in white flour. A little puddle of flour held an egg. She learned much later these were offerings to entice a *loa,* a voodoo spirit. Evidently Olinda was practicing to become a mambo. The candles were still warm, and she knew Olinda had recently come from there. She confronted the woman, but Olinda only said Evangeline would have to catch her if she could. Watching Olinda kept Evangeline from going crazy, as isolated in the country as she was and accustomed to the chaotic life with her mother. But she knew she was better off and would not leave with Felicia when she occasionally dropped in to visit.

Through the years, Evangeline inevitably learned about Olinda's trickery. Dahlia and Nicky said it was helpful Evangeline's thought processes were mostly formed before she moved there, or there was no telling how influential Olinda might have been. Evangeline liked to think she had a stronger mind than to believe in voodoo or hoodoo mumbo jumbo, but she didn't judge. Olinda believed, and that was what mattered.

On the one hand, living in a Southern Baptist household, and on the other hand, living with a hoodoo practitioner, Evangeline's teen years had been a total hoot. Evangeline was proud to say she never practiced the occult because she wasn't about to take a chance of her soul going to hell like Grandpop said.

If Grandpop knew Olinda lapsed into her old ways, and he would have to have been blind not to, the woman had become so entrenched in the family, he probably felt helpless to confront her. And Evangeline suspected there was more to the relationship than they let on. Maybe Olinda put a love whammy on him. Evangeline shook her head because that picture she could do without.

Felicia died two years ago. Before Grandpop passed last year, he made provisions for Olinda to remain in the house for the rest of her life. Evangeline inherited the house and the ten acres it sat upon, but as of now, she had no plans ever to return there to live.

She waved and parked the Bronco on the pea-gravel driveway in the shade of Paladin, the old oak, whose arms had often held her after Felicia dropped her there like one might drop a basket of dirty clothes at the laundry. Evangeline named the tree after reading that paladins were holy knights during the reign of

Charlemagne. They played a variety of different roles: healing, protection, and retribution, and were defenders of the weak. Evangeline needed those consoling elements during such a traumatic period.

The real slap came when she heard Felicia tell Grandpop her daughter was his responsibility now. After Evangeline learned the story of her birth, she thought about those words and decided Felicia considered her payback for Grandpop pressuring her to give her baby up for adoption.

Stop it. Wallowing in self-pity and dredging up those days isn't constructive. Therapy after Nicky left was supposed to have squashed her ghosts, rebuilt her self-esteem, but memories did not disappear during a few emotional months of baring one's soul.

She placed her purse under the front seat, a habit when leaving it in the car. Her tote, which she kept packed, also from habit, lay on the back floorboard. She exited the auto and clicked on the alarm. Even in the country, one couldn't be too careful, especially under the present circumstances. She glanced up and down the blacktop for suspicious sightings, but the road was empty and quiet.

Olinda, wearing a checkered scarf tied around her head in a topknot, a gray peasant skirt with a low v-neck collarless blouse tucked in and revealing an ample bosom, and sporting a sweater, met her halfway down the walk. A sense of peace fell over Evangeline. Home. The only root, however tentative, she had ever known.

Olinda said, "Had me a intuit you was coming."

Evangeline loved Olinda's velvety voice, so deep and sensual it could hypnotize you if you let it. The woman tried to control her Haiti patois but it, along with her thick Louisiana dialect, sometimes made her hard to understand. One's ear had to be attuned.

They embraced, and even though she was in her forties, Olinda's smooth, tawny face appeared unlined. "You never change. Still movie-star beautiful."

"You and dem movie stars. You the one should a done actressing. Such wasn't in my cards. If so, I wouldn't be here to fix up your problems."

"Now, Aunt Olinda, don't go causing me any trouble."

"Could I—a little?" she asked, a knowing, wicked expression passing across her unblemished face, the look she achieved prior to or after an unaccountable happening. Gently, she prodded Evangeline up the three wooden steps extending the length of the front porch. "Let's settle into de house. I'm pulsing to hear about your new poodle dog."

A gush of cold air, like stepping into a freezer, greeted Evangeline and almost knocked her back. "My God, it's freezing in here. Is the air conditioner broken? Is that why you have on a sweater?"

"Nah, Doc Hornie say . . ."

"Doctor Horne."

"He say I be in de middle of mini paws, and I get hot spells so bad they wets me all over. I keep it cold, wear a sweater, and when dem hots come on, I yank de ting off till it pass on to wheresomever it come from."

"Wouldn't it be easier to—what do you do when you go out? Never mind." Evangeline figured it was Olinda's body, so she couldn't fault her for how she wanted to care for it.

The smell of patchouli hung heavy at the door, and Evangeline half expected the living room to contain fetishes and such, but it remained as Grandpop had left it. The same frayed multicolored braided rug defined the seating area, and his tan leather chair, still missing two buttons on the backrest, sat in front of the eighteen-inch television. Even if an electronic wasn't made in America, it had better have an American name, or

Grandpop wouldn't own it.

Evangeline smiled, remembering his mantra about Americans buying too many foreign goods and outsourcing too much work to foreign countries and one day, but not in his lifetime, aye God, we would have a country filled with nothing except a bunch of white-collar computer nerds.

Evangeline did notice one difference in the room. A smaller version of Grandpop's chair, which must be Olinda's, sat on the other side of his end table that now sported two reading lamps. Could Olinda anticipate him returning from the dead? Anybody with any sense would realize such an event couldn't happen, but Evangeline wouldn't burst the hoodoo's bubble. Instead, she said, "Not much has changed around here."

"What you expect, *ma chère*?"

Obviously Olinda knew what she expected, but Evangeline said, "Just an observation."

Olinda let it go and beckoned her to the kitchen, where a drip coffee pot sputtered. A plate of scones lay on the 1950s yellow-and-chrome dinette table, along with two of Grandmother Beene's glass dessert plates and matching sugar bowl and creamer in a beautiful iridescent amethyst color. The matching cups had long been broken, but two brown mugs waited to be filled with coffee.

"I'll get eating ware," Olinda said.

She did know I was coming. "How did . . . ?"

"I told you I had a intuit."

Even now, the same pungent scent of mystery surrounded Olinda. Evangeline figured the incense had finally permeated her body. Evangeline knew that conjuring up spells and putting real curses on people wasn't possible, but Olinda disagreed and said anything was possible.

Still, unexplainable events had occurred. Once, when Olinda emerged from the woods, Evangeline could swear a shimmering glow, flaring from purples to reds, danced and dimmed around her and followed her as she moved, somewhat like the energy field everything in the universe is supposed to possess. One of these days she would check into an aura camera to detect electromagnetic energy that could supposedly be computerized into colors. Maybe Olinda had devised a way to bring that energy into viewable focus with the naked eye. But that must be beyond Olinda's capabilities.

Evangeline wrapped her arms around herself. "I'm going to need a sweater. Do you have an extra one?"

Olinda lifted a shoulder wrap from the back of a kitchen chair and handed it to Evangeline. "I keep 'em in every room in de house."

Evangeline shivered and snuggled into its warmth. She savored the aroma of the apple scone, then bit into it, hoping to catch Olinda in a fib about making them because of an intuit. It tasted warm and freshly baked. How did she do it? Olinda's predictions, more often than not, would come true.

Olinda poured the steaming coffee into their cups. Evangeline sipped and sputtered it back into the cup. "What is that?" she grumbled. "What happened to the chicory? This tastes like warmed over pee."

"My grocer quit selling it, so I've been buying regular grind."

"And here I was looking forward to cutting my coffee with a knife."

Olinda settled in the chair opposite her. "You want a different cup? You did spit in dat one."

"I'll get it."

After Evangeline had refreshed her coffee and returned to her chair, Olinda said, "Now, tell me about dis dog."

"You mean you don't already know?" Olinda was aware of her feelings about the hoodoo miscellany, and the two women sparred around it, sharing a mutual respect that put it in perspective. Until Evangeline had come to terms with the truth about her father and her mother's lie, she'd turned to Olinda, upon whose shoulder she had cried many a tear.

She remembered sitting at this same table while Olinda stood at the gas stove frying chicken and trying to console her with the tale of how a group of men viciously ripped her from her mother's arms when she was fourteen and forced her into slavery.

"My words can't express what dose people did to me. If I ever run into one, I swear one of us won't walk away alive."

Evangeline believed it then, and she believed it now.

"Child," she had told her, "you be lucky. Look what you come into. A whole new family. A rich one t'boot and proud to find you. I never had such luck till your grandpop found me, and I bless my *loa* every day for such a wonderful man. You need to get over what your mother did. She okay. Done the best she could."

So Evangeline had decided to get over it, but it had not been easy. Before, she had been a free spirit, ready for new challenges, the daughter of a war hero. After the truth emerged, she became free game for the gossip mill, no longer admired, but the illegitimate daughter of "that woman." She finally quit going to church because of the whispers. And praise God, as Grandpop said, she had only one more year of high school. How anyone gets through hurtful gossip without being scarred for life was a mystery, but Olinda was right. Although the time passed slowly, it did pass and had become nothing more than a small ripple in the scheme of things.

She glanced at Olinda, who observed her curiously.

"You remembering tings you need to leave alone?" Suddenly, she stiffened, sat up straight, and for several seconds her eyelids fluttered and her head weaved. Evangeline had seen this before and held her breath.

Olinda moaned, came out of her spell and said, "Oh, mercy, there's evil doings going on around you. Feel it in my bones. You need to watch out, girl." She laid her cold hand over Evangeline's and clasped it. "Stay here with Aunt Olinda. You be safe here."

Evangeline shivered and swallowed hard, trusting Olinda's instincts—or whatever they were. But she couldn't get sucked into her fortune telling premonitions.

She tightened the wrap around her shoulders. "My dog's name is Zelda," she said, shaking off her foreboding.

"I see what you're doing, changing the subject, but you better tink about it. I'm never wrong."

Evangeline segued into facts about Zelda, purposely omitting the part about the lightning and Zelda's somewhat odd actions afterward. Neither did she mention the phone calls, the fire at the motel, or Rossini's auto accident. With her intuition, Olinda would jump on those like fleas on a dog's back. She would be hoodooing all over the place.

"You must have picked one special dog, *chère*. Why not bring her to Aunt Olinda? Got plenty roaming space around here." She laughed her deep, rich laugh. "Maybe afraid I'd put a heebie-jeebie on her?"

The devil. She got right to it. And to tell the truth, that was exactly why Evangeline left Zelda at home. "With you reading my mind, I must be careful what I think."

"Or what you wish for?"

"One day you'll have to teach me how you do it."

"Oh, *chère,* you'd have to believe first. 'Sides, you oughten to know I don't need to see nothing to heebie-jeebie it. Fact is I been tinking . . ."

Chapter 16

On several occasions as she headed home, Evangeline had the feeling of being followed, but since it was a straight shot to Houston, many of the same cars were traveling the highway. She must guard against the paranoia that could make one imagine frightening scenarios. Maybe she was fearful because it was dark, and she was alone, and Aunt Olinda had creeped her out.

She worried about the woman, who had admitted she had the makings of an ulcer, but had assured Evangeline she would be fine. Since she was prone to little fibs, Evangeline planned to research the diagnosis, and try to get Olinda to Houston for a second opinion. Still, Olinda could be very stubborn and probably wouldn't come.

A hot flash passed over her to think Olinda might be seriously ill, because she loved her and couldn't imagine not having her to talk with, or that the Delacroixs might be her only living relatives. They abhorred her, but she must conquer her inferiority complex, and acquire a real backbone.

For some chilly reason, on a long dark stretch, she glanced in her rearview mirror and noticed a gap closing between her and two pinpoints of light. Somebody was certainly in a hurry. Her speedometer read sixty-five, but she eased up on the gas pedal. Maybe the driver was going to an emergency, so she would let him pass. The auto sped up beside her and swerved toward her front bumper.

"What the—"

She grasped the wheel, twisted it to the right and hit gravel. At fifty miles per hour, she fishtailed, bounced along the shoulder, had sense enough to not slam on her brakes, but coasted and thankfully stopped within a few feet of a concrete bridge culvert.

"Oh, God, what the devil just happened?"

She collapsed against the seat and sat for a few minutes until her body stopped shaking and she could come to terms with the situation. Coincidence? An accident? Or did someone deliberately try to kill her? Should she report it? But what could she tell the highway patrol? That a car had tried to run her off the road? They'd probably put the incident down as road rage, and decide she was somehow responsible.

The car was long gone, and the event had happened so fast she hadn't noticed the make, much less the color or license number. And there was no other driver in sight who could act as a witness.

She wiped sweaty hands on her pants legs, opened the door, tumbled out, bent over and inhaled deeply. *Walk it off. I'm not hurt, Atlas is okay, I hope. No major harm done.* The clicking of cicadas, buzzing insects, and an occasional car whizzing by were the only sounds, and it chagrinned her that not one of those autos stopped to render aide. When she had calmed sufficiently to drive, she reentered the Bronco, crossed her fingers and twisted the ignition key. Atlas fired right up.

"Thank you, God."

Tentatively, she pulled back onto the highway. Her world had turned upside down again, and she didn't know where the evil was coming from or why.

★ ★ ★ ★ ★

A little after midnight, the gate clanged shut behind Atlas, and it was only then Evangeline's teeth unclenched and her hands relaxed on the steering wheel. She sighed, safe at home at last. And she couldn't wait to see Zelda, because for the first time she realized how empty her life had been. Strecker had let Zelda out earlier and brought one of his dogs over to play. He said two were easier to handle because they kept each other company. She would think long and hard about adopting another, because it was difficult arranging for one. Two would be almost impossible.

She bent down and felt inside the mouth of the stone frog for the key. "Yep." Strecker replaced it. But as he'd cautioned, she would change hiding places. Everybody and his uncle knew about the frog.

Zelda was waiting at the back door, wagging her nub and grinning. Evangeline knelt, wrapped her arms around her, stroked her fur, and clamped her own mouth shut to ward off germs as she welcomed the kisses slurped over her face and neck. "God, you're sweet."

Zelda woofed, and the icy chill Evangeline had felt all evening slowly faded.

She checked her watch. "Baby Cakes, you've been cooped up for hours, and I've been in the car almost as long. Either the trip gets harder each time, or I'm getting old. Let's you and me go out and stretch." She opened the door wide as Zelda zoomed past.

Evangeline glanced up to see the Bernowitzes' window curtain move. *No, you old bat, Strecker isn't my lover, and I haven't been on a late date. In fact, I haven't been on a real date since the divorce.* The saving grace of her neighbors being so close was they could hear her yell if a problem arose. They were her backup alarm system.

She wondered whatever happened to Maximilian. He probably decided she wasn't interested because she left without so much as a good-bye. Maybe she'd call his gallery tomorrow to explain.

Zelda stood stiffly, nose pointing toward the back fence. A shadow flashed past on the horizontal beam. Evangeline's stomach dropped and she stumbled back. "Zelda, is it a rat?" But Zelda sat and wagged her nub as two yellow eyes attached to a fluffy gray body glared at them from behind a tall bush growing against the fence.

She held her stomach, relieved. "Oh, it's a cat. Probably somebody's pet out night prowling. Scat. Don't need another mouth to feed."

She perused the fence, but the cat was gone, and for some reason her insides felt empty—too many changes, people leaving, dying. What was next?

The trip and accident must have been rougher on her than she thought, because she tossed and turned the entire night. Her only memory of her dreams was that they were unsettling. The next morning, after a quick wakeup shower, she dressed in the walk-in closet, and when finished, she noticed Zelda at the window again.

"I can't leave you home alone so often, girl. We might have to find a doggie day care."

She watched Zelda for a moment, and it dawned on her the dog was probably bored out of her gourd because she was used to action. What to do?

"You'll come to work with me today and stay in the kneehole under the desk. Julian will never know unless blabbermouth Babs tells."

Zelda woofed and chased her stubby tail.

"Now, look here, Zelda, you're freaking me out. These are

coincidences. You can't possibly understand what I'm saying." She paused. "Maybe you're triggered by a word or the tone of my voice. That's probably it. Strecker said it's common knowledge that dogs respond to sound pitch. Then again, here I am talking to you like you're human."

In the rear parking area at Rembrandt, she wheeled the Bronco into her usual space, gathered the water bowl, leash and her purse, then she and Zelda quietly entered the building. Kreshon waved and gave her thumbs-up about Zelda. Babs wasn't in the anteroom, but Lance sat in his office with his back to the door, the phone to his ear.

She hurried directly to her office, pulled out the chair, snapped her fingers for attention and pointed under the desk. Without hesitating, Zelda obeyed and settled down.

"We'll see how it goes. Right now, I've got tons of paperwork, so be nice."

Later in the morning, Lance stuck his head through the door. "Your New York trip didn't produce results?"

"I wish."

"May I enter?"

She motioned him to the chair in front of the desk. "I'd love some company."

He unbuttoned his pinstriped charcoal-gray designer suit coat, sat primly in the chair in front of the desk and fiddled with the crease in his slacks. "Need any assistance?"

To her, the name Lance conjured up a macho, carefree guy. This man was the polar opposite, and nothing she imagined a detective to be, although he was a hunkish type. A curse word never fell from his lips, and the big words he used sounded forced and out of place. His politeness made one uncomfortable. He'd had the same girlfriend for six years, seemed happy, and excelled in his business. Julian depended on and trusted him implicitly.

On the surface, he appeared to respect and like her. Intuition told her that deep down, he was jealous of her and Julian's working relationship, so his offer to help was a surprise.

"Well, I did make a little headway. A possible contact," she said. "But I would like to check it out on the QT. I could sure use your expertise but don't want to interfere with your schedule. Julian's done what he can, checking on the Rossini accident, and I hate to bother him further." She threw up her hands, defeated. "And I don't have a clue where to begin."

"I'll expedite as soon as possible. The name, please."

She almost rolled her eyes. "You have no idea how much I appreciate this. His name is Abner Jacobson." She wrote it on a notepad, tore off the paper and handed it across the desk. "He painted the El Greco scene, but you're probably familiar with the story already."

"Some, but I've been in Mexico and haven't been thoroughly briefed."

Since this was the first occasion he'd offered more than a stiff good morning or good-bye, she wouldn't mention the automobile incident. "How did Mexico go?"

"Productive. We found the Mexican fence and discovered one painting in a closet inside one of those oversized kids' gift bags; the other is still missing, but I'm optimistic."

She frowned. "It amazes me the extent to which collectors will go to own what they alone can enjoy. A stolen work of art certainly can't be displayed openly."

Lance nodded. "In most cases it's thieves who hope to make a profit by selling it on the black market. In others, it's more an egocentric mentality of 'I've got it, and you don't,' or an obsession with a particular artist, or simply because they can. Who can fathom a thief's motives? Art theft can bring Herculean rewards to the perpetrators."

"Have any thoughts on what happened to my grandmother's paintings?"

"Not really. And forgive me for being skeptical, but they could have been destroyed, hidden, lost, sitting in a vault somewhere, or even right under our noses."

"Even if I find Grandmother's paintings, I probably can't afford to keep them." She mused, "At least I'll have the satisfaction of honoring a promise. And too, if I quit actively looking, isn't there some sort of statute of limitation?"

"Texas and most states have a statute of limitation rule of two to six years. You'll be fine as long as the discovery rule or due diligence rule applies."

"So since I'm actively searching, I'll be okay?"

"Right, but rules continuously change."

"And I must keep abreast. If I eventually succeed, I certainly don't need a drawn-out custody battle."

"So much World War Two art has never been found or returned because the rightful owners were killed, mostly in the Holocaust, and their heirs have no proof of ownership. You have photos and provenances. If the paintings eventually surface, we'll know." He paused. "Some treasures don't see the light of day for generations. I'm sure you're prepared for that." He shifted in the chair. "Now, what happened with the El Greco? Julian says you returned distressed."

Distressed? Spooked sounds more like it. She brought him up to date on both incidents. "The police say the fire was arson and suspect someone wanted to do me in. I'm hoping it was a grudge against the motel and they picked my door randomly, or maybe kids up to petty vandalism. I doubt they'll ever find the culprits."

"Petty arson has a way of getting lost in the system."

"Julian says the Rossini death might have been murder. What do you think?"

"I have no idea. Let me contact some sources." He scooted his chair back and rose.

Zelda sneezed.

He craned his neck and squinted. "What in the Sam Hill do you have under there?"

Did she hear cursing?

"A dog," she said, making a face and putting her finger to her lips for him to lower his voice.

"You brought it to work?"

She grinned. "Never know when I'll need major backup."

Chapter 17

The Memorial Park trail Evangeline usually jogged on appeared empty, which would allow for a chance to clear her mind and think. So much had been happening she hadn't had an opportunity to fully analyze the events.

It was the right thing to do, coming directly from work to the park. If she had gone home to change clothes she would have found a million reasons not to return.

She wheeled the Bronco into a parking space and after releasing Zelda from the seatbelt, climbed out. From the corner of her eye she watched the dog sniff around and relieve herself on a patch of grass. She pulled on white socks and laced up the gray tattered running shoes stored in the car for when she needed to do serious footwork. The wash-and-wear khaki cargo pants and white cotton blouse she had worn to the office wouldn't hamper her run. *Mental note, pack shorts, a T-shirt, and a towel to leave in the Bronco. Maybe even a sweat suit.* Zelda would need exercise, and now Evangeline would not have the excuse of not wanting to jog alone.

She had joined a gym, but couldn't force herself to go. At the sight and sound of Evangeline retrieving the leash from the door's side pocket, Zelda padded over and sat in front of her expectantly. She figured it was a Pavlov or Strecker conditioning response, like the whir of an electric can opener announcing dinner.

At least she and Zelda weren't totally alone. A ponytailed girl of about sixteen wearing white short shorts and a tight pink tank top leaned on the hood of a blue subcompact, stretching. Her companion, a skinny longhaired hippie-type in black bike shorts, leaned against the driver's side door ogling her.

While Zelda sat on her haunches and waited, Evangeline placed a hair band over her head, bent over and touched her toes, twisted her torso from side to side, and performed a few arm and leg stretches. She clicked on the car alarm, zipped the keys into the sports purse buckled around her waist and started off slowly. Cooped up in the office all day, Zelda panted excitedly, anticipating the run, ready to go full speed ahead. The leash deterred her, and she fell into step beside Evangeline.

"It's been a while since I've done this, girl, so go easy on me."

Zelda woofed.

"Do you automatically woof when I speak to you or do you really understand me?"

Zelda woofed.

The park had lost many trees during a devastating drought, but was recovering and still lovely in October. The leaves were turning to orange and gold, squirrels chattered and scattered hoarded nuts, and birds sang happily. A gust of wind from behind, plastered Evangeline's hair around her face, partially obscuring her view. But with the setting sun behind her, the atmosphere was quite pleasant.

They were halfway around the track, and with the monotony of her thudding shoes on the hard-packed trail, synchronized arm and leg movements, and the breeze now on her face, she was lulled into a sense of euphoria in which all she saw was the trail ahead disappearing into a long black tunnel between thick foliage.

Soon they entered the murky shadows that darkened the farther in they went, but Evangeline's mind felt light and clear for the first time in weeks. She followed the trail almost by rote, as her mind wandered back to her grandmother Danielle.

During the few years they had together, Grandmother told wonderful stories about her life. Like a soft, silken mantle of peace, great happiness overcame Evangeline as she remembered sitting and listening spellbound to the old woman reminiscing about her childhood in France before World War II and her adventures as a spy during the upheaval.

Grandmother told her that before the war, the Delacroixs were one of the wealthiest families in France. Evangeline thought Grandmother must have practically been royalty. But she'd been a rebel even before the word became popular. It was important to her to be productive and contribute to society and not rely solely upon her family's wealth, so she was living and working in Paris as an art curator when the Germans invaded in 1939. They forced her to work documenting looted art. Martin Ravel, who later became Evangeline's grandfather, recruited Danielle into the French Underground.

The family's art collection disappeared near the end of the war, about the time US. troops landed in Normandy and liberated Paris. It must have been a terrible period for her. At the mention of her father, Henri, she would become fragile and her hands would shake. After the war, Grandmother married Martin Ravel and they had one child, Evangeline's father, Aubert.

Grandmother searched years for her family's treasures but never found a trace. Her father had already transferred most of his finances to a Swiss bank, but when he recovered from a stroke, he couldn't remember where he stored the access data or even which bank he had used. Grandmother never found the money, which had been drawing interest ever since.

After Grandmother became ill with an enlarged heart, Evangeline made her a promise to continue the search. So far, she had not found one tangible clue. And at the time, she had no reason to doubt that her grandmother passed suddenly with a massive heart attack. Uncle Jacques and his lawyer handled the legalities, but that niggle in her brain was wiggling away.

When Grandfather Ravel, an American with money of his own, passed away, an unscrupulous financial advisor swindled Grandmother out of most of the family's fortune. She died with few liquid assets and, in Evangeline's opinion now, under odd circumstances. She left Evangeline with a few important items: an insurance policy covering tuition and expenses at a four-year university of her choice; the provenances of the lost treasures, along with the task of continuing the search; deeds to a family estate outside Paris and a château in the Loire Valley that Evangeline had never visited, along with a generational family trust for payment of the taxes and upkeep; Evangeline's cross to bear was a legacy of the Delacroix clan in Texas, who considered her an illegitimate outsider from a less-than-desirable family harboring a voodoo/hoodoo woman.

Close family members of her mother, Felicia, were gone now except for a few second or third cousins and Aunt Olinda, who wasn't a blood relative. Felicia passed still searching for Shangri-la. Evangeline wondered if she had any regrets while here on earth, although maturity had made her realize events probably worked out for the best. By leaving town, Felicia thought she was protecting her child by not letting her grow up with the stigma of being a bastard. Or she could have been a coward. Who knew what was right? Maybe her mother was wiser than all of them.

Suddenly, Zelda's deep growl and forceful jerk on the leash snapped Evangeline out of her musings. She halted. "What?" she whispered and peered into the inky surroundings.

"Zelda, stop it. You're scaring me," but the poodle barked furiously, heaved on the leash until her forepaws left the ground and she was suspended on her back legs. Evangeline stumbled forward as ice-cold panic zipped up her spine.

"Go, girl. Let's get out of here." Zelda started off, dragging Evangeline along until she was running full-out, pounding the trail through the tunnel as if the devil were on her heels. She stumbled, righted herself, rounded a curve on the path, and burst out into the open and onto the parking-area blacktop. Her heart beat like a sledgehammer and she thought it would explode.

She slowed her pace, looked down at Zelda, and scolded, "What in hell was that all about?" But Zelda offered no apology. Panting and chuffing, she strained relentlessly forward. Evangeline trusted the dog's instinct, picked up speed again, and before she reached the Bronco, fumbled for her keys and pressed the panic button. The siren screamed and she pushed the unlock button. At the car, she jerked the door open and Zelda sailed onto the passenger side, while Evangeline clawed up into the driver's seat.

She hit the lock button, gripped the steering wheel with one hand, and with the other, shakily inserted the key into the ignition and ground the engine to life. As she threw the gear into reverse, she twisted her head around, but saw nothing except the young couple emerging from the tunnel of trees onto the lot.

She collapsed against the backrest. "Well, crud, Zelda, you big wuss. You scared me to death. We need to have a serious talk. My heart can't take another episode like this."

Zelda pressed her nose against the side window and watched the couple who were bent over with their hands on their knees, catching their breaths.

"You call those two a threat? Some police dog you are."

Zelda adjusted her position on the front seat and faced Evangeline. Her ears pricked up and Evangeline swore the dog understood what she had said, because she appeared confused that her master doubted her. Then she dropped to her stomach, inched over the console, submissively propped her head on Evangeline's thigh and looked up at her with sad, soulful eyes.

"It's all right, girl. I forgive you," she said, while patting the dog's head, massaging her neck and scratching behind her ears. "Wish you could tell me what had you so frightened."

Chapter 18

After a long, lingering bath, hot enough to scald the peel off a tomato, and a supper of fried chicken tenders and coleslaw, Evangeline settled on the rolled-arm sofa in the family room with a glass of wine and tried to calm her frayed nerves. She could usually shake off unsettling events, but lately there had been so many so close together she didn't have time to recover. As Dahlia would say, she was bumfuzzled, couldn't put her finger on anything tangible that would refute or prove her feeling that she was being stalked, but intuition told her that was exactly what was happening. Why or by whom she hadn't the slightest idea.

Think about the good stuff. It isn't like me to become unhinged, but I can feel a fall coming. She shook it off, glanced around and decided she loved this room. Separated from the kitchen by the butcher-block island, the seating area was defined by a thick, shaggy white rug reminding one of tangled polar bear fur. The coffee table, made from an old Moroccan door she and Nicky found at an architectural outlet and had inset with a thick sheet of glass, was where they had lounged on floor pillows, eaten dinner and discussed the day's events over a glass or two of wine. Supposedly from a castle known as a Kasbah, the door was decorated with ornate geometric designs in faded jewel tones, and fascinated her because of its heritage. The two leather recliners were useless, because Nicky wanted her within touching distance when they found time to relax and watch their black-and-whites; chairs were too confining, he had said, and when they were not on the floor pillows, he would pat the sofa cushion for her to sit beside him. *Oh, well, so much for togetherness.*

If she thought about it, which she did daily, Nicky's presence permeated the house. He had wanted the wide-screen television that she never had time to watch because of grading school papers, then studying for her detective license and surfing the web for possible leads on the artwork. After he moved out, she had to learn to use the television's conveniences, and it was now her evening entertainment. It also broke the sound of silence.

So many memories surfaced that she thought of moving. But if she moved, Nick would know he'd won, that she couldn't live without him. Or maybe he would realize she *was* moving on. *The devil, you pathetic little twit! He isn't sitting home alone with a poodle, watching television. He's probably at Fallana B's wallowing in attention and thinking about whom he can seduce, although he wouldn't have to try very hard with Fallana around.*

Ready for a much needed bawling session, she sat back and clicked on a soapy black-and-white movie. Zelda sat on her haunches, watching her quizzically. "Okay, come on." She patted the cushion. The poodle placed her front paws gently on the pillow, eased up next to her and rolled onto her back, exposing her soft pink tummy.

"I'm still mad at you," Evangeline said, and tickled her belly. "Okay, I'll rub yours if you rub mine." She laughed, because talking to a dog had to be scraping the bottom of the barrel. But she also thanked God for the animal and her warmth. With Zelda near, a frozen place in her heart began to thaw, one she thought would never feel again.

She sipped the wine, trying to forget the park incident. But the niggle was still there, like an unseen force waiting to appear and knock her for a loop. Since Zelda was taught police tactics, it was odd she was so frightened. Maybe it was her way of protecting Evangeline, removing her from danger. Evangeline would never know, because Zelda couldn't tell her.

"Good stuff," she said, setting the wine glass on one of the six coasters Dahlia had brought her from England last summer.

She dozed, conjuring Nicky standing in the doorway clad in a starched white shirt and tight underwear. The sharp peal of the phone pierced the fog. She jumped, tipped sideways and her hand came down on Zelda's head. The dog yelped, adding to Evangeline's cobweb of confusion. "Damn, the dream was really getting good." *Maybe I can pick up where I left off.*

She stumbled to the bar, fumbled the receiver from its base, and glanced at the wall clock, which indicated ten p.m. She recognized the area code, but not the number. Cautiously, she said hello. Her heart sank. Doctor Horne, the family physician, said, "Evie, we had to rush Olinda to the ER. Her ulcer hasn't responded to treatment as we hoped, and I suspect a perforation. If I'm right, we need to get aggressive. She's the most pigheaded woman I ever dealt with. Can you come? She said not to bother you, but she'll listen to you."

"Oh, my God. Of course. I'll leave tonight. I can't stay, though. I must work to pay my bills." Without hesitation or thinking of the consequences, "Would it go against you if I brought her to Houston? I'm less than ten minutes from the medical center, and it would really help me."

"Don't mind a bit. It's a great idea. Might do her some good to get away from here. Let's do it this way. Instead of you coming tonight, I'll make the necessary arrangements and send her there by ambulance. She's kept up her insurance, so most of the journey should be covered. My wife will check on the house here. Make certain it's locked up tight. I'll touch base with the doctor who takes over there."

"Let me know where and when to meet the ambulance."

Long after hanging up, Evangeline slouched on the stool at the bar, her feet on the bottom rung. How could she handle her job, the dog, Aunt Olinda and the extra cost of the hospital stay, finding the lost art, having a life? But she would work it out. Like a recovering alcoholic, she would take one day at a time. What was it Grandpop used to say? "The Lord never piles so much on your shoulders you can't carry it," and Mamma would counter with, "Yeah, as long as you're made of stone."

Nurses were arranging Olinda's bed sheets and IV when Evangeline entered the hospital room. "Well, if you're not a mess," she said good-naturedly, taking the woman's hand and squeezing. "This is a helluva way to get attention."

"Now, girl, don't you go making fun of Aunt Olinda. I be feeling like something Scrounger drug up," she said, referring to the tomcat that had roamed her neighborhood for the last fifteen years, hanging out wherever it pleased, usually where the most food and affection were available.

"I'll be going home in a day or two. Can't stay long. Too much to do. Mr. Beene wouldn't like my being gone."

Evangeline rolled her eyes. "Where Grandpop is, he doesn't have a whole hell of a lot to say about this. I checked out perforated ulcers on the web, and this is serious. Frankly, if you don't do what the doctors say, you could get peritonitis and die."

"Pish. No way. I got a lot more trouble to cause afore I go see my *loa*."

Evangeline wondered what trouble she referred to, and hoped it didn't include her. The woman was incorrigible.

"Hand me that magazine. I feel a hot coming on."

Evangeline did as asked, but Olinda's face turned crimson and perspiration popped out on her face and arms. She was glad menopause was still many years away before she had to deal with it.

"Ask the doctor for some medication. I'm surprised Doctor Horne hasn't prescribed any."

"I don't take med'cine unless I know what's in it."

At a light rap at the door, a man wearing green scrubs with a mask hanging around his neck asked if he could enter. Evangeline motioned. Olinda said, "It's your hospital. We visiting."

He introduced himself as Doctor Petrie—fiftyish, gray at the temples, and wiry, as if he could run a thirty-mile marathon in his expensive running shoes—a brand beyond Evangeline's means.

"I'll be the attending physician, but will consult with Doctor Horne periodically. If you need anything, call my service and they'll notify me immediately. I'm here to serve you."

That's a switch.

He handed each of them a white linen-like card with his name and number. Evangeline inserted it into her purse and Olinda clenched hers in a white-knuckled fist.

Olinda afraid?

With a warm and inviting bedside manner, Dr. Petrie looked down at his patient, took her hand, patted it and said, "Miss Olinda, you are one fine-looking woman. We need to keep you healthy."

Olinda's face turned a deeper scarlet, and it was definitely not from menopause. Miz Toughie was smitten. Maybe she would behave.

After giving them a brief rundown on Olinda's prognosis, the doctor eased toward the door and was gone.

"I like him, don't you?" Evangeline said, glancing around. "The room is cozy."

"I need to get out of here soon as I can."

Her patience running thin trying to pacify Olinda, trying to think positively, to find neutral ground for the woman's predicament, Evangeline said, "You heard what he said. The perforation in your intestinal tract needs immediate attention. Fluids, bed rest, a special diet and an operation."

"Pish posh. I can take care of my own."

Evangeline lost it. "Listen, you stubborn old hoodoo. I don't intend to let you die so you can get your way, and then for the rest of my life blame myself for letting it happen."

Olinda's eyes narrowed devilishly. "Yes, 'um, guess you got me where you want me." She paused and a smile tilted the corners of her mouth. "At least for now."

She always gets the last freaking word.

Chapter 19

Although her grandmother's Uncle Jacques lived a few minutes away, Evangeline had not seen him in many months, and made an appointment to visit before bringing Olinda home from the hospital. Built on several acres, Uncle Jacques' French Tudor was a spectacular mansion in one of the most prestigious neighborhoods in the area.

After leaving France in the late thirties with a substantial inheritance, and when his dream of a productive horse ranch failed, Uncle Jacques moved the family to Houston, where he purchased the property in the 1960s. Eventually, servants' quarters and a guesthouse were built on the acreage, and most of his clan still resided in the compound behind brick-fenced walls.

The majority of Jacques' kin leached off his investments and vied for his attention as the favored one. In his late nineties, he was Evangeline's great-uncle. Age had finally taken a toll, and he was now too feeble to leave his suite except for occasional wheelchair jaunts onto the suite's balcony. He still possessed a sharp mind, but she realized this might be her last visit with the old gentleman, the only living Delacroix who actually cared about her.

With a jab of pain, she remembered the exact time and place of her first conversation with her grandmother's family. As a gesture of good faith, she had visited the mansion, and when the butler ushered her into the solarium, the reception she received felt cold as frostbite.

The illegitimate child of a common working-class family didn't fit into their idea of an acceptable and proper member of their elite group, especially a person with an aunt like Olinda. Uncle Jacques had been kind enough, although a little standoffish until he got to know her better. She supposed his first expectations of her weren't too high. But that was then; this was now.

Evangeline drove up to the call box and punched in a probably obsolete code. The gate didn't respond. She pressed the call button, identified herself to the voice, and the heavy iron gate with the ostentatious gold "D" swung open. She hurried through, remembering how quickly the gate closed, and proceeded through the tunnel of oaks bordering the driveway.

The crepe myrtles still bloomed, and she thought it was a shame the beautiful grounds were never used for anything constructive—just sat looking well kept and lonely.

Claudine, Evangeline's cousin, must have known she had an appointment, because she answered the door and stood tall and statuesque, blocking the entrance.

Evangeline was undaunted. The woman's clingy ink-blue dress—which showed the right amount of cleavage to intrigue a male real estate client, but not enough to intimidate a woman—high-heeled shoes, pearl earrings, and blond flaxen hair pulled back in a French twist were impeccable. But her stare pierced Evangeline like a laser.

Evangeline tried to laser it back, but could not muster the intensity. She had never loathed anyone to such a degree or so blatantly. "How are you, Claudine? You're looking spiffy today."

Claudine stepped aside. "Come in, if you must. I am on my way to meet a client."

Evangeline gave her credit for at least making an effort at selling high-end real estate. She certainly had the contacts, and

Evangeline admired her for ridding herself of the husband who had made an obscene gesture to Evangeline when they first met. Claudine had seen the suggestive hand-at-the-crotch movement, and although Evangeline was perfectly innocent and would never have acted upon it, the incident had since defined the two women's relationship. It was sad, because she and her spunky cousin neared the same age, and Evangeline felt she could truly like her.

"Knock 'em dead, Claudine," she said sincerely as the chauffeur pulled up to the front entrance in a silver BMW.

Claudine started down the steps, turned, and said, "Great-grandpère is very ill. Don't upset him with your stolen-art nonsense."

Witch. One thing she wouldn't do was take advice from Claudine. She would be careful, though, not wanting to be a catalyst for Uncle's relapse.

Upstairs, a woman who appeared to be in her early forties, wearing a starched white uniform, occupied a chair adjacent to Uncle Jacques' door. She rose and laid the paperback she had been reading on the seat.

Finally having come to terms with the Delacroix family's feelings about her, she retaliated by embarrassing them when the opportunity arose—not ladylike, but it gave her satisfaction and got her through the confrontation. Besides, there were more skeletons in the Delacroix closet than in an old country cemetery.

Never having seen the woman at the door, Evangeline said, "Hi, I'm Evangeline, the bastard—"

"He's expecting you," she said and rapped gently on the double doors. At the tinkle of a bell, she opened one side and motioned Evangeline through.

Uncle Jacques was propped on pillows against the headboard of a huge sleigh bed. His wrinkled, flabby skin hung on for dear life as though if it released its hold, he would go to bone. Once clear, his twinkling hazel eyes now held a faraway swimming look, and she knew it was only a matter of time.

He wiggled his fingers for her to come forward and she leaned down and kissed his brow. He was well kept except for the slight acrid smell of urine wafting past her nostrils.

"I'm bad off," he said, squeakily and yet with the wonderful French accent she loved.

"No," she said, sitting in the bedside chair and taking his hand. "You'll be around for many years."

"Yes." He sighed, although resigned to the truth. "I wondered if you would visit."

"Uncle Jacques, of course I would come."

"You are so like your grandmother. Tenacious, loyal, beautiful."

Tenacious, yes. Loyal, yes. Beautiful, debatable.

"Are you well, my dear?"

"Things are good. I'm still searching, of course, but not with any real hope. I suppose the paintings are gone forever."

"You will find them. You cannot do otherwise." He coughed, and she took a tissue from the stand and held it to his mouth. When he finished, she tossed it into the empty wastebasket beside the bed.

He said, "The lungs aren't what they used to be. But I did enjoy those Cuban cigars. I remember . . ." He stopped, tried for a breath, and began another chain of thought. "I've made a proviso for you when I'm—"

"Shhh," she said, pushing back a shock of white hair that had fallen over his forehead. "I can't think about it." She gulped a sob and *he* patted *her* hand. So like him to do the consoling.

"There, there, my dear, don't cry. It's my time. I've already lived too long. Must give the vultures their due. Now, let me hear about you."

"First, Uncle Jacques, may I ask a question that's been bothering me?"

"I'll answer, if I can."

"Grandmother passed so suddenly, I'm wondering about something. Have you seen a death certificate giving the exact cause of her death? I assumed it was a heart attack because she did have problems and took medicine, but now I'm trying to tie up loose ends in my mind."

"There was a certificate." His brow wrinkled and he stared into space, thinking. Then, referring to his attorney, he said, "I believe Kestner has it. Yes, I remember now. I saw it on his briefcase at the reading of Danielle's will."

"May I take a look, maybe get a copy?"

He pointed to the desk. "His number, in a drawer, there. Don't know what purpose it'll serve."

"Idle curiosity."

Evangeline went to the Italian rococo desk inlaid with ivory, removed the address book, dialed the number and told the secretary Jacques Delacroix would like to speak with Mr. Kestner. A male voice was immediate. She held the phone to Jacques' ear.

"Kirk, Jacques, here. Oh, doing fine. Not what I used to be, as you well know. Listen, Kirk, I'm calling for my niece Evangeline. She needs a copy of Danielle's death certificate. Will you handle it for me?" Jacques listened a moment and said, "In fact, give her access to anything regarding Danielle she needs. Umm. I will, and you take care, too. Done," Jacques said and nodded for Evangeline to hang up the phone. "But why the curiosity? It's been, what, seven years? More?"

"It isn't important enough to waste our time on."

She settled back and told him about Zelda, and that Olinda was in the hospital, and that she'd come to terms with the divorce, mentioning nothing about the odd occurrences of late.

Occasionally, he nodded or mumbled something, but she realized he wasn't hearing half of what she said. When his eyes drooped, she decided the visit had ended. He needed to conserve his remaining strength.

"Uncle Jacques, I love you and will see you soon. If I can do anything, have someone call."

He attempted another weak hand squeeze. Tears came to her eyes, so she rose, gazed down, kissed two of her fingers and pressed them to his lips. "Good night, Uncle Jacques."

She hurried from the room, but halfway down the stairs she tripped, and grabbed the banister with both hands to prevent a headfirst tumble. At the front door, she twisted the handles, jerked them open and, banging them behind her, stumbled to her Bronco. "Shit, shit, shit. Too many deaths, too many deaths. Please God, no more."

Chapter 20

The next day, after a quick visit to the hospital to check on Olinda, Evangeline was at her desk when Babs appeared in the doorway, leaving no avenue of escape.

"Busy?"

"Always," Evangeline said.

Babs, her hair in pigtails tied with pink ribbon, wore an above-the-knee pleated skirt and a cute little purple T-shirt with the words "Likee But Don't Touchee."

Evangeline and Lance had cautioned her about the clothes she wore to work, impressing on her the need to dress professionally. But it went in one ear, and Julian didn't seem to mind, so who were they to throw cold water on the situation? Evangeline's Bohemian attire was at least coordinated, with no writing.

Babs leaned against the doorjamb, crossed her arms in front and crossed one ankle over the other. "Have you ever thought about cyberdating?"

Taken aback, Evangeline sputtered, "Not really. You?"

"Maybe. Well, yeah. You can go to these online dating services and they match you up with another person you'll be compatible with."

"Babs, as far as I can tell, and from what you relate to me, you're never at a loss for male companionship."

"Thought I'd try a different scenario. Never know. I might meet Mr. Right."

"Honey, you need to be careful. I've heard horror stories about meeting online."

"The dating service is supposed to rule out the risk."

"Well, I wouldn't leave my safety in the hands of someone else."

"God, Evie, you're no fun. Always so serious."

Evangeline had heard that more than once. "All I'm saying is be careful. If you must, be sure to meet in a public place."

"Yes, Mamma." Babs craned her neck. "Is Zelda under there?"

Zelda woofed.

Babs grinned. "You gotta love a sassy dog."

"She's my baby, aren't you, Zelda girl?" Evangeline had removed her right shoe, and rubbed the dog's tummy with her toe. Zelda woofed again.

The phone rang. Babs said, "Whoops," and hurried off.

Evangeline wondered if the girl's parents knew her plan to meet someone she'd found online. "Lordy, I feel so old talking to her."

A short time before lunch break, Babs buzzed Evangeline's intercom and said she had a visitor. She hoped Dahlia had returned from cha-chaing with the deck hands, but as she rose, Maximilian Forbes appeared at the door.

He strode to the desk and clasped her hand in his. She felt a little off-balance at seeing him and was glad she had not weakened and called him first. She sputtered, "Max, what a pleasant surprise. Come in. It's good to see you."

"I'm in town on business and took a chance you'd be here. Wasn't sure you'd want to see me the way you disappeared in New York."

"Please have a seat and let me explain." She related the circumstances and gave a quick run-through on Olinda.

He settled back in the chair, seeming relieved and confused at the same time. "I flew the Cessna into Hobby this morning and plan to stay a day or two."

"Wonderful," Evangeline said over Zelda's soft growl that prompted a nudge from her toe.

"Is that Zelda?" He craned his neck to see over the desk.

"She's jealous of anyone new. And very protective."

"I had a dog like her once. Never could trust him. Very unpredictable."

She nodded and lifted her eyebrows questioningly.

"I only have a minute. Meeting a client for lunch, but keeping my fingers crossed you're free for dinner."

"Hmm. Let me check my calendar," she said playfully, thumbing through the daily on her desk. "Yes, I think I can make it. Nothing planned for dinner for the next six months."

He laughed. "I can't believe that."

As she walked him to the door, they agreed he would pick her up at seven. Back at her desk, Evangeline pulled the chair aside and snapped her fingers at Zelda, whose head lay between her front paws. "Come out from under there right now. What is wrong with you? He's a perfectly nice man. You should be ashamed of yourself."

Zelda came out from the kneehole, whined softly and nuzzled her hand.

"If you're going to act unruly, you'll have to stay home."

The dog looked at her quizzically.

"Oh, no you don't. You're not getting away with playing dumb. You know exactly what I'm saying."

Lance stuck his head through the door. "To whom are you conversing?"

Conversing? Why doesn't he simply say talking to?

He glanced down and saw Zelda. "You're losing it, Evie. It's an animal."

"But she isn't *any* animal."

Babs wheeled her little subcompact into a parking place in front of the cleaners. She couldn't believe she had forgotten to pick up her dress yesterday when she had more time, but lately it seemed she had become extremely absentminded. Her parents continually told her to pay attention, that her lapses in memory would get her into trouble, and they had been right about most things. Maybe it was the attention deficit problem she was diagnosed with in high school. She'd always had to study harder than any of her peers, but it wasn't her fault. Except, like now, when she tried to get off the medication, she really messed up.

She was excited about her date tonight with the new guy she met online and hoped he would be worth the effort. The last one was an absolute catastrophe. All he talked about was what he owned and the trips he had taken. She didn't get a word in edgewise, and she shuddered, because if there was one thing she had, it was a gift for gab.

Dan sounded like a winner, almost too good to be true. But she was an optimist and looked to the bright side. At twenty-two, she still had plenty of time to settle down, but going to singles bars sure got old. Maybe she should have tried a two-year college like her parents wanted, taken cosmetology or photography. Yep, she shot real good pictures. Maybe she'd submit a few to some contests, see what happened. The receptionist job was okay for now, but it offered no future. Maybe she could become a detective like Evangeline.

She meant to tell Evangeline she had seen Evangeline's friend at the car rental kiosk at the airport while picking up her mother a few days ago. From behind, the person's friend seemed familiar. Maybe she forgot to mention the incident because she had a secret Evangeline didn't know. Babs wasn't jealous of her. It was just that everyone liked Evangeline so much and respected her opinions; to know something she didn't was kind of a turn-on. Though Evangeline might already be privy to it.

At her apartment complex, she parked in her space and gathered her cleaning from the backseat. She had about an hour to make beautiful for Dan. It would be close, but she was confident she'd have time to wash and do her hair.

Due to the overcast sky, the evening had darkened earlier than usual. The gate to the walkway to her section was ajar and she gave it a swing with her foot. "Well, that's just great!" *The light's out again.* It had happened before, and she couldn't even see to put her key in the lock. This was no different. *Count your steps, Barbie, twelve in all, remember?* She peered into the unrelenting shadows and moved carefully lest she fall over an object left on the concrete path. One, two . . . eleven, twelve.

The dark wall of the apartment door loomed before her. Over the pittosporum bush, she carefully draped the plastic cleaner's sack containing her favorite sexy black minidress with the tie shoulder straps. She then felt around in the bottom of her purse for her house key. Why couldn't she remember to have it ready as the defense instructor had told them in class?

At a rustle behind her, she started to turn, but the chill that shot up her spine was quickly quashed as a lightning bolt exploded in her head and everything Barbie had tried to remember or wanted to say was quieted forever.

Chapter 21

Evangeline dressed carefully, anticipating a lovely dinner out and then who knew what would happen. For the first time in months, she felt like pursuing a relationship with someone other than Nicky. He had made his decision about what he wanted, and she must accept it.

Who was she kidding? Nicky was the love of her life, her soul mate. She would never get over the ache. Breakup was a bitch.

Max might not be the one, but he was a beginning.

The phone rang and showed *Unknown Caller.* She hesitated, but it was Max apologizing and asking if she could meet him at the restaurant. He had made reservations for eight o'clock but was just now leaving his appointment and it would take about forty-minutes to drive into town. She said she didn't mind but secretly resented them not driving together.

She was being seated when Max entered and waved. She wasn't exactly ugly, but he was such a good-looking specimen, she wondered what he saw in her. *It must be my charming personality, or maybe my money—not.*

At the table, he leaned down, kissed her cheek and sat opposite her. "I'm so sorry for this, especially on our first real date. I'm finalizing details on a major art deal and time got away from me."

"I understand completely."

The waiter came, and after Max consulted with Evangeline, he ordered an expensive bottle of wine. They made light conversation, finally turning to art, and she related what she had learned and ruled out in the quest for her grandmother's treasures. He seemed impressed at her familiarity with the inner workings of the government's World War II art recovery program.

She said, "The Nazis really did some plundering, and it's sinful, the number of artworks still missing or unclaimed."

"Your job is cut out for you."

"Grandmother listed her pieces with major lost art registries, but heard not a word."

Max stroked his chin. "Stolen art is big business. Though it's difficult to sell a famous piece because the buyer can't display it for fear of reprisal. Of course, if a person wants to own it for the sake of owning it, that's a different story."

"There is an artist, Abner Jacobson, who seems to have a connection of sorts. I'm not exactly sure how, but Julian and Lance plan to get involved, so maybe they'll discover a new lead."

He offered again. "I've a few well-placed contacts, so if I can—"

"I'm winging it at the moment, but appreciate the offer. As I said before, it wouldn't be fair to get you involved in this."

The waiter appeared, and Max ordered a T-bone medium rare and Evangeline ordered filet mignon medium well.

She said, "My Aunt Olinda is having surgery tomorrow. Not sure how it will go. I dropped by the hospital before I came here, and she's being really snippy."

She related a little more about Olinda, and he was amused at the voodoo/hoodoo reference and said, "I lived in New Orleans a few years, and encountered one or two mambo*s* and hungan*s*. Even studied the religion and visited Haiti. From what I understand, voodoo is a conglomeration of African beliefs and rites with a lot of Catholic practices mixed in. The dances and body possessions are what make it seem so dark and mysterious. Possession is probably good or bad acting, however you want to view it. Don't put much stock in any of it. But live and let live, I say."

Evangeline was relieved he didn't think they were weird, even though she was adamant hoodoo wasn't her belief, and Olinda was a cross she must bear. "Thanks for understanding. I love her, because she's been a source of affection and consolation for many years. But to keep the record straight, Olinda isn't a mambo. She's a hoodoo or root woman, because she uses herbs for magical purposes and knows just enough to get her in trouble."

He waved his hand in the air. "Hey, who am I to judge. Sounds like fun. And you have a new dog. You are one busy lady. Please, use me if you need me."

Any time, you handsome devil. "I'm open to suggestions."

He mulled it over and then a glimmer set in his eyes. "How about a change of scenery. Maybe a plane trip to wherever you choose."

She didn't have to think about it, and teasingly said, "Actually, I own a castle in France I've never seen. At least I own it along with the tax department."

He grinned. "Royalty! I'm impressed."

"I once thought so."

"Next week sound good for you?"

"I was kidding."

"I'm not."

Flustered, Evangeline said, "I don't even know if my passport is current. My plans were always spoiled before I could use it."

"Why don't you check it out?"

"You're serious."

"Whenever you're ready."

More than flabbergasted, but calling his bluff, she said, "It depends on how Olinda's surgery goes and if Julian will give me the time off."

Max asked the waiter for a pen and wrote numbers on a napkin. "I forgot to give you my cell phone number. All you have to do is call."

"Or maybe just whistle," she said, referring to Bacall's words to Bogart in the 1944 film *To Have and Have Not.*

"Uh, what?"

"Nothing."

Evangeline could not believe it. She might finally visit the château Grandmother Delacroix-Ravel spoke about so lovingly, roam the stone halls of the old castle fortress, descend to the underground vault and kitchen, walk out onto the ledge where so much happened.

Maybe she and Max could fly to Paris and visit Saint Lyra, the old homestead outside the city. The desire was partly idle curiosity, but mostly she needed a connection to her past, and Grandmother Delacroix-Ravel must have wanted it too, or she wouldn't have left the estate and château to Evangeline. On several occasions she had planned a trip to Europe, but events or someone always interfered, although it was mostly the financial factor. By now, the structures had probably deteriorated, but according to Grandmother's stipulation, monies were bequeathed for taxes and upkeep, and Evangeline received verification yearly from an attorney friend of the Delacroix-Ravel family.

The last Evangeline heard, both places were being rented out to vacationers or businessmen who wanted privacy or to get away from the rat race. The rentals helped with expenses and occasionally she would receive a royalty check. Not much, but always a nice surprise.

★ ★ ★ ★ ★

Zelda was waiting at the back door, lips back in a grin, nub and hind end wagging so hard it almost knocked Evangeline over.

"Easy, girl. I'm glad to see you, too." She ruffled her fur. "Oh, the devil, what will I do with you if I take a trip?"

After mulling it over, she decided it was probably a dream, anyway. And besides, she hardly knew Max, and here she was agreeing to fly around the world with him. She might have to rethink her decision, although nothing would probably come from it anyway. And, if it did, would she be a fool to turn down the offer? No use adding another weight to her shoulders. She'd decide when and if the time came.

With homeowner and dog ownership duties completed, back door and windows locked, she retired to the upstairs bedroom. She had given up trying to make Zelda sleep downstairs and had bought another dog bed and laid it inside the door.

Might as well check the passport. Never know when I'll need it. She went to her closet, flipped on the light and moved boxes around to get to the small waterproof safe. She had never owned anything important enough to keep in one, but Nicky had insisted, and it had come in handy. She probably should keep her Glock in there, but if she needed it, by the time she unlocked the safe to get to it, she'd probably be dead. Instead, she kept it in a locked metal container inserted into a nondescript keepsake box behind some shoeboxes on the top shelf of the closet. Probably the first place someone would look, but no children visited, so she'd be safe from an accidental shooting.

She punched in the code, pushed down on the handle and opened the door. The passport was tucked into the back in its original envelope so she pulled it out, crossed her fingers and looked at the expiration.

"*Voilà,* six months to go." A flutter of anticipation and excitement tickled her senses as she returned everything to their original places.

Exhausted, she changed into a gown, and without removing her makeup, fell into bed. Nicky didn't like pajamas, although she did own two pair. He said a gown was easy to manipulate and saved valuable time. *Where are you now, Nick, you jerk?*

Zelda sat and laid her nose on the edge, staring at Evangeline with soulful eyes. "No way, girl. You need to have some boundaries. At least for a while."

She turned her back to the dog and pulled the covers to her chin. She should have slept like a baby, but tossed all night, an uneasy blanket of foreboding shrouding her. She could feel a change coming. Even Zelda sensed it. Her occasional mousy yips disturbed what sleep Evangeline managed to succumb to, and each time she squinted one eye open, the dog was at the window, gazing out.

Finally, Evangeline went under, dreaming of kneeling in a slowly deflating rubber raft bobbing about in the middle of a shark-infested ocean. The shrill echo of the phone slammed her awake and she sat straight up. The illuminated dials of the night-stand alarm clock read five a.m.

Chapter 22

Evangeline jerked on a hoodie and sweat pants, and twisted her hair into a topknot. She slipped into backless canvas shoes, tripped over Zelda and said, "Scoot. Aunt Olinda's in trouble and I've got to get to the hospital, pronto."

Zelda bounded past her down the stairs and waited at the back door.

"No. Stay. You can't go." The dog tucked her rear and lowered her head. Evangeline softened, and patted the animal's head. "I'll be back soon as I can, girl. Be good. I love you."

In the car she careened around the corner, did rolling stops at the signs and fudged on a couple of caution lights. At the hospital, she pulled up to the drop-off entrance, killed the engine and hurried to Olinda's floor, thinking her Bronco would get towed, but she didn't care.

Dr. Petrie stood at the nurse's station. Evangeline grabbed hold of his coat. "What's happened?"

He shook his head. "I really don't know for sure. The night nurse went in to check on her and she wasn't there. We've searched most of the halls and rooms with no trace."

"Is there a surveillance tape? Can we see it?"

"A copy is on its way." He glanced up and down the corridor. "The floor is quiet this time of morning, but let's go to the nurses' lounge. It's more private and has a television with a DVD and VCR player."

"Something terrible has happened to her. I know it."

"Now don't jump to conclusions. She might be hiding. Patients are known to do that before major surgery."

"You have no idea what's been going on."

While they waited, Evangeline related the happenings. He looked skeptical.

"I'm not an alarmist, Dr. Petrie, anything but. My boss believes I'm in danger, so that's good enough for me."

A young volunteer brought the tape and inserted it into the VCR. Doctor Petrie pointed out Olinda's room. Evangeline sat forward stiffly when a figure in scrubs, a surgical mask and cap entered the camera's scope of the corridor and sidestepped through Olinda's door. A few minutes later two figures emerged, Olinda in a hospital gown, the other with an arm wrapped around her shoulders. As they neared the camera and before disappearing under it, Olinda raised her head and moved her lips in what looked like "help me." The other figure had slouched over, and his or her face was hidden by the surgical mask and cap. The camera was positioned too high up to tell the person's height.

Evangeline said, "Can't be certain, but it looks like a man." The realization hit her and she sucked in a breath. "Oh, my God. She's been kidnapped."

Dr. Petrie had already lifted the phone receiver. "I'll notify the police."

Evangeline and Doctor Petrie were giving an officer background information when Arlo Strecker exited the elevator. Evangeline met him halfway and deflated into his arms like a punctured balloon.

He placed a welcoming arm around her shoulders to comfort her.

"I was going off duty and came at once when I heard your name on the radio."

"Oh, Arlo, I don't know what to do or why anyone would want to kidnap Aunt Olinda. It must be mistaken identity."

"Have you had a ransom call?"

"Not on my cell. I came right here. Haven't checked my answering machine at home."

"Maybe the tape will enlighten us. We'll send it to the lab, and Officer O'Mally will question the staff, so you don't need to stay here. I'll follow you home, make sure the house is secure and wait until a suit gets there. We'll want to monitor your phone in case you're contacted."

"I might have to hitch a ride. I parked at the entrance and my car probably got towed."

"No. I knew you were here, and when I saw a Bronco out front, I looked inside and realized it was yours. I spoke with a staff member who's a buddy of mine, and he's keeping an eye on it."

She took a deep breath. "Thank you, thank you."

Doctor Petrie said he would let them know if they found out anything else.

At home, Evangeline and Arlo waited outside until two plainclothes detectives arrived. The first one, who must have seniority, introduced himself as Sergeant Finch. The heavyset redheaded one was McTavish.

She unlocked the back door and Zelda darted past them and careened around the corner of the house. "Probably has to potty. Actually, if anything was wrong, Zelda would alert me."

"She's smart," Arlo agreed, "but she can't talk."

Evangeline raised one eyebrow. "Almost can, and you know it. There are other ways of communicating."

"Yeah. You should probably wait outside until we're sure it's safe."

"No way. I'll follow you. Zelda will follow me." She turned to find the dog at her heels, and then she glanced up at the Bernowitzes' window. Like clockwork they were both there, peering down at them. She waved, and they disappeared from sight.

"No telling what they think or will tell my neighbors."

"Do you really care?" Arlo asked.

"Not particularly, just never liked gossip. It can be so harmful," she said, thinking about high school.

After a careful search of the first and second floors, they tromped to the attic where all seemed in order. Downstairs, the detectives hooked up equipment to monitor her phone, but by now the clock said seven a.m. and time for work. Arlo and the officers wanted her to stay near the phone, but she couldn't sit idly by and do nothing.

"I need to work. Been off too much as it is."

What am I thinking? This wasn't about her anymore. Now Olinda was involved, and she must consider her. Was she all right? Was the ulcer worse? How long could she go without surgery? According to Doctor Petrie, it should have been done yesterday, and now, time was of the essence. *And why Olinda?*

Babs didn't answer the phone at Rembrandt, so Evangeline called Julian's private number. He insisted she remain at home. Relieved, she removed the twelve-cup coffeemaker from the pantry, shoved the four-cup to the back of the counter, plugged in the other, and paced as the coffee dripped into the carafe like a slowly leaking faucet. "Oh, the devil, hurry. I'm getting a withdrawal headache."

Finally, the coffeemaker gurgled, and she poured a cup for her and one for each officer. The jolt of caffeine helped alleviate the slight pounding at the base of her skull.

She had to get off the stuff, but she had cultivated the habit in childhood. The camaraderie it engendered would make it nigh on to impossible to quit, even if she could get the caffeine out of her system.

When the phone jangled, anticipating the kidnapper, she grabbed it before Finch could stop her, but it was Julian. "Evangeline, please sit down. I have some devastating news."

Weak-kneed, she plopped on the bar stool. "Okay," she said meekly. "I'm sitting."

"It's Babs. Neighbors found her this morning—she's, uh, dead. A homicide."

Evangeline's hand went to her mouth. "Oh, my God! What happened?"

"They found her lying at her front door in a pool of blood. Her father called me. Wanted me to hear it from him before I saw it on the news. They think it was a robbery gone bad. Her purse and car are missing. Her cleaning was still on a bush by her door."

"This is unbelievable. Babs, of all people. Here I've been worried about me and Aunt Olinda's kidnapping, and all the time Babs lay in the cold damp night." Evangeline felt shame for the things she had thought about the girl who was too young to die. "Julian, do they have a cause of death or an approximate time?"

"Sorry to be so blunt, but her head was bashed in. Her parents are in shock, of course. That's all the info I have, but I'll keep you posted. I'm to pick up clients at Bush Intercontinental in about thirty minutes. Lance is holding down the fort, so don't worry about the office."

"Thank you. If I can do anything, anything at all, let me know. Babs was like family."

She hung up, debating on whether to call Babs' parents, and then noticed Arlo and the two officers watching her expectantly. She filled them in and directed her question to Arlo. "Do you think there might be a connection to Olinda's kidnapping?"

Arlo said, "Evangeline, I'm beginning to think you're on to a real mystery. The incidents seem totally unrelated, but my gut is telling me otherwise. I know one thing. You must be alert at all times and not take any unnecessary chances."

"I hear you, Arlo, and I promise to be careful."

"I couldn't stand it if anything happened to you. I mean, what would Zelda do?"

"I have no doubt you would take her back."

"Yeah, you're probably right. But still, be careful."

The detectives agreed to keep her apprised of new developments, and they settled down to wait.

Minutes turned into hours, but the phone didn't ring. Arlo had several appointments scheduled and said he would call her when he got a chance. The two detectives gleaned as much information as she knew about the strange happenings of late, and were at the kitchen island playing gin rummy. Evangeline leaned on the back door frame watching an angry mockingbird attack a squirrel that had managed to jump over the metal guard of the birdfeeder.

Freaking squirrel. "Shooo!" She kicked the doorframe. Squirrel and bird took to cover.

Waiting was not good for her. She was getting more nervous and distracted, thinking of all the possible scenarios Olinda could be encountering. And poor Babs. A robbery. You never knew when your time would be up. She debated again on calling Babs' parents, but family and friends probably surrounded them. *And why doesn't the kidnapper call?*

And then, as if on cue, came the shrill echo of the phone. Evangeline almost knocked McTavish over reaching for it, but his restraining hand on her wrist was quick.

"Wait till we're ready."

At his nod, she raised the receiver. "Yes?"

"You've been waiting for my call." It was a statement.

As before, the voice sounded digitally altered, squeaky high, like the person had ingested helium. It could be male or female. No way to tell. "Is Olinda okay?"

"Olinda's fine. Shaken, in some pain, but otherwise unharmed. For now."

"What do you want with her?"

"To let *you* know how close I can get to you and your loved ones whenever I choose."

Blood rushed to her head and she gripped the receiver, suddenly knowing this was about her. She gathered courage. "But why? Have I done you harm? Do I have something you want? If it's money, you should know I don't have any."

"No more questions. The hoodoo is sitting on a bench near the park. You can't miss her."

"Wait!"

The line went dead, and she looked intensely at Red. "Did you get a trace?"

He shook his head. "Not enough time."

They screeched to a halt at the curb where Olinda was sitting, her face chalk white. "Oh Lordy, child. I'm done for. Get me to your hospital quick."

At the hospital, Evangeline and the two detectives waited in the hallway until Dr. Petrie examined Olinda. He exited the room and told them she was none the worse, mostly shaken up, and the surgery would be postponed until the next morning.

Finch said, "Is she up to speaking to us?"

"A few minutes, but don't upset her."

"I'm going in with you," Evangeline said.

"Okay, but we'll do the interrogating."

The nurse was straightening the covers and before she left, adjusted the IV. Indicating the call button, she said, "If you need anything, press here."

"Miss Olinda, I'm Sergeant Finch." Nodding toward the

other detective, he said, "This is my partner, Sergeant McTavish. We need to ask you some questions."

Evangeline realized the medication was taking effect, but hoped Olinda could shed some light on her kidnapping.

Finch continued. "Can you describe your abductor? Anything stand out? A scar, the way he or she spoke, clothing, anything to help with identity?"

With a thick tongue, Olinda mumbled, "What I remember is the person never said a word. Kept the mask on, pointed, jerked and pushed me into one of them love wagons. I couldn't do a thing because of that med'cin they give me. Don't want any more of it. Don't need it."

Olinda began tugging at the sheets, and Evangeline feared she'd pull out the IV.

Finch laid a hand on her arm. "It's okay, Miz—mind if I call you Olinda?"

She ran her fingers through her hair. "Call me whatever you want. It doesn't make a never mind. I'm getting outta here soon as I can."

Evangeline eased in front of Finch, and with both her hands, clasped Olinda's icy one and rubbed it gently with her thumb. "Aunt Olinda, surely you can remember some little detail. Was it a man or woman?"

She shook her head. "It could have been a man, but that medication put me half asleep and I didn't pay attention."

"Are you afraid? Did the person threaten you?"

"Oh, child, you need to rethink this artsy stuff and get back to your grandpop's house. We both need to get back quick as we can. Don't like this city. Got me a bad, bad premo."

"It would help if you could remember any little detail."

Olinda tugged at her sheet and rocked from side to side. "I'll tell you this. My kidnapper tied my hands, showed me a note that said not to look, blindfolded me, pushed me onto the floor in the back of that love wagon, drove around for a while, and then pushed me out at that bench. Don't make sense, but it happened like that. Never said nothing to me."

She was quiet for a moment. "I'm through talking." Olinda closed her eyes, and her breathing became even and quiet.

"Well, officers, it looks as though my aunt has tuned us out. Shall we?" Evangeline said while ushering them to the door. "Come back in a few hours. Maybe she'll be more cooperative."

Finch said, "We'll station an officer outside the door as a precaution." He handed her a card. "Call me for anything. This is an odd case. A pointless kidnapping along with a threat, and you've no idea what it's all about?"

"Actually, it could be about the missing art I mentioned, but I have no clue who is involved."

After they left, Evangeline sat quietly by the window, staring into space. Olinda was petrified. Maybe her abductor had threatened their lives. Could all this really be about missing art? *Whoever it is doesn't know me very well. I'm not scared off that easily. And he, she, it, flat shouldn't have messed with Olinda.*

Chapter 23

Olinda came through the operation as if a voodoo *loa* had bewitched her, but the thought of her going home and living there alone did not sit well with Evangeline. Olinda would have to stay with her until she was well enough to drive or at least prepare her own meals. Even though temporary, it wouldn't be easy living with her again. The upside was that Olinda and Zelda could keep each other company, and Zelda could alert them to any danger. Too, Evangeline wouldn't be constantly worrying if one or the other was okay.

Should Olinda need medical attention, the old homestead was too isolated, and Dr. Petrie said to call him if a problem arose. Now, how to approach Olinda with the news? She'd already said she wanted to leave Houston immediately. But that would not happen.

In Olinda's hospital room Evangeline stood by the window out of harm's way. Olinda hit the roof as predicted.

"No way I'm living in dis town."

"Yes, you are," Evangeline said, her mind made up. "A nurse will come in once a day to help out until you heal. I'll take you home when you can stand and walk without hunching over and, more importantly, when you can drive." She moved to the bed and pulled Olinda's hospital gown up, pretending to see through the bandages. "You've a mean-looking incision."

"Stop it," Olinda said, swatting at Evangeline's hand. "Dat's private. And I knew you'd pull a stunt like dis. You and Mr.

Beene, one of a kind. Stubborn. Sneaky."

"Excuse me, maybe you should look in a mirror, because it sounds like you're describing yourself."

Olinda looked away, and then the corners of her mouth tilted in the devilish smile Evangeline dreaded because it always meant trouble.

"I got other ways to get what I want. So, we'll see about it all."

"Olinda, you better behave. I'm not putting up with any heebie-jeebie foolishness from you."

"We'll see."

The police interviewed all the employees at Rembrandt Art Investigations and the art gallery about Babs, but Evangeline couldn't add much to what everyone else told them.

She said to a detective, "The last time I saw Babs was at work the afternoon of her death. She had made a date with some guy she met through an online dating service."

"Do you know which dating service?" the lead detective asked.

"She didn't say," Tears welled. "But she promised to meet in a public place and to not get into his car. Too dangerous."

"Good advice. I wish everyone would take precautions."

"Oh, my god, you don't think—"

"We'll follow up on all leads, check her personal and office computer and find out about the online date. Right now this looks like a mugging gone bad."

Evangeline mentioned her own odd encounters, but again the detectives did not seem to draw parallels.

Evangeline dreaded the funeral, and although the church overflowed with flowers, the service was simple and tastefully done, nothing like the ostentation Uncle Jacques' funeral would exhibit. Of course, there had not been much time to prepare for

Babs. Nobody expected her to be bludgeoned by a mugger.

Evangeline didn't recognize any law enforcement, but they were probably mingling with the mourners and watching for anyone suspicious. Often a perpetrator had to satisfy a sick need to see how his actions had affected the family.

She could not imagine the grief Babs' poor parents were experiencing, because losing a child must be the worst loss in the world. It upset the order of life. The parents were supposed to go first. And it reminded Evangeline of those she'd lost and how fleeting life could be. It also reminded her to call Dahlia.

After giving condolences to the family, she spoke with a few acquaintances and then quietly exited the side door. Blinded by the sun's glare, she shaded her eyes, and took in the tall figure leaning against Atlas's hood. Nicky's arms were crossed over his chest, his legs at the ankles. He wore jeans, a black T-shirt and black athletic shoes. Her heart skipped a beat. "Shit."

As she approached, he pushed away from the car and grinned.

She said, "How did you know I was here?"

He raised an eyebrow. "How else?"

"Of course, the obituaries."

"Let's go home," he said, taking the car keys from her, unlocking the Bronco and opening the door.

"You mean *my* home?"

"Your home, our home, whatever."

"To clarify, it isn't *your* home anymore."

He ignored her comment as she climbed into the Bronco. But she would fly to the moon with him right now if he asked her.

At home, he pulled into the driveway behind her. She punched the gate closed and noticed that the squeaking and grating sound had gotten worse. She would oil it and hope it didn't need greasing—another expense.

At the patio back door she said, "You'll get to see Zelda. If she doesn't like you, you're outta here."

He clutched his heart and staggered back a step as though shot. "Sized up by a female canine. Can't get much lower on the food chain. But I'm looking forward to meeting this dog wonder."

He reached down to the frog for the house key.

"Sorry," she said. "I moved it."

"Do I get to know where?"

"I've been told by a reliable source not to tell anyone. I'm pretty sure that includes my ex-husband."

She opened the door with the key from her purse and Zelda bounded past them. They watched as she headed for her potty place, performed her business, circled around and sniffed at it. Then she trotted back to where they were and sat in front of Nicky as if to say who are you, and what is your connection here?

Nicky squatted, gave a hand signal and said, "Come here, girl." Zelda looked at Evangeline and she nodded. Zelda's whole body wiggled like an electrocuted worm. She went to Nicky and laid her rear end sideways on the ground, submissive. He extended a hand and she placed a paw in it. "Well, hello there. I'm Nicky, and I used to live here."

Under her breath Evangeline murmured, "But not anymore."

"I heard that."

Zelda took to Nicky immediately, and followed him into the house. "She's a beauty," he said, bending down and scratching her ears.

Zelda woofed. Evangeline smiled and went to turn off the alarm. The devil, she'd forgotten to set it this morning. No wonder it didn't sound when she opened the door. Such carelessness could be detrimental to her health.

"Want a beer, tea, coffee, soft drink? I'm offering to be polite, not like I'm inviting you to stay."

He ignored her last remark and sat on a stool at the butcher-block island. "A beer would be great."

Not having eaten lunch, she took a package of cream cheese from the refrigerator, placed it on a glass dish, slathered on some jalapeño pepper jelly and surrounded it with whole-grain crackers. She removed two wine glasses from the freezer, rimmed them with a slice of lime then swirled them around on a saucer of salt.

She filled the glasses from a cold bottle of beer and squeezed in a little of the lime, sort of like a Margarita. She had learned to drink it that way from a girlfriend in college whose father owned an icehouse. He thought it lent a little more class to the place.

From the corner of her eye, she saw Nicky watching her with his sex-on-my-mind look. If he thought it would happen, he was dreaming.

"Evangeline?" he said, his voice husky.

She placed her hand on her hip, glared at him. "What's wrong, Fallana pissed at you?"

He looked crestfallen. Too bad.

"I miss you is all. Miss touching you, talking with you. The whole *you* thing. I didn't realize how much until the other day at the lounge."

He came to her, wrapped his arms around her waist and drew her to him. Her heart lurched and she was weak against him. He leaned back on the counter, caressed her arms and wrapped them around his neck, fumbling to interlock her fingers. They were melded together. "Don't let go," he whispered.

"No, I won't." She couldn't let go if she wanted to. It felt too good, too familiar. And then memory clicked in and she stiffened. "I can't do this—can't trust you. It hurts too much after what you've done."

"Evie, I've been a stupid fool. You're the one for me."

"Oh, really?" She flattened her hands on each side of his chest and pushed him away. "Trust is important to me. You knew—know that."

"I'll spend my life proving it to you."

Get some backbone, Evangeline. Don't fall into his arms the first time he comes whining back. "Do not promise a certainty you can't deliver. You're probably having a bad day, feeling sentimental. It will pass and tomorrow you'll wake up in another world." It was difficult to do, but she moved to the back door and opened it. "For now, I'm due at the hospital."

His shoulders hunched, and at the door he turned and gave her his lopsided smile. "I am not having a bad day, and I'm not giving up."

She pushed the electronic gate opener lying on the desk, closed the door on him, grinned, and wondered what to do with the beer and cream cheese.

Chapter 24

Abner had never been so lonely. He always ended up at Rudy's where a sea of familiar faces washed over him, and Joe and Rudy seemed to be genuinely glad to see him.

Joe asked if he wanted the usual and Abner nodded, then headed for his table. Rudy waved to him from the kitchen door, then glanced toward the entrance and beckoned to a man entering.

Rudy approached Abner's table. "Here comes Siegel," he said and grinned as a tall, rather handsome man wended his way through the tables. "You have to meet Siegel. He knows a little about art. Haven't talked to him extensively, but I'm sure you two will hit it off."

Not really into meeting anyone new, but not wanting to offend Rudy, Abner agreed to the introduction.

After courtesies were dispensed with and Rudy's friend occupied the chair across from him, Abner decided this Mark Siegel was actually an interesting fellow. He spoke intelligently and knew many of the names Abner tossed out. Rudy brought Siegel up to date on Abner's interest in art and his retirement from the museum, and then excused himself to see about a customer.

Siegel ordered a bottled beer and said, "I spent a summer in Paris, and took a few side trips, and I travel abroad often now. But Abner, I'm curious. How did you become such an art aficionado?"

For a moment Abner had second thoughts about revealing personal information to a complete stranger. "Rudy gives me too much credit, and it's really a boring subject, so when you've heard enough, say so. It won't hurt my feelings." *Why do I always belittle myself?*

"Don't worry," Siegel said. "I am not in the least masochistic. Life's too short."

Abner settled back and told Siegel about his assignment during the war and learning auto mechanics.

The waiter brought Siegel's beer, and he said, "You must've been a kid."

"Sixteen, but I had false ID papers. Besides, the army didn't really give a rip." He stretched his legs out onto the vacant seat, and remembered that he laughed a lot in those days. Now, few things made him smile, and he hadn't enjoyed a good belly roll since he couldn't remember when.

Siegel's expression indicated he waited for more, and Abner continued. "When I was discharged and returned home, a local private museum needed a driver and auto mechanic and hired me. Later they promoted me to the warehouse and eventually, when I proved myself, I received a fulltime custodianship."

"I'm impressed," Siegel said, draining his beer.

If he could keep this young man's interest, Abner supposed he wasn't so boring after all.

"Through the years, I've seen many masterpieces come and go."

"All this time and you've held one job? Amazing."

"By the way," Abner questioned, "what did you say your line of work was?"

"Oh, this and that, but art collecting is my real passion. If you ever run across a swinging deal, say an old master or even a new up-and-coming artist with investment potential, I might be interested."

He removed a card from his billfold and handed it to Abner. "Since I travel a lot, you can usually catch me on my cell phone or leave a callback number." He glanced at his watch. "But I must go now as I'm late for an appointment. I stopped in to say hi to Rudy." He thumbed a twenty-dollar bill from a gold money clip, laid the bill on the table, scooted his chair back and stood. "My treat, Abner. It was worth the interesting conversation."

Abner rose and extended his hand. "I enjoyed meeting you, Mark. Maybe we'll cross paths again."

"You can count on it, my friend. You can count on it."

Chapter 25

Before bringing the hoodoo queen home, Evangeline called Strecker to find out about developments in the kidnapping. He said he'd been keeping tabs with the detectives handling the case, but since there hadn't been any more calls or incidents, they were at a standstill.

"Did they follow up on Babs' dating service?"

"The guy has an alibi. He waited from seven to eight-thirty at the restaurant where they were to meet, but she never showed. Witnesses verify his whereabouts later. And the dating service doesn't give out home addresses, but I guess Barbie could have." Accusingly he asked, "Did you ever get an updated alarm system?"

"They'll be out to install one tomorrow afternoon."

"Did you move the house key to a better hiding place?"

"Yes, sir, Sergeant, sir! I did as commanded."

"It's best not to leave one outside, period. It's an invitation for disaster. Heard too many horror stories. Thieves know most places to look."

"But what if I lose mine, or you need to see about Zelda? I've always hidden a key and I can't see changing habits because of some creep. I can't let fear rule my life."

"Then you better hide it good," Strecker said. "Especially so your neighbors don't know. They moved in after you did, didn't they?"

"The Bernowitzes?"

"Yeah, the ones behind you whose upstairs window conveniently has a view to your backyard."

"Yes, but I can't imagine they would have anything to do with this. They're nosy. Nothing else to do but live vicariously through me. Start gossip. You know the type."

"Still, you need to be careful. Everyone is suspect, and positively don't tell anyone about the key. Not even your aunt."

"Yeah, right. And I'll tell the earth not to turn. She knows what I'm doing before I do. Uh, I'm curious. Do you like old movies? Black-and-white ones, I mean?"

He named a few of the old-timers and those from the forties and said, "Is that what you mean?"

She grinned and gave a little giggle. "Yes sir, exactly what I mean."

After hanging up, she thought she might have something else in common with Strecker other than Zelda. And if everyone was suspect, that would include a number of people: Julian, Lance, Sada, about everyone she knew through the investigation firm. The Bernowitzes and other neighbors, Dahlia, Nick, Strecker, even Max. She wouldn't put anything past the Delacroixs. Especially Claudine. What an exasperating mess.

Through the process of elimination, she didn't believe Nicky was the culprit; why would he start wrongdoing so late in the game? Max she had just met, and he didn't know about her circumstances; Julian had been the most supportive; Lance was prim and full of himself, so she couldn't see him breaking a sweat; Sada had more money than she would ever need and had never been interested in the art scene; Dahlia was absolutely out; the Bernowitzes, maybe, but not likely; one of the Delacroixs, also a maybe, but not likely. It had to be someone she didn't know, but why? If she were remotely close to finding the art, then maybe she could understand. But since she did not have a clue, it didn't make sense.

★ ★ ★ ★ ★

Later in the day, Evangeline checked Olinda out of the hospital, filled her prescriptions at the pharmacy and they headed for home. She stopped Atlas in the driveway, pushed the close button to the gate and cringed at the worsening sound. "Got to remember to oil the hinges." After killing the engine, she opened the car door and said to Olinda, "I will not take you home, and that's final."

"Why you such a hard head? I never did anyting to you. I just wanna go home. Recuperatin'll be easier than in this smog- and traffic-filled hellhole. A body could get a lung disease."

"I will drive you home when the doctor says you can care for yourself, and not before."

"You think because you got one of them fancy college doctorates you know what's best for me?"

"I'm following Petrie's orders, so suck it up and live with it."

"Messing with me can get you in trouble, girl. Don'tcha know?"

"Give it a rest, Olinda. Get out of the car and into the house, now!"

"Well, since I'm an invalid, you going to open the car door, or what?"

Evangeline grinned to herself, got out and went around to the passenger side and helped Olinda to the back patio. When she opened the door, Zelda bounced out and almost knocked them down.

"Oh, my *loa*! What was that?"

"Olinda, meet Zelda."

Zelda immediately sat and waited to be greeted.

"Well, aren't you a fine-looking specimen? And so well behaved." And under her breath, "Nuting like your master." Looking at Evangeline, she said smugly, "Maybe I did good after all."

"Good? How? What did you do?"

"Never you mind."

Olinda always spoke gibberish. Evangeline would have to get used to it all over again and ignore most of it, because she believed the woman did it on purpose for amusement and to torment her. She hoped she could weather this storm, because Olinda managed to bring out the worst in her.

In the house Olinda said, "I need to call Mizress Horne and find out about the place. Mr. Beene won't like me being gone this long."

"Grandpop won't care."

"Harrumph! Tink what you want."

"Cut it out, Olinda. Grandpop is dead and you know it. This supernatural stuff won't cut it here."

Olinda faltered and fumbled for the back of a bar stool. "Is my room ready? I need to rest a spell."

Evangeline almost said, "I told you so," but it would only add fuel. And besides, she could use a little privacy and some Zelda time. It'd been a long day and she had heard, but never realized, how soothing dog therapy could be. And she needed it, because thinking about Aunt Olinda and her heebie-jeebies, Babs' death, Nicky's supposed change of heart, stolen art, Uncle Jacques' imminent death, and the Delacroix clan, was more stress than mind and body could handle. She'd had problems, but not so many dumped on her at once. And the thought of a perp trying to cause her harm was really scary. It was more than scary. It could be deadly.

After getting Olinda settled upstairs, she and Zelda had playtime outside, then they lay on the polar bear–style rug in the den and she caressed the dog's ears and gave her a massage—legs, hips, back. Zelda wallowed in the attention and licked and nuzzled Evangeline's neck. If only life were always this simple, with not a care or worry in the world.

Evangeline's stomach growled loudly and Zelda's ears pricked up. "That was me," she said, realizing she was starving, and feeling the urge to test her culinary skills. She'd have to check Olinda's food menu, but personally, she craved eggs, so an omelet it was. She'd eaten cold pizza for breakfast; why not an omelet and toast for dinner?

She turned on the country-and-western oldies station now playing a tearjerker about losing one's lover. Too late, she thought, Nicky didn't just let their love go, he shoved it right off the cliff. She assembled the omelet ingredients and equipment on the counter. From the refrigerator she took out the bottle of Chardonnay she'd opened a few days before, turned it up and sipped. *Might as well get soused, eat and go to bed. I sure can't go anywhere tonight.*

She grated cheese, chopped a bell pepper, and sniffed as tears came to her eyes—from the onion, she decided. This would be more fun if she had a friend to share the meal, or even if Olinda woke up. Zelda was company, but she couldn't talk. Although the poodle sat watching her, she probably wondered what Evangeline was doing in the kitchen, since all she'd seen her do was zap food in the microwave or bring home takeout.

"I can cook when I want to," she said to the dog.

Zelda placed her paws over her eyes.

"Good grief, dog, you freak me out sometimes." She mixed the egg ingredients, poured them into the pan and visually remembered how Nicky swished with his wrist movements. *Not bad. Who needs him?*

She leaned against the counter and took another sip of wine. The alcohol hit quickly, giving her a relaxing, pleasurable buzz. *Probably because of an empty stomach.*

Zelda had sprawled out near the back door, and Evangeline said, "Zelda, wait till you taste my omelet. Umm, umm, good." The dog woofed low as if chastising her. "Okay, I forgot, onions are poisonous to dogs, so I'll set aside a little without them."

After the eggs had almost set, she added the cheese, bell pepper and onion to one side and ran a spatula around to loosen the omelet. "Now comes the hard part." In deep concentration, she chewed on her bottom lip, and used the spatula and her fingers to gently and carefully lift one edge and fold it over.

"Well, the devil, I tore it. How does Nicky keep from doing that?" Just when things were going well, she messed up. Tough. Deal with it—so she slid the omelet onto the warm plate. It might not be as perfect as Mr. Perfect's, but it would taste as good. And who but she would ever know she couldn't even make a flawless omelet? "Now for yours, Miss Prissy," she said to Zelda, who was now sitting on her haunches, waiting.

"I take mine with salsa," Olinda said from the doorway.

Oh, dear Lord, Evangeline thought. She didn't want to prepare another one, so she'd have to share hers.

"By the way," Olinda said, "did you know you have a broken window upstairs?"

"No, which one?"

"The one in the bathroom facing the street. I tink somebody threw a rock, but I couldn't bend over to pick it up."

"God, what else is going to happen? Let's eat first, then I'll check it out."

When they finished dinner, Olinda and Zelda followed Evangeline upstairs to the bathroom but waited at the door. The window had been broken, and a rock the size of her fist lay on the rug with a piece of paper and a rubber band wrapped around it. Hands trembling, heart thudding, she picked up the rock and freed the paper.

From behind Olinda said, "What is it?"

"A note."

"I figured that. What do it say?"

Evangeline's voice trembled. " 'See how easily I can get to you.' "

Olinda blurted out, "Oh, Evie, I told you we gotta get out of here quick. Somebody's gonna get us."

Zelda let out a low whine.

Evangeline turned to Olinda and encircled the woman in her arms. And although she didn't totally believe it, and her stomach was flip-flopping, she said soothingly, "It's okay, sweetheart. We're going to be fine. Please calm down. It isn't good for you to be upset. We can't let a little broken window and a thrown rock unnerve us like this. Maybe you're right, though, maybe I should at least take you home." She pulled up staunchly. "But nobody is making me leave my house. Besides, the new alarm system will alert the central security people, and a patrol car will be here in minutes."

"But those systems aren't foolproof. They can be disconnected."

"True, but somebody would have to climb a fence to do it, and I've told you about the Bernowitzes, who see everything. The culprit did make one mistake. I'm thinking it's a man because it would take a pretty good arm and eye to hurl a rock over an iron fence into a small second-story window."

Partially satisfied, Olinda asked, "Well, if we have to stay, mind bringing me a butcher knife from the kitchen?"

Evangeline grinned and said if it would make her feel better, she sure would. "I'll call Sergeant Strecker in the morning about the note."

"I've been kidnapped, had a operation—which, by the way, is beginning to ache a bit—and if my first day in this house is an ind'cation of how the rest of it will go, don't think I can take it. Ain't been through anything like this since your Grandpappy found me."

Evangeline knew it was the truth and didn't quite believe her own rhetoric. She wished whoever was doing these things would show themselves before she came completely undone.

Chapter 26

Arlo came by early the next morning and picked up the rock and the note for forensic analysis but said it probably wouldn't lead to a perp. He would make a report, and told her it wouldn't hurt to set the alarm even when she was home. She said she would teach Olinda how, and assured him the new alarm system would be installed that afternoon. The next project was to have the window repaired.

Evangeline had another nagging worry but rationalized it away. Since Olinda arrived in Houston by ambulance, she couldn't have brought hoodoo paraphernalia with her. And since she couldn't drive until her stitches healed, she probably couldn't acquire any incantation paraphernalia, so maybe it was safe to leave her home alone for the next few days while she went to work. Olinda was resourceful, though, so who knew?

It would not matter anyway. It was all nonsense. So if it kept her occupied, Olinda wouldn't be butting into Evangeline's business. Zelda had taken up with her, so she must not sense any mystical or evil intentions.

In the balmy morning, Olinda sat in a lounge chair near the fig tree with a cup of hot green tea and nibbled on toast. She seemed to have recovered from the kidnapping and the rock incident, and Zelda lay in the grass beside the chair with eyes shut.

Olinda had arrived in Houston wearing a hospital gown, so Evangeline had purchased some casual wear for her. This morning she wore the comfortable pink seersucker zip-up housecoat.

Evangeline stepped onto the back patio and called, "Can I do anything else before I head to work? I've a lot of research to do for Lance, and interviews are set up for a new receptionist. I might be a little late this evening. A list of phone numbers where I can be reached is lying on the island, as well as those for emergencies. The nurse should be here shortly."

"You run along. Miss Zelda and I will be fine." Olinda patted her lap. "I'm packing your trusty butcher knife in case my kidnapper and the rock thrower comes a callin'. And like you said, with Zelda and those two nosy neighbors, I got plenty of company."

Zelda tilted her head and lazily opened one eye.

"Bernowitzes. Their name is Bernowitz. I left their number, too."

Satisfied Olinda was taken care of but wondering about her attitude change since last night, Evangeline headed to work. Thank God the office wasn't far, because sitting in traffic for an hour would rip apart her already frayed nerves.

Her cell phone chimed. She fumbled it from her purse and glanced at the caller ID. "Max, I've been thinking about you."

He asked where she was, and she told him on the way to work and thanks for asking, but she was fine. "Trying to juggle work and deal with Olinda. And our receptionist was mugged and"—she stifled a moan—"killed the other night. It was horrible."

"A mugging, you say? I'm so sorry. She was cute in a dumb-blond sort of way. Do they have any suspects?"

She was certain he didn't mean to sound callous. "Not that I know of, but I'm hoping they catch the creep. As a matter of fact, it happened the night we had dinner. Oh, God, while I was enjoying myself, Babs was lying on cold concrete." She hesitated. "Dead or dying."

"Don't chastise yourself. How were you to know?"

"Intuition should have given me a warning. I didn't have a clue."

"Do you usually have intuitions?"

"Sometimes."

"I wish I could help. Maybe put out feelers for a new receptionist?"

"Thanks, but an employment agency is sending some prospects for interviews today, and I'm not particularly looking forward to it. Julian will still have to okay her. Lance too."

"Not changing the subject, but have you thought about the plane trip I mentioned?"

She had totally forgotten, because in her mind she knew she couldn't go. "Max, I'm sorry, no. With everything that's been happening, I'm lucky to remember to eat. Can I take a rain check until things calm down? I really, really do want to visit the Loire Valley. It sounds like a wonderful vacation."

"Let me know when."

"Are you in town? Houston?"

"Wish I were, but alas, I'm in Taos looking at the work of an excellent upcoming artist." His voice rose with excitement. "The flow of her brush and blending of colors are clear, vibrant, simply lovely. I don't usually handle the modernist style, but I might make an exception with this one."

"I know you'll decide wisely."

"Well, I wanted to make sure you didn't forget me."

"I could never—holy cow." The car in front of her braked, she stomped down on her brakes and grabbed the wheel with both hands. Atlas fishtailed to a stop inches from the car's bumper. The phone sailed onto the floorboard on the passenger side.

"Jerk," she mumbled, then bent over as far as she could without unbuckling her seat belt and groped to retrieve the phone. Naturally it was out of reach. She said loudly so Max could hear, "I'm okay, can't reach phone. We'll talk later."

Julian had dropped the job of hiring another receptionist into Evangeline's lap. It was now eleven o'clock, and three women had passed through the door, none of whom were remotely qualified or knew anything about Rembrandt's sort of work. Babs was more than a receptionist and would be hard to replace; she was Girl Friday to Lance and Evangeline and usually handled problems with the building, ordering supplies and doing day-to-day routines. Lydia, Julian's secretary, handled his personal and business ventures and did the bookkeeping, so Lydia or Lance should be the ones doing the hiring or firing.

Each time Evangeline answered the phone, she thought about Babs and wondered if her own search had anything to do with the girl's untimely death or the strange happenings of late: Rossini's death, the phone calls, the fire, Olinda's kidnapping, the incident in the park, the broken window, and those weird feelings she had been getting, like someone was watching her and her hair standing up on the nape of her neck. Taken individually, the events seemed random, unrelated, but taken collectively, instinct told her there was a connection, if she could find the missing piece. As Grandpop used to say about coincidences, if it looks like a duck and walks like a duck, it usually is a duck. Time would tell if it quacked like a duck.

And then into the office five minutes early walked Francie Bascomb—late twenties, petite, heart-shaped face, dark bobbed hair, and big, round blue eyes set off with thick dark lashes, and one smart-ass attitude. A shot of adrenaline the office needed.

"I'm here for the job," she said.

Evangeline believed her, for the handshake was firm and her face was filled with confidence. Evangeline motioned her to the chair at Babs' desk while she perched on its corner and thumbed through the woman's resume, liking what she saw.

She looked up. "I see you were at your last job for less than a year. Mind telling me why you left?"

"Don't mind at all. The office manager and I didn't see eye-to-eye. He thought he could play touchy feely, and I knew my hotheaded hubby wanted to be the one to touchy feely me. To ward off a confrontation, I decided it best I find other employment."

"Good thinking, but you could have filed a complaint."

"If the job had been worth it I would have. It flat wasn't."

"I see. Will you mind taking a typing test?"

"My forte," she said and tapped the computer monitor awake.

Francie's fingers flew across the keyboard, and when Evangeline checked for spelling errors she found none. "You're hired, with the understanding your references check out." She paused, and teasingly said, "Please tell me you don't chew gum."

"I haven't had bubblegum plastered over my face and hair since junior high."

"Excellent. When can you start?"

"Right now if you need me. Uh, I heard what happened to your other receptionist." A look of compassion passed over her face. "I'm so sorry."

The comment caught Evangeline by surprise. "It was a terrible thing. I'm hoping they catch whoever did it. Justice for Babs and closure for her family."

"Yes, I would want that, too."

It seemed inappropriate to discuss Babs with a stranger, so Evangeline said she had a ton of work to do and she'd better get busy. And she surmised Francie couldn't do much damage between now and five o'clock, so she would check her references later.

She handed her a red folder. "Julian—Mr. Krystos—will have final say, but for now, here's a list of phone extensions and a copy of office procedures to peruse. If you have any questions, I'm in the office to the right. I'd rather you ask than guess."

"Gotcha. Uh, Miz Raines, shall I call employment and tell them I might be a go?"

"Absolutely." Francie being there would allow Evangeline to concentrate on work. She wished the police could catch Babs' killer, then she would know one way or another if her death and the stolen paintings were connected. And if someone wanted to harm her, why didn't they just kill her? None of it made any sense.

Chapter 27

The security company had come and gone by the time Evangeline arrived home. The operating instructions, along with the invoice, were lying on the desk. Evangeline did a double take at an amount that would take a huge bite out of her bank account, but it had to be done.

She flipped through the mail and saw nothing but advertisements, an electric bill and an envelope with no return address. Not in the mood to deal with any of it, she tossed the envelopes on the desk along with her keys and purse, and went in search of Olinda and Zelda—odd the latter hadn't greeted her.

Voices emanated from the front of the house, and because the nurse's car wasn't out front, Evangeline wondered if someone had dropped her off.

"Hey," she called, "I'm home."

Silence.

"Olinda? Zelda?"

"We're in the living room."

Evangeline stood in the doorway with her mouth open at the scene before her. Olinda sat in one of the stuffed high-back chairs placed around the fireplace; a girl who looked like a rock-star wannabe with dyed black-and-orange spiked hair and eyes rimmed in smudged black shadow, sat on the floor at Olinda's feet; Zelda lay contentedly next to the girl, who toyed with the dog's ears.

"Olinda, what's going on?"

"This is Penelope," she said, beaming and nodding toward the girl.

Penelope looked up and smiled.

"Who is Penelope, and where did she come from?"

"I found her sitting outside the fence, drinking a beer."

"But what is she doing in my house?"

"Don't be mad," Penelope said, rising from the floor like a Botticelli Venus rising from the sea. "Miss Olinda asked if I was hungry. I hadn't eaten since last night, so, of course, I said yes. Beer fills a hollow space, but has no fiber. I'll go if you want me to."

"Haven't I seen you out on the street corner? Are you from the homeless shelter?"

"I stay there sometimes, but mostly I'm on my own. And yeah, I've seen you drive by."

"I'm sorry, Penelope, but you can't stay here."

"Naturally. I didn't plan on it. But did appreciate the offer of a square meal." She gestured around. "You really have a nice pad. And I love your serigraphs and prints. And your art glass is lovely."

"Olinda, we need to talk."

"I'll make myself scarce," Penelope said. "Come on, Zelda, let's you and me go for a walk outside."

When Evangeline heard the back door open and close, she stood before Olinda with hands on her hips. "What are you thinking? You've given a complete stranger the run of my house and you know absolutely nothing about her. She could steal me blind. I swear, Olinda, I wonder if you have a screw loose somewhere."

"Now don't go getting lathered up. I'm a pretty good judge of people. She's a smart one, knows about art and the value of stuff. Not your regular runaway."

"I'll bet she does. And what do you know about runaways?"

Olinda's lips pressed tightly together. "A lot. Don't forget, slavers jerked me from my mamma's arms and practically held me in chains till I escaped into the swamp where Mr. Beene saved me. Oh, I know, all right. Haven't ever been so scared."

"I understand," Evangeline said softly, and then, because Olinda often played the "poor me" card, she straightened her spine. "Life can be a bitch, but living alone, I can't have strangers in my house. It's dangerous, and I'm leery enough without you bringing in riffraff off the street."

"You sound like you're better'n everybody else. Judgmental like."

Evangeline began to pace. "I am not judgmental. It's called being cautious. And don't turn it around on me. I understand how you work."

"Well, maybe you ought to lighten up a bit. Open those arms and accept that everybody's connected by that energy field pulsing through the universe you so keen on. Tink about it. Penelope was sitting on your curb for a reason. Zelda almost ran into your car for a reason. I got this stomach ulcer for a reason. We're all threaded together, and the sooner you realize it, the easier your life'll be."

"Those are coincidences."

"I don't believe in coincidences. What's the word they call it?"

"Synchronicity?"

"Yes, sync—What you said. Stop trying to control the uncontrollable. You get in a dither over the littlest."

"*You* put me in dithers. When you're around, I can't decide which end is up."

"That's 'cause you're believing I might be right, but feeling guilty because it goes against Mr. Beene's 'going to hell' talk."

"Well, that might be so, but it has nothing to do with you letting a stranger into my house. What if she's involved with the kidnapper? Did you consider that?"

"Harrumph. She isn't. Trust me. And I reckon if you want her to go, you'll have to tell her."

Evangeline shook her head and raised her hand, palm out in a stop position. "Oh, no I won't. You let her in and you will get her out, energy field or not."

In the backyard, Penelope said, "Miss Evangeline, I don't want to get Olinda in trouble. I'll go if you want."

"It's probably for the best," Evangeline said, having figured all along she would be the one to do the dirty work.

Penelope appeared crestfallen as she turned, shuffled toward the gate and waved her hand. "You'll have to let me out—push a button or a code."

"Oh, for goodness sake. You can stay for supper, then you have to go for sure."

Penelope turned back, and a smile cracked her anxious face; she clapped her hands and in a high-pitched, singsong voice said, "Zelda, I can stay. Isn't that wonderful?"

Zelda woofed, wagged her nub, and trotted over to Penelope.

"Supper only."

"Right."

A look of triumph crossed Penelope's face.

Evangeline decided *this isn't right. She is too well groomed, with freshly dyed hair and manicured and painted nails. I'm going to be sorry for this. I know it.*

Evangeline opened a bottle of red wine and poured herself a glass. "I'm going to turn into an alchy," she mumbled. While two steaks for her and Penelope marinated, she sliced up salad fixings. On the opposite side of the sink, Penelope grated cheese for baked potatoes, two for Olinda, who was on a soft-food diet.

"So," Evangeline said, "is Penelope your real name?"

"Maybe not, but it's kind of classy, don't you think?"

"Shall I call you Penny?"

"No! God, no. Penelope, please."

"How old are you?"

"Eighteen."

Evangeline raised an eyebrow.

"Okay, seventeen."

"Umm. How long have you been on the streets?"

"About a year."

"May I ask why?"

Penelope's eyes hooded. "If you don't mind, I'd rather not answer. It's too upsetting."

Olinda, who sat at the end of the butcher-block island, said, "You sure ask lots of questions. Let the girl be to enjoy herself afore you kick her out. I believe the word is compassion."

"I simply want to know who I'm harboring in my own home. That isn't too much to ask."

"I hate to mention this," Penelope said, "but you have a major draft in this house."

"What do you mean?"

"Well, remember when I was at the top of the stairs?" She sputtered. "Sightseeing, mind you. Well, a strong wind almost knocked me back down, and I had to grab the handrail to keep from falling."

Evangeline dropped the knife in the sink.

Olinda mumbled, "Umm-humm. That be the ghost we don't talk about."

Penelope's face lit up. "Not a ghost, too? Fantastic. Can you see it?"

"Sometimes our owner here sees a shadow and feels a cold place. But we're not supposed to talk about it in public."

"I do not believe in ghosts," Evangeline said.

"Yes you do, but you won't admit it. Penelope, you prob'ly

felt it cause you're new to the house and it wanted to check you out. Make sure you worthy to be here, sort of like Evie's new kinfolks feel about her."

"Oh, good grief, Olinda, stop it. She'll have nightmares, and that last comment was uncalled for."

"Diddywah. Ghosts. Can you beat it? Had a feeling this was an interesting place. That calls for a drink," Penelope eyed the Merlot, took a goblet from the dish rack and wiggled it. "Can I have one?"

"No way. I'm not about to contribute to the delinquency of a minor. There's a Pepsi in the fridge."

"I could sure use a beer, then."

"Not in my house."

"Have any cigs?"

"You're having dinner here, nothing else."

"Okay. Can't blame me for asking."

"Teenagers are all alike. You'll try anything to get what you want." Evangeline looked at Penelope from the corner of her eye and she was grinning. "I can't imagine your home life being so bad you'd rather be bumming on the streets."

"There's more of us out there than you would imagine," Penelope said. And then softly, "Usually a man's involved."

"Figures." Evangeline sliced down hard on a radish and wished she could be instrumental in helping kids at risk. Maybe she could when her own life became more settled, or as her mother used to say, when her ship came in—if it ever did.

The aura that surrounded Olinda when she left the woods after a witchcraft session crossed Evangeline's mind, and she wondered if Olinda could be right about the energy field concept.

If nothing else, her life had certainly taken a strange turn. What happened to her vine-covered cottage and picket fence with kids, dog, cat and husband? Her interim one-person sanctuary now included a talking poodle, a hoodoo queen and a pointy-haired homeless Goth. What else was God going to send her?

The hour was late when they finished the supper dishes, and Evangeline didn't have the heart to turn Penelope out. She wouldn't send a dog to the pitch-dark streets at ten o'clock at night. And quite frankly, she found Penelope to be one of the most intelligent young people she'd ever met. She was charming and enjoyable to be around, *if* one could get past the bizarre getup. It proved the old adage that you can't judge a book by its cover.

With Penelope following, Evangeline headed up the stairs. Near the top the girl called, "Hey ghost, I'm coming up, and I don't need another blast from the past."

Evangeline almost giggled out loud. The girl was uninhibited and really fun to be around. At the landing they entered the bedroom situated next to Olinda's. Olinda had retired after supper. Evangeline handed Penelope a pair of pajamas and insisted she take a shower. No telling where her body had been.

After peeking in on Olinda, she returned downstairs and locked up for the night. As she was gathering her purse, keys and several valuable items—simply as a precaution, she told herself—she noticed the mail lying on the desk. "Guess I better take a look." She sat in the secretary chair she had found at a used office supply, and when she came to the envelope, she slit it open with her grandmother's mother-of-pearl letter opener. It contained a single sheet of paper written in childlike block printing.

Dear Ms. Raines,

Regarding several paintings stolen from the Delacroix family, I have inside info on their whereabouts, but must be cautious before divulging said info. Be warned, you aren't the only one searching, and I fear for my life and yours. If my identity is discovered, the paintings will go underground and be lost to you forever. Wait for further contact.

Concerned.

Her fingers trembling, she dropped the note on the desktop and clutched her chest, trying to catch her breath. "Oh, the devil." She reached for the phone, needing to share this with someone. Her hand paused in midair. The desk clock read eleven, too late to call Julian, and she wouldn't give Nicky the satisfaction. Dahlia was probably in the throes of a love fest at this very moment, and Arlo could be anywhere.

What could this mean? Was it a hoax? Did someone actually know the whereabouts of her grandmother's paintings? Was there really a killer out there and, if so, what was to stop him or her from doing a number on Olinda and herself? Should she contact the police? What to do? She wouldn't sleep a wink.

At this moment, she wished sheltering arms were holding her, making her feel childlike safe. She needed Nicky, but their marriage was over and done with. And with no loving male figure in her life other than her short-lived time with Grandpop Beene, she'd never felt really safe. She felt more like she was always in an adrenaline high waiting for the shoe to drop. And she must learn to deal with never reveling in the security of a father's loving embrace. Thousands, millions of children never had a caring male figure and turned out fine. Maybe she was too possessive of Nicky, used him as a surrogate father to fill that empty space, and depended on his undying love. If so, she had grown in the last year and realized she must not expect a replacement for what she never had.

Zelda laid her head on Evangeline's knee and looked at her soulfully. She massaged the dog's ears. "It's okay, girl, it's either good news or really, really bad news. It's the quack I've been waiting for, and time will tell if it's a real live duck or a rubber one."

Chapter 28

In answer to Evangeline's phone call the next morning, Arlo arrived at the house to investigate the note. He stooped and read it from where it lay on the desktop. Then he gingerly picked up the sheet of paper by its tip and inserted it and the envelope into a clear plastic evidence bag. "Guess you touched it."

Evangeline shrugged. "Before I read it, I had no reason to do otherwise. Can it be genuine, or another prank?"

"D.C. is a far piece for a prankster," he said, referring to the postmark. "I'll take it to the HPD lab. Maybe forensics can pull up a latent print. Doubtful, though."

"So, basically, all I can do is wait for another contact."

"That would be my guess." He frowned. "And you might have to start paying rent at forensics."

"What—oh, because of the other note?"

"Yeah."

"Not funny."

Penelope padded into the kitchen in Evangeline's pajamas and pink-striped socks. When she saw the uniform, she hesitated, and then plopped on the corner bar stool. With a sour expression on her face, she said, "Why'd you call the pigs? I haven't done anything."

"He isn't here about you, Penelope. It's another matter entirely."

Arlo eyed the girl. "A friend of yours?"

"Actually, Penelope is Aunt Olinda's friend. I let her stay the night."

"You need to be careful, Evangeline."

"That's what I keep telling everyone."

"Excuse me, I'm sitting right here," Penelope said.

"Be cool, kid." Arlo pointed two fingers at his eyes, then at hers. "I've got my sights on you. And you need to be more respectful of authority."

"All you pigs are alike, throwing your weight around."

Evangeline placed her hands on her hips. "Penelope, Sergeant Strecker is a guest in my home. Mind your manners."

Arlo shook his head in disgust and, to Evangeline, said. "I have to go, but will let you know the results on the note."

Outside, Evangeline touched his arm. "She's leaving after breakfast. I feel sorry for her."

"I hate to sound so cynical, but street kids usually have two things on their minds. Who they can screw over and where their next meal is coming from. Watch your back."

"Definitely." She gave him a sisterly peck on the cheek. "I, we, owe you big-time."

He blushed. "Please be careful."

Inside, Penelope said to Evangeline, "What's with the HPD, or is it personal?"

"Not what you're insinuating. I've been getting threats, and other incidents have happened. The sergeant is concerned. And he was instrumental in my getting Zelda. It's grown into a comfortable friendship."

"Yeah. It's more than friendship to him. I saw how he looked at you."

"Ridiculous. He's my friend."

Penelope snickered. "Not like any friend I ever knew."

"I don't have to explain myself to you, Penelope. Now, please get dressed. I'll drop you off at the shelter on my way to work."

"I thought maybe I could stay a little longer."

"Not gonna happen. Olinda is enough of a headache without adding another."

"I meant to say I *thought* I wanted to stay longer until I heard about threats. That's one aggravation I don't need."

Because she was compassionate by nature, a pang of conscience hit Evangeline for being so hateful and brusque. And she sensed that Penelope's words were a cover-up at being turned out. Evangeline wished she could think of a constructive avenue to help the many runaways, but she felt like Sisyphus, who continually pushed a boulder up a hill only to watch it tumble down again.

Chapter 29

Abner Jacobson hoped he hadn't made a mistake, sending the note to Evangeline, but he thought he had been extremely cautious by driving into Washington so it would have a D.C. postmark and not one from his hometown. He had learned about her shortly after her grandmother Danielle Delacroix-Ravel found her. He knew about Danielle from when she listed her missing treasures with international registries.

He had always intended to make himself known to the family, but then Danielle died and he needed money, so he sold one or two of the canvases. Now, before it was too late, he must make amends. He must be discreet about revealing his identity, because he suspected another factor was looking for the artwork. He couldn't exactly put his finger on it or why he thought it, but he had the strangest feeling he was being watched or followed.

In his apartment, he sat at the small desk positioned before the window fronting the thoroughfare and gazed into space. He would never survive prison, or even a long trial, so he must be careful how he handled the situation. Right now, Rudy and his attorney were his only friends, but he could not trust even them. He wished it were different, but there it was.

It was actually in his best interest to move away, but he could not abide leaving his hometown of familiar faces and places. Nowhere in the world did he feel more at ease, and strangely, at this time in his life, he needed roots more than adventure.

Perhaps he had waited too long to retire, maybe he should have done it years before when his health was still good. Maybe he should have married, but a wife would have complicated his goal. In retrospect, marriage would have made it impossible.

A sharp pain stabbed at him and he clutched his chest with one hand and with the other removed the tortoiseshell pill box from his shirt pocket, flipped the cap, and fumbled out a small white tablet. He inserted it under his tongue and prayed, *God, let it work yet again. I have much more to do.*

As quickly as it hit, the pain subsided, and he tried to relax. An idle mind might possibly be the cause of his feeling the weight of the years and imagining that someone monitored his movements. While working at the museum, he was so immersed in his job and long-term plan, he paid little attention to outside events. He had heard about men retiring, and then dropping dead from boredom. With no reason to get up in the morning, what good was he to himself or anyone? Maybe he should pursue Teresa, the lady on the next floor who flirted with him.

The custodial work at the museum had been mildly strenuous, consisting of keeping the paintings in good repair. He cleaned, dusted, reframed and rewired, glued on new backs, and changed their locations often. If a painting remained in one place too long, and light rays touched the pigments at the same angle, they could cause fading.

The physical aspect of stretching and bending and exercise in general had kept his weight down. Now the disgusting results of inactivity were a sagging paunch and shortness of breath. He stretched the waistband of his slacks. It was perplexing, having to resort to elastic to be comfortable.

And he abhorred the thought of taking his annual fishing trip. The pluses were breathing clean air and sleeping under a sky studded with stars that blinked like fireflies and seemed close enough to pluck. The Jeep ride was the killer, bouncing roughly over ruts while trying to control the steering wheel. His strength wasn't what it used to be.

He picked up the pen lying ready and let his hand hover over the lined legal tablet. It was now or never, he decided, and so he began. After a page or two, he realized it would take forever to write it all out, so he ripped up what he had penned, went to the kitchen sink, ignited the torn sheets, and watched as they curled into ashes.

He set up his computer on the table by his lounge chair, inserted a disk, adjusted the chair to reclining and spoke into the microphone. Later, after several stops and starts, he removed the CD, rose, stretched and went to his desk. With a felt-tipped pen, he labeled the disk, placed it into a clear case and inserted it, along with the note and the key, into the padded envelope. He addressed and sealed it with several drops of sealing wax, and murmured, "May God forgive me for the trouble I've caused."

After locking his apartment, he walked the several blocks to his bank, glancing back occasionally for someone suspicious. At the bank, he accessed his safe-deposit box and placed the envelope inside on top of his last will and testament. He had given his attorney, Jonas Messner, access to the box and his bank records should he die.

"There," he said. "It's done."

CHAPTER 30

Francie was already at the receptionist desk when Evangeline arrived at work, and Lance was in his office with the phone pressed to his ear.

"G'morning, Ms. Raines," Francie said perkily. "Can I get you some coffee? Fresh made from the beans."

"Thank you, but I'm gurgling in it already and will lay claim to the ladies' room any minute now. And for heaven's sake, call me Evangeline. We don't stand on ceremony around here."

Francie ducked her head. "I hoped you'd say that."

"Unless," said Evangeline, stressing the word, "a client comes in. Then Julian is a stickler for propriety."

"I can do propriety. When do I meet this elusive Mr. Julian?"

"At his convenience, I suppose."

As she passed Lance's office, he was hanging up the phone. She stopped and leaned against the doorjamb. He acknowledged her with a nod, and she said, "I've received the strangest note."

He motioned her to the chair opposite the desk. After she quoted the contents, Lance said, "I haven't had a chance to check out the Abner Jacobson who's copying old masters—and not particularly well, I must say. But I can work on it this afternoon. The name sounds fairly common, which might prove to be a problem in finding the right man."

"Any help is appreciated."

"*De nada.* Uh, Evangeline, Francie seems to be reliable, and Julian left the final say up to me. Anything I should know about references?"

"The devil, I forgot to check them. I'll do it today."

In her office, she automatically glanced under the desk kneehole for Zelda. She missed having her at work. *The darned dog grows on you.*

After checking out Francie's suitable references, and then trying to concentrate on a file about a missing jade dragon carved in the late Chou Dynasty and worth seven figures, Evangeline placed the folder in the top desk drawer and wandered to the reception area.

"Have you met Kreshon, our daytime security?" she asked Francie.

"I waved to him and he waved back, but not a formal intro."

"Come with me. We'll remedy that right now."

Kreshon was at his station by the front door and rose when he saw them.

After introductions, Francie said she better get back to work, and Evangeline went across the hall to the art gallery.

Marion, one of the sales women, was spraying the glass countertop and wiping it clean. Lydia, Julian's private secretary/bookkeeper, was straightening an askew surrealist painting.

Nearing fifty, Lydia had finally ditched her glasses and gotten contacts. And she seemed to be coming out of her shell by wearing a little more makeup and less severely tailored outfits. Open-toed wedges instead of clunky-heeled pumps softened her austere look. Nice combinations, Evangeline thought.

"Is he here?" she asked as Lydia tapped the right side of the frame into place, stepped back, and scrutinized the painting.

Without looking at her, Lydia said, "He left. I don't know where. What do you want?"

"I was wondering if he heard any news about Mr. Rossini."

"I wouldn't know." She paused and turned. "And personally, Evangeline, I don't give a rip."

Taken aback, Evangeline said, "Excuse me?" Lydia's attitude was out-of-character with her prim and proper persona, and Evangeline wondered what was going on. At Lydia's frosty silence, Evangeline forced a calm voice. "Need help with that?"

Lydia ran her fingers through her hair. "This frigging place is driving me crazy. Julian acts like it runs by itself. Quarterlies are due. A shipment from Europe came in this morning. Stanley quit yesterday, saying life was too short to spend it unloading boxes, so I have no muscle to help me. And I will not—I repeat, will *not*—do heavy lifting along with using my fricking brain all day to keep up with the machinations around here."

She spun around, stomped off into her office and slammed the door, leaving Evangeline with her mouth agape. "Wow!" she said to Marion, whose eyes were wide. "What in the world happened?"

"You don't know, do you?"

"What?" Evangeline's stomach made a nosedive. "Is she sick?"

"Sick in love."

With an exaggerated swipe to her brow, she said, "Phew, that's a relief. Anyone I know?"

"Probably, but I'd rather not say."

Respecting Marion's no-gossip policy, Evangeline said, "It'll bother me till I figure it out."

"Shouldn't be too hard."

And for the first time, Evangeline realized she wasn't privy to the personal lives of the people she worked with. She had tried to maintain professional relationships, but maybe she'd gone overboard. She would try to be more interested, beginning with Francie.

Chapter 31

At home, Evangeline leaned against the kitchen sink, thinking. Well, of course, Lydia must be in love with Julian. If so, the poor woman had to realize hers was a hopeless situation. Julian would probably never divorce Sada, and would probably always have a roving eye. Not Evangeline's problem, though. Lydia would have to learn it for herself. The resulting crash would be heartbreaking. To lose the love of one's life was devastating. She was a walking-talking commercial to the fact.

That reminded her to call Nicky. After the way she had acted the other day, she hated for him to think she needed him, but maybe he would know why the Bronco had started clattering and coughing, or at least go with her to an auto shop so she wouldn't get ripped off.

She picked up her cell and pushed in Nicky's number. Smoke, the cat that had taken them into its circle of friends, purred and swished around and through her legs. She should take it to the vet, but so far it wouldn't allow her to pick it up. It sat royally on the windowsill or paraded through the house wherever it wished to go.

At first, she hesitated to let the cat inside because of Zelda, but the poodle seemed comfortable with the feline.

Nicky answered on the third ring. "Nicholas here."

"It's me. I might have a problem with the Bronco and wonder . . ." She paused. "Will you go with me to the auto repair shop?"

"Of course. Come by here later today and I'll test-drive it.

Maybe it's a minor glitch like bad gas."

She got sick to her stomach thinking about going to Fallana B's, because she might run into the hussy, but Nicky was doing her a favor. "I'll be there about six."

Nicky realized Evangeline wouldn't call him unless absolutely necessary. He also realized he missed her more than he wanted to admit. After seeing her at Fallana B's, he thought about her constantly, of holding her in his arms, burying his face between her breasts and hearing her say she forgave him for what he had done to her, to both of them.

It might be too late, but he would keep trying. He wouldn't push her, and hoped she would eventually forgive him. He was a stupid, stupid, selfish fool.

Evangeline backed out of the driveway and noticed Penelope sitting on the curb at the corner. She pulled up, rolled down the window and said, "Okay, get in. We'll get a bite to eat after Nicky checks out Atlas."

"Who's Atlas?" Penelope asked, settling in the front seat as though she'd expected the ride.

Evangeline turned the corner and headed to Fallana B's. "You're sitting in him, and buckle up. When you're with me, obey the rules."

"Yeah, yeah, being an ex-schoolteacher and all."

"Penelope, what happened to make you so pessimistic?"

"You don't really want to know or, for that matter, really care. You're playing the do-gooder role. Someone who never had to fight for survival but smugly thinks she knows it all. Right?"

"I'll ignore that remark, because you've no idea what you're talking about. Someday I'll tell you about my childhood, but right now your circumstances are more important. Be aware you're not the only one who's had it tough."

"You ever been—raped—more than once?"

Evangeline swallowed hard, realizing what she had suspected was true. And she also thought how lucky she had been all those years when she practically raised herself. In retrospect, her mother never brought home her male friends. Still, Evangeline had often been in harm's way and due to her own initiative, had survived with no major damage. She said to Penelope, "No, I haven't."

"Okay, then, you won't understand my circumstances."

"Did you report it?"

"Sure, I told my counselor at school, and my mom, but since my stepdad denied it, they thought I wanted to cause trouble. So after a couple months, I split."

"I'm so sorry. Not being believed, especially by a parent who's supposed to protect you, must be devastating."

"It's okay. I'm fine, learned to defend myself so nobody messes with me now. One thing about the shelter, they teach the girls self-defense. And besides, if I can hide out for a couple more months I'll be eighteen, then I'm legally on my own."

"I wish I could help you, but—"

"Yeah, I heard somebody wants to kill you."

"God, did Olinda tell you that? She is such a blabbermouth."

"Olinda's okay. Weird, but I like her. Voodoo isn't so mysterious."

"Don't get caught up in hocus-pocus. It will cause you trouble."

"If I've got it right, one spirit can inhabit sixteen live bodies. Eight females and eight males. When one body dies, the spirit returns to the sea to wait for a body it thinks worthy. Guess that's where they get the zombies, because the spirits of the dead are always around."

"It's mumbo jumbo, and zombies are not real," Evangeline insisted.

"Maybe. The *loa,* the voodoo spirit, is what I can't wrap my brain around."

"Olinda better not ever do conjuring in my house."

"Yeah, I can see how closed-minded you are." Silence. "Not changing the subject, but where're we going?"

"Like I said, to get Atlas checked out," Evangeline said. "He cuts out sometimes and is beginning to clatter."

Evangeline pulled into Fallana B's parking lot and wheeled into a space in front.

"Hey, I've been here before," Penelope said. "They wouldn't serve me a drink even with my fake ID."

"Well, thank goodness for small wonders."

"I've heard about your Nicky. Does he play the sax here?"

"I need to speak to Olinda about her big mouth. And yes, that's the Nicky."

Penelope unbuckled her seat belt and opened the car door.

"No. We're not going in. He'll come out."

"Shoot."

She punched in Nicky's number, and he said he was on his way.

When he walked out, Penelope said, "Diddywah. He's a hunk. How'd you lose him?"

When Nicky was in charisma mode he could charm the devil, so entertainment suited him. Women wanted to take him home, and even a few men had tried. He never met a rock he couldn't melt with a smile.

"Shut up, and mind your manners."

"Yes, Mamma."

Evangeline released the hood and she and Penelope exited the car. "Thanks for the favor," she said to Nicky and then introduced Penelope.

"Hey, dude," Penelope said, high-fiving.

He did not high-five her back. "Seems Penelope and I have met. Uh, had a short disagreement about a fake ID."

"Can't blame a girl for trying."

Nicky raised an eyebrow. "How do you two know each other?"

Evangeline gave the particulars and Nicky said, "Now, let's have a look at Atlas."

After a few minutes of tinkering, he stood up straight and dropped the hood. "Probably bad gas. Wait till the tank is almost empty to fill up again. If new gas doesn't solve the problem, I'll look deeper."

"I'm hoping it's that simple. Can't afford a major overhaul."

"This baby is good for another hundred thousand."

Uh-huh. She felt smug, because buying Atlas was her idea. "We better get going. Olinda is home alone."

"Do you two want to come into the club for a bite? We'll package up a meal for her."

Penelope nudged Evangeline's shoulder as if to say why not, but not wanting to come face-to-face with Fallana, Evangeline said, "We're headed to the mall, but I appreciate the offer."

"The mall? You said—"

Evangeline gave Penelope a little shove. "Get in the car, Penny."

Chapter 32

"Mr. Jacobson?" the voice on the other end of the phone asked.

"Yes," Abner said. "May I help you?"

"You don't know me, but I'll get right to it. Through a mutual acquaintance, I've learned you might have an objet d'art for purchase."

Abner hesitated. "What kind of object? What are you talking about? Who would tell you such a thing?"

"Maybe we shouldn't discuss it over the phone."

"We have nothing to discuss, because I have nothing to sell. Don't call me again."

"I'm certain my offer will be to your satisfaction. Please consider it, and if you change your mind about meeting, my phone number is in your calls box."

There was no way Abner would agree to meet a complete stranger to negotiate any kind of deal. And who told this person about him? Had he slipped up somewhere? Been too enthusiastic and cocky and caused someone to investigate him? Had someone traced the note he wrote to Evangeline back to him? Or was this a real opportunity to sell another painting? He would ponder it, and if he decided to pursue the matter, he did have the phone number. The caller gave no name, which was suspicious, but Abner was suspicious by nature.

★ ★ ★ ★ ★

The cobweb in Abner's mind began to clear, but along with it came a blinding headache with every muscle in his body feeling like it had been pounded with a sledgehammer. He lay on his back on a hard surface, with arms extended behind his head. He was extremely uncomfortable, so he tried to move, but his arms felt weighted down, and wouldn't budge.

Finally able to focus with one eye shut and the other squinting, he managed to turn his head enough to see that his wrists were handcuffed to a water pipe. Panic shot through him, and he jerked at the bracelets, bucked and squirmed, but merely succeeded in making clanking noises and hurting himself.

I knew I should've joined a gym. What will I do? I can't get loose this way, and my back and arms are killing me.

With great effort he wiggled to a sitting position and surveyed his surroundings. It looked like a cellar with light from a basement window the only illumination. Intuition told him he was about to die.

But what happened? He remembered being groggy after sipping a cup of tea offered him by the Buyer, but after that, nothing. And then it hit him. He must have been drugged, and with every bone in his body hurting, he was either dragged or thrown down the basement stairs. But why? *Come on, Abner, think. Why are you here?*

If it was about the Botticelli, he was in major trouble.

From the shadows he saw movement and the Buyer said, "Ah, Abner, I see you're awake. Sorry I had to drug you, but you were easier to handle that way."

With his faculties returning, Abner peered intently at the figure. In a voice squeaky to his own ears, he said, "Why are you doing this?"

"Isn't it obvious? The art you've kept hidden for years."

"I don't know what you're talking about."

The Buyer materialized from the gloom and loomed over him with arms crossed. "Abner, let's not play games. You have them. I want them. And I will get them. It's as simple as that."

"No way in hell."

"I don't want to kill you, but trust me, I will if you don't co-operate."

Abner had no doubt about that. "Do what you want. I'm practically dead anyway."

"You're a sensible man. What good is the cache to you? All you can do is look at it occasionally, and I can do so much more. You're an old man, and I'm wondering what will become of those priceless artifacts if you die. Why not enjoy the amenities the money can bring? Tell me where they are and I'll make it worth your while. More money than you can spend in the time you have left. Then you won't have to travel the country trying to make a sale and looking over your shoulder."

This person must think Abner an absolute idiot to believe he would have his freedom if he revealed the paintings' location.

"I'd rather they rot in hell than tell you."

"Abner, Abner, you won't let that happen."

"Wait and see. And besides, they aren't mine to give."

"But you kept them these many years. So what makes me any different than you? Oh, maybe because I'm willing to pay—or to kill."

Abner wondered how he could have been so stupid as to come to this house, based on a call to purchase a Botticelli, with no questions asked. He'd always been careful, gauging each step by what he might or might not reveal, yearning to, but never making, a close friend, forever on the fringes. Now, the one time he let his guard down might cost him his life. He should have told someone where he was going.

If he died here, the site of the paintings would also die unless Evangeline deciphered the clue. She was smart. He had faith she would figure it out.

Prepared for the worst, Abner yelped and gritted his teeth at the sudden kick to his thigh.

"A small sample. Eventually you'll tell me what I want to know."

"Never. All your torture won't make me give in."

"Surely, you jest. For now, though, I'll leave you to your thoughts. When I return, I trust you'll see it my way. Oh, and I must inform you, it's useless to scream. As you know from driving here, we're quite isolated."

The Buyer disappeared up the stairs and shut the door. Abner was alone, cold and hungry. Why didn't he take Rudy up on the dinner offer? He knew why. He was greedy, thought he could make a swinging deal without a middleman. Stupid, stupid decision. Maybe the last one he'd ever make.

Chapter 33

"Max, I've been wondering what happened to you," Evangeline said into the phone.

"I had to leave the country for a few days on business, a death in the family, etcetera."

"I'm so sorry for your loss. Were you and the deceased close?"

"A distant cousin living in Europe. I stayed a few days—wished you were there. We could've taken in a few sights, gone on to Paris, your château."

"Drat! I always miss out."

"I'll be in Houston this evening and I'd really like to see you. Catch up on what's been happening there."

"Sounds good to me. I seem to have inherited a few houseguests since we spoke, but I'll tell you about them later. Where, when? Want to come to the house and meet everyone?"

"This is another one of those business-before-pleasure trips. Can we meet for dinner again? I promise a real date soon."

After a sumptuous dinner of buttered lobster and a shared bottle of fine wine with Max, Evangeline felt a little amorous, especially when he took her hand and caressed it with his thumb. She'd never been promiscuous, but was a healthy hormonal female who missed making love. And if asked, she would consider accompanying Max to his hotel room. Instead, he surprised her with a different invitation.

"I'm meeting a client later tonight. Think you could stand

more art talk? It's in the area, so you won't be too late getting home."

It's your loss, fella. "I'll call Olinda. Tell her to let the animals out and to lock up."

Olinda said Penelope was snuggled up on the sofa watching television about dog training. Zelda was asleep under the coffee table, and Smoke was somewhere around, so not to worry about her, she had plenty of company.

Evangeline hated the idea of Olinda going home. It'd been nice having her there. Of course, she couldn't let her know that, for it would give her a wedge to torment her with. Olinda had been extra cooperative, but knowing her, this could be the lull before the storm.

They were leaving the client's home when Evangeline's phone chimed. Olinda said breathlessly, "We got a problem going on outside. Somebody's messing with the window. Zelda's going crazy and Penelope got out de butcher knife. Maybe it be the kidnapper. What'll I do?"

"Call nine-one-one. I'm on my way."

"A problem at home?" Max grinned, and she knew it was because there was always a problem at home.

"I'm the only sane one in my family. And stop grinning. Somebody's trying to break in and Olinda's in a panic, thinking it's the kidnapper."

"I'll drive and we'll pick up your car later."

Although Max broke many traffic rules, the drive still took longer than expected. Surprisingly, when they arrived, no police cars were in sight. Evangeline pushed the remote gate opener she kept in her purse, threw open her door and bolted from the auto. Olinda and Penelope were sitting on the back steps looking sheepish. Zelda and Smoke lay on the indoor-outdoor carpet.

Evangeline rushed up to the pair. "Okay, what happened?"

Penelope put her hand up, palm out, as if to say *don't ask me.*

Olinda said, "What took you so long? We coulda been killed dead."

"But you weren't. Where are the responders?"

"Uh, we kinda jumped the gun on dat one. A justaful mistake."

"What do you mean justifiable?"

"Well, you see, when we looked at the window that was being messed with, we saw two eyes peering in at us and we both started screaming and I called you and nine-one-one. After checking again, we realized it was Smoke scratching to get in."

Penelope interjected, "We'd put the little stinker outside and forgot about him. To get our attention, the cat batted and scratched at the window."

"We guess Zelda went haywire because she wanted Smoke inside or because we were freaking out," Olinda said.

Evangeline glared at Smoke, who lay on his side licking his paw, and his green eyes appeared to smile at her deviously.

Can't be. I'm going crazy. "What about the police and the nine-one-one call?"

"They were here immediately, and after we told them about the cat, they walked around the house to make sure wasn't nobody lurking. They filed a report but got another call and hightailed it out of here."

Evangeline shook her head. "Our neighbors will think we're criminals, with the police coming and going." She glanced up at the Bernowitzes' window, but it was dark. Evidently they'd seen all they needed to.

"Okay, you two. I'm sure you've heard of the 'The Boy Who Cried Wolf.' "

"I never heard of no such person."

Penelope snickered.

"Watch it, girl. You know what I can do."

Evangeline said, "Forget it. It won't do any good to explain."

Batting her eyelashes and trying to appear seductive, Penelope craned her neck and asked, "Who have we here?"

Evangeline turned to Max standing slightly behind her. "Penelope, this is my friend Maximilian Forbes."

Penelope said, "Good gawd, how do you do it? He's one big hunk. You need to give me some lessons."

Zelda was acting strange, sort of cowed, her lips in a slight snarl, teeth showing.

"It's okay, Zelda. I'm home now. You'll be fine."

The dog slunk off the porch and around the house.

"She must hear a noise," Evangeline said. "She's one strange animal sometimes. But maybe we should go see."

Max said, "I'll do it. You wait here, and then I'll take you to get your car. I do believe the evening is over."

A minute later, Zelda appeared around the opposite corner of the house, approached with rear tucked, sat at Evangeline's feet and gazed up at her.

"What was that about?" she said to the dog.

Zelda whined, rose and deposited herself next to Olinda.

The next day, a pink phone message was on Evangeline's spindle to call Mr. Jonas Messner of Messner & Messner, Attorneys at Law, in Washington, D.C. Evangeline wondered what it was about. Surely not Uncle Jacques. She dialed the number and was immediately connected to Messner, Sr.

"Miss Raines, thanks for responding so quickly. I was afraid you might not call."

"What can I do for you, Mr. Messner? Do I know you?"

"Not me personally, but a client of mine who recently passed away has included you in his last will and testament."

"Who in the world do I know there?" And then she remembered the anonymous envelope. Could this be connected?

"The client lives outside the Washington, D.C. area and wished to remain anonymous until you received the package that would answer your questions. My question is, where shall I send a special delivery, signature-required, parcel? Your home, the office, or will you come here?"

"You may send it to my home. Someone will be there to sign." For a while, she thought. She must remember to tell Olinda to expect it.

"Thank you. I hope you'll find the contents of the package to your satisfaction. It should arrive within the week."

"Uh, Mr. Messner, can you tell me anything else? Who it's from, what it's about?"

"Sorry, those were my instructions."

She gave him the address, which, if he'd done his homework, he already knew. She disconnected and said, "What now?"

Chapter 34

She had been expecting it, but when the news came about Great Uncle Jacques' passing, Evangeline's tears flowed easily. He was her one ally in the Delacroix family and a kind and gentle soul. She imagined the vultures, as he had called them, were already circling, ready to swoop in for control, and wondering how much of the fortune they would inherit. The inevitable fight would probably tear the family apart, and she'd be watching to see how it played out—which one became the victor. The eldest usually gained control, but Uncle Jacques didn't play by the rules when it came to family. He would do what he thought best by passing on the role as head of household to the one who deserved it.

She was informed of Jacques' death after the funeral arrangements had already been made, and then only because Uncle had insisted she be told. The parking lot overflowed with gleaming chromed, newly washed and waxed automobiles. If it cost over fifty thousand, it was accounted for. She had run her Bronco through the cheapie carwash, but it stood out like an elephant in an antique store, so she was glad she had to park on the street, allowing for a quick getaway.

As she entered the funeral home for the viewing, Randall, the eldest grandchild, eyes bloodshot, was situated at the door, greeting mourners.

"Hello, Evangeline," he said, a reproachful smile playing at his mouth. "What are you doing here?"

Evangeline brushed past him without commenting. Every one of them abhorred her and she understood some of their animosity, but not to such a ridiculous degree. Could they really believe she was a gold digger when she had never asked one of them for a nickel?

As she perused the crowd of furs and diamonds, she did see a friendly face, Uncle's lawyer, Kirk Kestner. He glanced up, spied her, waved, and wended his large frame to her.

"Dear Evangeline, so good to see you," he said, taking both her hands in his and squeezing them warmly. And then he said quickly, "Wish it weren't under such sad circumstances."

"I know. It's the end of an era, isn't it?"

"Jacques was a fine man. Ninety-six years young and my friend for fifty of those years." As though just remembering, he said, "As Jacques instructed, I made a copy of Danielle's death certificate for you. Was I supposed to mail it?"

Her hand went to her mouth in embarrassment. "Oh, no, please forgive me. With everything that's been happening, it slipped my mind."

He patted her shoulder. "There, there, no harm done. You can get it at the reading of the will. You are coming?"

"I have no reason," she said, shaking her head.

"But most of the relatives will attend. And you *are* blood kin."

"Even if Great-Uncle Jacques remembered me, when the bickering about it ends, there won't be anything remaining. Or I'll return whatever it is to get some peace."

Kestner circled her shoulders with his arm and held her close to his side, a nice comfortable feeling, and one she hadn't felt for some time.

"My dear, it was Jacques' last wish that you attend. I insist." He whispered in her ear. "Don't let the hounds get you down. They aren't worth it. Hang in there a little while longer, a new wind is blowing."

She sighed, wanting as few encounters with the Delacroix clan as possible because she always came away feeling dirty and unworthy, although in reality, many of them were the unworthy ones. And she'd probably get her wish sooner than later. "If you think I must. When?"

He gave her the details.

Claudine, hair perfectly coiffed, makeup applied with air-brush perfection and wearing wrinkle-free attire, walked over and planted herself before Evangeline. "Come to let everyone see how grieved you are?"

Heat rose to Evangeline's face.

"Nice shoes," Claudine said, referring to Evangeline's six-year-old pumps. "What are they, faux alligator?"

Not in the mood for ridicule, and aware she wouldn't have to endure it much longer, Evangeline said, while smiling sweetly, "If you don't get away from me, I'll jerk that phony chignon right off your bleached-blond head."

Claudine sputtered. "You wouldn't dare."

"Try me. I've had enough of your condescending attitude. Get out of my face and leave me alone."

"Well, I never. I was attempting civility, trying to give you a compliment. Lord knows you need one."

"No, you were being sanctimonious, as usual."

"Your days are numbered with this family."

"Your days are numbered with me, and that suits me fine."

Kestner's mouth hung open, flabbergasted, but his blue eyes twinkled.

Evangeline could not believe she had spoken to Claudine in such a manner. As long as she'd lived, she had never treated another human that disparagingly, no matter the circumstances. Her nature was to turn the other cheek, but she was fuming as she pushed through the crowd and headed for the viewing room.

She didn't really need to see Jacques' body because it was only the physical vessel for his beautiful soul, but out of respect for him, she had to be etiquette appropriate.

Calm down, and don't go in there miffed. It wouldn't be fair to Uncle. She hesitated at the door, taking in deep breaths, and slowly, as though a burden had lifted once she had finally expressed her viewpoint, she also realized she had probably severed the Delacroix relationships for good. *My God, I'm turning into my mother.*

The gilded casket lined with burgundy satin was quite ostentatious, but it was covered with white roses, Uncle Jacques' favorite. The mortician had done a nice job on his face, filled in some of the wrinkles, although she had loved his character lines. She reached into her pocket for a tissue, tempted to wipe the rouge from his cheeks and the pinkish lipstick from his mouth, but decided that would be inappropriate.

After paying her respects, kissing two of her fingers, and touching them to his cold hard forehead, she eased out a side door, hurried to her car where, with the windows rolled down, she sat for a long while weeping silently. Then, wiping away the tears and blowing her nose with a tissue from the console, she headed for home, where Olinda was probably conjuring and hexing. She might even have put a curse on her and Zelda, or for that matter, the entire city of Houston.

Chapter 35

That same evening, Evangeline was sitting at the kitchen island researching lost art on her laptop and looked up when Olinda entered the den holding a white padded envelope.

"I signed for this. If I was the sneaky kind, I would've opened it, but tell truth I was afraid to. There's a daub of sealing wax closing the flap, and with all the goings on around here, that wax might be poisoned or explode in my face."

Absently, Evangeline said, "Thank you, Olinda. Put it on the bar. I'll get to it when I'm finished here."

"You heard any more about the Babs girl?"

"Nothing. The police have no real clues. Her credit card's never been used, but they did find her car. No fingerprints, of course, no witnesses, except for a grainy spy camera set up on a building nearby."

"How about dem notes we received?"

"Nothing."

"Not changing the subject, but when can I go home? I don't mind it here with Zelda, Penelope, and Smoke—and you. But I best be getting back to see about things for Mr. Beene."

"If you get a clean bill of health, we can go next weekend." Evangeline ducked her head, not wanting Olinda to see her despondency at the prospect of her leaving.

Olinda nodded. "Okay, then. I'm going to lie down a spell. Don't bother with supper. And be careful opening that envelope."

When she was gone, Evangeline wondered what she had for lunch. Maybe Penelope brought in fast food.

Finding nothing new on the Internet, she shut off the computer, rose, stretched, and went to the back door to watch Smoke stalk a bird. Zelda lay in her bed under the desk, but opened one eye to monitor Evangeline's movements. And with Olinda asleep, all seemed well.

Evangeline wondered what Penelope was doing, if she was safe.

She noticed the white envelope on the bar, picked it up and saw a return address from Messner & Messner, Attorneys at Law. Distracted by Uncle Jacques' funeral, she had completely forgotten about her call to the attorney.

She took the letter opener from the pencil holder on the bar and sliced through the flap, leaving the wax intact. No use taking a chance. Inside was another envelope addressed to her with no postage and also sealed with wax. Inside this was a plastic bag containing a disk in a clear, hard plastic cover, a key, and a sheet of paper.

"What in the world?"

She fingered the odd-looking, old rusty key, and turned the disk over, hoping for information. Her printed name appeared. She leaned against the island, unfolded the paper and read the brief note.

Evangeline,

On the CD you will hear my confession. The key should be self-explanatory when you decipher the following numbers. I pray to God you do it before someone else does. Good luck. 4193084.

"Confession? A puzzle of numbers?" Was somebody scamming her? *One way to find out.* She sat at the bar, booted up the laptop, inserted the CD and pressed the appropriate keys.

An elderly man began to speak.

"Dear Evangeline, since you're listening to this, my attorney has contacted you and informed you of my death. I've asked him not to mention my name or the circumstances of my demise until you've received the envelope and listened to my message. You are then to call him, and he will give you the details you need.

"They say confession is good for the soul, and for what it's worth, I never intended to harm you or your family. After hearing this, I hope you will forgive this old fool for his indiscretion."

Evangeline leaned forward on her elbows. "Okay, now what is this all about?"

The speaker continued. "My name is Abner Jacobson."

"Holy . . . Abner Jacobson! Who are you, Abner? And what have you done?"

"Family background isn't important. What is important is how I went from being an experienced auto mechanic with no artistic background to becoming an art custodian. I had recently been discharged from the army when I answered an advertisement for a driver for our local museum and was hired immediately. Eventually, after proving myself, I was promoted to the warehouse and later to custodian. Surrounded by such beauty and doing a job I had come to love and enjoy, I gave it my all.

"For one reason or another, larger museums would send paintings to us as a gesture of good faith or to allow for more space at their facility—some of the objects were valuable, others not so much. Anyway, a couple of years after World War Two ended, I was in the warehouse when a truckload of paintings came in. I noticed that one crate contained faded French writing but no shipping label. I guessed it had been shipped by mistake, and decided to trace it back when I had time."

Abner coughed. "I unpacked and checked off each crate's contents, and when I took the crowbar to that last one, I never dreamed how it would affect my life. I unwrapped the first painting and thumbed through the shipping form, but the piece wasn't listed there either. I thought I'd made a mistake, but in a hurry to leave work, I quickly unwrapped several more paintings and realized none of them were listed. Upon inspection, I understood why. Whoever had painted them was a terrible artist. I figured that was why the other museum sent them to us without documentation or an invoice. Maybe they were never even removed from the crate, but I never inquired or learned the reason why. Anyway, I repacked the box and shoved it against a back wall.

"A few weeks later, I took a closer look, and noticed the surface layer on one was fairly new and smudged, and dried paint showed through. I don't excite easily, but my stomach did an uptake—I'd seen this before—someone trying to disguise a valuable painting. These days, infrared reflectography is one of the ways to look beneath layers of paint, but back in the forties all I did was soak a small cloth with a special pigment-removal solution, and dabbed at a tiny section where artists often signed their names. Letters began appearing that eventually spelled Botticelli. As I daubed away paint from each piece, I knew my discovery was extraordinary—actually astonishing.

"You cannot imagine my excitement, and the need to share the find. To my credit, I dialed the head custodian's extension, but as fate would have it, he had left for the day. Since this was too important for transom gossip, I decided to wait to speak with him personally.

"I returned the paintings to the original crate, slid it into a dark corner and covered it with a tarpaulin. This was a discovery so huge, it would go down in history with my name attached."

Evangeline, so intent on listening to the recording, jumped

when her cell phone chimed. Nicky was on the other end saying he was around the corner and wanted to stop by to see if his nail gun was in the garage. Anxious to hear the rest of the recording, she almost told him she was busy. But deep down she wanted to see him, so she closed the laptop and inserted the envelope containing the key and note into a kitchen drawer.

When Nicky arrived, Evangeline did not invite him inside, but stepped out onto the patio and shut the storm door. The devil, her face felt like an inferno, because seeing him sent heat from the top of her head to the tips of her toes.

Nicky grinned as if he knew what she was feeling, and his smugness ticked her off enough to dampen the fire.

He greeted her and Zelda and said, "How's Atlas doing?"

"You were right, new gas, new Atlas."

"And, how's our Miz Olinda?"

"About to drive me nuts. She wants to go home, and is feeling good enough to let strangers into the house." On each hand she put two fingers up in the air for quote marks. "Penelope, for one."

"Oh, yes, our girl Penelope."

"And now we've inherited a cat we're calling Smoke. Guess why."

He laughed. "Because it's gray?"

"Exactly."

"I guess Zelda's okay with it."

"Matter of fact, they sleep together. It's skittish with other people and has such long fur, I really can't tell if it's male or female. Makes use of the litter box, so maybe it got lost."

"Your life has sure changed, uh, in a good way. We were so into each other we didn't have time for anything or anyone else."

"Didn't last, though, did it?"

His eyes hooded. "No, my fault entirely. But I'm hoping . . ." He looked away and then back. "And what's this about a package and your life being in danger?"

"Well, good grief. It's like I'm living in a fish bowl."

"Word gets around."

"It wouldn't if Olinda wasn't here, or Penelope." She brought him up to date on a few things, but still did not mention Maximilian and his offer of a trip to Europe. It probably wouldn't materialize anyway.

"The garage is unlocked," she said. "Need any help looking?"

"I can probably manage."

She milled around the patio, checking the bird feeder and watching Smoke stalk a blue jay. "Big mistake, cat," she murmured. "That blue jay will peck your eyes out."

She noticed Nicky watching her from the garage door, and said, "What?"

"Remembering . . . never mind. The nail gun seems to have disappeared. I'll buy a new one."

She wondered if he actually needed the tool, or if it was a pretext to visit. If so, it was useless as she still would not invite him inside.

After Nicky left, Evangeline was about to return to the recording, but Olinda entered the kitchen and headed for the refrigerator where she retrieved a bottle of water.

"Was that Nicky?"

"Yes, it was."

"Where is he?"

"He needed the nail gun, but couldn't find it. I didn't feel like company, so don't ask."

"You're one big smarty. You know that?"

"I wish I didn't have to be."

"I'll be out of your hair soon enough. My doctor's appointment next week will be my last in this town."

Evangeline swallowed hard. She'd gotten used to having her around—as long as she didn't start hexing.

Her cell phone chimed. Arlo.

"I need to answer this."

"Hint, hint." Olinda headed back upstairs with the bottle of water.

Evangeline threw a pillow on the floor between the sofa and the coffee table and sat there while talking and rubbing Zelda's tummy.

Arlo said, "Thought I'd check on you. Is Zelda okay? Are you okay?"

They talked for a while about nothing in particular, and he said he'd stop by soon and show her another dog command. Zelda was snoring, and when Evangeline heard Smoke scratching to get in, she told Arlo she had to go. Smoke sat at the glass storm door with the blue jay in its mouth. The freaking cat was scary. She understood the dead bird was a gift to her, but said, "You're not coming in here with that."

Anxious to hear the rest of Abner's speech, she returned to the computer and the recording. Abner's message continued.

"The next day I learned the curator had gone to a conference in Europe for a week. I'm usually patient, but this time, curiosity got the better of me. It took a few days, but working discreetly, I wiped at the fresh paint on the Botticelli. When Phillips returned, I resisted telling him. In my own pathetic, selfish way, I wanted to keep it my secret a little longer.

"Weeks passed before the entire scene unfolded. I'd seen it on Greek vases and in art books. With your art history background, you probably learned Botticelli painted allegorical religious figures and mythological characters. The linear movements of the figures, as though floating, and the emphasis on outline, were definitely his style. I was almost positive it was an original.

"While cleaning the second one, I sometimes had to stand and walk around to catch my breath, because it was becoming obvious the elongated figure of Jesus with the angels above him was an El Greco.

"Rembrandt painted the third. His use of color and mastery of light and shadow is unrivaled. The figures of the old man and woman sitting by a hearth seemed to glow from within.

"Before it was over, I'd uncovered several more masters. In my heart I knew the paintings were originals. How could such a thing have happened? It completely mystified me. The only explanation was that during the chaos of the last days of the war, they were accidently loaded onto a ship in France and brought to the United States. How that wooden crate ended up in my museum is one for the books—it was meant to be. Fate. And I hadn't planned to keep it a secret forever, but time passed and so did the window of opportunity for telling anyone. Trust would be broken, and my job meant everything. Not knowing what else to do, I stored them away, moving the container to different niches within plain sight, as if those priceless masterpieces were worthless pieces of junk.

"I had a real scare one morning because the crate had disappeared. I searched everywhere, becoming fainthearted. Thank God I found it in a corner, moved by a workman, I assumed."

Abner's voice caught, he coughed, and it sounded to Evangeline like he choked up with emotion, and then silence. She thought he'd stopped the recording, but his voice resumed.

"Sorry. I needed a breather. Even now I get emotional, remembering. These are trivial details, but please understand how some of what happened was out of my control. Maybe one day you will come to terms with what I did or didn't do.

"I could have contacted different museums about a missing crate, but to be completely honest, I dreaded the thought. I did check lost art lists, and when those first grainy photographs of the Delacroix paintings appeared, I became nauseated, had to leave work, stayed in bed for two days, sick to my stomach. I hadn't stolen the paintings, but was guilty of omission.

"Finally, I decided to ignore the situation, to purge the Delacroix name from my mind. And for years that was what I did. Eventually my conscience won and I researched the Delacroix name and history and found out about your grandmother."

The reality hit Evangeline like a brick. "Oh, my God." She shut the laptop, stood, bent over and tried to take a deep breath, but could only gasp for air.

"Grandmother's lost art. Unbelievable. This man, Abner Jacobson, has had Grandmother's paintings for years, and the bastard never came forward—unless someone is scamming me." She took a small glass from the cabinet, turned on the tap, filled it and chugged it down. "Water won't do it."

From the refrigerator she selected a half-full bottle of Chardonnay, uncorked it and took a swig. Its warming effects soothed her. "Abner Jacobson, you freaking thief, you're going to make me a freaking alcoholic."

Calmed, she set the bottle on the counter, settled at the island, lifted the laptop lid, and with a trembling finger, pressed the resume key.

Abner said, "Years passed before the idea came to me. Maybe it'd always been there. The establishment trusted me, and I had earned that trust, except for this one little indiscretion."

"No excuse," Evangeline murmured. "No excuse."

"I'll never forget the exact moment of my decision. I'd been dusting the Rubens and thinking what a shame it was that no one could enjoy it. And then it popped into my head what to do. I could sell it as a forgery or reproduction.

"I knew several dealers who trafficked in forgeries, and the painting I'd choose would be the most genuine forgery in the world. Even at one-third the value, I'd reap a windfall. I could never sell it as an original. I'm a terrible liar, so questions would quickly trip me up. If I did get caught, I could pretend I thought it a reproduction, and the other paintings would be safe. Greed's been the downfall of men smarter than me, and I didn't intend for that to happen. If I were careful, I'd have enough money to live out the rest of my days in comfort."

Evangeline stood and began to pace as Abner's confession continued.

"How to remove the paintings from the building seemed problematic, but in the end, it was simple. Since I routinely transported museum pieces to different locations for numerous reasons, I would merely walk out with one. Through the years, I took art lessons, and amazingly found I had talent. I practiced the technique of each artist, and then painted reproductions that I substituted for those I'd taken home. Of course, anyone could tell they weren't worth much, but what did it matter? They replaced some insignificant art pieces acquired by the gallery. It was so easy it was ludicrous.

"When I brought home an original, I signed my name over the artist's, made incidental paint-overs and hung it in plain sight. The few guests I entertained were impressed with my artistic ability. I'm ashamed of this, but when they'd leave, I'd buckle over laughing at having pulled off the greatest ruse of the century. Old masters hung on my apartment walls and nobody was the wiser.

"After retirement, I needed money, so I decided to sell one—a difficult decision, because I'd be losing a member of my family."

Evangeline mumbled, "Harrumph, your paintings? You mean Grandmother's paintings."

"But I couldn't be certain I had a genuine Vermeer, so it went first. The second one to go was the Seurat."

Abner choked up again. "Sorry, can't help myself. Anyway, the dealer who agreed to buy the Vermeer asked few questions the first time. He quizzed me up and down about the Seurat, but he was greedy and paid nice prices for both. I wasn't greedy, simply wanted enough money to live on."

Evangeline said, "On somebody else's dollar."

"I flooded the market with reproductions so that tracing the originals would be more difficult. It was an ingenious idea, with only the dealer and the purchaser privy to which was which.

"My downfall? Selling the two pieces in the first place. Someone got wind of it and has been dogging me. My health isn't good, and I need to tie up loose ends, to make amends, to make certain the rightful owner gets the art. You, Evangeline. I'm sorry we never met, and if I die under unusual circumstances, you need to be vigilant. Whoever is stalking me wants the paintings and will stop at nothing."

Silence. "Well, that is my story. My one regret is that no one will mourn me. I spent my life with objects, devoted it to a place that did not appreciate me or even send me a Christmas card." Another pause. "My choice, of course, so I must put blame where it belongs.

"I purposely have not mentioned the dealer's name who bought the Vermeer and the Seurat. Maybe you can figure it out and retrieve them one day. Two masterpieces are floating around as excellent forgeries. The Vermeer that went to the Arab at the auction was not yours. Oh, and by the way, I almost introduced myself to you there, but lost my nerve. I even followed you and your friend to the Italian restaurant, but realized I couldn't face you. Your beauty shines through, and you seem kind and sincere. I wish your grandmother's other pieces were in my collection. They may be lost forever, but at least you will have the art I saved for you."

Evangeline shook her head. "Abner Jacobson, you're in total

denial of what you've done."

He said, "And now for a final bit of information. From what I've learned, you have a quick mind. Not long ago, I moved the paintings to a new location for safety. The envelope contains a key and a note with a clue to their whereabouts. Guard the key and clue well. Wish I could be there to see your face when you find them.

"*Ciao,* dear Evangeline, and good luck."

"Unbelievable." Evangeline sat at the kitchen island trying to absorb exactly what she had heard, but it was so preposterous that it didn't seem plausible. And yet, for that reason, she believed it. She removed the envelope from the drawer, emptied the contents onto the counter, fingered the key and stared at the numbers *4193084*. Nothing about them came to memory or made any sense. But Jacobson felt certain she would know, so it had to be simple and logical. "Think, Evie. Think."

Zelda, who was lying on the kitchen floor, rose, came to her, laid her chin on her knee and whined.

She rubbed the dog's ear. "I know, girl, it's unsettling, and I don't know what to do. Maybe some sleep will help, because the old brain sure isn't working tonight."

She ejected the disk, dropped all the items back into the envelope and placed it in the kitchen drawer under a dishtowel. Tomorrow she'd call Mr. Messner. Maybe enlightenment would come to her then.

Chapter 36

"Miz Raines, so glad you called. Abner would be pleased."

"Mr. Messner, after receiving the package, I couldn't have done otherwise. The recording unsettled me. Did you listen to it?"

"Abner wanted me to explain the details of his death and to make certain you received the package. He had sealed the envelope with wax, so all I did was have my secretary insert it into a padded one and send it to you."

"So you aren't privy to the contents?"

"No, Miz Raines, I'm not."

Interesting. Abner kept secrets even from his attorney. "You said you'd give me the details after I received the package."

"Umm. Yes. Really sad. Abner was not in good health, so he was careful with his activities. A hiker found him in the ravine of a jogging trail, dead from an apparent heart attack. Umm—which I thought strange because I'd never known Abner to hike or even jog. He fished now and then."

"Did you suspect foul play?"

"At first, yes. But since he had no relatives, and when the autopsy indicated he died of natural causes, I laid my misgivings aside. Assumed I was being paranoid."

Evangeline remembered some kind of chemical that imitated heart attacks, and she made a mental note to check with a chemist friend of hers. "Did Mr. Jacobson own a home or have a storage shed?"

"A condo that he left to a charity, but that's all I'm positive of. If he had a storage facility, it's news to me. Why are you asking these questions? Did the package contain bad news?"

"I hate to say this, but in his note, Mr. Jacobson insinuated his death might not be accidental, that it might be a homicide. Did he ever give any indication of that?"

"Oh, my word, no, except . . . except . . ."

"Yes?"

"If I think about it, he had been acting strangely, more secretive than ever. Upon one occasion he hugged me and said he'd always thought highly of me. I thought he was being sentimental. In his note did he say why he was afraid?"

"I'm not at liberty to say at this time, but I assure you, you'll be one of the first to know if it's true. May I contact you if I have more questions?"

"Yes, yes. Abner and I go way back, so if I can help, I'm here."

"The Houston police might contact your police, so you could be getting a call."

"Whatever it takes, although I don't really know much. Abner was a private person."

I can just imagine. "One more thing, Mr. Messner, did he mention the names of friends or establishments?"

There was silence for a moment.

"Umm. He did mention a restaurant called Rudy's, said he liked its food and camaraderie, and Rudy introduced him to a very interesting fellow."

On a pad, Evangeline wrote down the name, thanked Mr. Messner, disconnected and sat back in her office chair. "Now what?" *Where do I go from here?*

Lance passed by her door, and she called, "Lance, you got a minute? I need to pick your brain."

He backed up. "Sure. Where? In there?"

She motioned. "I have something to show you."

He sat primly in her guest chair in front of the desk and predictably unbuttoned his suit coat and adjusted the crease in his pants.

Evangeline said, "I like your tie. Muted red and gray checks go great with your gray suit."

"Thanks," he said absently.

Evangeline passed the envelope across to him.

"What do we have here?"

"Take a look and tell me what you think."

He removed the items and perused them curiously while Evangeline explained about Abner Jacobson and the envelope's contents. She said, "I have no idea what the numbers mean, or what the key belongs to. The note says I should be able to figure it out, but I've racked my brain and nothing makes sense."

"Well, at least now you know who Abner Jacobson is. One mystery solved." He fingered the slip of paper and turned the key over in his palm. "The key is old. Looks like it belongs to one of those old-timey locks, like a heavy wrought-iron gate or door. In fact, I'd say it is every bit over a hundred years old or more. Check with a locksmith, or look for a photo on the Internet."

"Do the numbers mean anything to you?"

He studied the note and then tapped it with his pointing finger. "They could be scrambled. Try rearranging them in various sequences, or put each sequence on a separate index card, and let time pass. When you look again, a light might dawn. I do that when I'm writing up a report."

"Good idea. I did the same thing in college. We called the process 'letting it lie.' " He returned the envelope, and she said, "Not changing the subject, but heard any news about Babs?"

"No, and it doesn't seem possible the perpetrator could get away so clean."

"I feel so sad about that situation. I never really got to know her."

"Babs was Babs. What you saw, etcetera," he said, rising. "Uh, by the way, will you be around to answer the phone? Francie has an errand to run, and I need to help in the gallery unwrapping a new shipment. Lydia is on another rampage. What's with her? I've never seen her so stressed. She practically castrated me this morning."

"I know what you mean. I was on the bruising end the other day." If Lance did not know Lydia was in love with Julian, then Evangeline wasn't going to tell him. Hopefully Lydia would come to her senses, but it was doubtful. You can't help who you love or how deeply. Or, maybe what she felt wasn't love, but habit, the proximity of working together for so long.

She said, "All I need to do is drop the envelope at police headquarters, but I can do that any time today."

"Keep me apprised, and Evangeline, make copies of everything."

"Gotcha."

While Francie was gone, Evangeline made duplicates of the three items, and for good measure, photographed them with her cell phone. She then took out a stack of three-by-five index cards and began to arrange the numbers in various sequences, but they were endless, and she decided to try another course. Not wanting to discard what she'd already done, she shuffled them and went through the pile one by one. Nothing rang a bell. "Let it lie. Let it lie."

She secured the cards with a rubber band, dropped the bundle and some blank ones into her executive tote—actually her oilcloth super tote from her teaching days—and then punched in Arlo's number to tell him about the package. He would come by the office to have a look and take it to the station. She picked up her gel pen, leaned back in her chair and started clicking.

Right now she needed a diversion, a change of scenery, fun. And she knew exactly where to find them. The problem, her responsibilities, were mounting, and she had promised Kirk Kestner to be at the reading of Uncle Jacques' will next week. On the other hand, if she didn't do it now, when Olinda returned home, she'd have Zelda and Smoke to worry about.

Her cell phone chimed, illuminating Dahlia's name. She grabbed it and pressed talk. "Thank God, you're back from wherever you went?"

Dahlia giggled. "I live to be needed and wanted. Makes life worthwhile."

"Are you drinking?"

"Probably. That's what you do on a cruise."

"No, that's what *you* do on a cruise, but I'm hungry to see you, sober or not."

"How about this evening, your house. I'm dying to meet the dog and have a heebie-jeebie slapped on me. And I promise to be sober by then."

Evangeline chuckled. "Olinda hasn't been hexing lately . . . uh, that I know of. The dog's name is Zelda, and I've added a few more bodies to the mix. We're one big happy dysfunctional family."

Chapter 37

When Arlo arrived to take the envelope to the police station, Evangeline decided to keep the key but sent the paper copy with the numbers inked out, and a photo taken with the detective's cell phone.

Later, she stopped at her favorite Mexican restaurant, ordered snacks to go and while they were being prepared, walked next door to the liquor store for Margarita fixings.

She opened her gate at home, and was surprised when Dahlia pulled in behind her. Usually her friend was fashionably late.

Evangeline, Dahlia and Olinda talked about old times and caught up on Dahlia's newest escapades. She believed she had finally met someone she could be with. Evangeline prayed it was true, but she had heard it before. Her friend had grieved too long and was becoming more destructive to herself.

Aunt Olinda was on extra-good behavior, probably trying to prove she was able-bodied and trustworthy enough to go home. Zelda was in heaven with the company, and immediately took up with Dahlia, lying by her on the sofa, basking in a belly rub.

Smoke disappeared the minute Dahlia walked through the back door, and had not come out, not even for a bowl of milk or a can of tuna. Evangeline noticed the cat peeking over the top of the credenza in the hall. The animal was too smart for her. She'd tried caging it to take it to the vet, but Smoke wasn't having it. Until proven wrong, Evangeline referred to Smoke as him.

The sidewalk-gate bell jingled, and through the glass in the front door, Evangeline saw Penelope peeping through the wrought-iron gate. She used the remote to unlock it and released the deadbolt on the door. It was discomforting to use such safety features, but under the circumstances, necessary.

"Hey," Penelope said, "you didn't tell me we were having a party. Looks like I'm right on time."

Evangeline rolled her eyes. "Come on in."

Penelope greeted Olinda, met Dahlia, and laid a rolled-up package on the desk at the back door.

"What do you have there?" Evangeline asked.

Penelope placed her hand on the item protectively. "It's for later."

"Okay."

Evangeline popped the chicken quesadillas in the oven to warm, and prepared a tray with the salsa, guacamole, cheese queso and tortilla chips.

While they talked, she performed a fairly decent job of making a pitcher of Nicky's slush Margaritas with crushed ice, tequila, Cointreau and lime juice. A stack of plastic glasses went into the freezer to frost, and when she finished with them, she would toss them out. Her agenda did not include dishwashing.

They dined around the coffee table: Penelope on a pillow on the floor, Dahlia and Olinda on the sofa and Evangeline in the lounge chair. Penelope was satisfied with a virgin Margarita.

Penelope smacked her lips. "It's the salt and lime on the rim that really make it a Margarita."

"And you know all about Margaritas," Evangeline said.

Penelope raised an eyebrow.

After munching, and a glass or two of alcohol, Evangeline said, "I hate to ask, but I've got a project for us if everyone's game."

Penelope volunteered first.

Dahlia complained, "Leave it to you to spoil a perfectly good buzz." But she and Olinda reluctantly agreed.

Evangeline pulled the index cards from her super tote and explained about Abner, and that she had no idea what the numbers represented.

The group gathered excitedly around the end of the island. Evangeline wrote the original numbers on four index cards and passed them out. She then distributed the cards she'd already filled in and a stack of blank ones.

"Please take a look at the original and tell me what you think it could represent. Lance says the numbers are probably scrambled and will have importance only to me, but Dahlia, you and Olinda know my life history, so maybe you can come up with the answer."

Penelope said, "Well, I'll tell you right now, it's a date."

"Lance thinks so too, but I need other feedback. My brain is pickled."

Dahlia scrutinized the numbers. "Maybe it's the code number to a safe or deposit box. Or, holy shit, a Swiss bank account."

"Tsk, tsk," Olinda admonished.

Penelope clapped her hands. "Yeah! We'll all be rich."

Evangeline smiled at Penelope for including herself in the concerns of the household. "If the numbers are scrambled and they are to Grandfather Henri's Swiss bank, a lot can happen in sixty-plus years; the account might have disappeared by now."

"Can that be what it is?" Dahlia asked.

"Anything is possible, but how in the world would this Abner Jacobson get the code to a Swiss bank account? Instinct tells me it's for the location of Grandmother's artwork."

Olinda said, "Or, maybe it's the formula for a fountain of youth. Or, how to bring the dead back to life."

"Be serious," Evangeline said. "This could be the clue I need to find Grandmother's treasures. It might be a scam, but I feel in my bones it's the real deal. Anyway, I thought you already knew how to bring people back from the dead."

Olinda stuck her tongue out at Evangeline. "I am being serious, and you're one big smarty pants, you know that?"

They laughed.

Evangeline directed her next comment to Penelope. "Who wants to jot down some dates?"

Penelope grinned, raised one hand. *"Moi?"*

"Great." Evangeline handed a pen to her and she began to write down sequences of months, days, and years.

"It'll take forever to do this," Penelope said, but seemed genuinely content with keeping busy. She occasionally glanced up and interjected an amusing comment when the conversation lulled.

It was past midnight when, with nothing accomplished, they decided to call it a day.

Dahlia said, "Well, I've had my family fix for a while, but I promise to ring you tomorrow or at least the day after. Enjoyed catching up. And please, tell me if you decode the numbers. Don't go off half-cocked on some dangerous mission."

Evangeline crossed her heart. "I promise."

Penelope took for granted she was spending the night. Olinda wandered off to bed. Penelope and Evangeline straightened the den and cleaned the kitchen, and Smoke finally came out for dinner. When Evangeline locked up and set the alarm, she noticed the package on the desk at the back door.

"Is this for me?" she asked.

"Yes, but I didn't want you to open it with everyone here."

Curious, Evangeline started unrolling what felt like a canvas or heavy drawing paper.

"Oh, my God," she gasped. "It's me."

"Yeah." Penelope grinned and puffed up, a tinge of red coloring her cheeks.

"Penelope, did you do this? It's absolutely wonderful. Looks exactly like me. Watercolor is a difficult medium because the paint runs so easily, but this is perfect. When did you do it? Where did you do it? You didn't tell me you could draw."

"A lot you don't know about me. And, yes, I drew it, here and at the shelter."

"How could you afford the supplies?"

She did not hesitate. "I stole the watercolors. Olinda swung for the paper."

"Oh, my word. We're going to hell in a breadbasket, but I don't care. This is quality stuff. I'll have it framed and hang it in my office at work. Everyone coming in will see it there." She hugged Penelope to her and felt the woman-child's craving for closeness. "You have talent, honey-bun. We need to give that a lot of thought. My boss might even have a suggestion. Maybe we can get you an agent or a sponsor to help make you some money."

"How else do you think I support myself? I stand on a street corner or in a park and hawk my wares. It keeps me from standing on a corner or in a park hawking my body like a lot of runaways have to do."

"Oh, Pen, I can't stand to hear that. It's so dangerous." Secretly, it relieved Evangeline's mind that Penelope wasn't on the streets selling her body. Deep down she'd known that wasn't the case, but now it was out in the open. And she decided it explained one mystery about Penelope.

The girl pulled up straight. "Well, unless somebody is packing a gun, I can take them out with self-defense tactics, the one good thing my stepfather taught me. He was really sorry when I used a few moves on him. The shelter's taught me even more. I can pretty much decimate anybody I want to."

"You're scary, you know that?"

"Yeah, gotta love it."

"I've learned Krav Maga. Ever heard of it?"

Penelope scrunched the corner of her mouth. "Self-defense Israeli style? Yes, ma'am. We call it Dirty Dancing. An attacker doesn't expect to be pummeled with elbows, fists, fingers, anything you got."

Evangeline laughed. "My favorite is to charge in like a bull. A perp never anticipates that from a puny woman. I'll show you sometime."

"Great. Anyway, I'm glad you like the portrait. I needed to show my appreciation for all you do. And wanted you to realize mooching isn't who I am."

"That's quite obvious, and you don't owe me anything, except maybe loyalty and, umm, a little behavior modification."

Penelope laughed. "Gotcha."

Evangeline yawned. "I'm beat, though, so I'll head off to bed. And sweetheart, I'll treasure the portrait always."

"I'm not real sleepy, so can I work on the numbers in bed?"

"Absolutely. Wake me if you find anything." If anyone could decipher the puzzle, Penelope could. Young minds seemed to grasp riddles easier than those of people Evangeline's age. Ugh, thirty wasn't old, but it sure wasn't seventeen.

Not used to the tequila she had consumed, Evangeline curled up in bed and fell asleep before her head relaxed on the pillow. Her dream was pleasant. Max and Nicky were dining at the same table trying to out-barb each other.

"Psst."

Evangeline mumbled, "Umm."

"No, not umm. Get up. I've found something."

Evangeline jerked awake to see Penelope standing over her. "Found what?" She propped up on her elbow.

"I want to run these dates by you. See if any click."

"What time is it?" She closed one eye and focused her bleary one on the clock face. "Three-thirty? Have you been up the entire night?"

"It's gonna be worth your while to get out of that bed."

Chapter 38

Evangeline threw back the covers, swung her legs over the side of the bed, and jammed her feet into her bunny slippers. "What's so important it can't wait till morning?"

"Time waits for no one," Penelope quoted. "First, I could've used your computer without permission, but I figured that wouldn't fit in with my"—she raised her hands and made quotes in the air—"behavior modification."

"Oh, pulease, tell me."

"Let's go downstairs and boot up your computer."

The girl was incorrigible, but since Evangeline would never get back to sleep, they went to the first floor to her desk where she sat in the chair and Penelope scooted up a stool.

While the computer booted, Penelope said, "I took each one of the numbers that corresponded to a month and used those first. I figured the days of the month weren't important yet, so secondly, I went for the year.

"After several reviews, my mind wandered, and for some reason I thought about my father and how much I missed him."

Evangeline's breath caught.

"Before he died, he enjoyed talking about his dad's exploits in World War Two. Grandpa was one of the soldiers who marched into Paris when we liberated it, and that triggered the memory of your grandmother being French and having homes in Paris and the Loire Valley. I decided maybe there was a connection to the numbers. I couldn't remember the exact date of liberation, but I knew the year nineteen forty-four was important. I wanted to figure it out for you, but needed your computer."

Evangeline's hand went to her mouth. "Oh, my God, you might be on the right track. I never in a million years would have thought of that, but it makes sense."

She clicked on World War II, Paris Liberation, and the two of them said the date simultaneously.

"August twenty-fifth, nineteen forty-four."

"There it is," Penelope squealed.

"I see the year, and the month, but the clue numbers don't have a two or five."

"Maybe the day of whatever happened is different, but it's got to be the same time period. Come on, Miss Evie, think."

Penelope was practically on top of Evangeline, bending over with her head blocking the monitor.

"Penelope, I can't concentrate with you in my face."

"Sorry." She scooted the stool back. "I'll give you some space. Make a pot of coffee. Maybe a jolt of caffeine for both of us will help."

From the stairwell, Olinda called, "What's going on down there at four o'clock in the morning? Whatever it be is exactly why I need to get outta here. Too much calamity. A body can't rest."

Evangeline ignored her, her mind spinning. What happened in August of 1944? Was that date what the numbers were about? And that was a big *if*.

"Are you thinking?" Penelope asked while puttering at the coffee pot.

Smoke, the cat, sailed through the air from the top of a cabinet, landed on the island and puffed up, ready to tangle with whatever or whoever got in his way. Zelda pawed at the back door wanting out, so Evangeline got up, punched off the house alarm, unlocked and opened the wooden and storm doors. Smoke sailed out with Zelda at his heels.

Penelope insisted. "Well, are you thinking? I know what, let's get settled and go over everything your grandmother told you about that year. There has to be a clue there."

"Okay, but it will take time and it's already Thursday morning." Evangeline had planned to call Max to see if the trip was still on, but it probably wouldn't happen now.

"What's Thursday got to do with it? We have four hours until you have to be at work. We can get a lot done between now and then."

"You're a slave driver, you know that?"

"Yeah, but a cute one, and I like the saying on your new mug, 'Dancin' to a Different Beat'."

They settled at the island with cups of coffee, pencils and paper. "Let's isolate the numbers already used," Evangeline suggested.

"That's a no-brainer. All that's left are three and zero."

Evangeline said, "August third or the thirtieth of nineteen forty-four. Why is August important?"

"Where was Grandma then?"

"I don't remember." She tapped her lips with her finger. "Wait, I believe the German colonel took her prisoner in August. But how would Abner Jacobson know that down to the date?"

"Let it jell for a while. Maybe that'll help."

"I do my best planning in the bathtub, so I'm headed upstairs. Then I have to get dressed for work. I can't be late because I've a big favor to ask Julian."

"I guess I'll have to do the heavy lifting, then."

In the upstairs bathroom, Evangeline turned on the bathtub water, added bubble bath, stepped into the tub, and submerged up to her nose, racking her brain to make sense of it all. *Relax, don't try so hard; let it come.* Suddenly, she sat up, hurriedly climbed from the tub, dried off, and donned her robe. She padded out into the hall and called, "Penelope, get up here quick."

Penelope took the steps two at a time. "What's the matter? Are you okay?"

"Follow me." At the end of the hall she ascended the second flight of stairs to the attic. She and Nicky had spent days cleaning, mopping, dusting, disinfecting, and installing fluorescent light fixtures. They planned to make a workout room and office, but it hadn't seemed important since Nicky left. And, too, remodeling cost money.

Olinda's voice came from below. "What you doing up there?"

"Nothing. Go back to sleep."

She heard grumbling and Olinda's bedroom door slam.

To Penelope, Evangeline said, "I stored Grandmother Danielle's important papers up here in a water- and fireproof trunk. One day I plan to make a scrapbook of her exploits and life." She knelt, flipped the latch and rummaged until she found what she was looking for—Danielle Delacroix-Ravel's two journals.

"Whatcha got?" Penelope asked.

Evangeline handed Penelope one of the old musty journals. "See if you can find anything helpful. Be careful, though. I want to preserve these as best I can."

They sat on the floor, carefully turning pages, stopping to read a particularly interesting passage. Penelope was intrigued. "Your grandmother had a fascinating life. Here she writes about her and Martin Ravel trying to escape from the Nazis. Exciting stuff."

"Read about that later. Right now look for some dates. It would be later by almost a year. My journal starts after the war, which probably won't tell us much." When Evangeline finished, she sat with her arms around her knees watching Penelope. When her face lit up, Evangeline realized she'd found a clue.

★ ★ ★ ★ ★

At Fallana B's, Nicky shoved the bar stool back so hard it tilted and he fumbled to keep it upright. The bartender who was busy wiping the other end of the counter, looked up and grinned. Nicky straightened, put his hands on his hips and glared at Evangeline.

"You're going where, with who?"

"Whom," Evangeline said, her face screwing up at his reaction.

"Whatever."

"Wow. I thought you'd be happy I'm finally getting a life. The reason I'm telling you is in case of an emergency at home."

"This is the dumbest stunt I've ever heard. You don't even know this Max what's-his-name. Two, three weeks at the most?"

"Give me a break. He's perfectly respectable, owns a gallery in Dallas, flies a plane, has met Julian, and I must say, is quite handsome." She could not resist rubbing it in. "This is a once-in-a-lifetime opportunity, Nick, and I'm taking it."

"He's probably some kind of pervert wanting to woo you from your loved ones."

"I thought that about Fallana," she said under her breath. "Aunt Olinda will stay at the house with Zelda and Smoke. My friend Arlo will check on them every day. I can't depend on Dahlia, who might get on a boat or jet and flit off into the wild blue yonder."

"Who the hell is Smoke?"

Evangeline chuckled. "The cat."

He appeared relieved. "Oh, yeah. Stop laughing."

The bartender now leaned against the back counter with his arms around his middle, watching them. "Now children," he chided.

"Keep out of it," Nicky ordered.

The bartender put up his hand in surrender.

Evangeline planted herself staunchly before Nicky with her fists on her hips, and they stood staring at each other as though in a standoff.

"Nicholas Montgomery Raines, you have nothing to say about what I do. You've made it clear you're moving on, going into partnership with Fallana in a lounge, of all things. That doesn't make sense to me, but I'm sure not raising a ruckus about it. It's your life, do with it what you will."

He appeared crestfallen and stared at the floor. "Worrying about you is a hard habit to break."

Evangeline shouldn't, but she touched his arm, and even through the starched white shirtsleeve, felt fire. She jerked her hand away and stepped back.

It was his turn to grin. "Still feel it, don'tcha?"

Quickly, before she melted into his arms. "I have to go. I'll e-mail or call with my itinerary, and I'd appreciate your checking on Olinda. Make sure the house is safe. You know how she is."

"I sure do know how she is, and I'll bet if she could really hoodoo stuff, she'd hex our house right back to East Texas."

Our house? As she rushed out the door to the parking lot, she heard him call, "Be careful. I love you."

She stumbled to Atlas and grabbed the door handle. There must be somebody somewhere to give her the heat she and Nicky shared. *Then again, maybe not.*

Chapter 39

Evangeline felt like a teenager on her first date, excited, giddy, yet apprehensive. They were driving to the airport in Dahlia's new sports car to meet Max at the hangar while he handled flight plans. She had hesitated to ask him, but when she made up her mind, he said he could leave immediately, fly to Houston and meet her.

Olinda had tried to guilt-trip her; how could she leave while Olinda was ill and somebody was stalking them? But the nurse, Dahlia, and Nicky would visit, and she had their numbers in case of an emergency. Evangeline filled Olinda's prescriptions and went shopping for groceries, dog and cat food. Olinda could call a taxi if she needed to go somewhere, and moneywise, Dahlia would contribute if need be. Lydia, Julian's secretary, would always have a contact number. What could happen in a couple of days?

Evangeline had hidden the keys to Atlas and locked the garage door. She wouldn't take a chance on Olinda skipping out or Penelope taking a joy ride, wrecking the car, or getting a ticket, and making Evangeline legally responsible.

"Don't worry your pretty head," Dahlia said. "I'll check on them every day and drive by at night. Make certain the house is buckled down."

"I appreciate it, because I'm actually looking forward to this. I'm killing two birds, as they say. Thanks to Penelope and my gut instinct, I believe the numbers in the note refer to a date while Grandmother lived in France. Specifically the one when the treasures left the château. I can't figure out the connection yet, but hopefully it will click while I'm there. Maybe jump out and say 'this is it.' Right now it's anybody's guess. If the trip doesn't bear fruit, I'll visit D.C. when I return."

"Would you be up to a confession?"

Evangeline shifted in her seat toward Dahlia. "Okay."

"I've been to your château. Umm, it's a lovely place."

"When? Recently?"

"Nah, a couple years ago."

"It's okay. I would've visited if I could've gotten away. The circumstances weren't right. Anyway, as always, *mi casa es su casa.*"

Her friend was probably trying for a connection after Carlo and her children were killed in a car accident. Since she was in Italy, and the Loire Valley in France was convenient, it was natural to visit the château.

"So, you trust this Max?" Dahlia said seriously.

Dahlia had the habit of shifting a conversation into an entirely different direction to wherever her mind went, making keeping up difficult.

"He's never given me a cause not to. And what would be his motive? Julian says his reputation is above reproach; he keeps his word and tries not to cheat clients. Gossip has it he inherited a bundle. Besides, he seems interested in me, and I'm thinking I might see where it leads."

"Well, thank God. Nicky has monopolized your life for too long. I don't understand him. You are so special."

"As far as Nicky goes, I guess you could say he's going through a midlife crisis, except he isn't in midlife yet."

"Ha, ha, that would mean you and I were, too, and I ain't ready for no stinkin' midlife crisis."

They pulled into the airport where many private planes were

hangared and searched for the number Max gave her. He stood outside the tall, wide doors, waving.

Dahlia swung into a parking space in front of the office, turned off the engine and stared at Max. "Wow! What a hunk."

"Yeah." Evangeline giggled.

"Look at those shoulders. Wonder how he measures up underneath those britches?"

"Dahlia, stop it. He might hear you."

"God, Evangeline, you are so serious. I hope you loosen up on this trip. Stop grieving about Nicky and worrying so much."

Evangeline let it go because they'd already been down that road.

They exited the car and introductions were made. After small talk, Dahlia said, "Sorry to abandon such good company, but I'm late for an appointment. Nice meeting you, Max. Take care of my baby. Evie, please have fun and call me when you land so I'll know you didn't ditch somewhere over the Atlantic."

"Don't even say such a thing."

"Ciao, adios, gut Wiedersehen and *au revoir."* They hugged and kissed each other's cheeks. As Dahlia settled into the front seat, she rolled down the window, threw a kiss and called, "Travel safe. I love you."

Evangeline swallowed hard and waved back, because it was usually her friend who left while she stayed on familiar ground. This time, she would be alone in a strange land with a man she barely knew.

Instead of taking Max's plane, he had chartered a private jet service that included a pilot and flight attendant.

"I prefer to spend as much time with you as possible, and I can't do that bogged down with technical data. I am signed on as an extra copilot, but that shouldn't be a problem."

Evangeline indicated the airplane. "This has to be expensive.

I'll be indebted to you for the rest of my life."

"Promise?" He raised an eyebrow. "To be perfectly honest, I have business in Paris."

The jet interior was equipped with all the amenities. The chairs were so plush Evangeline thought she'd sink so far into one she wouldn't be able to extricate herself. She settled into a leather swivel, and Max sat opposite her—intimate, comfortable.

When airborne, Evangeline said, "I could get used to this."

"That's what I'm hoping."

The flight attendant asked if they would like a drink. Evangeline ordered a spicy Bloody Mary. Max ordered the same.

When the woman brought the drinks, Evangeline took a sip. "Perfect."

The attendant smiled and wandered off to the galley.

Max said, "I am curious why you decided to accept my offer. The last we spoke, you were adamant you couldn't go."

"As I told someone yesterday, this is the opportunity of a lifetime. I've never had enough leisure time or money, and probably never would, to visit Saint Lyra, where Grandmother grew up, or the château in the Loire Valley. I needed a break, needed to clear my head of stolen art."

"And here I thought it was my charming good looks." He grinned.

"Well, I must say that was part of it. If you weren't good-looking and charming, I probably wouldn't have agreed to come."

"Oh."

At his downcast expression, she said, "I'm teasing you now. Anyway, I called ahead, and the attorney handling both locations leased the château for a month beginning next week. Guests are vacating Saint Lyra today, so this works out perfectly. I cannot wait."

"I hope this trip fulfills all your expectations. I'm pretty sure it will mine."

She swiveled to face him, their knees brushed, and the touch, although light, startled her. Her mind wandered for a second. *What if . . . control yourself, don't appear so obviously smitten.*

"Max, you know quite a bit about me, personal and otherwise, but all I know about you is that you have an art gallery in Dallas, which must be successful to judge by these accoutrements. You own a plane, have relatives in Germany, and you are darned handsome."

He was flustered. "Woman, you are blunt, and flattery will get you everywhere. You are right, though. I've been so interested in you, my life seems mundane, boring."

"Nothing boring about you or your life. I envy your means to come and go as you please."

He was silent as though gathering his thoughts.

"So?"

"Ask me questions, because I don't know where to begin."

"At the beginning. Where were you born? Where'd you grow up, go to school?"

"Boston, Boston, Harvard."

"Harvard? I'm impressed."

"My parents were both architects and, I'm embarrassed to say, did quite well financially. I tried to follow in their profession as they wanted, but the art scene held more intrigue, and I get a kick out of making deals. Mom and Dad blamed themselves for my passion, being the avid collectors they were. I can't draw worth a damn, but immersed in art growing up, I developed a discerning eye."

"How did you get from Boston to Dallas?"

"When I graduated with a PhD in Gothic Art, my parents floated a loan and I opened my first gallery at twenty-three. One position led to another, and here I am."

"Would I know the gallery name?"

"Probably not. When I moved to Dallas, I changed it."

"I like Maximilian Forbes Fine Art."

"I agree."

"Do your parents still live in Boston or did they follow you to Dallas?"

"They died in an auto accident a few years back and left me a nice inheritance. Of course, I'd give it all back to have them walk through the door."

"I'm so sorry. Death is seldom easy to accept." She touched his arm warmly.

"I've gradually come to terms."

"Each one of us—you, me, Dahlia—has lost someone important."

They were quiet until she asked, "Ever been married, engaged?"

"A brief marriage four years ago. She said I was too driven, involved in my work. She was probably right. Uh, Evangeline, if I may ask, what happened with you and your ex?"

"Nicky? Umm, let's see. He married too young, hadn't sown any wild oats. You know, the same old story."

"He's a damned fool." He leaned over and fingered a wayward curl from her forehead. "If I had you, I wouldn't let you go."

Oh Lord, she was getting in deep. Her ego was flying high at the moment and she wanted to jump him and kiss him all over. She'd been a virgin when she and Nicky met, and she hadn't had sex with him in over a year. She wondered how it would be with someone else.

The flight attendant called from the galley, "I'm preparing a light lunch. Can I get you anything in the meantime? We still have hours before landing."

The spell was broken. Max gave an almost inaudible moan,

and to Evangeline's ears, her voice sounded high, squeaky. "No, thank you. Actually, the Bloody Mary did me in." She leaned her head back against the cushion, reclined the seat and placed her hand over her mouth to stifle a yawn. "I've been up almost twenty-four-seven. Mind if I take a short nap?"

Max said, "I say we both rest. The next few days will be hectic, eventful." He raised his glass in a sort of toast. "And that's a promise."

CHAPTER 40

Evangeline and Max checked into their Paris hotel in the shadows of the Place de la Concorde, and decided to spend the rest of the day sightseeing. Max ordered a private car that waited while they visited as many tourist attractions as time allowed. Evangeline spoke passable French, but Max's fluency rolled off his tongue like a native Parisian.

First, they drove the wide tree-lined Champs-Élysées to the Arc de Triomphe, where they lingered at the Tomb of the Unknown Soldier, climbed the inside stairs to the top and viewed the streets extending from it like the spokes of a wheel. They rode the elevator to the top of the Eiffel Tower and looked out upon a panoramic view of the city. It was there she realized the width and breadth of the bustling metropolis and its ever-flowing Seine. At the Louvre, she wished they could linger, but the *Mona Lisa* was a must-see, so they walked directly there—a second visit to the museum would be necessary.

They passed Notre Dame Cathedral on the Île de la Cité sitting in the middle of the Seine and where the first settlement of Paris really began. They drove through the Latin Quarter on the Left Bank, and visited the Musée D'Orsay. So many places Evangeline had read about; she could not absorb them all at once. Even then, they barely scratched the surface.

If their schedule allowed on their return to Paris, she wanted to spend a few more hours in the Louvre—not nearly enough to see the entire collection, which would take weeks.

On Butte Montmartre, they passed the Sacre-Coeur Basilica, the Waxworks Museum, and the Moulin-Rouge, where Toulouse-Lautrec painted the performers and habitués. The Butte was where she had the most engaging moments.

The driver dropped them at a small sidewalk café to freshen up and have a bite to eat. Tables were fitted together tightly to accommodate more customers. Next to theirs sat a well-put-together woman and a well-behaved Irish setter. The friendly dog sat quietly and waited patiently for table scraps. The woman nodded okay for Evangeline to pet the animal, and she realized how much she missed Zelda and Smoke. After stroking the setter, she needed to wash up and use the bathroom.

The *salle de bains* barely had enough room to turn around. A snicker escaped her lips, then she giggled and soon was enveloped in a full-blown fit of laughter so strong, she almost passed urine. She was no prude, and had gone to the bathroom in the woods, behind bushes, and even in a chili can, but that was the funniest incident she'd ever experienced. Old tiles covered the floor with a hole in the middle that she was expected to squat over to do her business. She struggled with her slacks and finally surrendered and took them off so they didn't get soiled. There wasn't a hanger, so she wrapped them around her shoulders and placed her feet in the indicated spaces. Now she knew one reason French women had traditionally worn skirts or dresses.

When finished, she tugged on the hanging chain to flush, stepped into her slacks, and washed her hands. In an old stained mirror, puffy cheeks and red eyes stared back, so she dabbed at her face with a tissue from her purse to remove the laughter tears.

When she returned to the table, Max rose, pulled out her chair, squinted at her face and grinned. "I see you found the ladies' room. A new experience, huh?"

Afraid she would begin another laughing session, because that's how it worked when she got tickled, she clamped her lips together and nodded. She was also embarrassed because café patrons were scrutinizing her and probably believed her to be another idiot American. To tell the truth, she wouldn't take anything for the experience. She had needed a good laugh, and now felt like she had truly toured Paris.

Both Max and Evangeline were exhausted when they returned to the hotel and decided to order in and get an early morning start. The rooms had a connecting door, but Evangeline trusted Max to remain a gentleman.

She stripped off her clothes, turned on the shower and stepped into the tub, where she lathered with the hotel's wonderful-smelling soap and shampoo and washed away the day's grime. Then she lolled in a long, leisurely hot bath sprinkled with bath salts and mulled over the preceding events. Afterward she dried off with a fluffy white towel and applied the hotel's special lotion.

She wanted to get comfortable but, not wanting Max to see her in her nightie, she donned the satin lounging pajamas she had bought especially for a costume ball a couple of years before. It consisted of a full-length vest, pantaloons and chain belt. Second-hand sequined mules finished it off—sort of an "I Dream of Jeanie" costume.

"Not bad," she said, slowly turning before the freestanding full-length mirror.

When room service brought their dinner, she knocked on Max's door. He tipped the bellboy and popped the champagne he had ordered, an expensive and rare brand.

He rolled out her chair and they settled at the table. He poured and tested the bubbly while eyeing her admiringly. "To you and your unusual outfit. It fits you and your personality perfectly."

She hoped it was a compliment.

"Thank you, kind sir, and I would like to make a toast to you and a fruitful journey." They pinged glasses.

"This is an unbelievable adventure," she said. "Never thought I'd be toasting with champagne in a Paris hotel. And I owe it all to you."

"My pleasure, but if anyone deserves it, you do."

"You've been the most gracious host, going to places you've probably seen once too often, and never acting bored."

"I enjoyed watching you and your sparkling enthusiasm."

"Never thought of me as sparkly."

They discussed the day's events over a light meal of Quiche Lorraine, fresh fruit salad and an after-dinner aperitif. Evangeline's eyes widened when he checked his watch, rose, kissed her cheek and said, "I've enjoyed this so much and hate to call it a night, but you are as exhausted as I am, and we both need sleep. Tomorrow will be hectic." He headed for the connecting door, where he bowed. "If you need anything, knock twice."

When he shut the door on her, she sat dumbfounded, wondering if she was utterly boring. Or had she misinterpreted his interest in her? She at least expected a few seductive words or a little romancing, whether they led to the bed or not. Didn't movies depict it like that? Not that she was naïve enough to believe in that kind of romance. But come on, get real: Paris, two people in a hotel room, champagne, da-da, da-da, da-da.

Maybe he did not have a romantic interest in her, or didn't want to intimidate her. Or maybe the yawn she tried to suppress turned him off, or maybe the outfit was too much. Maybe, maybe, maybe. He could be waiting for her to make the first serious move.

Well, sorry. He would have a long wait, because she wasn't positive she was feeling it either. Nicky kept popping into her mind. She wished he'd give up and get out of her head.

She kicked off her mules, removed the costume, folded it over a chair, fell into bed in her undies, and scrunched under the covers. The mattress was heavenly and the room temperature perfect, allowing her to sleep so soundly that when the alarm buzzed, she had difficulty opening her eyes. Her mouth felt like cotton, and she needed caffeine. She staggered to the bathroom to the two-cup coffeepot and pushed brew. She splashed cold water on her face and decided to take a quick shower to get her adrenaline flowing.

When dressed, she knocked on Max's door, but there was no answer. *Okay, he's probably in the shower.*

After several tries, she piddled around arranging her makeup and clothes for a quick departure, a habit from when she and her mother would skip out on the rent or for whatever reason found it necessary to leave town quickly. Actually, she probably stayed packed most of her adolescent life until Felicia dropped her off at Grandpop's. Afterward, Felicia couldn't have gotten her out of there with a bulldozer.

She reclined on the bed and read some of the room literature. Surely Max went for a paper.

The package of index cards in the side pocket of her tote called to her, so she took them out and studied the one on top with the August dates. Hopefully the clues would fall into place when she got to Saint Lyra or the château.

"Shoot." She had been so enraptured with the trip, she had forgotten to contact Aunt Olinda and the others. She looked at her watch, calculated the time in Houston, and punched in the number. Olinda answered. "What you calling this time of day for? I be napping and dreaming of home and Scrounger."

The same old, same old—Olinda's false bravado, not wanting anyone to think she was needy.

"Well, at least you weren't pining for Grandpop. And I love

you too. Is the house still there?"

"What house?"

"I'm teasing. Are you okay?"

"As if you cared."

"Olinda, please be nice. I need to do this."

Silence. "Well, Penelope spent the night. Smoke slept with me, and Zelda slept with Penelope. Zelda don't like your being gone."

Evangeline ignored the comment because Zelda wasn't the one minding her departure. "Have you heard from Dahlia?"

"She brought fried chicken and the fixings last night and stayed for a spell. Nick called. Wanted your itin'ry, but I told him he'd have to check with you, cause I didn't know where you were."

"I'll call him later."

"Arlo What's-His-Name stopped by and played with Zelda. Said he'd keep an eye on us. You got him trained good."

"I have not trained Arlo. As a policeman, he is primarily concerned with our safety."

"Yeah, okay, whatever."

"You're beginning to sound more like Penelope every day. One of her and one of you is enough."

"Leave me and the girl alone. Anyway, is your Max behaving himself? Have you . . . ?"

"He is not *my* Max. No, I haven't, and yes, he's behaving. You'd think I was five years old, the way you try to insinuate your ideas into my thoughts."

"You can fool some of the people . . ."

"I have to go. We're driving to Saint Lyra this morning, will spend the night, then drive to the château. Oh, Lindy, it's simply beautiful here. I wish you could've come. Next time you will."

Olinda's voice caught. "I got to go, girl. You take care of yourself."

Evangeline felt a hollow emptiness when she hung up. Loved ones were hard to come by, and her family and friends at home were her lifelines. She shook the feeling off, determined to enjoy today. She was disappointed when Mr. Lamont, her grandmother's attorney, said he had out-of-town business, but to contact him when she returned to Paris. He would have returned by then and they could visit. He was sure she'd have many questions about the properties, and had notified the caretakers of both places to expect her.

She paced the room and was hanging the strap of her purse over her shoulder to go out when Max rapped on the outside door. She unlatched the security chain, and he entered juggling a *boulangerie* sack, two cups of coffee and clutching a stack of papers to his body with his elbow.

"I've rented a car and got directions to Saint Lyra. Also picked up some tour brochures. Thought maybe you'd like to visit a few places on the way."

Evangeline relieved him of the sack. "You are a sweetheart; you brought bakery. I'm so hungry I could eat a dozen *aigs* and drink a quart *o malk.*"

"I'm sorry. What?" He appeared totally confused at her wordplay.

"Grandpop's saying. Don't you get it? So hungry, eat a dozen eggs, drink a quart of milk."

"Oh."

He was still undone, and she decided *this man has no sense of humor.*

She ripped the sack down the seam, revealing four Danish pastries, and two ham and cheese crepes. "Max, you are spoiling me. I'm as useless as a newborn, letting you pamper me the way you do."

He grinned. "I'm having fun showing you off. You do realize

you're a beautiful woman? And I love watching your enthusiasm."

"Well, I am enthusiastic. Haven't enjoyed myself this much in ages—well, never." She bit into a crepe. "Umm, so good. But I'm wondering, should we check out now because no telling where we'll end up?"

"Done. I'm packed, and while you do the same and have breakfast, I need to make a few phone calls. Take your time. We aren't on a schedule."

Dahlia's caution rang in her ears. She said while chewing a mouthful, "Umm, maybe we should also contact the American Embassy and give them our itinerary." She washed down the crepe with a sip of coffee. "I've heard that's the safest procedure when traveling on one's own."

"You are absolutely right. I'll do it immediately."

Chapter 41

The new rental sedan hugged the road like a dream. Saint Lyra lay outside the city, and the farther they went, the lovelier the French countryside became with its rolling hills, quaint cottages, and mercurial properties with partially hidden estates.

"I understand why Grandmother loved it here and why the Nazis wanted a piece of it."

Max was driving, relaxed and unconcerned. "You could be right," he said and shifted in the seat.

Evangeline sat forward expectantly when they arrived at the Delacroix acreage protected by a wrought-iron gate with a fancy gold "D". Max pushed the call button, gave her name to the voice, and the gate swung inward. The long winding driveway cut through a tunnel of trees that had a fresh trimming and reminded Evangeline of Uncle Jacques' home. Saint Lyra might have been his inspiration.

"Oh, my word. The grass is so green it looks like a watercolor painting. And not a leaf is out of place on the bushes. This is absolutely beautiful."

The house appeared and Evangeline gasped. "Good Lord, I'm speechless. Grandmother's photo doesn't do it justice. She told me her great-grandfather built the structure in the Renaissance Revival Style."

"Okay."

Evidently Max wasn't familiar with the period. "In other words, it's based on the Italian and French architecture of the sixteenth century. Each side of the house is balanced symmetrically, but this one has a middle arched entrance versus one to each side. Builders use smooth cut stone for the walls, large stone blocks at the corners and ornately carved windows. There's a lot more to it, but this one looks like a good example."

"Sounds like you've done your homework."

"There may be more, but I count seven chimneys, making it twice, or maybe three times, as large as Uncle Jacques' home." She paused. "My gosh, it must take a houseful of servants to keep this baby in shape."

"It's quite impressive. Must also take a fortune to maintain the grounds."

"Grandmother left money for taxes and upkeep, and her lawyer in Paris leases it out to tourists, which helps."

Max parked the car in the circular driveway at the entrance to the mansion. The front doors opened and a slight little man in a black butler's uniform appeared, bounced down the two steps, opened Evangeline's door and helped her out. His wiry frame and energetic movements belied his age. Deep wrinkles lined his brow, and his hands revealed large blue veins. Evangeline guessed him to be in his middle or late seventies.

He bowed and kissed the top of her hand. "Mademoiselle Delacroix, so glad to finally meet you. I am Renaud Felon, and I am honored to be keeper of this lovely estate." A heavyset woman wearing a red apron and white chef's cap appeared at the door. "This is my wife, Emma. We are at your service."

I'm practically royalty. This is too much. And she would not embarrass the little man by correcting her name. By all rights, she *was* a Delacroix.

Evangeline was anxious to walk the perimeter and view the places her grandmother spoke about. Saint Lyra's grounds had probably changed through the years: trees had grown and died, stables had been rebuilt, and new fences installed. Great Grandmother Adelene's variegated white-granite mausoleum glittered in the sunlight. Henri was buried in the back pasture where a monument marked his grave.

For now, she sucked in a deep breath and stepped across the threshold into a massive marbled foyer with a magnificent crystal chandelier hanging from the second-story ceiling. After the war, Grandmother had fun bringing the home into the twentieth century, by shopping for antiques and such. Except for selling off an acre now and then to pay for incidentals, the estate remained as it did when she lived there.

Max followed her inside and they gaped in awe of the grand old place. Grandmother had told her transient Germans used the facilities at the end of the war and hauled off whatever wasn't nailed down. Evidently, the chandelier was too burdensome. Evangeline crossed her fingers that she could find the secret Grandmother told her about. Others who knew of it had probably died long ago, unless it was common knowledge.

Renaud asked, "May I show you to your quarters, or would it please you to explore first?"

"I'd like to freshen up a bit," Evangeline said. "Max, you?"

"I'm easy. But that's a good idea. Let's settle in, and then we can enjoy the rest of the day poking around. I'm sure your grandmother reminisced about her childhood, and you'll want to do some investigating."

"True."

As Renaud led the way, Evangeline helped him and Max carry their luggage up the wide central staircase. Halls branched off right, left and center from the landing that was more spacious than Evangeline's house. As Renaud directed them down the center hall, he nodded toward an elevator to their right. "Wouldn't you know, the lift quit working last week, but the repairman is due here today, and I'm hoping he can fix her. She is slow, but gets us up and down. Those stairs can be a killer."

"I can imagine," Evangeline said, "but I don't mind. The exercise will do me good. Traveling entails a lot of sitting."

"Emma is preparing a snack to tide you over until dinner. Please inform us if we can make your stay more comfortable."

"Thank you, Renaud, but our time is limited. We plan to leave for the Loire Valley tomorrow. On this trip, I want to see as much of France as possible. On my next visit, I plan to stay longer and talk to some of the locals, maybe to someone who knew Grandmother during the war."

"I understand," he said, stopping, opening a door and indicating for her to enter. "Mademoiselle, you will have Madame Delacroix's old suite, and Monsieur will have the accommodations across the hall. Madame gave specific orders for her father's suite to be off-limits to guests." He sputtered, and pink rose into his cheeks. "Not that you are one, Monsieur. Speaking thus is the habit of an old fool."

Max waved it off. "And I respect her wishes. Any place is fine."

Renaud appeared relieved.

Evangeline said, "Henri was a special man. Grandmother loved him dearly."

"*Oui,* Mademoiselle. Monsieur Henri Delacroix's heroics are talked about to this day. He protected his daughter and aided many Jewish refugees to escape the Nazis. Our Danielle is a hero in her own right. When many of us failed to do so, she stood up and said no to the blasphemous Nazis by joining the underground. The Delacroix story is legendary. You must be very proud."

Evangeline's throat caught, and tears came to her eyes when she realized the extent to which the French people respected and practically eulogized her family. Such high esteem would be difficult to reach.

Max had remained silent during the discussion, but had placed his arm around her shoulders in a comforting gesture. She figured Renaud's admiration touched him also.

The little man gave a slight bow. "I'll leave you now. I hope you have a pleasant rest." He indicated the intercom by the door. "The names are self-explanatory, Mademoiselle. The kitchen is button number two, as you can see."

Max said he'd see her in a few minutes. She shut the door and collapsed against it. This had to be a dream. In a million years she wouldn't have thought this could happen to her, an illegitimate commoner from East Texas, USA. There must be a catch, or someone, or an incident waiting in the wings to burst her bubble.

Okay, Evangeline, stop being pessimistic and asking for trouble. Enjoy the ride for as long as it lasts.

After hanging her suit bag in the armoire, she busied herself in the bathroom freshening up, and then walked into the bedroom, sat on the edge of the bed and started to bounce, testing the mattress. *Feels firm enough. A good night's sleep and I'll be ready to tackle whatever tomorrow brings.*

Right now, a caffeine jolt was a must, and then she'd go exploring. It had been a long time coming, but she was finally here, and she owed it to Max. She hated to keep secrets from him because he'd been nothing but supportive, but this was her life, so when she had a few minutes alone, she'd check out one of the main reasons she wanted to come.

The afternoon was gorgeous, with a French blue sky, the sun dappling through the trees and a cool breeze ruffling the leaves and playing with Evangeline's hair. She had never imagined Max's tall, masculine physique on a horse. He would look more at home in a skimpy swimsuit, like the hero on the cover of a romance novel, but he had taken to the gelding like a pro. She gave her mare free rein, because she seemed to know where to go.

They rode to the back pasture by the woods where the airplane bunker and the monument to Henri were located. Evangeline felt certain the events that took place during the war were as exciting and heartbreaking as Grandmother had told her.

They dismounted, and while Max waited silently with his arm draped over the horse's neck to steady him, Evangeline knelt and said a prayer. Afterward her mare took the lead and trotted to the pond. Evangeline pointed. "There's the willow tree Grandmother used to lie under. Yet it doesn't look old enough. I guess they planted another one in her memory."

They decided to rest under its branches, and let the horses drink and cool off. Once they mounted up again and made the rounds of the pasture, the sun had set, and the wind had picked up.

After removing the tack from the horses and giving them a good brush down, Evangeline glanced at her watch, and they headed for the house to wash up for dinner. Emma had outdone herself. The table was set with the best china and crystal, and they enjoyed a pleasant meal of lettuce wedges with blue cheese dressing, homemade rolls, pasta with a white truffle sauce, and a dessert of fresh berries and cream.

Evangeline said, "Emma, I think I've died and gone to heaven. That meal was delicious."

The woman giggled and curtsied.

Max concurred as they rose and retired to the drawing room with small-stemmed crystal glasses filled with a liqueur Renaud said was made with all natural ingredients on the premises of a Loire Valley château.

Evangeline settled into an overstuffed, squishy leather chair, propped her feet on the ottoman and sipped the liqueur.

"Mmm. I could get *so* used to this."

Max, who leaned against the mantel, grinned. "I've known you for a short time, but figure within a week you'd get antsy for work."

"You're probably right." They were quiet for an interim, each with their own thoughts. Finally, when the liqueur kicked in, Evangeline said, "Max, I'm fading fast. Don't feel you have to, but I'm turning in. Tomorrow will be another busy one."

"I'm for bed if you are. Uh, I mean . . ."

Evangeline smiled, "I understand what you mean." Poor Max; he was so afraid of being disrespectful, he didn't realize how boring and wearisome he'd become.

She was pleased he would follow her lead and retire early, because after Renaud and Emma did the same, she would have an opportunity to explore alone. A pang of guilt shot through her for not including Max in her plan, but she needed to do this privately. Maybe a trip was a good test for a blossoming relationship.

Later, when the alcohol wore off and the downstairs clock bonged the witching hour, Evangeline slipped on her bedroom slippers and zipped up her robe. Quietly, she opened her door and listened. Max must be asleep, because all was silent. Night-lights illuminated the hall, and the long oriental carpet muffled any sound as she headed toward Henri's suite.

Earlier, when giving them a tour of the house, Renaud unlocked the suite's door and forgot to relock it when they continued on. She pressed down on the antique lever handle and cringed at the squeak when she nudged the door ajar. She paused for a moment, praying she hadn't been heard, and then slipped through. Renaud had also left the draperies open, and moonlight bathed the interior in a soft glow.

Evangeline stood in front of the wide three-section bookcase. It had been almost eight years, but she had been trying the entire evening to recall exactly where Grandmother said to look. Under a bottom shelf popped into her mind. She knelt at the left section and began carefully, so as not to get a splinter, sliding her fingers under the shelf and along the wall behind it. Nothing. She did the same to the second section, and again nothing. Her stomach clenched at the thought that someone had found it or accidentally removed or plastered over it.

"Come on," she mumbled, "be here." And then, in the corner of the last section on the back wall, she felt a thumb-sized indentation. She got down on all fours and peered under the shelf to see brush strokes where the recess had been carelessly painted over, and more than once, according to several different colors. If you weren't looking, you'd never notice it.

She held her breath and pushed with her thumb. Nothing. "The devil, what am I missing?" Then she remembered you had to push three times in consecutive order. Starting over she mashed, one, two, three. Her stomach lurched at the scraping of a pocket door sliding behind the bookshelf.

"Oh, Lordy. It's still here." She shoved quickly to her feet and peered inside a dark cavern. She couldn't see the back wall, but the area appeared to be about the size of a walk-in closet, five feet wide by eight feet long and seven feet high. This was where Grandmother said her father kept his private art collection along with trinkets, jewelry and items of sentimental value.

She started to walk into it, decided better, and propped a chair half in and out of the room. Wouldn't do to get trapped in there.

As moonlight penetrated the interior, her eyes became accustomed to the dimness; shelves materialized along one wall, but the rest appeared empty. Now she was here, what did she expect to find? If the room contained items of value, Grandmother or Grandfather would've found them long ago. But she thought of the old saying about a fresh pair of eyes.

The hair on the back of her neck stood up at the sound of a door opening. She froze in place, but after a bit decided the house was settling, the way hers did, like a ghost sighing.

There must be ventilation, because the air wasn't as musty as one would expect. She pulled another chair into the small room to stand on, and in a grid-like pattern, much like detectives walk a crime scene, she methodically examined along the crown molding and baseboards. With not a clue of what to look for, she would be glad for any find.

She checked the entire room and, disappointed, decided it was a useless endeavor. She picked up the chair she'd been standing on, and toted it back into the bedroom, making certain the legs occupied the same carpet hollows.

She returned to the vault, took hold of the chair blocking the door, and stopped. *Okay, think about it.* If the outside bookcase had a notch, there might be one on the shelves inside. She reentered and began to painstakingly feel along the inside ledges of the bookcase.

Her hand moved past it before it registered—an indentation. "Oh, my God, I can't be this lucky." She pushed three times and a drawer rolled out. It was about twenty-four inches long, eight inches wide and four inches deep. Her heart was in her throat and she could barely breathe. Henri must have hidden small valuables and papers in there, but after his stroke his memory failed him about certain details, so he must have forgotten the drawer.

She peered inside, but it seemed empty. Not trusting her eyes, she probed around in the grid pattern.

"What's this?"

A small piece of paper was wedged in a corner, so she carefully fingered it out. Once rolled like a cigarette, it was now creased and flattened with age. She pushed to her feet, went to the window, gently unrolled the brittle yellow paper and gazed at what might be the answer to her future.

CHAPTER 42

Without better light, the faded numbers on the note were barely discernible, but this could be what Evangeline had been hoping to find. The letters *IBOS* were written below the numbers.

"My God, can this be it?"

Another sound like a door clicking closed changed her excitement to panic. Fingers trembling, she decided not to push her luck, and went quickly to the closet, shut the drawer, and moved the chair to its original position. She pushed the recess twice and the door slid into place.

She peeked into the hall, saw it was empty and hurried along the corridor to her suite. When safely behind locked doors, she collapsed into the bedside chair.

This is ridiculous. Why am I so creeped out? Why do I feel guilty? I've done nothing wrong. I'm not breaking any laws. By rights, this house is mine, as is everything in it.

She was not ready to deal with the questions, wanted to be certain. It would all come out in due time. To tell truth, she wasn't sure what she'd found or whom to trust. She rose and stood in the middle of the room, trying to decide where to hide the document. Why not the obvious? She opened her tote and, as she had done with Abner's old key, tucked it into the little secret pocket sewn into the lining. *If you have an idea what you're looking for, it will be easy enough to find, but who in the world would be looking?*

She crawled into bed and slipped between the sheets,

prepared for a sleepless night. She lay stiff, jaws clenched, so keyed up her heart thumped like a motorboat.

Grandmother had said her father, Henri, had transferred most of his holdings to a Swiss bank, but after his stroke he couldn't remember where he'd hidden the paperwork or the bank's name. Without an account number, Grandmother could not gain access to it even if she knew which depository it was in. The money and God knows what else had been drawing interest for over sixty years. If Evangeline could figure it out, the institution wasn't going to be happy or helpful when she showed up asking.

Cross that bridge when you come to it. Now, do I tell Max, or wait till I get home and let Kirk Kestner, Uncle Jacques' lawyer, handle it? It would probably be best to wait till she was back in the United States. She might be totally wrong about everything and didn't want Max to feel used. He had been nothing but supportive, and they still had the château to visit with two days left before returning to the states.

The bedside clock indicated two a.m. She contemplated calling Olinda or Dahlia, but all she could tell them was she'd found a piece of paper with some more numbers on it along with four letters of the alphabet. If the letters represented a repository, Dahlia would probably know. *Patience, Evangeline. You've lived till now without money or status. A while longer won't matter.*

Fidgety, she couldn't lie there staring at the ceiling, so she flipped on the bedside lamp, rose from the bed and retrieved the paper from her tote. She needed to memorize the numbers in case she lost the note or had to destroy it. And the challenge would make the time pass quicker.

She sat in the chair with her legs propped on the bed, trying to think of an easy way to do it. She had a fairly good memory, but eleven numbers plus four letters were too many to keep straight. What if she got a brain concussion or Alzheimer's or some other cognitive disease and forgot them?

One of the tricks she learned in science class popped into her mind, so she took a pencil and corresponded each number with the letter of the alphabet.

"Hallelujah!" When she'd finished, only she knew how to decipher the letters to spell *BANDIDAJOAN*. That plus the *IBOS* was easy enough to recall. She rubbed out the words with the pencil eraser. *No use in broadcasting all my secrets. I'll record them when I get home. What can happen between now and then?*

She hated this feeling of suspicion, but she didn't completely trust anyone here. Max seemed legitimate, helpful, sincerely interested in her. The Paris lawyer, Emma and Renaud were the only other people she knew in France. But her gut instinct and an icy prickle at the base of her spine were telling her to be wary. Her mother's advice wasn't always reliable, but the one Evangeline heeded to this day was "Keep out of trouble by trusting your instincts." That bit of advice helped her on many occasions growing up, because when a situation was getting out of control, she would make sure she had an exit strategy.

Once when she was fourteen, she and a group of her peers were hanging in the neighborhood park swinging, seesawing and generally acting silly. One boy lit up a marijuana cigarette and started passing it around. Not wanting to be perceived as a prude, but certain she wasn't going to smoke it, she pretended to get sick to her stomach and made herself throw up the hot dog she'd eaten earlier—a good ploy that allowed her to vacate the premises. Several kids who stayed got busted, but she was home safely tucked in bed.

She usually had a sixth sense about trouble, could feel it coming a mile off. And tonight she had that peculiar vibe, like someone was trampling her grave, as Grandpop used to say. Tomorrow she would send Olinda and Dahlia some postcards along with an envelope addressed to herself that would contain the paper. She would probably beat the mail home. Dahlia generally arrived in Houston before her letters did.

The next morning, groggy after a sleepless night, she felt let down having to leave the estate. In one night, it seemed like home. But on the bright side, she had the Loire Valley château to look forward to. And she had it in her mind that the château held the key to the missing art. She would find out soon enough if the date she and Penelope deciphered from Abner's note proved significant.

Emma prepared a picnic basket for them: wine, bottled water, tea, and some little pineapple-and-cream-cheese sandwiches along with a liver pâté and crackers. Lord, when Emma cooked the liver, its odor permeated the whole house. Evangeline grew up liking liver and onions, but she might never eat it again.

After bidding the couple good-bye, with them hugging and patting and bowing, and telling her to please hurry back, Evangeline said, "Max, I'd like to stop and purchase some postcards to send home. Would you mind?"

"Not a bit, although you could probably hand the cards to them when you see them."

"It wouldn't be the same. I enjoy receiving Dahlia's notes, even if she's already home when I get them. I've saved every one."

They stopped at a petrol station with a nice little gift shop and grocery store. While Max filled up the tank, she purchased cards, a couple of envelopes, and stamps. She had stuck the paper with the numbers in her pocket and now inserted it into the envelope addressed to her. She wrote greetings from France on the postcards to Dahlia and Olinda, and the attendant said he would send them along with his outgoing mail. That done, she must remember *BANDIDAJOAN IBOS*. Even if Olinda opened the envelope, she wouldn't know what the two words meant.

The sun was setting when they arrived at the cutoff from the main highway to the château perched on a limestone cliff overlooking the river.

Stunned, Evangeline said, "It's exactly as Grandmother Danielle described, like a dreamy painting."

Max agreed. "It is beautiful."

"It was built in the late sixteenth century, but my family has owned it for almost two hundred years. Great-grandfather Henri refurbished the main living areas with modern conveniences, and my grandparents maintained it until they both passed away. Supposedly the caretakers are keeping it in working condition. I hope they're as nice as Renaud and Emma."

"I'm sure they will be."

Max drove slowly and carefully as they rumbled across the moat drawbridge. Evangeline craned her neck out the window for a glimpse of the slow-moving water fed by an underground spring. "There's a secret gate under the water leading into the château courtyard. That's how my grandfather entered to save Grandmother from the German.

"Who is this German you keep referring to?"

Even now, thinking or talking about the man sent shivers through her body. "He was a colonel who selected Grandmother to work at a loot repository and became infatuated with her. But I don't want to think about him right now. I will say that if you had met Grandmother, you would understand—beautiful, smart, and rich, a lethal combination. He ended up stealing the family's art work, which has never been found."

"Exciting stuff. Did she ever find out anything about him or his family?"

"I don't believe so. It wouldn't have mattered. They had nothing to do with the episode, and it was better to leave it that way."

"She was probably right."

Evangeline wasn't ready to mention Abner Jacobson and his note. Although in Max's defense, with his background, he might be helpful.

Evangeline's heart thumped faster. "We're almost there. It's exciting to finally see the places I've heard about. Most have been as Grandmother described, except much, much more than I expected."

If she couldn't find the clue at the château, she had no other direction to follow. But she knew to the core of her being this would be the place. And yet, as they drove through the gate, she had the eyelid twitch, her warning that trouble was brewing. And she remembered Olinda's saying that situations aren't necessarily as they seem.

Chapter 43

Awestruck at the compound's grounds and castle facade, Evangeline twisted to view the panorama.

Since the Delacroix château was built several centuries before, it did not resemble more recent French country estates, but was actually considered a Middle Ages castle or fortress. It perched on a plateau surrounded on three sides by a ten-foot wall of stone, with the fourth side a straight drop to the river below.

The courtyard retained various paving stones laid over time, and a grassy lawn yawned to the left along with a huge garden to supply the tenants with fresh vegetables and fruit. A formation of ducks waddled toward a central water fountain.

"Holy cow, no way I own this. It's totally unbelievable."

"Evangeline, you are one lucky woman. Didn't you realize the extent of your family's wealth?"

"Remember me telling you the French properties are all that are left, along with monies for upkeep? Grandmother died almost penniless."

"Yes, but if you had to, you could sell one of the properties."

"No. The will stipulates they are to remain in the family. I couldn't bear doing otherwise."

At that moment she noticed a man waving to them from an inconspicuous alcove. She pointed. "He must be one of the caretakers, and I'll bet that's the outside entrance to the kitchen."

They exited the auto as the tall slim man hurried up to them, and, like Renaud, expressed his happiness at her visit. His body bent noticeably, as though with a pronounced curvature of the spine. Evangeline remembered his name was Didier, and he had worked there for almost forty years. She marveled that people stayed at one job for so long. Maybe there weren't many to be had, or living in luxury without the hassle of owning it suited them. Not a bad life.

"My wife, Ginette, is at the market in the village and should return shortly," Didier said. "Pierre, our part-time handyman, will take your luggage to your rooms."

Didier led them through the front portico into a black-and-white checkerboard-tiled entry hall with a wide staircase against the right wall. "Oh, my gosh, I can picture Grandmother making a grand entrance from the top, floating down the carpeted stairs, wearing a satin, formfitting ball gown and dripping in jewels. It's what dreams are made of."

"Mademoiselle, you will occupy Madame Delacroix's rooms. And you, Monsieur Max, will have Monsieur Henri's suite. I am sorry to say, for the price we charge, guests who come for the ambience and luxury of a castle are allowed to use those rooms. Many others are cordoned off, but there is still enough access to the castle to make one's stay interesting and worthwhile." He raised one eyebrow. "I hope you approve."

As they began the staircase climb, Evangeline said, "You do what you have to do, Didier. If that helps pay the taxes, then I'm sure Grandmother would understand. I know I do."

The sun had set, and deep shadows filled the castle when Evangeline settled into her room. Moonlight beamed softly through various uncovered windows, but all in all an odd, unsettling feeling nipped at her heels as she knocked on Max's door.

They wanted to be comfortable while touring as much of the château as possible before bedtime, so she had changed into her aqua-colored warm-up suit, white socks and gray walking shoes with the aqua shoelaces to match the outfit.

She eyed Max appreciatively. He was movie-star quality in a camel-colored warm-up that accentuated his strong thighs and broad chest muscles. Dark, wavy hair curled behind his ears, and a five o'clock shadow gave him an exotic, Latin-lover appearance.

She wondered what she would do if he made a serious advance toward her.

He said, "Where would you like to start? The kitchen, maybe?"

"Actually, I'm starving. Didier said they are preparing a nice meal and to tell him when we're ready."

They descended the wide staircase to the marble foyer and then to a lower level where the huge stone kitchen chamber held the ovens, storage bins, a wine storage area and a most enticing aroma.

Evangeline's mouth watered as she casually glanced over at the stone facade Grandmother had told her about. Behind it was the hidden wine closet, where the priceless Delacroix art was secreted before it was stolen.

Ginette proudly gave them a tour of her domain, but Evangeline could not wait to see the other places she'd heard about.

Thankfully, Didier and Ginette shooed them out so they could prepare the dinner table. From the kitchen, Max and Evangeline held tightly to the stair rail leading down worn stone steps to the next level. The cavern, protected from the outside elements by folding doors, was still damp and at least ten degrees cooler than above.

They folded back the double accordion doors for light and a better view. A gust of wind assaulted them. Testing the ground, they carefully moved out onto the ledge now restricted by a metal fence. The gusts had ceased, but a nippy breeze continued to blow from the north, so Evangeline crossed her arms and rubbed her hands up and down them for warmth. She leaned out and peered over the fence, half expecting to see Grandmother's nemesis, the German colonel, crawling up the sheer face of the abyss. Of course, no one was there. "It's a long way down."

Max grabbed her arm. "Evangeline, be careful. Don't lean over so far. It's dangerous."

"This is where it all ended. Even now I feel Grandmother's panic."

"Umm. Your grandmother must have been unusually brave."

"Yes, but she always downplayed it. She said fear for her life had triggered adrenaline she didn't realize she had. Not sure I could be that brave."

He turned her to face him, pushed the wayward curl away from her forehead, and wispily traced his fingers down her cheek. "You are brave, dedicating your life to honor a promise."

"Is that bravery, selfishness, or stupidity? I don't know. I will certainly benefit if I find the paintings. And I've tried to analyze my motive, but it keeps coming back to my promise and not letting someone take what is rightfully mine. Not in my nature, and difficult to go against."

"True, and I understand a little about revenge."

"You, Max?"

"Nothing to talk about now."

She let it go, and they continued down to the boat ramp, where a small outboard hung in straps ready to be lowered with a pulley into the water. It was still a long way down.

Didier's voice echoed down the stairs and through the tunnel that dinner was ready, so they returned to the kitchen. She had asked him earlier not to set up the dining room for the two of them. They would all eat together at the chef's table in the kitchen.

After a lovely meal of duck a l'orange and rice pilaf, along with a big taste of gossip about château guests and the local villagers below, Evangeline said, "Ginette, your duck is the best I've ever tasted. Can't wait to see what you prepare tomorrow."

She blushed. "*Merci, Mademoiselle.* You are too kind."

"Didier, would you mind if we went up to the turret where Grandmother spent much of her time?"

"Of course not, Mademoiselle. Whatever you wish. That part of the château isn't lit, but you can manage with a good flashlight." He scooted his chair back. "I'll show you the way."

Evangeline offered to help Ginette clean the kitchen, but she would hear none of it. Didier retrieved a lantern and escorted them through musty stone corridors up several flights of stairs and a spiraling staircase. At the apex, he unlatched a trapdoor and they climbed out onto the circular turret open to the elements, with a three-hundred-sixty-degree view of the landscape.

The wind blew much stronger up there, but Evangeline barely noticed. In the moonlight, a mesmerizing sight greeted them. Low-lying fields were backdropped by trees looming like hulking black mushrooms. The river glistened in moon glow like a long, winding flow of quicksilver.

"My God, it's awesome. Makes you feel like you own the world. I can see why Grandmother sat up here contemplating and conjuring Grandfather to arrive. You could lose all your worries."

A gust of wind grabbed Evangeline's hair and whistled past her ears. "At least you could if the wind wasn't trying to take you over the edge." She clasped her hands. "But think, this used to be a castle fortress with hundreds of servants and soldiers protecting it, along with the drama of affairs and machinations you read about."

Max took her hands and kissed both her palms. "You're a dreamer with a great imagination."

The act startled her, and she realized he probably expected more from her than she wanted to give. Shame washed over her for using him, because he was so nice and polite and had gone out of his way to make the trip enjoyable.

Why can't I get down and dirty and quit being so frickin' moralistic? She could not put her finger on the reason, except her body didn't respond to Max—no warmth and giddiness inside. When they first met, she thought there might be more between them, but there seemed to be no real sparks. She attributed the dullness to Nicky swimming around in her head telling her to be careful, and Olinda warning her situations were seldom as they seemed.

Instead, she laughed at his dreamer comment and said, "Noooo, not me."

Max said, "Truthfully, it's a little lonely out here."

"All in the eyes of the beholder, but I'm ready to go in if you are."

She had forgotten about Didier until he spoke. "Mademoiselle, a cold front is due in the morning. It might be a problem traveling. I wish you could stay longer than one night."

She shivered and wrapped her arms around herself. "I feel it in the air. And I wish we could, but our schedule is set, and we have obligations in the States. We must return to Paris by tomorrow night and fly home then. I'll be back soon, though."

"Ah, well. It was worth an attempt."

Evangeline looked at Max. "Ready?"

He nodded.

In the corridor of their rooms, Evangeline thanked Didier for the pleasant evening. "When daylight comes, I'd like to explore on my own unless that's a problem."

"It is your castle, so you may do whatever you wish. But be

vigilant; the château is old and deteriorating. We are shoring up obvious problems, and have cordoned off or locked the doors of especially dangerous places we're aware of. The problem is, there may be others we haven't discovered."

"I promise to be careful."

"Oh, yes, and please don't forget to sign the guest book in the foyer. You are not a visitor, but for posterity. The estate people like to keep a record of who has visited. We have quite an impressive list."

"I'll definitely sign it in the morning."

She rose on tiptoe, pecked Max's cheek, bade him good night, and entered her suite. The whole experience was more than Evangeline could absorb. She needed to be alone to analyze her next step. Max had been a rock, chauffeuring her around, and believing she was in France simply for a visit, but she had to go with her instincts and be careful whom she trusted.

She unzipped her tote and fingered the old key in the secret compartment. If she had calculated correctly, she knew exactly which keyhole it would fit. Her main problem was how to explore without Max or the caretakers seeing her. She wanted to do it tonight, but the château wasn't Saint Lyra—too many unknowns hid among the shadows, and her eyelid wouldn't quit twitching.

Chapter 44

Chimes awakened Evangeline from a deep sleep, and she realized it was her cell phone in the charger on the nightstand. She opened one eye, propped on her right elbow and fumbled for the phone. Her home number came into focus along with the clock—two a.m. She shook away the cobwebs. "Oh, Lord, what's happened?"

She jabbed the talk button and raked her fingers through tangled hair. "Olinda, Penelope, are you okay?"

Olinda's concerned voice said, "Girl, is everyting okay with you? I got me a notion tings ain't right. Danger be floating around that foreign place."

A sigh of relief and, "I'm fine, trying to get some sleep."

"Where are you now?"

"We're at the château, had a nice meal, did some exploring and plan to do more tomorrow before we return to Paris. Why, am I in danger?"

"De *loa* . . . never mind. You don't believe anyhow, so let's say I had me a intuit."

Evangeline had mixed emotions about Olinda's intuits, which the hoodoo woman truly believed were the results of black magic.

"*Chère,* I need to know where you be every minute."

Evangeline had to smile. Sometimes Olinda acted like she couldn't tolerate Evangeline, but she was the first to worry about her. It was then her Haiti-Louisiana swamp brogue became more pronounced. Other times, it was passable.

"I'll call you when I can, and positively will when we leave the château for Paris and when we get on the plane. Everything all right there?"

"We okay. You be the one to worry. If I be knowing where the danger's coming from, I'd slam a trick on it. I will send a protection cloak. Uh, you wearing what I put in your suitcase?"

"No, what?" A light flipped on in Evangeline's brain. "Did you put a mojo bag in there?"

"Maybe a little red one. It got some herbs, a couple Zelda's hairs, a bird feather, couple your nail clippings, a dab of oil . . ."

"Great. Fantastic. I feel so much better and do appreciate it."

Not catching Evangeline's subtle ridicule, and seemingly satisfied, Olinda said, "Good. Keep it with you. Zelda say she misses you. Penelope. Nick-lus, too."

"Nicky? Have you spoken to him? Did he mention my leaving the country with Max?"

"Nick-lus will tell you sooner 'en you tink."

"What do you mean, sooner than I think?"

"I got to go. Zelda and Smoke need to pee. Oh, excuse me, urinate."

"Wait." But there was silence, and Evangeline realized Olinda had disconnected. *Now what could she mean by that?*

She scooted back under the covers and tried to fall asleep. Olinda's intuits were usually on target, but what kind of trouble could Evangeline be headed for? She would keep one eye open and a hand on her cell phone. She wondered if France had an emergency number like 911. Didier would know.

Exhausted, she finally went under and did not awaken until sunlight through the window cast soft beams across her face. "Eight o'clock? Oh, the devil!" She threw the covers off and bounced out of bed, ready to get started.

Rested and more clearheaded than the night before, Olinda's

warning barely registered as Evangeline hurried to dress.

She padded down to the kitchen, expecting to see Ginette busy cooking. "Hey, anybody here?" She looked around, but the room seemed empty. "Where is everybody?" Then she noticed a note on the table. Max and Didier were driving into the village to get supplies and would be back soon. Ginette would be in the vegetable garden.

"Perfect." She sped back up to her suite, removed the key from her tote and flew back to the kitchen. At the bottom of the stairs, she held on to the banister, bent over and gulped air. "Anybody here?" Silence.

She hurried over to the stone wall and counted twelve blocks. She inserted her fingers into a recess, pressed around until she felt a release and heard a click. The facade slowly swung open.

"Oh, my God, it's really here." Unbelievable. Grandmother was telling the truth. Behind the facade was an iron door. She breathed deeply to calm herself, but decided she must hurry before someone came. Her hand shaking, she fumbled the key into the lock and turned. The lock released and she pushed on the door, but it did not budge. She pulled, pushed, shoved, kicked, cried and cursed, but it was useless.

Now what? She might need help, but whom could she trust? And maybe it would be for nothing. But why would Abner send her the key, and how did he get it?

She decided she'd better close up and that she might have to wait until she returned to France, but did she have the patience to wait? "I wanted to do this on my own." She closed the facade and heard Ginette at the top of the stairs to the outside.

As the cook descended, she said, "*Bonjour Ma'mselle.* Did you sleep well?"

"Like a log, *et vous*?"

"*Tres bien, merci.* I made beignets and French-pressed coffee." Ginette raised an eyebrow. "Would you prefer ham and eggs?"

Evangeline decided not to push her luck. "Beignets and coffee are fine. When can we expect the men to return?"

"Any minute now. We needed a few groceries and petrol for the jeep. Later, *M'sieu* Max wants to take a ride outside the château walls."

"Do I own more than the château?"

"Of course, *Ma'mselle.* About fifty acres with more fruit trees, caves and other interesting sights."

"There is so much I want to see. Wish I had more time, but we're locked in on the plane trip back to the States. We both have responsibilities there."

After breakfast, Evangeline wandered through the old castle, being careful not to enter cordoned-off areas. She didn't need to have an accident, but she did need to decide whether to include Max in her quest or return to France without him.

Julian would probably finance the trip, because he would benefit if she found the artwork. His support had been invaluable, and since he had the money, contacts and knowledge, he was the perfect one to help her with claiming the pieces, if she found them.

With all the twists and turns of the dark corridors, it was a miracle she found her way back to her suite. Chilled to the bone, she donned a heavier sweater and then remembered she hadn't signed the guest book. More than an hour had passed and Max and Didier hadn't returned, so she headed to the foyer. Except for an inkwell with pen, the gem-encrusted book sat alone on an elegant seventeenth-century rococo commode. Evangeline casually thumbed through a few pages and was impressed as she read the names of a broad sampling of visitors: celebrities, countesses, dukes, earls, lords, emirs, US congressmen, even the presidents of several European and Asian countries.

An idea niggled at her, so she flipped back several years and speed-read forward. She almost missed it, but stopped, scanned up the page, and there it was: the childlike signature of Abner Jacobson, who visited the château this year.

"Son of a . . . I knew it." It was the most plausible way for him to get the key.

Her heart pounded, and her hand trembled. "Now what?"

"Ma'mselle," Ginette called from the door to the kitchen below. "May I prepare a snack for you until lunchtime?"

"Uh, no thank you, Ginette. Beignets and coffee'll tide me over." Actually, she was so excited she couldn't swallow another morsel.

Evangeline closed the book and approached Ginette, who stood inside the hall. "Have you heard from the men?"

"*Oui, Ma'mselle.* Didier rang and said they were at the petrol station and would be here shortly."

"Great." Evangeline followed Ginette down to the kitchen, sat at the table and propped her feet on a chair.

From a teapot the cook poured Evangeline a cup of hot water and plopped in a tea bag. "Did you have fun exploring?"

"I sure did, but it'll be more fun with Max. And Didier was right, it's getting really cold."

"My husband usually predicts the weather correctly."

Using the subtlest tone she could muster, Evangeline said, "Grandmother told me about a secret room down here where they stored wine. Are you familiar with it?"

"Of course, *Ma'mselle.* It is common knowledge."

Evangeline's stomach sank. Someone might have already absconded with the treasures if they were ever there in the first place.

"I'll show you." Ginette went directly to the wall and pressed her fingers into the indentation. The wall swung slowly open revealing the iron door. "Not long ago, we noticed the old key was missing. For years we stored it safely on the ledge up there." She pointed to a place where the stone jutted out about two inches. "Its disappearance is a mystery, but since the room was empty because of structural damage, like many of the rooms in these old castles, we haven't bothered with another key. If you wish, though, we'll have one made before your next visit."

Relieved that the door hadn't been opened since Jacobson's stay, Evangeline said, "Not necessary. I was just wondering. Trying to put all my eggs in the basket as we Americans say."

Ginette smiled. "Your little American idioms are hard to understand sometimes, but they usually amuse me. As to the key, we will definitely call a locksmith, though the lock is so old it might need to be replaced."

"Oh, I hope not. I want it to remain the same. So please leave it alone until I return. I'll decide what do then. Surely, if we can send a man into space we can replace a rusty old key. Oh, and please don't forget to tell Didier not to replace the lock."

"As you wish, *Ma'mselle.*"

Evangeline realized she needed to be more assertive. Not come off as an a-hole, but at least command a modicum of respect by pretending to take charge. Except one could gain more cooperation with honey than with the sting of a bee—and also by playing dumb.

"Shall we close the facade? Wouldn't want it to fall in on us."

"Of course, *Ma'mselle.*"

"You and Didier have been here a long time."

"Yes. We love our jobs. But some guests are not as cooperative as you and *M'sieur* Max. It often gets to be too much. Occasionally we gripe that we can't take anymore." She sighed. "But thankfully, the feeling soon passes and we look forward to the next visitor."

"I'm glad. You and Didier are wonderful hosts."

Ginette beamed. "Thank you, *Ma'mselle.*"

"I noticed some really impressive names in the guest book upstairs, and wonder if you were here for the more recent ones."

Ginette pulled up proudly. "I have cooked almost every meal for every guest for the past twenty-five years."

Evangeline mentioned some signatures of famous people and some not so famous and then said casually, "The name Abner Jacobson sounds familiar. Were you here when he visited? Did he spend the night, or do you even remember him?"

"Abner Jacobson?" Ginette put her finger to her chin and scrunched her mouth to one side. "*Oui,* I recall him. A pleasant little man. He rented the château for two weeks. I believe he is an artist because he received several large packages containing art supplies, paints, canvases and such."

"I'll bet," Evangeline murmured under her breath.

"Is he the same person?"

"Um-hum. Sounds like it."

"I admit I had to leave for a few days to nurse *ma seur* after her operation. *M'sieur* Jacobson didn't mind since it was my sister. In fact, he almost seemed glad. Said he was most happy with croissants and *la soupe.* Didier stayed outside most of the time repairing the wall around the château. *M'sieur* Jacobson took day trips and said he enjoyed himself immensely."

So that's how he did it, Evangeline surmised. The paintings were delivered here, and since the wine closet was off-limits, he stored them there while no one was about. When he left, he took the key and mailed it to me, though the chance of losing the paintings was huge.

Then she considered maybe it was a ruse and he was toying with her. Maybe there weren't treasures behind the iron door. Even so, when she was ready to open it, she'd make certain a gendarme was nearby. If she found even a few of the lost art, Julian had told her the cache would be worth millions upon millions of dollars.

Heat rose in Evangeline's cheeks. She couldn't imagine that kind of money. How would she handle the process? The responsibility would be overwhelming, too much to cope with. But she was getting ahead of herself. There might be absolutely nothing behind the door.

"Evangeline?" Julian's voice was so loud and clear over her cell phone, he could've been in the next room. "Just checking on you. Have you had a good trip? Pleasant, fruitful?"

She read meaning in his tone, and she almost told him what she'd learned but didn't want to disappoint him if it didn't pan out. "I'm having a wonderful time. Seen many places Grandmother spoke about and I do have a couple leads but nothing I want to mention yet."

"Please be careful. You're important to us."

"Thank you, Julian. I appreciate your concern, but Max is an excellent tour guide, and the caretakers are amiable. I couldn't feel more welcome."

"Will you make it to work Monday?"

Evangeline had been taking liberties, and although Julian seemed okay with it, there was a limit to his generosity. "I'll be there." She paused. "I might need to take off the middle of next week for the reading of Uncle Jacques' will. Kestner wanted me to attend, probably for posterity, so I said I would. It'll really unnerve the Delacroixs, though."

"Of course. Not a problem. Take care, and if all goes well, I'll see you Monday."

After disconnecting, she wondered where Max and Didier were. Then she heard an engine rumble across the moat bridge and went to the front door to greet them.

Max unfolded from the front seat and she waved. He waved back.

"Where's Didier?" she called.

From the back seat he took a couple totes filled with supplies and then approached her. "He ran into an old friend and wanted to commiserate. He's to ring when he's ready to go."

"Oh, okay. Ginette's going to flip. She has honey-do's for him. Umm, do you still want to take a jeep ride?"

"Since Didier gave me a running commentary while we were driving, I can wait till another visit." His expression was one of uncertainty. "Unless you want to."

"Actually it's quite chilly out here. Maybe we better hang at the château until we're ready to head back to Paris."

"Suits me."

Evangeline itched to know the contents of the wine room and was torn between involving Max, calling for a gendarme, waiting for Didier, or postponing it until her next trip. *Screw it.* She swallowed a knot. "Max, I have a confession."

He raised an eyebrow. "Uh-oh, sounds serious." He grinned. "Are you breaking up with me?"

"No, silly. It's about Grandmother's stolen art."

"Okay."

"I might have found it."

"What? Here?"

"Yes."

"Well, that's wonderful."

"If I'm right, I'll need your help."

"Let's get to it, then. Where . . . ?"

"In the kitchen. Come on, I'll show you."

She led him to the kitchen below, where Ginette, who was chopping vegetables for a salad, stopped and craned her neck to see behind them.

"Where's Didier?"

It dawned on Evangeline that she had returned the key to her tote, so she said to Max, "Wait here and explain Didier to

Ginette, and I'll be right back." She flew to her suite, and as she rummaged for the key, her hand brushed against the soft material of the red mojo bag. "What the hey, might as well try for all the luck I can get." With the tips of her fingers she gently removed it from the tote, sniffed for any rank odor, and dropped it and the key into her sweater pocket.

She headed downstairs to the foyer where she heard another car in the driveway. "No, not company now." She cracked one side of the front door, peeked out and her mouth dropped open. "Nicky?" She threw the door wide and he waved to her. "What the hell are you doing here?"

He approached and grabbed her in a bear hug. "Why, I came to see you, my love."

She stiffened, brought her arms up between them, pushed on his chest, breaking the hold, and backed up several steps. "I didn't invite you here."

Amused and with a devilish glint in his eyes, he said, "Since when do I need an invitation to visit my wife?"

"I'm not . . . Dammit, leave right now."

"Nope, not going to happen. And where is this Max I've been hearing about?"

"You're the most exasperating . . ."

"Man I've ever known. Yeah, that's what you always say."

She would never admit it, but she was secretly glad he had come, and felt a little woozy at his touch. "How . . . ?"

"Olinda's intuit."

He always finished her sentences. How did he do that? "I should've known she'd be involved."

"Sort of expected it, didn't you?"

"Yes, and you have some major explaining to do." She shivered and noticed he was wearing a lightweight jacket. "But I'm freezing, so you might as well come inside. We were getting ready to unlock a door."

His eyes squinted. "And this door is important why?"

"You'll see."

In the kitchen, Evangeline introduced Nicholas to Ginette and a shocked Maximilian. Max recovered quickly and Nicky seemed amused.

Nicky explained about business in France, said he knew Evangeline was at the château, so he drove up to surprise her.

Evangeline decided she must act upset for Max's sake. "I was surprised, all right."

"Convenient," Max said.

"Okay, guys, enough chitchat. Let's get to the business at hand." Evangeline produced the key from her pocket and strolled to the wall. "Watch this." She inserted her fingers into the crevice, pressed, and as the wall slowly opened, she watched the two men gawk with their mouths open.

"Man, oh man, Grandmother Delacroix was telling the truth," Nicky said.

"Amazing," Max uttered. "Fake walls, secret iron doors and rooms. It's like a real live Gothic tale."

"There's more." Evangeline held up her crossed fingers for luck and inserted the key into the lock. "Okay, I'll need some muscle because the door's stuck."

"How do you know?" Max asked.

She lowered her eyes. "I tried it earlier."

She turned the key and they heard the click.

Ginette came over and gently moved Evangeline out of the way. "*Ma'mselle,* you have to give 'er a little push right here." She placed her ample hip against the door and shoved. The door creaked inward.

Nicky said, "Amazing what a woman can do with the swing of a hip."

Evangeline glared at him.

The cavern was dark, but an oil lantern sat to the door's left, along with a package of matches. Ginette struck one, lit the wick and the room came alive with dancing shadows.

"You first, *Ma'mselle,* but be careful. Part of the ceiling is crumbling." Ginette moved aside and Evangeline stepped tentatively through the open doorway. When her eyes adjusted to the shadows, she surveyed the room and her stomach plummeted. The cavern was empty except for a large rectangular drop-leaf table.

"Well, the devil. There's nothing here."

Max was by her side. "Maybe there is." He moved to the table and raised one of the leaves. Underneath lay a long plastic container much like a wrapping paper storage box.

Max dragged it from beneath, and he and Nicky took hold of the handles, carried it into the kitchen and deposited it gently on the floor. Evangeline couldn't catch her breath.

"You may do the honors," Max said.

"I—I can't."

Nicky wrapped his arm around her shoulders and she leaned into him. "Evie, this might be what you've been looking for."

"And it might not."

They grouped in a circle around the container, dumbly staring down at it and waiting for Evangeline to take the initiative. But she hesitated, wondering how many more disappointments she could endure.

"Oh, for heaven sakes. I'll do it," Ginette said, as she unclasped both ends and raised the lid.

They all stared into the container.

"What's that?" Ginette asked.

"My future," Evangeline whispered as tears filled her eyes.

Nicky hugged her tightly. "Oh, honey, please don't cry. I knew they'd turn up one day."

Max shifted from one leg to the other, seemingly undecided what to do.

"Now I know how Jason felt when he went searching for the Golden Fleece, always beyond his reach until . . ."

Nicky patted her shoulder. "Yeah, and he found it, didn't he?"

Ginette placed her hands on her hips. "Well, are we going to stand here or take it out and look at it?"

Evangeline broke into laughter, and Ginette said, "Americans. Crazy as loons. Let me."

Max said, "No, let me." He gingerly lifted the plastic-wrapped package from the container and laid it on the table. "Ginette, do you have scissors?"

She fetched a pair and he carefully sliced the wrapping.

Evangeline held her breath and squeezed Nicky's hand. "God, let it be."

Max peeled back the covering and they stared speechless at six heavy-duty cardboard tube rolls. Evangeline's hands trembled as she picked one up and tried to pry the lid off. It finally popped loose and she reached in and withdrew a rolled up canvas. Nicky helped her unroll it and they spread it out on the table.

"Oh, my word, look."

Max leaned forward. "My God, this is a Rubens. I'd know his work anywhere."

"Is it really?" She shook her head. "If it is an original, this is unbelievable because it's back where it started from. Is that poetic justice or what?"

They proceeded to open the tubes and unroll the other canvases, revealing six old masters' paintings in all.

The excitement in the room fairly sizzled. Even Ginette, who professed ignorance about art, tried to get in on the discovery. "Are they real?" she asked.

"I'd stake my life on it," Max said. "But we'll have to wait till the tests come back."

"The Seurat, Vermeer and van der Weyden triptych are missing, but my God, so what?"

"Now what do we do?" Nicky wondered out loud.

"I have no idea," Evangeline said. "Do we declare them with the government, take them home on the plane, or what?"

"They are yours," Max said. "Seems like you could keep them."

"Yes, but I want to do this by the book. I'll call Julian for advice."

While the men carefully examined the paintings, she climbed to the top of the stairs to the outside where she leaned against the door to prop it open. She reached into her pocket for her cell phone and her fingers wrapped around the mojo bag. She grinned, patted it and said, "Yeah, Mama."

She punched in Julian's private number and he answered on the first ring. "Evangeline?"

She could barely breathe. "I found six," she said. "Now what do I do with them?"

CHAPTER 45

Evangeline returned to the kitchen where Max and Nicky waited for her to report the phone conversation. "Julian suggested I take the paintings to Paris. He will call the embassy there and relate the situation. I'm to phone when we arrive and leave the decision up to them."

Max said, "Sounds good, but if we're going to make it back to Paris in time to board the plane, we probably need to wind this up pretty soon."

Evangeline agreed.

"Nick, you're welcome to fly back with us," Max said.

"Great. I'll drop the rental car off and hitch a ride to the airport with you guys."

"Tell us where you'll be and we'll pick you up on the way out."

Evangeline caught Max's attention and mouthed, "Thank you."

Nicky called information, found an auto rental drop off in the next village, gave Max directions and went on ahead. Evangeline and Max gathered their belongings and set them in the foyer along with the container of paintings.

"I'm ready when you are," she said. "But I've looked everywhere for Ginette, and she has totally disappeared. I'd also like to say good-bye to Didier."

"Maybe Ginette's in the garden. Want me to check?"

"She'll probably show when we start packing the trunk. But I do wish Didier were here. I hate to leave without speaking to him."

"You know how we men are when meeting up with old friends."

"I guess, but he's aware we have to go soon. Anyway Max, I've said it before, but I sincerely appreciate everything you've done. This trip has been the culmination of a dream and I owe it to you."

He turned his back to her. "You might not say that shortly."

She frowned. "What do you mean?"

"Maybe I haven't been completely honest with you. In fact, I haven't been truthful at all."

He slowly faced her, holding a revolver and pointing it directly at her.

Not quite registering the reality of the situation, she stepped back. "What in the world?"

A smirk played across his mouth. "Come on, Evangeline. I've been playing cat-and-mouse with you, letting you do the work of finding the art." He wiggled the gun at the container on the floor.

Her skin prickled, "I don't understand. Is this a joke? If so, it's not amusing."

"I'll spell it out for you. The day was bound to come when you'd find the paintings, and I bided my time until I thought you were getting warm."

"This is about my family's treasures?"

"Partly."

"You're telling me you've known all along about me?"

"I have, and you were so easy. Gullible, really."

"But we met accidentally, didn't we?"

"Planned. My accomplice informed me of your every move."

"Accomplice? Who . . . ?"

"I even let you wait and wonder if I was going to call. You

never suspected a thing."

"There has to be more to it. I might never have found the paintings. Why were you so sure? And why my treasures? Why not someone else's?"

Voice bitter, Max said, "You think they're yours. By rights, they should be mine."

"How? Why? Are we kin?"

He started pacing, waving the gun. "Not kin, but we have mutual acquaintances."

"What does that have to do with it?"

"Shut up. Your asinine questions bore me. I'll tell you everything when I'm ready. I've wanted to confront you before, but that would've blown my cover—the whole plan. I did almost let it slip a couple of times. Remember in the Italian restaurant in New York when I said I knew of the Delacroixs? You had never mentioned them, so how would I know you were related? Some detective you are."

Her cell phone chimed and they both jumped. She looked inquiringly at Max.

His eyes narrowed. "Answer it, but if you so much as mention your little predicament, I won't hesitate to blow your head off and abscond with the paintings. You'll die never knowing why."

"It's Nicky," she said, punching talk before Max changed his mind. She leaned against the stair rail and forced a light tone, "Hey, you. Are you ready?"

He said he was, the paperwork was done, and he'd make some calls home while waiting.

"We'll be leaving shortly." Pause. "What? Fredric March in his nineteen-thirties Academy Award film role? I don't remember. Research it. Listen, I have to go. We still have packing to do."

She disconnected as Nicky's voice trailed off, "What are you—?"

God, she hoped he got it, and dropped the phone into her pocket.

"Good girl," Max said and arched an eyebrow. "But what about Fredric March?"

"He was trying to remember some movie role. Not important. Now where were we? Oh, you were planning to tell me more."

"No, I've decided to wait. It'll be a surprise. Now hand over the phone."

Shoot. She'd hoped he'd forget about it. She reached into her pocket for the cell and extended it to him.

He pocketed it and motioned her down the hall to the kitchen stairs. "Let's take a walk, then I'll tell you everything."

That didn't sound good. If he planned to steal the paintings, he could not afford to let her live.

"Why are we going to the kitchen? Ginette might be there by now."

"We aren't stopping in the kitchen, and Ginette won't be there. She's tied up and locked in her room."

"Then where are we—?" A cold knot of fear squeezed around her heart. Oh, my God, he was taking her to the cave.

"Yes, I see from your expression you've figured out that part."

As they descended the second flight of stairs to the cavern, her mind whirled. How could she get out of this? Didier was her one hope. Maybe he'd come to her rescue. Nicky was at the car rental waiting, so he wouldn't be any help.

"This is crazy. How do you hope to get away with it?"

"Don't worry your pretty head about that."

In the cavern, he motioned for her to stop in the middle of the room as he strode to the folding doors and pulled them back. She noticed for the first time how beady his eyes were as he watched her shift from one foot to the other.

"Max, you don't have to do this."

"Oh, but I do."

He had the advantage, but he seemed nervous and began pacing again.

She had to play for time. Hadn't her mother always told her that time healed all wounds, and situations could change in an instant? She had been six-kinds-of-a-fool where Max was concerned, but it wouldn't happen again.

She weighed her options. He was much stronger than she, but the *Krav Maga* techniques of kick, bite, grab, might give her a small advantage, because he would never expect it from her. She had to wait for the perfect moment.

"At least Nicky is safe. Did you hurt Didier?"

"Matter of fact, Didier is in a ravine where I left him after he told me where he kept his gun. Bringing one on the plane was too risky."

Her hand went to her mouth. "He's . . . he's dead?"

"I'm pretty sure he is."

"You are one cold SOB."

"Yes, I am." He stopped pacing, pulled up straight, scrutinized her and smiled ruefully. "Now for the real kicker. It's so obvious if you think about it."

He paused and she waited.

"Ready?"

"Yes, Max, tell me. Or do you need a drum roll?"

"You'll soon lose your smart-ass attitude. But no matter." He preened. "My grandfather was Rutger Ludecke. Ring a bell?"

"Rutger Ludecke?" It took Evangeline a minute to process the name. "The German?"

"Bingo! Yes, the German. The one your grandmother thought loved her, but she was a plaything, a means to an end. Sort of like you were. The love of his life was my grandmother."

Evangeline was speechless, dumbfounded. Could that be

true? But why would he lie?

A stool was positioned against the wall near the opening to the outside, so he placed one hip on the seat, one foot on the rung and the other on the floor. Waving the gun around again, he said, "I was told the story of how the Delacroix woman was the cause of Grandfather's death. Also about the art and finances that should have been ours."

His eyes hooded when he glared at her. Pure unadulterated hatred pierced her. She had never felt such a chill.

"Even though he lived and made it back to Germany, he was a broken man and never recovered mentally or physically. He died too young because of your whore of a grandmother, and my family has vowed retribution ever since. Through the years we've managed a few triumphs against the Delacroixs, but I'm the one with the balls to finish it."

"That's crazy. And actually, they weren't Ludecke's to take. They belonged to my family."

"According to my father, in war anything goes."

"But after these many years—how long have you known about me?"

"Evangeline, I've tracked you since your grandmother found you, and I've always known about her, had revenge drummed into my head since I can remember. But I started planning seriously when you came into the picture."

She decided he was a brainwashed crazy man. "My God, Max, you've wasted your life searching for artworks that aren't even yours?"

"As much mine as yours. And who are you? An illegitimate backwoods bitch who can't keep a relationship because all you think about is finding lost treasure and belonging to a family who wouldn't spit on you if you were lying in the gutter."

That did it. How could this man have taken her in so easily? She'd actually believed his sincerity about how sweet her mother was to have named her Evangeline, and when she told the story of her grandmother being a spy, he didn't bat an eye. And now, how could she even the odds?

"I've heard enough. Let me out of here."

He was off the stool and in front of her, blocking her exit. With a deadly smile, he said, "Oh, no. You still don't get it. I'm going to kill you like I did the others."

"The others?"

"The art dealer, Babs . . ."

Acid burned up into her throat. "You killed Mr. Rossini and sweet Babs. What did Mr. Rossini have to do with anything?"

"He had one of Abner Jacobson's Seurat fakes. I was hoping to find Jacobson before you did, but changed my plans and decided to let you do the work."

"Then you're the one who bought the Seurat the next day."

"Yes. The daughter was at the gallery, so I went in and paid top dollar for the useless piece of junk, but at the time it was worth it for you not to learn his name."

"And Babs. She was an innocent bystander, wasn't she?"

"Yeah. I hated to kill her, but she saw me with someone, and I couldn't take a chance of her telling you or the police later."

"Your accomplice?"

"Maybe."

"But I don't understand—we were having dinner when she was killed."

"Evangeline, it doesn't take long to crush somebody's skull, and I purposely picked a restaurant near her apartment."

How could he be so nonchalant about murder? "Who else did you kill?"

"You're really going to flip out with this one." He emphasized, "Your grandmother."

"My . . . my grandmother?"

"Actually, she was the easiest. A heart attack? Nope. Digitalis did the trick. Since she was being treated for heart problems anyway, the doctor never thought to check for the overdose I gave her. Never knew what hit her."

Through clenched teeth, she said, "You, you killed my grandmother?" Growling, she lunged at him with fingers stretched into claws. He sidestepped and laughed. She stumbled to her knees.

"You are so pathetic. Naïve. Ridiculous. Wanting to be accepted by the Delacroixs, who are nothing but a bunch of leeches. Revenge is my first motivating factor; the art is a bonus."

He squeezed her arm, jerked her up and pushed her onto the stool. Reality sank in. Max seriously intended to kill her. And she saw no way out. *Olinda, where is that protection cloak you were sending?*

CHAPTER 46

A strong gust from outside teetered Max off balance. Evangeline started to make a move, but he quickly recovered and growled, "Don't even consider it. A bullet'll find you before you make it to those stairs."

She raised her hands, palms out. "Whoa. Take it easy. Running is the farthest thing from my mind." Under her breath, she murmured, "For now." Then louder, she said, "But since you plan to kill me, why not tell me all of it. Who's your accomplice and who's been following me?"

"I started the fire at the motel, was in the park when that bitch dog scared you to death, added water to your gas tank, and managed several other incidents to panic you."

"Did you try to run me off the road on the Interstate?"

"Yeah. It was dangerous, but I couldn't resist. You weren't paying enough attention, so I gave you a wakeup call."

"You woke me up, all right. Almost killed me. Did you kidnap Aunt Olinda?"

"Yes, I did. Called you a couple times and even had my accomplice contact that old fool Abner Jacobson. I discovered who he was, and arranged an accidental meeting with him at a restaurant. My accomplice tried everything to find out about the paintings, but he was too stubborn to give them up. Wanted to repent for what he did to you, I suppose. I sent him to his grave believing they were safe."

"All this for the art?"

"You aren't listening. The art is a bonus. I did it mostly to avenge my family, and I must say, it was more fun than anticipated."

She shook her head. "Max, you're deluding yourself. It's about the art and the money it could bring."

"Think what you want. In a few minutes it won't matter."

"Your plan won't succeed. Too many people know I'm with you in France. Questions will be asked."

"When Nick showed, I had to change plans, which in the long run will work out better. A jealous ex-husband comes to claim his woman from the new boyfriend. The situation escalates; the ex goes berserk and tries to murder everyone at the château. The new beau is forced to protect himself by killing the ex. It's a plan made in heaven."

"You wouldn't."

"Oh, yes I would."

"Surely Ginette's been on the phone gossiping to her sister about our find."

"I confiscated her phone, and Didier was already dead in the ravine. Nick is the only other person who knows."

Max had forgotten about Julian, and Evangeline wouldn't remind him.

"You've overlooked a few things," she said.

"I'll worry about them later. Now get up. We're taking a little walk out onto the ledge."

Evangeline grasped the stool seat with both hands. "You'll have to drag me out feet first."

"I wanted the satisfaction of pitching you off the cliff, but shooting you is fine with me. Or should I say, Nick shoots you, kills Ginette and Didier and wounds me. It'll hurt, but will be more persuasive to the police. I shoot Nick, and that's that."

"But Nicky isn't here."

"He'll be back when we don't show or answer the phone.

Now get your ass up." He grabbed her bicep, squeezed until her arm tingled.

She slid from the stool. "Okay, big boy, let's get it on." With her one free hand she gripped the stool's leg, swung it around and connected with his hip.

"Bitch." He released his hold on her arm and slapped her hard, snapping her head to the side.

Dazed, cheek stinging, she shook her head to clear her vision. Through clenched teeth she warned, "Max, you're beginning to tick me off."

She counterattacked by charging and knee-kicking his groin. He bent over, moaning in agony, one hand holding his privates. She chopped the back of his neck and he fell to his knees but quickly recovered and managed to retain control of the revolver. He rose slowly, staggered back a few steps and she rushed in with arm outstretched, fingers pointed and stiff, and jabbed at his throat. Her other arm chopped the gun from his hand and it skittered across the floor.

"Let's see how lethal you are without a weapon."

He gagged and coughed, and clasped his throat.

"Damn you. I'll kill—"

"Not today, you won't."

Whomph. He gut-punched her with his fist, she gasped and wrapped her arms protectively around her stomach, feeling Olinda's mojo bag in her sweater pocket.

"How'd you like that?" Max said triumphantly.

"I didn't," she said, fumbling for and wrapping her fingers around the talisman. Smoothly she removed it from her pocket and clutched it in her hand. When he came for her again, she pitched it underhanded to the ground in front of his foot and prayed. He stepped down, slipped on the bag and teetered off balance. She rounded off, karate-kicked him in the stomach and sent him sprawling.

She stumbled toward the gun, but he crawled after her and, before she reached it lying in the corner, he grabbed her ankle and she fell flat, the wind knocked from her. He stood over her in an instant, drew back his leg and aimed, and she knew if he connected this time, she might not recover. One chance. She rolled, came to her knees, donkey-kicked his shin and heard bone crack. He howled in pain and plopped to the ground.

She reached back for the gun, and with probing fingers felt the cold metal. In a fluid movement, she came to a sitting position with legs spread and pointed the gun at him.

"Now who's going to kill whom?"

He groaned. "You wouldn't."

"Give me one good reason why not."

"Don't have it in you."

"Wanna bet?" Her finger closed on the trigger and pulled, the echo of the blast resounding through the cavern.

Eyes wild, he grabbed where his earlobe should be. "You crazy . . . Now look what you've done. You've shot off my ear."

"I was aiming at your head. Want more?"

"Get a doctor. Call an ambulance. I'm bleeding to death and you broke my shin bone."

"You big whiner. You won't bleed to death. Duct tape will fix it. Grandpop used it for his leather chair, wrapped water pipes in winter, and even held together the car muffler. I heard astronauts even used it to make repairs in space. But if you want, I'll oblige by shooting the other ear to make 'em even." She was an excellent shot, but said, "I must tell you, though, my accuracy isn't always true. Probably seventy-five percent, so you never know where the bullet'll hit."

"You are one crazy bitch."

"Yes, I am," she said, quoting his earlier comment. "You shouldn't have messed with me or my loved ones."

He whimpered that he was dying and the pain was excruciating and he needed a doctor.

She heard the clomping and clatter of footsteps descending the stairs and Nicky's voice, "Evie?"

"Down here."

He skimmed the last few steps, hurried to kneel before her and began probing her for wounds. "My God, sweetheart, I heard a shot. Are you all right?"

"I think so, but you better phone an ambulance for the whiner over there." She nodded toward Max, who groaned and moaned. "Biggest baby I ever saw. Fights like a girl."

"What did you do to him?"

"A few *Krav Maga* tricks."

"The police are on their way. They can handle the ambulance. But we need to have paramedics look you over to make sure you're okay."

"I do feel like I've been pulled through a knothole backward, even though the only times he touched me were to squeeze my bicep, slap me upside the head, and gut-punch me. I'm pretty sure I'd know if I had a broken rib or a concussion."

Nicky stared in awe at Max lying on the floor. "You did all that?"

"Believe so."

Nicky laughed till his eyes glistened, a habit when he was relieved. "Remind me never to pick a fight with you, Miz Evangeline Raines."

She grinned. "Yes, and don't you forget it."

"Uh, Fallana needs a bouncer. Want a job?"

She socked him lightly on the arm. "Watch it, Tonto. I'm not in any mood to hear her name. Curious, though, did you understand my code message?"

"I finally remembered that Frederic March won the Academy Award for his portrayal of Dr. Jekyll and Mr. Hyde. I put two and two together and figured you were talking about Max and I better get back here quick." He looked sheepish. "Uh, I might be in trouble for stealing a rental car, but hopefully they'll understand when I tell them my woman was in jeopardy."

His woman? "Olinda will have a field day when she finds out the mojo bag helped save my life. I'll never live it down."

CHAPTER 47

The gendarmes interrogated Evangeline and Nicky for hours. If her grandmother's lawyer in Paris and the American ambassador to France had not intervened, they would probably still be stranded at the French police station.

Max hadn't succeeded in killing Didier. Someone found him in a ravine near the château, and he was expected to make a full recovery. Ginette, gagged and tied to a chair in her room, was unharmed, and both were eager to give evidence against Max, who they said was a devil.

The last Evangeline heard, Max was under heavy guard in the hospital, recuperating from his non-life-threatening wounds. After some major haggling, the French authorities slashed through the red tape, and agreed to extradite him to the United States for the murders he committed on American soil.

The lawyer explained to the auto rental company why Nicky took the car without completing the renewal paperwork, and they decided not to press charges.

The authorities also agreed to let the paintings return to America with Evangeline. With that last piece of legality cleared up, she and Nicky were considered innocent of any crime and were released. All in all, and contrary to what Evangeline had heard, the French were highly accommodating.

After crating and labeling the art, Evangeline and Nicky loaded it on the jet and flew to Houston. They shared a taxi to Rembrandt's, where Julian offered to store the paintings in his vault until she decided how to proceed. She figured they would be ninety-nine percent safe there, and waited while Lydia entered each one into the inventory ledger in the On Consignment column.

In the backseat of a taxi driving to their respective homes, Nicky asked "What now?" and put his arm around her shoulder.

She snuggled to his side. "I'm so tired, it'll take a day or two to recuperate, then maybe I can think about the future. Although I promised Kestner I'd attend the reading of Uncle Jacques' will, I'm not looking forward to it. To deal with the Delacroix bunch is worse than trying to ride a pogo stick in quicksand."

He squeezed her affectionately. "You can do it."

"Yeah."

"Uh, what I really meant was what about us."

She pulled away and scrutinized his face. "I do love you, Nicky." She leaned over and kissed his cheek. "Forever and ever, but it's different now."

"I understand. My fault entirely. Before, it was wild, passionate love, us against the world."

"We've grown in different directions, which happens more often than not. I want to continue working with Julian, because it's interesting, challenging." She grinned. "And the adrenaline rush is almost as good as our sex." The minute she said it, she regretted it.

He groaned and shifted in the seat. "Evangeline, you're killing me. Now isn't the time to remind me of lying next to you, skin to skin, making love. When we were apart, all I could think about was getting home to you."

She felt a stirring in the pit of her stomach. *Hold on, Evangeline; do not give in to lust.* She swallowed hard, and swiftly changed the subject. "A project is jelling in my mind that will require hours and days of research. But I don't want to talk about it yet."

"Whatever it is, it'll be successful."

"And then, too, there's Fallana."

He stiffened. "I can find other work."

"And be as miserable as before?" She snuggled back under his arm. "Can't we leave it like it is for now, being friends and letting time take its course?"

"Do I have a choice?"

She didn't answer, and they were quiet until Evangeline sniffled. "He killed Grandmother."

"I heard at the police station." He rubbed her shoulder. "I'm so sorry, Evie. Wish I could make it better for you. She was a wonderful person."

"It's senseless. So many lives lost over revenge and painted canvases. And Max's accomplice is still out there."

"How could I forget?"

Evangeline's hands clenched. "When I find him, he'll wish he were dead."

"Are you sure it's a him?"

"Well, no, but from all indications it is."

"If Max is offered a good enough deal, such as life in prison versus the death penalty, surely he'll give up his accomplice."

"You would think so, but I can't depend on it. I plan to investigate anyone who might possibly be Max's partner. He said Babs saw him with someone who would be a dead giveaway if she revealed it, so she had to die."

The taxi pulled up to the front of her house, Nicky and the driver set her luggage inside the gate, and she said she could handle it from there.

"I hate to leave you with a murderer still on the loose, ready to do you harm."

"I'm pretty sure I'll be safe here." She kissed him good-bye, and gave him a gentle shove. "Now go." And under her breath added, "To Fallana."

As the taxi pulled away from the curb, the front door burst open and Olinda, Penelope, Zelda and Smoke rushed down the steps and enveloped Evangeline in hugs, chatter, barking and purring. It was the most satisfying sensation.

Dahlia, craving Olinda's shrimp jambalaya, had stopped at the market and purchased the ingredients. Jambalaya, along with a salad, crusty French bread and a robust red wine, suited Evangeline fine. She rehashed the trip almost minute by minute, with Dahlia constantly rubbing and patting her arm and murmuring heartfelt sympathy. After dinner, Dahlia made a quick departure, saying life was too short to hang around, so she was meeting friends and flying to Vegas.

With the kitchen cleaned and dishes put away, the three sat at the island, Evangeline nursing the last of the wine, Olinda and Penelope with glasses of iced tea. Zelda, on her belly with back legs splayed, had settled partway under Evangeline's stool, and Smoke lay on the counter on his back, legs spread like a teddy bear with lost stuffing.

"Olinda, that meal was delicious. What's it called again?" Penelope asked.

"Child, where you from? You don't know about jambalaya? I learned how to make dat in the swamp."

"Well, one good thing came from the swamp." And she quickly added, "Uh, and only one good thing. But I wish Dahlia could've stayed longer. She's a hoot."

Evangeline laughed. "She couldn't wait to get out of here. I was worried she'd leave town while I was gone. Usually, she's on a plane, train or boat heading off to a new adventure. And, too, kitchen duty isn't her forte."

"I'm still wondering how you knew where to find the loot," Olinda said.

"Penelope didn't tell you? She's the one who figured it out."

Penelope placed her hand over her heart as though wounded. "I can zip it when I need to."

Evangeline said, "All along Pen thought the numbers referred to a date, but what date? She woke me up one night, saying she might have the answer. We went to the attic and read through Grandmother's journals. The ones I read were mostly about the post-war years, but Penelope noticed a page about the paintings and the day they went missing at the château. Or should I say, when the German stole them. Grandmother wrote the date in her journal as August thirtieth, nineteen forty-four. Our little runaway here"—Evangeline reached over and patted Penelope's hand—"noticed that the dates were in the code numbers that Abner had written in his note."

Olinda acknowledged Penelope admiringly. "But Evie, how did you know they were in the wine cellar?"

"The key. Old and rusty, it probably belonged to an iron door. Grandmother had told me about the château, and I had a hunch. Thanks to Penelope, it turned out to be correct."

Penelope tapped her temple. "Am I a brain, or what?"

"Smart aleck is more like it," Olinda chided.

"Anyway, that's how we found the paintings." Evangeline sipped her wine. "Uh, I sent postcards from France, and an envelope addressed to me. Have they arrived?"

"Haven't seen them," Olinda said. "You, Pen?"

"You know I don't check your mail."

"Sure you don't. Maybe they'll arrive tomorrow."

"I do not check the mail."

"Okay. Stop pouting. I believe you."

Evangeline nodded toward Smoke. "We really must keep the cat off the counters. It isn't sanitary."

"Nuh-uh, not me. I'm not telling Smoke nothing. You do it."

Evangeline ignored her and took a bite of cheese and crackers from the tray on the island.

"Well?" Olinda said.

"Well what?" Evangeline asked, but had an idea what Olinda wanted to hear.

"What about your mojo bag? Where is it?"

She knew this was coming, and might as well tell it, because Olinda would never let up. "It got sort of crushed when I threw it under Max's foot. He stepped on it, slipped and lost his balance, allowing me to chop the gun from his hand."

Olinda leaned back triumphantly. "Aha, see there. It helped save your life."

To argue with Olinda was like arguing with a fence post, but for some reason Evangeline jumped right in. "Believing mojo bags have magical qualities is like believing Grandpop will return from the dead. It's utter nonsense."

"Uh-huh, if you say so."

In an attempt to get Olinda's mind off the mojo bag, Evangeline said, "What happened to the protection cloak you were supposed to send me?"

"Well, I needed your body to be here and since it wasn't, the best I could do was dress Zelda up in your shirt and sprinkle her with a little magic dust. It weren't perfect, but evidently it did help."

"Oh, please. Protection cloak and mojo bag, my foot. *Krav Maga* saved me."

"Naw, child. Mojo works in mysterious ways."

"Nothing mysterious about throwing that bag under Max's feet."

"But if you didn't have it to throw, he mighta killed you." She turned to Penelope. "What do you think, Penelope?"

"Sorry, Evangeline, I'm with Olinda on this."

"And I'm not the only one believes in *nonsense* as you call it. What about Fleecy?"

"Felicia," Evangeline corrected. "And what about my mother?"

"Seems I remember hearing about a ghost fire out in the swamps."

"What?" Penelope asked eagerly and shifted on her stool for a better view of Olinda.

"Fleecy say she visiting a friend out near the swamp. Dark came on them when they was walking back from buying Cokes at a gas station country store. Didn't have streetlights. Anyway, Fleecy got them cold chills down her spine like evil coming down."

If Evangeline thought about it, she had faced her own dark places and déjà vu moments, but never thought of them as mystical or possessing magical powers.

She reached over to pet Smoke. He raised his head with lips back, showing two front teeth and *grreowed.* She jerked her hand away. "Okay, you stupid animal. Your days are numbered."

"See," Olinda said. "He's your cat. You the one has to rep . . . repri . . . fuss at him."

"My cat? How do you get that?"

"You named him, and you know what they say."

"No, what do they say?" Evangeline kicked off her slide and rubbed the sole of her foot along Zelda's back. The dog wiggled and sighed. "Nice doggie," she cooed.

"If you ever name a stray animal, it's yours for life."

"You made that up."

"Did not."

Evangeline said, "It's true Mamma had premonitions, but that's not the same as believing in witchcraft. She'd say 'I have a feeling so-and-so needs me.' Then she'd call and it would be the truth."

"Funny you believe in Fleecy's premos but not mine."

"The difference is that Mamma didn't claim to be a hoodoo queen."

"Harrumph. Anyways Penelope, Fleecy turned around, looked behind her and saw this fireball traveling lickety-split down the middle of the road headed straight for them. She and her friend started running like bats outta . . ."

"Watch it." Evangeline nodded toward Penelope. "No cursing in front of the kid."

Penelope rolled her eyes upward. "Oh, for criminy sakes."

"She ain't like any kid I ever come across. And don't interrupt. They was running and this fireball came whizzing right over their heads and disappeared around a bend in the road." A triumphant grin lit her face. "Now what you think that was?"

"My mother telling ghost stories to scare me. And even if it were true, there are several theories about swamp fire, ghost lights, whatever you want to call them."

"Name one," Penelope said smugly.

"Swamp gas is when methane, created by dead-plant decay, ignites by spontaneous combustion and causes a ball of fire. I've even heard of people spontaneously combusting and burning to ashes."

"Nope, that part would be a mambo doing a dirty trick," Olinda said. "And even if it was this methane gas exploding, and by the way, I haven't heard proof that happens, why would it follow them down the road?"

"Olinda, fireballs are not mystical phenomena. Logically, roads are clear open spaces. Don't fill Penelope's head with your hocus-pocus stuff."

"But it's fun and I like it," Penelope said.

Disgusted, Evangeline rose. "Fuggeddaboudit! I'm going to bed."

"Spoilsport," Penelope called after her. "Can I have the rest of your wine?"

As she headed up the stairs with Zelda trailing, Evangeline grinned to herself and mumbled, "Welcome home, Evangeline. And thank you, God, nothing's changed."

Now if she could get through the reading of Uncle Jacques' will, she could concentrate on Max's accomplice. According to him, if Babs mentioned seeing him with a certain person, Evangeline would know immediately who his accomplice was. Surely it was not someone close to her.

CHAPTER 48

The next morning, after a quick shower and hastily applied makeup, Evangeline flipped through the clothes hangers at the back of her closet. She decided on the five-year-old princess-style, red boatneck with the box jacket. The extravagant purchase had been for a daytime charity luncheon where red was mandatory. Nicky hated those affairs as much as she, but his boss had given him tickets and more or less insisted they attend. And it was for a worthy cause. It took six months to pay off the credit card bill, and she hadn't worn the dress since. Most of their money, and Nicky made good money at the time, went to updating the house.

Red wasn't appropriate for the occasion, but Uncle Jacques would love it, and shock value was her one victory to wave over the Delacroixs. Since they never knew what she would do, the apprehension in their eyes when she appeared was priceless and almost made dealing with them worthwhile.

She twirled quickly in front of the full-length mirror in her bathroom. Although a little loose, the dress fit well enough to get by. *Now where are those red shoes?* After tearing through her closet, she decided the shoes had disappeared, so she settled on beige sling pumps. Tacky, but what the heck? With pearl studs in her ears, a brush to her hair, and a change of purses, she was ready for whatever they threw at her.

She made a hurried stop at Rembrandt to check on the paintings, but Julian had not arrived, and he possessed the combination to the vault. Lydia was her usual harried self, and today she wore an especially anxious countenance, and would not look at Evangeline.

The woman needed to get a life other than Julian Krystos and Rembrandt, because it was a hopeless situation. She probably didn't want to walk away from a lucrative job. Besides, when you are in love, you don't always make the best choices.

Evangeline pulled out of Rembrandt's parking lot and realized she would be late for the will reading. She made a shortcut through a neighborhood, but to her chagrin, the streets were under repair and it took twice as long to navigate to the freeway.

When she drove into the parking garage of Kestner's office building near the Galleria, there were no parking spaces available. She wound around almost to the top floor, and finally noticed a car backing out. She stepped on the gas and wheeled Atlas into the vacated space. In her side-view mirror, a man in a luxury sedan presented her with his middle finger, and she almost returned the gesture.

In the elevator she had another bout of second thoughts and wished she had not told Kestner she would attend. The green light pinged and the door slid open. She breathed deeply and stepped directly into the massive foyer of Kestner, Bevins and Padilla, Attorneys at Law. A beautiful floor mosaic with the initials *KBP* anchored the area. The company leased the entire sixth floor, no small expense given the location and square footage. As a client, Uncle Jacques probably helped pay for a large portion of it.

The receptionist, pretending to be busy, sat primly behind the arc-shaped glass-and-brushed-chrome desk. If the poor thing smiled too broadly, Evangeline decided, her flawlessly painted-on makeup might crack and she would look like a sugar cookie crushed in the bottom of the cookie jar. *For shame,*

Evangeline; cattiness does not become you. She is probably a nice lady who could be a friend someday. Stop justifying your own inadequacies.

The woman looked up and evidently recognized her, because she gestured to the right, said precisely, "They are waiting for you in the conference room."

Well, you can dill my pickle.

At the door, Evangeline's stomach lurched. She took another deep breath, gathered courage and entered. The group chatting around the long, oval mahogany conference table consisted of a few of Jacques' adult offspring—his son Dimitri's daughter, her husband and their children Lucien and Micheline; Dimitri's son Randall and his children Claudine and Sebastian. Randall's wife, Portia, was not present.

The cacophony stopped abruptly, and she hoped they couldn't hear her heart thumping. She gave a partial fan wave and said, "Hello, everyone. Hope I haven't held up the proceedings."

There were "harrumphs" and shuffling of feet. Except for Kirk Kestner, Lucien's friendly smile bolstered her.

Kestner rose, came to her, took and patted her hand. "Glad you're here, Evangeline dear. I heard what happened in France and wasn't sure you'd make it."

He escorted her to a chair at the end of the table, pulled it out, and because she hadn't the strength to do otherwise, she obediently sat between Claudine and Lucien. She hugged her arms tightly to her sides and primly clasped her hands in her lap to shrink into the chair's back. Thinking better of it, she unclasped her hands. No need to appear completely intimidated.

Voice oozing derision, Claudine whispered, "Nice vintage outfit, but where are the matching red shoes?"

Bitch.

"I believe all those planning to attend are here," Kestner said from the other end of the table. "This is a sad occasion, but one that must be met. Jacques has been specific in his bequeathals and as far as I can see, they are indisputable. Since you're all anxious to get this over with, I won't waste time with amenities, but will get right to it."

He thumbed through a folder on the desk and extracted several pages.

"As we all expected, until the will is probated, my firm and I will serve as executor of the estate. If there are any objections, we'll take them up after the reading."

Kestner read through small incidental bequeathals and finally came to the children and grandchildren.

" 'To my great-granddaughter Claudine, I leave five hundred thousand dollars, the auto she loves, and . . . percent of my estate.' "

Evangeline's mind was on Olinda, hoping she and Penelope were behaving, and attempting to remember what happened to her red shoes, so she heard smidgens of Kestner's reading.

" 'To my great-granddaughter Micheline, I leave five hundred thousand dollars and . . . percent of my estate. To my great-grandson Lucien, I leave five hundred thousand dollars, and the . . .' "

" 'To my Granddaughter . . . twenty percent . . . To Randall, the eldest of my grandchildren, fifty-one percent of the business and title of CEO . . .' "

Evangeline, wishing she were anywhere but here, slumped in her chair and let her mind wander as Kestner droned on about bequeathals, estates, percentages, etc.

" 'To Evangeline . . .' "

"What?" It took a moment to realize Kestner had said her name and that a shuffling of bodies and a hum of voices vibrated the room.

"Excuse me," Kestner said. "I would appreciate attention and quiet. You can squabble after I'm finished."

Evangeline sat up straight amid immediate silence, like shutting the door inside a soundproof booth. This bunch didn't mess with Kestner.

"To continue with the reading, 'to Evangeline, whom I have grown to love and who I know will be fair in undertakings regarding the Delacroix family, I leave the remainder of my estate, which includes the keys to my homestead. Family members who remain or decide to reside there will honor her directives, or, at her discretion, she is authorized to take measures deemed necessary. From my estate, a lifetime bequeathal of monies will be kept in escrow to handle all liabilities and financial aspects with regard to the property. This bequeathal is binding and can never be contested or overthrown.' "

Evangeline uttered, "Holy sh—"

"This is ridiculous," Claudine said. She jerked a thumb at Evangeline. "And I'm not taking orders or asking *her* for anything."

Lucien clapped his hands. "Bravo, I want to know how you did it."

If Randall's eyes could shoot nails, Evangeline would be pinned to the wall. He rose abruptly and shoved his chair back so forcefully that it tilted. Lucien grabbed it before it hit the floor. "We'll see about that," Randall growled. "She must have coerced him when we weren't around."

Kestner said, "I assure you this was Jacques' wish. Because I knew there would be ramifications, I recorded the transaction on video and tape and asked Jacques on several occasions if he really wanted this. You're each welcome to a copy."

Too stunned to comment, Evangeline sagged into the chair, limp as a rag doll while the bickering back and forth continued.

Randall demanded, "I want a copy of the video and the will

before I leave these premises. What's the date?"

Kestner nodded. "August of last year." He directed his next words to her. "Please stay. We need to talk."

Evangeline sat across from Kestner in his office, one leg crossed over the other, foot jiggling, so mad she could chew rawhide.

"Why," she asked, "would Uncle Jacques do this? He knew how his family felt—feels about me—and vice versa!"

"Calm down, Evangeline. It might not be as bad as you imagine. Jacques trusted your character enough to know you would be unbiased in family matters and would do what was best for all concerned."

"How could he be so certain? We didn't spend much time together, and someone always hovered around, making sure I didn't run off with the family silver."

Kestner laughed. "Jacques lived a long time and understood his family well. He also had an uncanny sense of human nature, and it amused him to watch how afraid of you they were."

"Afraid? Of me? But why? I couldn't cause any harm, and I'm certainly not a thief."

"Because you are so different from the lot. On the tape, he said his family needed a wakeup call, and giving you this opportunity would insert new blood and shake the bunch up."

"It's certainly shaken me up."

"Between you and me, you must have noticed how selfish and self-centered they can be."

"Oh, I've noticed. Lucien treats me halfway decently, but the others—"

"Well, there you go. You have one ally already. The others will come around eventually. And I'm always here for you."

She covered her face with her hands. "Oh, God, I can't. I planned to distance myself from them ASAP."

"You would have been okay financially, especially since you

found Danielle's paintings. But with the remainder of Jacques' estate, you'll be set for life if you continue to invest wisely. The others will probably spend their share before they leave the building. That's why he bequeathed each one a percentage of the business and left the great-great-grandchildren trust funds. At least everyone will have an income unless the companies go bust, and I don't see Randall letting that happen."

"How mu—? No, I don't want to know, because I'm not taking it."

"Jacques was quite wealthy. If my memory serves correctly, your share will be in the mil—"

"Million dollars! Oh, my God, unbelievable. There must be some mistake."

"You can hear the tape. Judge for yourself."

She threw up her hands. "So what did Uncle Jacques think I would do? Run home, pack my bags, put my house on the market and become a Delacroix?"

"The will doesn't stipulate that you must live there. But don't make hasty decisions. Much needs to be settled first, and time is an excellent problem solver. Give it a month or so, then we'll talk again. By then you may have changed your mind."

"Doubtful. Actually, I can't see it happening."

"You can put the money to good use, maybe start a foundation, help the poor, be productive. And I'm sure Randall will come around. He is really levelheaded and not as cantankerous as he tries to pretend. It's an act to keep everyone in tow. Otherwise they would eat him alive."

"Like they try to do me."

He tapped his pencil on the desk. "Other than Dimitri, who is on the down side of Alzheimer's, Randall is now the eldest capable Delacroix, and that brings a huge responsibility. I wouldn't want to be in his shoes." He coughed and said under his breath, "Or yours, for that matter."

"It's obvious he hates me."

"You can help each other." Kestner glanced at his watch. "I'm due in court just about now. Please think before you make a decision that will affect the rest of your life."

Realizing the conversation had ended and she was being dismissed, Evangeline made a move to rise. Time was also money to him.

He put out his hand to stop her. "Please, stay here as long as you want to collect yourself. This is a great shock, and you need to come to terms with it. Oh, I almost forgot." He removed an envelope from his top desk drawer and handed it to her. "Here is Danielle's death certificate, which you might need for the future." He rose and moved around the desk to where she sat, kissed her cheek and exited the room. She heard the door click shut.

With a throb beginning above her right eye, Evangeline plopped back in the chair and opened the manila envelope. Already aware of its contents, she was not surprised, given that Max gave her grandmother Danielle an overdose of digitalis and that caused a massive heart attack.

Stuffing the form back into the envelope, she rubbed her temple to ease the twitching and throbbing of her eye, but it didn't help. Maybe she had too much to absorb all at once. She should be jumping for joy at the turn of events, but felt trapped. *Uncle Jacques, how could you? When my life is looking pretty good, you throw me a curve. What am I going to do? And what will the Delacroixs do?*

Chapter 49

In Rembrandt's parking lot, Evangeline said to her friend's voice mail, "Dahlia, when will you be back in Houston? I need you."

After the reading of the will at Kestner's office, Evangeline found it difficult to concentrate, but a stack of work waited on her desk from last week. Francie wanted to learn some of the grunt work, but now was not a convenient time to teach her.

Kreshon was at his station at the front door, so she waved and called good afternoon. He waved back. She poked her head into the Rembrandt gallery, noticed Julian with a client, and decided to speak to him later. In the investigative offices, Francie, who was brushing the computer keys, looked up and nodded. Lance wasn't in, so she went directly to her office.

The inheritances were a worry. The ones from her grandmother were rightfully hers, but not Uncle Jacques' money. That money would oblige contact with the Delacroixs, and she had prided herself on being independent, not relying on anyone. She shivered as though someone had walked over her grave. *The Delacroixs are going to eat me alive and spit me out bite by bite until nothing is left.*

She dove into the paperwork, and except for munching on a bag of potato chips and sipping a diet drink at her desk, didn't come up for air until Francie buzzed quitting time.

Julian's clients had vacated the premises, so Evangeline walked across the hall to speak with him.

He was leaning against Marion's receptionist desk, staring into space. When she approached, he smiled. "Evangeline, how are you? Coping with all your adventures?"

"I had a shock at Uncle Jacques' will-reading, but I'll tell you about it later. I'm wondering if you've thought about what I should do with Grandmother's paintings?"

"Sorry, no. I've been negotiating with a new watercolorist. Looks like a go."

"Great." Memory of Max's watercolorist fleetingly clicked into her mind. "Uh, that reminds me. I've found a young artist you might be interested in mentoring. Her watercolor portrait of me is fantastic."

"Bring it in and I'll take a look." He paused. "I'm not promising a contract."

"Of course, I understand, but it's unbelievably good."

"As for your family's art pieces, they are safely ensconced in the vault. Want to see?"

"If you don't mind."

He turned to Marion, who was clearing her desk. "Please ask Kreshon to lock up."

Evangeline appreciated Julian's precaution in not opening the vault with the public around. One couldn't be too careful. She would hate to lose the paintings after finding them.

When Julian slid the container into the gallery light, she peeked into the vault's dark abyss but was greeted with shadows. They unlatched each end of the container and she perused the cache. Satisfied they were all there, she nodded to Julian, who dragged the box back to the walk-in, closed the doors and spun the combination lock.

She had reached the door to leave when Lydia caught her arm. "Got a minute, Evangeline? I'd like to speak with you."

Evangeline decided Lydia better not get pissy with her, but the woman seemed genuinely concerned about her well-being.

"My dear, I heard about your ordeal in France. I hope that terrible man didn't harm you."

"Well, thank you, Lydia. He did scare the bejesus out of me, but I probably hurt him more than he did me."

"How in the world did he pull off those murders alone?"

"Oh, he had an accomplice."

"Did he say who?"

"He wouldn't spill. But like Nicky said, when the authorities fly him to Houston today, he might be willing to cooperate if he can cut a good enough deal."

"I see. I hope it's nobody close to us."

"I agree. That would be too much."

Seated in the kitchen at home, Evangeline enlightened Olinda and Penelope about Uncle Jacques' will.

Olinda moaned, "You mean we got to move into that big old, cold mansion?"

"No, we don't. And we're not going to. It'd be like country hicks moving in."

"Watch your mouth, girl. We aren't country hicks."

"Exactly. So I'm not accepting the inheritance. It will bring trouble and heartache."

"You're not? You gotta be kidding me?" Olinda said.

"I'm dead serious."

"Well, if that don't put pepper in the gumbo."

Penelope chimed in, "I'll take it."

Olinda and Evangeline each raised an eyebrow.

"Not changing the subject, but did we get any mail?"

"I been too busy to look," Olinda chided.

"Doing what?"

Penelope said, "I cleaned the kitchen."

"By the way, Penelope, do you live here now?"

The girl's expression brightened. "Can I?"

"Honey, you are still considered a juvenile. The authorities won't approve of my harboring a runaway."

"I'll be eighteen in two more months. If I can hang till then, I'll be legal. Uh, does your cop friend know my age?"

"Arlo? No, I've never had a reason to mention it."

Olinda interjected, "If she did, he'd be on us like beans on rice."

"But Penelope, I'm curious. Where exactly is your family?"

"Do you promise not to contact them?"

For her grownup talk and tough attitude, Penelope was really a scared young girl, Evangeline realized. "I can't promise, but I won't do it unless it's absolutely necessary. And, of course, I'd notify you first."

"Florida. But they probably moved by now."

"My God. How did you get from Florida to Houston?"

"Hitched, walked, whatever it took."

"Your mother must be out of her mind with worry."

"Nah, she's, like, cool with it." Sheepishly she added, "Even gave me bus fare to shag out. Got me as far as Biloxi. I told you the creep she's with has her under his thumb."

Evangeline wanted to, but found it difficult to believe a mother would give a seventeen-year-old money to leave home.

"Don't sweat it. If you don't want me here, I'll split. I just feel safe with you, Olinda, Zelda and Smoke."

Oh, God, she hits below the belt. Evangeline placed her arm around Penelope's shoulders. "Honey, it's a tough world out there." She paused. "But I guess that's obvious to you."

"Yeah."

"I have nothing else to say except we'll let time decide. Now, I have a project to do before I forget."

Penelope followed Evangeline to the walk-in closet under the stairs, where she retrieved the watercolor painting, carried it to the back door and laid it on the desk.

Penelope grimaced. "Where's it going?"

Not wanting to disappoint Penelope if Julian wasn't interested, she said, "I'm having it framed and hanging it in my office the way I planned."

"That reminds me. I was watching one of your black-and-whites yesterday and did a double take at a movie star who is your spitting image."

"I'm flattered. Who?"

"Heady something or other."

Evangeline chuckled. "Hedy Lamarr?"

"Yeah."

"I don't see the resemblance, but Nicky agrees with you."

"She's one fine looking *chica.*"

"Why, thank you, Pen, but those movies are my personal collection and I would appreciate your asking before touching them."

"Sorry. They looked like old VCR tapes. Glad I didn't copy over one."

Evangeline covered her mouth with her hand. "Oh, my word. I would have totally killed you."

"Geez, how can you watch those creepy things?"

"All in the eyes of the beholder. And it'd be a heck of a world if everybody liked the same thing."

"Who spit in your tea?"

"At the moment, my whole situation."

Olinda had been silent, watching the proceedings from the kitchen stool. "Tsk, tsk, selfish, selfish."

"Mind your business, Olinda. And that's the second time you've called me selfish. I share almost everything I own. What should I do, open the doors and let everyone in?"

"Not a bad idea. What else is money good for?"

"A question to ponder."

The germ of an idea took root in Evangeline's mind.

Because of the foot traffic along their street, and because they'd lost correspondence, Nicky had installed a slotted mailbox to be opened with a key from inside the fence. They hadn't lost mail since it had been installed. Evangeline thumbed through circulars and bills and saw the cards and envelope she'd sent from France. When Dahlia returned, maybe she would recognize whether the numbers were actually to a Swiss bank account, or if that was wishful thinking.

It would be too good to be true. Then unbidden tears came to her eyes. Her grandmother could have lived her last days in comfort if she'd found the paintings and the account number. Max, the SOB, had killed her, and it would be hard to get over that. Evangeline hoped he burned in hell.

Maybe she wouldn't wait for Dahlia. One could find most anything on the Internet. Swiss banks shouldn't be too difficult to research, and maybe the letters *IBOS* would signify one of them.

First, she wanted to figure out who'd joined Max in his crazy scheme. To do that, she'd make a list of names, and by the process of elimination, if God were willing and the planets were aligned, she'd come up with the right person.

In the kitchen she laid several sheets of lined paper on the island and penciled in a heading on each: Family, Friends, Business, Miscellaneous. She, Olinda, and Penelope began to list people she knew who could possibly be the culprit.

Olinda said, "Want folks from home?"

"Let's concentrate on Houston. I've been over names in my mind, but can't come up with a viable suspect. Maybe if I see them written down and do some pros and cons, I'll have the answer."

When finished with the list, Evangeline put an *X* by those to cross out—a daunting task, but Penelope and Olinda seemed into it.

After eliminating half the names, Olinda tapped her pen on the island. "Humm, wouldn't it make sense to check out who all would know where you'd be going? Max seemed to show up wherever you went."

Evangeline brightened. "Great idea. Never entered my mind."

Olinda beamed smugly and high-fived Penelope. "Thought you was the detective. Seems like it's been up to Penelope and me to figure this stuff out."

Evangeline grinned. "Couldn't have done it without you." She ran her finger down the list, and with a highlighter marked each possibility. The list now consisted mostly of names close to home and business associates. Among them were Julian, Lydia, Marion, Babs, Francie, Lance, and Kreshon.

Olinda said, "How about your nosy neighbors, the Bam-witz's?"

With her hand, Evangeline turned Olinda's chin toward her and held it. "Olinda, watch my mouth and listen." Slowly and with emphasis, Evangeline said, "Ber-no-witz."

"Whatever. Would the Ber-no-witzes know where you were going?"

"Before you came, I usually asked them to watch the house, which they did anyway, and informed them when I'd return. I seldom told them where I'd be. They were to call my cell or the office if a problem arose."

Olinda said, "Next on your list is Dahlia."

Evangeline shook her head. "Impossible. I've known her for fifteen years and would trust her with my life."

"Scratch Dahlia. How about Nicky?"

"Not Nicky. He would've made a move in France or before."

Suddenly a dark tide of exhaustion spread through Evangeline. She shoved the stool back. "I need a breather. This is making me sick to my stomach, analyzing my friends as though they were common criminals."

Olinda said, "Come sit back down, Evie. You've involved all of us in this, and you're not the only one sick to her stomach. This accomplice talk is making me so nervous, I could thread a sewing machine while it's running."

Evangeline chuckled and returned to the stool. "Where do you get those one-liners?"

"What you talking about?"

Evangeline rolled her eyes. Penelope grinned.

Olinda continued. "Next is Fallana, Nicky's . . ."

"Go on, say it. Nicky's lover." Evangeline grabbed the page from Olinda and highlighted Fallana's name with a flourish. Not really believing it, she said, "Fallana is a good prospect."

Olinda continued. "What about Claudine or one of those Delacroixs?"

"We'll do them last. It'll take hours to decipher that bunch. But they probably figured they'd inherit enough of Uncle Jacques' money to maintain their status quo."

Penelope chimed in, "The more you have, the more you want."

"We're not doing too good here," said Olinda. "You always think the best about people. Get serious. Now, how about Julian? He seems mighty interested in your paintings."

"Julian is my boss and is usually aware of where I am. But he is richer than God and has helped me through some difficult times."

"And Julian's wife, the one not his wife no more? You know, the one he don't sleep with."

"Sada? And it's called a separation. I don't have thoughts about her. She doesn't want a divorce. I guess status is more important to her than her freedom. But I can't see her involved.

And we can probably mark out Kreshon, who wouldn't know Adam from Eve unless Marion or Lydia told him."

Olinda scooted closer to the island and importantly tapped her pencil on the butcher-block. "Let's pro and con Lydia."

"Lydia is miserable. Julian works her to death, and she's stressed to the max. She does know my whereabouts, because she makes the reservations. She's sort of mousy, not gutsy like I think an accomplice would be." Evangeline's mind began to work. "But that might be the kind of person to get involved with Max. She always needs a raise for one reason or another. And I do believe she's in love with Julian. Maybe she thinks if she's his equal, he'll notice her. Babs also knew my comings and goings, and Marion, and now Francie."

Olinda closed her eyes and pressed her temples. "My mind is warping like a wet cardboard box. The *loa* say it's time for a break."

"Penelope? Are you okay?" Evangeline asked, frowning.

Penelope had been quiet and was staring into space. Now she rose like a zombie, glided to the back door and looked out.

"What?" Olinda asked.

Penelope waved a silencing hand. "I thought of an idea, and now it's gone. I need to walk around." She opened the storm door and went outside, with Zelda and Smoke following in duck formation.

Olinda snorted. "Our girl will come up with something. Mark it in your book."

"I hope one of us does." Evangeline went to the refrigerator and popped the top on a Diet Pepsi. "Want one?"

"No tanks."

Penelope burst through the back door with the animals scooting in behind her. "I got it, I got it. We need to decide who can profit the most by stealing your paintings."

"But Pen, that's what we've been doing."

"Not really. We've just been eliminating people. Who would have the connections to fence the stuff, and who wants money bad enough to kill for it? Someone determined enough and without a conscience."

"See? I told you our Penelope is a smarty, and I don't mean smart-alecky."

Evangeline touched her lips with her finger. "Well, I guess we could concentrate on that. Nothing else seems to be working. Except almost everyone could use more money."

Penelope said, "But I wonder who's willing to kill four or five people for it?"

Chapter 50

An hour later, the trio had exhausted the suspect list. Evangeline clicked the orange highlighter and dropped it onto the bar. "Well, I'm all in. We have two pages of names, and still not a clue who the accomplice is."

"How do they go about solving crimes in books and movies?" Penelope asked.

Evangeline was thoughtful. "Well, if we're talking about fiction, forensics or sting operations are often used."

"Since forensics isn't our forte, we can set up a sting."

"But we need specific suspects. Right now, we're flapping in the wind."

Penelope looked at Olinda and said smugly, "Maybe that's where Olinda comes in."

Startled, Olinda shook her head. "Nuh-uh, not me. I am not setting up no sting. My *loa* say not to set up no sting."

"You wouldn't really be the bait. We'd just spread the word you had seen a vision."

"Sounds like me being the lamb led to altar. Nuh-uh, no way. I'm not doing it."

"Slaughter," Evangeline corrected. "Led to the slaughter." She glanced at Penelope and raised an eyebrow. Penelope raised hers back. Realizing Penelope was into it, Evangeline decided to play along.

Olinda wrung her hands. "I seen what you did. Now stop it. Mr. Beene say I need to get myself home to check on the house and Scrounger."

Evangeline glanced down at Zelda, whose lips were drawn back over her teeth as though she were grinning.

"What kinda sting you talking about?" Olinda asked. "You better not be planning for me to be it."

Evangeline could barely keep a straight face. "Do you have any ideas, Penelope?"

"Not yet, but I'll come up with one. You can bet on it." She shot Evangeline a mischievous look. "Maybe Olinda can be the bait after all. What do you think?"

"Sounds like a sting to me."

Olinda practically fell off the bar stool, stood and paced. "Not me, I'm not gonna be no sting."

Penelope said, "Why, Miz Olinda, I thought you could lay a trick on the killer, and he wouldn't have power to do you any harm."

"You mind your manners, young lady. And leave my tricks be. You be surprised what I can do."

Penelope said, "When do I get to see one of these tricks?"

"You won't see it coming."

"Right now I'm starving. Do we have anything to eat around here?"

Evangeline got up and checked out the refrigerator and freezer. "Frozen TV dinners. I'm wondering, since I've been gone all day, why one of you hasn't started cooking something."

Olinda fretted and mumbled to herself while Smoke, on top of the built-ins, paced in unison with her.

Penelope said, "Well, it seems to me, since we're going to be rich, why don't we go out to eat? I feel a sting coming on, and I always think better on a full stomach."

Olinda stopped, straightened, and planted her hands on her hips. "There ain't gonna be no sting with me in it."

Penelope and Evangeline burst out laughing. Zelda rose and

turned in circles. Smoke made a long, raspy, high-pitched howl.

Olinda's face softened and she sighed with relief. "Very funny. Why you trying to fool an old woman? Even the dang dog and cat were in on it."

Evangeline moved to Olinda, and from behind wrapped her arms around the woman's waist and pecked her on the neck.

"I'm sorry we teased you, but the laugh did me good."

"Okay, but you had me going. Thought I'd be the sting for sure."

"Seriously, though, we do need a plan to flush out the killer." Evangeline wondered if Olinda could be the answer.

After Olinda retired, Penelope and Evangeline sat in the den with their feet propped on the coffee table watching a black-and-white movie.

Penelope took a sip of iced tea. "I don't get what's so great about these things. They sort of creep me out, and the music is weird."

"They have stood the test of time, my dear. Classic storytelling and acting."

"I think they are a bunch of cr—"

"We do not curse in this house."

"You do."

"But I'm not seventeen." Evangeline pushed the pause button on the remote. "I've been thinking. If we do spread a rumor that Olinda's had a vision, maybe the perp will make a move. What do you think?"

Penelope swelled, seemingly proud that Evangeline respected her opinion. "On second thought, I wouldn't want a killer stalking me, believing I could finger him. Besides, whoever it is probably doesn't believe in hoodoo."

"I guess you're right. It was a stupid idea and much too dangerous. But I can't live my life afraid I could be the next murder victim."

"What about talking to your cop friend? Maybe he can help."

"Arlo? Good idea. I'll call him right now."

Evangeline reached for the phone and speed-dialed Arlo's number. He was on duty but about to sign out and would be there shortly.

About twenty minutes later, Zelda went berserk, sensing Arlo's presence. When he entered, she ran excited circles around him. He knelt and she slurped kisses over his face and hands and whined pitifully.

He ruffled her head. "Easy girl. I love you, too."

Smoke dove from the built-in, thudded onto the counter, then silently hit the floor and slunk from the room.

After greetings all around, and agreeing to a cold beer, Arlo settled on the end bar stool. He leaned back, and with fingers laced behind his curly blond head, one foot on the floor and the other on the rung, said, "Okay, now what is this about a sting?"

Evangeline had never seen him in street attire, and the tight jeans and T-shirt revealed that his heftiness was pure muscle from his neck to his calves. The part in between sizzled her brain. She shook her head to concentrate on the sting and not his well-developed torso and other assets, but mainly to shake the desire that she would like to jump his bones. *God, Evangeline, you're becoming a pervert. All you can think about is sex.*

He raised an eyebrow. "Well?"

"Er, we . . ." she sputtered. "We want to bring the perp into the open before he has a chance to harm anyone else."

She relaxed when Arlo unclasped his hands and sat up straight. He pulled on the beer and rocked the bottom of the bottle on the island.

"Evangeline, with your training, you should realize that playing games with killers is dangerous. I'd leave it to the authorities. They are giving it number-one priority. This case is now an international incident, and they don't want any more deaths."

"I understand, but I can't sit here and wait for God knows what to happen. Not in my nature. We've tossed around a few scenarios, but most sound too complicated, and as you said, too dangerous." And she'd always been attracted to men with dark hair. Arlo's was blond and curly. *What's the deal?*

"If someone wants the paintings badly enough to be involved in four murders, he won't have any qualms about making it one or two or even three more."

Penelope had been silent, but interjected, "Yikes. It doesn't sound so exciting the way you put it. I'm with what you said, Mr. Arlo."

"Well, thank you, Penelope. And I'm proud your attitude toward the law is changing."

Penelope scrunched the corner of her mouth as though ready with a comeback.

Quickly Evangeline said, "Penelope's been a great help with Olinda and the house. I couldn't have done without her."

"You can bet your tin badge on that," Penelope mumbled. "And don't push it."

"There you go again, Penelope. Anyway, Evangeline, what you want to do might not be necessary. The perp could be watching your every move." He raised an eyebrow. "In fact, you need protection. I'll speak to the captain tomorrow and arrange for surveillance."

"What about tonight?" Penelope asked.

Evangeline patted her hand and glanced at the clock on the wall. "The night is almost over. What can happen?"

After Arlo left, Olinda staggered into the kitchen, rubbing her eyes. "A body can't sleep around here with such racket. Did I hear the cop leave?"

"Yes, ma'am. Tomorrow he's having a patrol car assigned to our house for surveillance in case the perp decides to make an appearance."

"But what about tonight?"

Penelope did her mouth-pucker. "Exactly what I asked. Uh, can I sleep with you, Evangeline?"

"Don't be ridiculous. Nobody's coming in this house, not with Zelda on duty and the alarm system armed. Arlo is being cautious. Besides, Smoke can scratch their eyes out and Olinda can conjure a protection cloak for the doors. The windows stick and are hard to open from the outside."

"What about the attic?"

"Uh, Penelope, maybe you'd feel safer out on the streets or at the shelter."

"Very funny. And thanks for the PJs. The little pink bunnies are totally my style. Now all I need are your bunny slippers."

Evangeline ignored the dig. "I figured if you were going to sleep here half the time, you needed your own pajamas. Umm, mind if I ask where you get the money for your changes of wardrobe, and where do you keep it?"

"I told you, I sell my art on the street. Mostly I keep my duds and drawing supplies in a locker at the bus station."

"The one in town? How do you get there?"

"Hitch."

Evangeline clasped her hand over her heart. "Oh, my word, you're going to die. Hitching is so dangerous."

"Yeah," Olinda said. "It'd be about like a cat at the dog pound. My money's on the cat."

"Don't worry about me. I'm careful, and with these throw-away phones," she wiggled hers in the air, "I can keep in touch."

Evangeline mused. "If you create a thing for good, before long, someone will figure a way to use it for evil. Criminals get away with a lot, and their names and locations remain anonymous because they use throwaways. The tech age might be the end of us."

"Tsk, tsk. You sure are being pessi . . . uh . . . resorting to your old ways, aren't you?"

Evangeline ignored Olinda, opened the storm door and looked out. Zelda squeezed by her and headed for her potty place behind the fig tree. "It's so dark I can't see the moon or stars, and the back porch light is burnt out. Remind me to change the bulb tomorrow. Or one of you could do it while I'm at work."

At the sound of a low rumble, she rubbed her arms. "Feels and sounds like rain. I love rain. It cleans out the pollen and makes the earth fresh and new. Thank goodness Zelda isn't afraid of thunder, like many animals. I thought sure the lightning strike would warp her mind, but she seems smarter, calmer."

Olinda pulled up proudly. "Lightning strike? I might take credit for that."

"Olinda, you think you heebie-jeebied her, and I hate to break your bubble, but professionals trained her. I never told you she's a retired police dog."

"I don't care what she's retired from."

Logically, Evangeline knew Olinda could not have put a trick on Zelda, but Evangeline's receptive mind often wondered if her claims might be justified. Still, she couldn't wrap her mind around contradictions to her Christian teachings.

Penelope said, "I've heard that animals react to our energy field. If we're afraid, we send out impulses they can feel. My little brother was scared to death of storms, so our Chihuahua would literally chew through the sheet rock to get to us or to get into the closet to hide. Once, we thought for sure she got lost, but we found her buried behind some old clothes in the closet. The poor dog almost shook to death. To get her to stop, I had to climb into bed and let her burrow under the covers down to my feet. Really sad to be so frightened."

Evangeline rubbed her arm soothingly. "Sweetheart, you

sound nostalgic. You're missing your family, aren't you?"

"Sure, but Mom is hung so high on that dude, she can't see straight. Maybe I'll go home when he dumps her."

"But how will you know?"

"I keep in touch with my aunt. When I use up the minutes on the cell, I call and give her the new number. She knows how to reach me if she wants to."

"Good." Evangeline rubbed Penelope's back in a loving gesture. "Before I go up, I'm having a glass of milk and a couple of those peanut butter cookies we baked. Anybody else?"

Olinda and Penelope raised their hands.

Afterward, Evangeline had let Zelda inside, locked up and set the alarm, when the bottom fell out of the sky.

"Oh, my *loa,*" Olinda moaned. "When the animals start pairing up, we'll know it's gonna rain a long time."

Penelope snickered. "You must be referring to Noah's ark."

"I read, too," Olinda scolded.

"The Bible? I thought you believed in voodoo/hoodoo stuff," Penelope said playfully.

Not wanting to get into another discussion about spirits, Evangeline said, "I'm turning off the lights. Everybody upstairs."

Evangeline slept deeply, dreaming about Arlo in tight jeans, no shirt, his abs rippling. He was bent over her bed, grinning seductively.

"Evangeline, wake up."

The voice wasn't Arlo's—someone was shaking her arm, ruining the dream.

"Evangeline, wake up. I hear a noise."

"Nooo, Pelope," she slurred. "Go back to bed. You're imaging things."

"No, I'm not. Listen."

Evangeline opened one eye and felt for Zelda, who she had

finally allowed to sleep with her. The dog usually took up Nicky's deserted side of the bed, but the space was empty.

Alert, Evangeline raised her head. "Where's Zelda? She'll tell us if somebody's trying to get in."

"She growled, then nothing."

"Remember the story about the boy who cried wolf? Before we call the police, let's first see about Zelda."

Evangeline slipped on her bunny slippers, and from the top shelf in her closet, took down her firearms case and opened it. She removed the subcompact Glock, holster, magazine and a small high-beam flashlight.

Penelope's eyes widened. "Be careful. Glocks are known to shoot off toes."

"How do you know?"

"My pervert stepfather is a cop."

"That explains a lot. And yes, your statement is true. Glocks have hair triggers with no separate safety lever that you slide like many firearms, such as Sigs or Berettas. They do have a lever within the trigger mechanism that you have to depress at the same time you pull the trigger. I keep mine unloaded under lock and key." She waved the gun. "If this sucker is loaded, the slightest pressure can cause it to fire, so when I'm carrying, I keep it holstered."

Evangeline shoved the magazine into the bottom of the handle, and inserted the gun into the holster. With the flashlight in one hand and the Glock in the other, she and Penelope tiptoed to the top of the stairs.

Evangeline flicked on the beam and shined it down into the foyer. Penelope's mouth worked overtime. "Shouldn't we turn on some real lights? I think we should, don't you? Then we can see better."

"Shh. If anyone's here, they can hear you blabbering."

Penelope whispered and pointed to the pistol. "Does that

thing shoot straight?"

"It does if the shooter does."

"Oh. Had much training?"

"Don't worry. I can handle it. This one has nine rounds, and if I can't hit my target with that many, I need to quit."

"Gotcha."

"I don't hear anything. Are you sure it was Zelda?"

"It could've been the wind, but where is she?"

A low growl.

Penelope held tightly to Evangeline's Glock-toting arm.

"Let go of my shooting arm!"

"Sorry." She grabbed Evangeline's pajama top. "Where's the sound coming from?"

"I don't know."

Another low growl.

Penelope halted and pulled back on Evangeline's shirt. "They're in the attic. And you can bet your booty, I'm not going up there."

"Penelope, if anyone was up there, Zelda would be raising Cain." *I hope.* "Now let go of my clothes." She mumbled under her breath, "God, I feel so old."

They moved to the attic stairs and climbed. Maneuvering on the steps wasn't easy because both of Evangeline's hands were full, and Penelope had such a grip on Evangeline's pajama top, she kept tilting off balance. At the landing, Zelda sat by the door with a sheepish look on her face. Evangeline felt the house's cold place and a swish of air. She grinned to herself and couldn't resist saying, "Okay, ghost. Whaddaya want?"

Zelda whined and placed a paw over her eyes.

Penelope moaned, "Oh, no. Not the ghost."

"I told you, it's friendly. Now stand back. I'm opening the door."

"Nooo, don't open it."

Evangeline held the penlight between her teeth, turned the doorknob and gently shoved. A flash of lightning illuminated the attic room, and two beady eyes stared at her. Her stomach double rolled, and she caught the creature in a beam. A bandit-masked raccoon stood on its hind legs, ready to attack.

"Git! Shoo!" she yelled and stomped her foot. Zelda streaked past them, but the creature scampered behind a stack of suitcases. The dog plunged in, suitcases tumbling to the floor. After a quick search, all they found was broken glass from a small window.

"This must be its path in and out. I'm sure it's escaped, but hope it didn't leave babies up here. I guess the security technicians didn't bother with such a small window."

Rain poured in, so they blocked the window with a sheet of cardboard torn from a box, and squeezed in an old duffle bag. "Hopefully this'll hold out the rain until I can get it fixed. But now I'm freezing. Let's go back down and see what the rest of the night holds for us."

Chapter 51

In her bedroom, Evangeline laid the flashlight and the holstered Glock on the nightstand just in case she needed them again. She crawled into bed, patted the other side for Zelda and turned out the lamp. She was almost under when her cell phone chimed. The clock indicated four a.m. and the caller ID showed it was Lydia. "Sheesh. No sleep for me tonight."

"Lydia, what's the matter? Are you okay?"

Lydia's squeaky, stressed voice said, "There's been a break-in at the gallery. The police and Julian are on the premises. You need to get down here, now."

"Give me twenty."

She threw on jeans, a heavy slipover sweater and running shoes. She dropped her phone into her purse, picked up the holstered Glock and practically slid down the banister. Zelda sat at the back door waiting.

"Okay, girl. You can go." She scribbled a note that she'd gone to Rembrandt's and left it on the bar.

By the time they got on the road, the rain had slacked, but gutters overflowed and puddles of water slowed her down. Of all the times for a break-in, it had to be when her paintings were stored there. At least only Julian knew the combination to the vault. When she finally pulled into Rembrandt's parking lot, three cars were there belonging to Lydia, the night watchman, Gino, and Julian's farm Jeep. She surmised the police had come and gone; a good sign.

She shoved her purse under the front seat, took the Glock and her car keys, and clicked on the alarm. The back door to Rembrandt was unlocked and the hall was empty. Strange no one was on duty, she thought as she hurried to the gallery door with Zelda padding along beside her.

She scanned the dimly lit interior. "Hello! Julian. Lydia. Anyone here?"

Julian called, "In my office."

The situation must be under control, so she motioned for Zelda to sit-stay at the entrance. She laid the holstered Glock on the chair seat in front of Miriam's desk, pocketed her keys, and noticed that the walk-in safe door stood ajar. Her stomach plummeted. Julian never opened the vault with the outside doors unlocked. Something was drastically wrong here.

He sat behind his desk in the shadowy office, wearing a hunting vest and a long-sleeved checkered shirt.

"What in the world's happened? Lydia sounded like it was life or death."

"Actually, Evangeline, it is. We have a little problem."

"Lydia said there'd been a break-in. Have the police come and gone? Where is Gino? Oh, my God, is it my paintings?"

His tone sounded almost accusatory. "Whoa. You always were too spastic for your own good."

"What?"

A muffled groan came from somewhere outside his office.

"Is that Lydia? Is she hurt?" She partially turned to go in search of the sound.

In a cold and commanding voice, Julian said, "Stay right there."

She whirled back to see him pointing a gun at her. "Julian, what are you doing?"

"Isn't it obvious by now? I'm Max's accomplice you've been racking your brain to find."

She grinned. "Yeah, right, and I'm the Pope."

"Oh, Evie, Evie, Evie. Some detective you are. You haven't a clue, and I'm not playing games anymore."

Her mouth dropped open. "Playing games? Accomplice? That's ridiculous. Not you. Anybody else. Lydia, maybe. Not you, Julian, my friend, mentor, confidante."

"Biding time until now." He rose, walked around the desk and indicated for her to stand still while he patted her down. "Where's your cell phone?"

Stunned, she sputtered, "In my car."

"Good. Wouldn't want my girl making a nine-one-one call."

"This is about Grandmother's art, isn't it?"

"Of course. Why else would I give an incompetent employee free rein to go traipsing around the world on my dime?"

"Now wait a darned minute. I am not incompetent. I have as much savvy as the next guy. All I need is some experience."

"Sorry, but you'll never have the chance."

"Have you thought this through? Everyone knows the art is mine."

"It will disappear for a while. When I'm in the clear, I might sell off a piece the same way Abner Jacobson did. And then again, having it might be satisfaction enough."

"It seems I've been down this same road with Max."

"I assure you the outcome will be quite different this time."

Not if she could help it. *Krav Maga* probably wouldn't work here, because he would be watching for it.

"Why did Lydia call me?"

"My plan to get you here. To her credit, she didn't want to, but I can be very persuasive."

"I'll bet. Where is she now—and Gino?"

"In her office tied and gagged. Gino's in the vault."

"Alive?"

"Lydia is for now."

"Gino's dead?" She clasped her hand to her mouth and calculated: five people dead, and all for the paintings. "This is too much."

He waved the gun and glanced at his watch. "Sit. We have a few minutes, so I'll explain it. Wouldn't want you to die in ignorance."

She shook her head. "Like hell I will. I'm not about to make it easy, so I'll stand." Still trying to absorb the ramifications, she asked, "So you are Max's collaborator?"

He stepped back from her and perched on the edge of his desk. He crossed his right arm over the left, balancing the gun. Evangeline stood awkwardly in front of him.

"Wake up, Evangeline. Max was *my* accomplice. He took credit for stalking you and for the murders. Since Jacobson had met Max, I was the one who lured him into a death trap. After I questioned him, Max did the dirty deed, but I pulled the strings. Max never would have gotten as far as he did without me. I even financed your European trip." He smirked. "Sada would really be upset if she knew you were having fun on her dime."

"Max led me to believe the caper was his idea and he was the mastermind."

"Max wouldn't know what to do with that many masterpieces. He'd stick them in some vault and let them rot. I have the connections. He was simply a means, as were you. His mind was set on revenge."

Evangeline's brain spun, and she started to pace. Julian seemed not to mind, probably confident she couldn't escape. She would play to his inflated ego. "Pretty ingenious plan. With me working here, my whereabouts were always known, and you had access to my leads. Dumb me, I thought you were being generous, kind, but you had an ulterior motive all along, hiring me back, letting me do the work to find Grandmother's treasures so you could steal them."

He puffed up. "Yes, Evangeline, I had you and Max jumping through hoops. Sort of amusing, and if it's any consolation, I do respect you a tiny bit. Occasionally my conscience would ping because I'd never been party to murder before. But then I'd think about owning those paintings, and couldn't help myself."

"Lance warned me about people like you. I wonder what he would say now."

"I really don't care what he thinks."

"Is anyone else involved?"

"Just *moi.*"

"But Julian, you can never bring one of those paintings out in the open. The law will come down like—"

"So naïve. Small-time view. Hundreds of collectors will salivate at owning an old master, no matter the circumstances. I know I would."

"You'll be first on the suspect list."

"Maybe for a while, but it will eventually blow over and become another cold case. Then I'll be free to do what I want."

Still pacing slowly, she stopped in front of him and glared. "You plan to kill Lydia and me, right?"

"Step back, Evangeline. Don't want you using that self-defense technique on me."

She did as told. "I repeat, you plan to kill me and Lydia."

"Of course. But it will appear that Lydia kills you and Gino, steals the art and disappears, never to be heard from again. I have a dumping site where her body will never be found. Nobody will be the wiser or suspect me."

"What if Max gives you up?"

"Me, a respected businessman and philanthropist? I'm above reproach, never even had a speeding ticket. Oh, maybe I like the women a little too much, but *c'est la vie.*"

"Yeah, *c'est la vie,* because there are a thousand holes in your plan."

"Even if Max does squeal, I'll convince the authorities he's a desperate man trying to save his own skin, trying to implicate an innocent person so he can cut a deal. Besides, there isn't a shred of evidence linking us. We met once when he came into the gallery, and afterward communicated with those wonderful throw-away phones."

"Why doesn't Lydia kill you, too?"

"Good question, and my answer will be that I was never here. I've been at my country place since last night."

Keep him talking. The longer he talks, the more chances there'll be. "You're bound to slip up. Forensics can discover evidence we never dreamed of. They'll check car mileage, gas receipts, telephone calls, everything. And what about the building's surveillance cameras?"

"The Jeep's panel controls are broken, and I took a chance with the gallery's safety and turned off the surveillance equipment yesterday. Of course, Lydia will get credit because I'm practically computer illiterate. Poor me. Lydia is the computer whiz with an uncanny ability to manipulate files. I have proof she's often taken advantage of my generosity. We never told anybody that I'm familiar with the alarm system. And I'll say I have no idea why she called you."

"Think you've got it figured out, huh? I've said it more than once: you're richer than God. How much money can one person spend? It doesn't make sense."

Then her recent windfalls flashed through her mind. If she didn't take control of this situation, her decisions about them wouldn't matter. She didn't even have a will.

Julian's attitude was nonchalant. "Like I said, I want more, and I get what I want."

She knew the statement to be true, had even said so herself. *Oh, Arlo, where are you?* "The police and my friends will get to the truth."

"Evangeline. You aren't as important as you believe."

"It makes sense now. I felt an elusive itch I couldn't scratch."

"You were right. I was that itch."

"I thought it odd that Max wasn't concerned about me calling you when I discovered the art. He knew you wouldn't tell, and those in France who knew would be dead."

"Exactly," he said icily. "Your time is up. Now get out there in the gallery and we'll finish this. Miriam will arrive soon to open up. I hate to do this to her, but she'll be the one to discover two dead bodies. I haven't decided whether to do Lydia now or later. Though if I wait, her blubbering will drive me insane."

My God, this man has no compunction or compassion.

Suddenly, it dawned on Evangeline that in a few minutes she might cease to exist. The shock was finally wearing off. She shook uncontrollably and moved falteringly, grasping first the doorjamb for support, next the sales counter and then the back of a chair. She glanced down, and noticed the pistol in its holster lying in the seat, but realized she couldn't reach it, remove it from the holster and aim before he shot her. She needed a distraction.

Julian nodded toward the vault. "Stand over there where I can see you. Have to stage this perfectly."

She didn't move, wanting to remain within reach of the gun. "You're one cold son of a bitch."

"So I've been told. Sada could talk on that subject until your ears burn."

This was the third time she'd been fooled by a man. If she got out of this, she would swear off them for eternity. Zelda. Where was Zelda? She glanced toward the door and saw she had obeyed the sit-stay command. But tremors were visible throughout her body, because instinct told her to charge.

She's waiting for my signal. I hope. But what is it?

At her hesitation, Julian's voice chastised. "No use trying to figure a way out. You are a dead woman." He caught sight of Zelda and, waving the gun, said, "What's your dumb-ass poodle doing here?"

"You'd be surprised at how dumb-ass Zelda is." The click of the safety on Julian's gun sent ice through her veins and initiated a snarl from her dog. "Is—is that a Beretta?"

"My God, Evangeline. You are so stupid. Don't you realize you're going to die? For heaven's sake, asking the make of the weapon that's going to kill you! What an imbecile." He again motioned her away from the chair and toward the vault. "Now move it."

"Don't I get any last words? Every prisoner gets a dying request."

"Move, dammit!"

It was now or never. Her knees weakened and she took hold of the chair back. *The attack word?* She didn't remember the attack word Arlo used for Zelda. *My God, what is the freaking attack word? Sit, stay, heel, shake.* Then she visualized a crushed orange—*got it.* Half turning toward the door where Zelda was alert, waiting, she firmly commanded, "Zelda! Crush!"

The animal barked once, burst forward, clearing the space within seconds, and launched herself at Julian, who yelled and raised his hands to ward her off. The dog's front paws connected with his chest, and the force of her lunge knocked him backward to the floor. The gun discharged with an earsplitting boom that echoed throughout the gallery. Julian dropped the weapon, and it skittered under a cabinet.

Evangeline grabbed her Glock, jerked it from its holster and in one swift movement brought it into shooting position. "Oh, Zelda, are you hurt, girl?" But Zelda guarded Julian, baring her teeth and growling viciously, daring him to move. The fear and surprise on his face was priceless as he spat out pieces of sheetrock floating down from the ceiling where the bullet had hit.

The dog's actions and reactions flabbergasted Evangeline. "Way to go, Zelda. Good girl. My hero. Didn't know you could do that." And then to Julian, "How's that for a dumb-ass dog, creep?"

He spat and demanded, "Get this beast off me."

"Excuse me? Zelda doesn't take kindly to a gruff tone of voice."

Zelda placed her paw on his chest and with her nose directly over his face, she snarled.

Julian whimpered. "Call her off, please. Don't let her maul me."

"Men." Evangeline snickered. "I must warn you, Julian, my Glock has a hair trigger, and is extremely touchy. One wrong move from either of us, and it might accidently discharge."

His voice trembled. "Okay. Take it easy. I'm not moving."

"Zelda, stay." She punched in 911 on Miriam's desk phone and told the operator she had a cold-blooded murderer in custody and gave the address.

Almost immediately she heard sirens, doors slamming and feet stomping into the building. "Wow! Talk about instant gratification."

Arlo exploded through the door, gun drawn, followed by armed men in camouflage gear who moved through the gallery. A uniform handcuffed Julian, and as they ushered him out the door, he mumbled, "Fucking dog."

Lydia was released from her bonds and whisked to an ambulance. The medical examiner was called to examine Gino's body.

With uniforms still milling about, Arlo and Evangeline stood in the middle of the gallery while she finished giving a preliminary report. "But Arlo, how did you get here so quickly? I no more than hung up from calling nine-one-one when I heard sirens."

"When Max coughed up Krystos as his accomplice in exchange for a life versus death plea bargain, we went to the man's penthouse but, of course, he wasn't there. I decided to call you and head over here. You didn't answer your cell, so I tried your house phone and Penelope told me your note said you'd gone to Rembrandt's. I had a bad feeling and called for backup. Good thing I did." He gently placed his palm on her forehead. "You look a little peaked. How about a trip to the ER?"

"No, I don't need a hospital. Julian never touched me except to pat me down." She pulled up proudly. "Zelda and I make a great team, don't we? The two of us pretty much had things under control when you arrived." She grinned. "Julian's the one who might need a doctor, though—specifically a psychiatrist after Zelda scared him half to death."

"That's my girl," Arlo cooed, motioning for Zelda to come. The poodle wagged her nub, rubbed against his legs, gazed into his eyes and whined happily. "You did good, girl. Saved your mamma's life." He knelt down, stroked the length of the dog's body lovingly, and gently clasped her head in his hands. They rubbed noses.

The tenderness in those actions melted Evangeline's heart, but she stood with hands on her hips and said, "Sorry, but you can't have her back."

"Personally, I wouldn't dare try to break up such a dynamic duo."

She peered down at the dog. "Yes we are, aren't we, Zelda? Well, girl, our job here is done. Time to go to the *casa,* unless I'm needed for an official report."

"Nah, it's okay to come in tomorrow and sign a statement. Want me to drive or follow you home?"

She leaned over and kissed his cheek. "You are a good friend, and I appreciate everything, but I think the danger is over and I can take it from here. I've several tough decisions to make about my future."

He gazed sheepishly at her. "Might they include me?"

Evangeline winked, but didn't answer. She lowered her hand to her side, turned and motioned for Zelda to follow. The dog trotted into step; Evangeline glanced down, and Zelda looked up. "Yep, Zelda, we make a good team, all right." They both grinned.

Epilogue

Evangeline lay in bed and stared at the ceiling. Her nerves were stretched tighter than a voodoo drum. Zelda slept next to her, but each time Evangeline made the slightest move, the dog opened one eye until satisfied her master was still there. Then she went happily back to sleep. The animal was quite protective and Evangeline hoped it wouldn't become a problem.

She had cleared up as many loose ends as was humanly possible in the course of a few days, and upon occasion even found the strength for humor. On the morning she left for the police station to give a written statement, she noticed a "For Sale" sign in front of the Bernowitzes' house. The poor dears probably couldn't take all the traffic at her corner. It would be interesting to see who moved in.

After she left the police station, she drove by Rembrandt's, but the building was secured with police tape, and a security patrol car was parked in the lot. With so many valuable items in the gallery, the level of security didn't surprise Evangeline. Lance was hopeful the outcome of the whole art-theft affair wouldn't affect their jobs, but if Sada was the sole heir, which was logical because she and Julian had no children, then the detective agency was probably doomed.

Arlo called up a few favors and brought her paintings to the house. She contacted a friend at a Houston art museum, who agreed to hold them until Evangeline decided what direction to take. Kirk Kestner advised her it would be to her advantage financially and for security purposes to lend them to a museum, so that's what she decided to do.

After researching Swiss banks, she found one matching the letters on Great-grandfather Henri's note. If the bank gave her any problems, Kestner would file a testamentary of her as the legal heir to the Henri Delacroix holdings, an amount he believed to be substantial. The money had been drawing interest for more than half a century, so there wasn't any hurry. But the red tape to get the Swiss on board might prove more difficult than finding the account number.

Evangeline's mind was pickled from thinking about the financial gains she would receive, because along with them came a huge responsibility. The inheritance from Uncle Jacques had placed a major burden on her. The thought of dealing with the Delacroix family made her physically ill. What was he thinking? His bequest wasn't fair to anyone, and she didn't want the added accountability that would be mandatory if she accepted his legacy.

Never in a million years had she imagined such an inheritance, but now she realized it must be put to good use. Should the Swiss bank windfall come to pass, she already had plans for that. And she owed it all to Penelope and Aunt Olinda.

And then there were Arlo and Nicky. Who knew where romance would lead? Or, as her mother used to say, when they would pack up their belongings and move. We never know what's waiting for us around the next corner.

Evangeline glanced at Zelda, who had turned away from her. She eased onto her side, laid her arm across the dog's neck, snuggled to its warmth, and whispered, "One thing's for sure, Zelda girl, we've got each other." At those words, tension ebbed from the animal's body, along with a long contented sigh.

As Evangeline relaxed and sleep slowly covered the day's cares with a warm blanket, she hoped that whoever or whatever waited around the corner would be good for them.

ABOUT THE AUTHOR

Jacqueline Pelham is the award-winning author of *Under the Rose,* a World War II suspense novel. She has published short stories and poetry in many literary journals, with articles appearing in *Fiction Writer's Market,* newspapers, and newsletters/bulletins. Her reviews have appeared in *Small Press Review, Review of Texas Books,* and Amazon.com. Her editorial endeavors include founder/editor of *Suddenly,* an anthology of poetry and flash fiction, co-editor *Fall From Innocence, Memoirs of the Great Depression,* editor of *Food for Thought/EZ Recipes & Poetry by Texas Poets* and editor of *Vittles & Champagne*—proceeds of which are donated to Abandoned Animal Rescue, a nonprofit. Jackie has lived in the Houston area most of her life and now resides north of Houston with her husband, Joel.